T0066943

S.K. Langin

Order this book online at www.trafford.com
or email orders@trafford.com

Most Trafford titles are also available at major online book retailers.

Printed in the United States of America.

ISBN: 978-1-4907-4151-2 (sc)
ISBN: 978-1-4907-4150-5 (e)

Trafford rev. 07/07/2014

Trafford PUBLISHING® www.trafford.com
North America & international
toll-free: 1 888 232 4444 (USA & Canada)
fax: 812 355 4082

Chapter One

With a slight, cool breeze the morning was extremely pleasant after the warmth of yesterday's late afternoon sun when the five guests had first arrived. They were guests of the Jute Valley Guest Ranch in the Wind River Mountain area of Wyoming. After staying their first night in comfortable accommodations and refreshed from their flight; they were hoping for some good trail riding to start out their stay.

Gathered in a semi-circle near the large horse corrals, they were listening intently to the ranch foreman as he described the various assortment of trail rides that were available to the Jute Valley guests.

Of the five guests, two were women; one, a tall, slender light-brown haired woman; the second, a tall dark-haired woman. On the reservations it had stated that they were from the mid-west. The dark-haired woman was married to the tall, handsome almost blonde-haired man standing close to her side. The couple, Tim and Linda Winters, had made all the arrangements for the group. A group that were planning to stay for two and a half months, almost three.

Grinning in a friendly manner, the foreman; otherwise known as the Ranch Manager, explained quietly, "All our horses are well trained and of the best quality, Mrs. Winters. And concerning our trail guides; well, we have some of the finest riders around this area. Tyler McKay, my trail foreman and horse trainer, will be going with you. He's busy just now, so I'll have Jessie help you to get your mounts and equipment. Jessie is also one of our guides. We usually send at least two riders with a group.

From the other side of Linda Winters, a dark-haired man that looked enough like her to be a twin, spoke up. His voice slightly condescending, "Sounds fine to me. Except, I'd like to get started."

"Of course, Mister Drake." Turning toward the huge stables, the ranch manager called to the guide.

Joseph Drake turned his dark head in the same direction as did the others. From around the corner of the nearby stable, a slight figure appeared. Joe, being of slender build and just under six foot, and rather sensitive to that fact; noted that the guide was small enough to be a jockey. As the rider came nearer, Drake looked more closely at the slim figure.

Tim Winters jabbed an elbow into Joe's side, remarking in an amazed whisper. "A girl."

Nodding mutely Joe continued to watch as the slip of a girl vaulted seemingly effortlessly over the corral fence. She couldn't be much over five foot; and still managed to stride with purpose and at the same time almost a cat-like grace.

A gray flat-crowned hat shaded the small lightly-tanned face and a long copper-red braid swung back and forth down the slender back. A blue cotton shirt was tucked into snug-fitting faded jeans.

A smile curved her lips as she glanced over at the ranch foreman, but as her gaze swept the group, the steady stride faulted slightly. Squaring the slim shoulders, she moved closer, finally halting beside the foreman. The hat kept her features in shadow and the smile had changed to a grim line.

The manager gave her a quick squeeze, smiling broadly. "Well, this is Jessie." Looking down at her, he said, "I want you to help this group with their horses and decide which trail ride they would like."

The voice was soft and husky as she answered him. Then lifting the small, determined chin; sunlight flooded the delicate tanned features.

Recognition whispered over four of the five guests as the cold, misty-gray eyes surveyed them stonily. The dark-haired woman was the first to speak. "Jessica!"

A stiff smile pulled at the corners of the fine lips. "Hello, Linda."

The manager stared hard at the group and then at the young woman beside him. "You know each other?"

Jessie laughed dryly. "You could say that, Phil. They're from my hometown. When Tyler gets back, send him on over, please?"

Phil smiled slowly, but nodded. "Sure thing, Jess."

As the foreman disappeared around one of the buildings, Linda Winters stepped forward hesitantly, "It's been a long time, Jessica."

"Almost three years." agreed the redhead. "You look great. Hello, Tim."

Winters grinned as he put an arm around Linda. Tim was in his late twenties with straight, almost-blonde hair and very blue eyes. Looking down into the dark-brown eyes of his wife, he answered softly, "We are married now."

"That's great. Not really surprised. Saw it happening."

When Jessie came face to face with Linda's brother Joe, the small oval face hardened, just managing to keep a stiff smile pasted on her lips. Joe would be around thirty-one and his dark hair and eyes were almost the exact same shade as his sister's.

"Joe. How have you been?"

He smiled with difficulty. "Just fine, Jessica."

A rich baritone voice sounded from behind her. "Cooper, say hello to this retired Army man."

Jessie Cooper twisted around, lips parting in a real smile this time. "Larry Connors. It has been awhile. How could the Army ever let you get away?"

"Had to talk real fast." Laughed the tall, platinum-blonde haired man. Larry had been a close friend to Tim and had joined the service not long before meeting the Drakes and Jessie. He had been home on leave and both men had been out celebrating. The Army had put a little more weight on the lean six-foot plus frame, broadening the muscled shoulders and deepening the wide chest. Connors was a couple of years older than Tim, closer to Joe's age and had always been of a more serious nature.

Seeing the tall, slender woman standing next to him, Jessie questioned quietly, "And who is this, Larry?"

Dull color tinted the tanned features as the blonde man looked down at the young woman at his left. "This is Cindy Tanner. We're engaged." Then smiling softly at the tall young woman, he added, "Cindy, this is Jessica Cooper. I've told you about her a number of times."

Cindy smiled and shook Jessie's small hand. "Hi. I've heard so much about you. It's nice to finally get to meet you."

The redhead shook her head and laughed gently, "Remind me to ask you just what you heard. And congratulations on your engagement. You're getting a fine man."

Once again Cooper turned back to her one-time best friend, Linda. She was an unusually beautiful, very classy young woman with long dark-brown hair that was almost black in color and very straight. Olive-colored complexion that had always tanned easily, and that Jess had envied. Eyes that were large and coffee-brown with long, spiky dark lashes. With the slim figure and tall five-foot-six height, Jessie had always thought that she would have made a wonderful model.

Remembering her assigned job, Cooper sighed deeply, then remarked in a flat, business-like tone. "Well, first we should get your mounts. Come with me. If we don't get a move on, Tyler will be here before we even get started."

Following the slender jean-clad woman, they finally halted in front of another corral filled with around fifteen to eighteen horses. All sizes and colors. Slipping between the fence rails, Jessie carefully eyed each one in turn; then turning back to the gathered group, she stated pointedly, "The horse that I give you now will be your responsibility and in your care until your stay is over."

One by one, she led out the horses; two bays, one a flashy paint she gave to Tim Winters. The last two were almost identical in markings and build. One, a large black and the other a dark-liver chestnut. "This is Warsaw." Commented Jess as she handed the chestnut to Larry.

"And, Joe, the black is Warsaw's half-brother, Dunkirk. They are both very good horses. Two of the best."

"Except possibly for Confederate, Rebel and Shiloh." interrupted a husky male voice from behind the group.

Turning, Joe found himself staring at a broad shouldered, lean-built man around his own age. A deep tanned handsome face harbored a pleasant smile; and sharp hazel-green eyes carefully studied the different faces before him. He was dressed in a gold-brown cotton shirt and snug-fitting soft denim jeans, boots and a tan flat-crowned hat. He was close to six foot or a little taller, it was hard to tell by the lean muscled shoulders and deep chest that narrowed down to a lean waist and hips. He reminded Joe of an athlete.

Carelessly the newcomer pushed back his hat, exposing thick, coal-black hair. Joe unconsciously angered by this cowboy's cool appearance, straightened up his own lean form and questioned rather sharply, "And who exactly are the three that you mentioned?"

The cowboy was about to answer, when Jessie spoke up harshly. "They happen to be horses, Joe. This is my boss, Tyler McKay, trail foreman."

Giving the redhead a puzzled glance, McKay cut in with a soft, easy drawl. "Nice to meet you. Sorry, I wasn't able to be here when you first arrived, but had some business to take care of. While we're on the subject, I'll explain a little about those three horses that I mentioned. Each summer there is a rodeo, an open horse show and a race. The race is mostly among the area ranches. Our entry has won the last three years in a row. He's a tall white Arabian stallion that is named Confederate.

"Besides being one hell of a race horse, he has also sired some fine colts. Two are still at the ranch. The older of the two is a red roan half-appaloosa gelding, which happens to be my mount, Rebel.

"Finally, there is Shiloh. He is a blue-gray Morab gelding. The breed is a half Morgan and half Arabian. Up until a year or so ago, no one could handle him without all kinds of trouble. Jess changed that and now she owns him."

Cindy cocked her head to one side and then asked, "Which one of the geldings is the faster?"

Jessie laughed softly, "No idea. We've never had the desire to race them full out. Beside the two horses are different. But none are as fast as Fed. Even though, Wes Wilcox believes his black, Gunfire, can outrun him."

Again the cool drawl sounded, "No chance of that. But, enough of the future events. Right now we have to get all of you out-fitted and on our way. What did you decide on?"

His intent gaze remained on the delicate features of the redhead as she questioned the dark-haired Linda. Smiling and with a slight nod of her head, she replied, "The two-day ride. Each one will have to take their mount over to that low, long building. There will be someone there to help you get ready. Tell them that it is for Tyler's trail group and the kind of ride. We'll meet you there."

As the five guests moved away leading their horses, Tyler glanced again at the young woman beside him. He saw the friendliness drain out of the gray-blue eyes, leaving them cold and hard. Shaking his head, he frowned to himself. "Jessie?"

As the coppery-haired girl looked up, he asked softly, "What's the matter?"

"Nothing, Ty, just old memories." Answered the small woman quietly.

When she went to move away, he hesitantly touched her slender arm, halting her. Hazel eyes looked deep into her gray ones, he questioned slowly, "I had the impression that you knew those people. And hadn't expected to see them again. Well?"

Cooper nodded shortly. She had never been able to lie to McKay; not in the three years that she had known him, and she wasn't about to start now. He was her friend, a real friend. And she, better than anyone, knew just how rare they were.

"Yes, something like that. Linda Winters, she's married now, it was Drake; she had been my best friend then. Or what I had thought was a best friend. And I had been fairly close friends with the others, except Cindy. This was the first time I've ever met her. One of those so-called friends was one of the reasons that I left home and came out here. The best thing that I have ever done." Sighing softly, she looked up into the ruggedly handsome face. "Well, come on, we have to get our horses. And, Tyler, forget about it. It's in the past, I want to keep it that way. The Jessica Cooper they knew is no longer. She got smart and grew up."

McKay smiled in return and together they headed for their horses and equipment. Behind the reassuring smile, doubt lurked. Tyler remembered the first day he had met her as a guest that had only been going to stay for a few weeks. She had been very shy, very unsure of herself; withdrawn and remote. The hurt had been there for anyone to see and he had found himself wanting to protect her. As the months had progressed she had gradually become more out-going, friendly; yet, there had remained that protective shield she seemed to keep close at hand. To all appearances it came across as a calm, cool reserve. To some people that didn't really know her, she appeared almost aloof, indifferent. But her friends knew better.

This small slip of a woman was great with children and animals. They trusted and loved her unconditionally. And she returned it.

Looking once more at the down bent head of the slender redhead, he solemnly promised himself that no one would hurt her again if there were any way that he could prevent it.

They each had a small cabin very near the two large bunkhouses and the horses were in a small corral behind them. At their approach, both horses whinnied greetings while moving up next to the fence.

Rebel gently nosed Tyler as he stepped into the corral. The red horse was of average size of about fifteen hands, with powerful shoulders and a muscled neck. Small pointed ears topped a proud, wise head with dark-brown eyes that watched everything about him.

Shiloh was closer to fourteen hands, but built a little more compact than the red horse. His fine-shaped head was molded beauty. A slender nose, wide-set intelligent dark-brown eyes and small, alert pointed ears. A blue-gray coat gleamed over strong, flowing muscles that was accented by the thick, rippling snow-white mane and tail. At seeing the young woman, the gelding playfully tugged at her shirt collar.

"Shi, cut it out, silly." Chuckled Jessie.

Tyler choked back the laughter that was threatening to spill out and shaking his head in amusement. "That horse is something else. Not exactly sure what. You two make quiet a pair."

Laughing blue-gray eyes turned on him and she took a mock swing at his retreating back.

Chapter Two

Leaning up against the outside wall of the outfitter's building, where he had been directed to go, Larry Connors quietly watched the large chestnut horse as it impatiently pawed the ground. Smiling, Larry rubbed a hand over the glossy neck and questioned softly of the gelding. "Ready to go, aren't you?"

The horse turned the large head and eyed the tall, platinum-haired man. His dark eyes intent and searching, Warsaw finally nudged Larry with his velvety-soft nose.

"Better watch that, Connors, you're talking to animals." Snickered Joseph Drake as he, Tim and Linda Winters moved up with their horses; Cindy a short distance behind them.

Before Larry could answer for himself, Cindy's soft voice sounded, "That's only bad if they answer you back, Joe."

Larry moved forward and wrapped an arm around the tall woman and hugged her slender body close to his. For two cents he would plant a good-sized fist in that pretty-boy face if he did anything even a little hurtful to Cindy. And from the look on Joe's face, the man was getting ready to do just that.

Hearing a shrill neigh of an excited horse, everyone looked up to watch McKay and Cooper as they neared the group. Both riders appeared almost a part of their mounts, completely at ease on the beautiful geldings.

Watching the little by-play between the three guests, Tyler frowned to himself. Something was wrong here; and he would have to find out later what it was. As Tyler halted Rebel, he carefully examined each guest's equipment. Finally turning to face Jess, he grinned knowingly as Shiloh nervously side-stepped with impatience. "What do you think, Jessie, are they ready for the two-day ride?"

The redhead flashed a brilliant smile. "As ready as they'll ever be."

McKay nodded agreement, then turned the red horse into the building. Watching him disappear into the shaded interior, Linda questioned of the mounted woman, "Where's he going, Jessica?"

Controlled gray eyes turned to the dark-haired woman. "To get the pack horses. Better get mounted. And by the way, I'm never called 'Jessica' here. I'd prefer that you call me Jessie or Jess." Glancing up she caught sight of McKay and added in a forced lightness of tone. "Well, here's Ty. Form a double line and follow us out at a walk, please. Is everyone ready? Good, let's go."

Much like a small cavalry patrol they filed out of the ranch yard. Moving past the manager's office, Phil appeared in the doorway and waved a casual farewell. Jess forced a tight smile onto her stiff lips and waved back in return. Letting a cool glance sweep the line of guests, she touched Shiloh's sides with her heels and the gelding broke into a slow lope.

Tyler moved up beside her, leading the two pack animals. The roan sided up next to the gray gelding, matching his pace to that of the gray. "How about letting them out for a real gallop before we start the upward climb?"

Jessie nodded approval at his suggestion, as Ty moved back to inform the others. "Last one to that stand of trees has to do the chores at camp tonight!"

With yells of challenge they kicked the all-too-eager horses into rapid motion. Jessie held Shiloh in check until the others had raced past and Tyler then yelled for her to get the lead out. Easing forward in the stock saddle, she let up on the rein and the gray gelding rocketed forward with her low over his slender neck.

Stride for stride the gray swept past the running group until the reddish nose of Rebel came up on his rear hip. Briefly the gray stayed even with the roan then took it upon himself to edge ahead just before reaching the border of the trees.

Sliding to a halt, Jess twisted around in the saddle to smile back at Tyler as he pulled the smooth moving red roan in beside her. They always raced like that; neither one ever really winning. Most of the time it was in fun, sort of a game they played. Sometimes Jessie thought that the two horses were playing the game themselves.

Soon the others reached them and again they started on their way. It was not long before the guests started seeing some of the really beautiful sights. Sights that could only be found in the high mountain country. Breathe taking sights like deep crevasses, high-towering mountains and waterfalls tumbling into cold, clear water-filled streams. They seemed to climb endlessly and at every turn in the trail something wild and exciting would never fail to show itself. By noon they took time out to eat the sandwiches and cold food the cooks had prepared for them. Then they were once again on their way.

Only now the terrain leveled out to some degree and they went down into lush green valleys and across deep-blue creeks where the wildlife seemed almost endless. It was nearing late afternoon when they came across their campsite. For the unaccustomed guests the long ride on horseback spelt only soreness in the sitting department for a while to come. But to their pleased surprise, after taking care of the horses and gathering firewood, they were not nearly as stiff as they had been.

As the fire started to come to life, Tyler stood up and faced the group. "How about a little fishing before we eat? I see that some of you brought rifles; please leave them in the scabbards. There is no shooting on this land. Only with cameras."

"If any of you would like to go camera hunting with me, you are now invited." declared Jessie with a smile.

Seeing disappointment on the two women's faces, Tyler suggested quietly, "I'm guessing, but I'd say off-hand that you didn't bring a camera along? Right, well no problem. We have enough in the backpack for each of you. So who wants one? And who wants to go fishing?"

Cooper looked at the other women as they looked back at her, then they all started to laugh. "I think all of us females will take the cameras and let you 'he-men' handle the fish."

Watching the three women head out of camp, Jess in the lead, Tyler bent to pick up his pole. As he straightened he came face to face with Larry Connors. "She has changed since I last seen her. For the better, I'd say. Prettier, for one thing. She used to wear her hair short and was very slender, almost like a boy. I know it's none of my business, but you seem to care about her. Never mind, you don't need to answer that. Would you believe that when I knew her she would have let both Linda and Joe more or less walk all over her? I don't mean that they were cruel or anything like that; but, that she would not have done anything to displease them. Not even a difference of an opinion. She was their errand boy. I bet you wouldn't catch her doing something like that now. She appears to be more sure of herself. If someone doesn't like the way she is; well, too bad. It's their loss. I like that."

At first Tyler had been taken by surprise, then as what the blonde-haired man had to say sank in, he listened more closely. Studying the clear-cut features, McKay realized that this man had no hang-ups about himself, so had been able to recognize the same traits in Jess.

Once again looking over at the tall man, Tyler had to admit that he liked him and a deep-gut feeling declared that it wasn't Larry Connors that had sent Jessie away hurting and trying to hide.

Nodding, Ty laid a gentle hand on the man's shoulder. "Thanks for telling me. I think your girlfriend is another one of those strong-minded people. Cindy seems very nice."

"One thing, when we rode up to the barn, I noted a tenseness. What was going on? I need to know if there is going to be any trouble?" questioned Tyler softly.

A sheepish grin flickered across the handsome face. "Nothing to really worry about. Joe can be a pain in the butt and I didn't want him giving Cindy a bad time. He has some bias opinions and I didn't want him voicing them to her by word or deed. I'll let you know if I can't take care of it. Alright?"

"I don't seriously think you will have any trouble in handling him." Chuckled the trail foreman.

Glancing up as the others brought up their poles, he added loudly enough that they could all hear. "Well, let's see if we can catch something for supper? Or we'll never, and I do mean never hear the end of it if we don't."

As they neared the creek shore, Joe moved off by himself. He, too, was thinking just how much Jessica Cooper had changed. It disturbed him a little to know that she had turned into a small knock-out. Not quite beautiful, but she had her own delicate beauty. He had been a damn fool to have once thought that she was not good enough for him to be seen escorting her with his friends. Maybe she still felt something for him? If so, maybe he could try his hand at getting her back? Hell, at one time she had adored him; why should that have changed? He had been the one to break off the relationship, not her.

Even as he thought out his next move, he couldn't help but remember just how she had acted toward him earlier. Not a good sign.

A short while later the camera-shooting party returned to camp, just as the men were starting to cook their catch of trout. And the aroma was mouth-watering. Putting their cameras away, the women helped with the rest of the preparation of the evening meal.

The sun had long since disappeared and darkness seemed to envelop them. The guests were stretched out in various places around the glowing campfire. Jessie sat a short distance away from Tyler, remaining remote and dangerously quiet. McKay glanced at the small tense body; moving to the guests, the greenish-gold eyes pausing momentarily on the dark-tanned features of Joseph Drake. The dark eyes were pinned intently on the slender redhead.

If Tyler wondered about that he gave no visual sign; but McKay was not the kind that showed his inner thoughts or emotions. He had been brought up in a male dominated life, hard and with no frills. A life where a show of emotions was also a sign of weakness. Even though Tyler gave the impression of an easy-going individual, he also had a dangerously short, volatile temper. Most of his friends had forgotten what kind of temper he had as he had learned to control it; but then he let it simmer until an explosion was imminent. He had the appearance of refined hardness; but his friends knew just how loyal and gentle he really was, but only his friends. On the whole, he was an easy-going, take-it-or-leave-it sort of man; but underneath that charm there was a hard core of reality.

Resting back on his forearms, Larry Connors studied the trail guide through lowered lids. McKay was gazing into the darkness, the fire's soft light flickering over the bronzed planes of his handsome face. True, it was a handsome face, ruggedly handsome, not pretty-boy handsome. But it was more than just bones and flesh; it was a face with character. No one was going to pull anything over on a man that possessed character like that of McKay. Connors liked what he had seen of the trail foreman so far; and he had met all sorts in his life.

Trying to read something of the expressionless features and seeing a slight frown mar the strong forehead, Larry had the feeling that McKay was thinking about Joe Drake. Now there was a typical pretty-boy face and an I-know-it attitude. Larry had never taken to Linda's brother. Larry didn't think that the cowboy particularly cared for the dark-haired Drake either. And to Connor's way of thinking the less McKay trusted the moody Joe the better off the cowboy would be.

Glancing up suddenly, Larry found himself looking into the cat-green eyes and knew that the trail foreman had sensed his gaze on him.

Tyler stretched his lean frame and then rose to his feet. Sweeping the group with a cool glance, he suggested quietly, "I think that it would be to everyone's benefit to climb into the sleeping bags. Morning comes way too early as it is."

A few grumbled, but nonetheless they curled up in their blankets. Within a very few minutes all were sound asleep.

By morning when the cold met their lazy efforts to get up, most would have preferred to have remained snug and warm inside their sleeping bags. Tyler got the men up and about; while Jess did the same with the women. She already had bacon sizzling and coffee bubbling to help in combined efforts to arouse the five guests. Eventually their prodding succeeded and one and all were sitting around the campfire eating freshly caught trout, crisp bacon, biscuits and steaming coffee or hot chocolate.

After stuffing themselves, they found that getting the horses ready for riding was not half so difficult. Amazingly by the time they were all mounted, it did not feel quite so chilly either. Tyler gathered the two pack horses and followed the group as Jessie took the lead.

If the first part of the trail ride had produced beautiful scenery, then the country they were traveling through now was pure heaven, or as close as they could get. The day before they had traveled up into the high country, now they were going down among the hidden valleys. Lush deep-green grasses reached to the horses' bellies, brushing the legs of the riders. Tall, towering pine dotted the ever changing landscape and suddenly a long, deep, very blue lake opened up in front of the astonished riders.

At the back of the lake; tall, rugged mountain walls cut jaggedly into the cloudless blue sky. Their magnificence reflected in the calm, crystal-clear waters of the lake. Tyler drew rein and the others followed suit.

Cooper watched the different expressions that played across the five faces. Some showed surprise, others amazement. But Cindy's was the most overwhelmed. Turning a bright face that hid nothing of her pleasure and wonder, Cindy breathed excitedly, "I've never seen anything half so lovely. I can't find words – it's just --- Wow!"

Jessie laughed softly. "I've seen it many times, but it still affects me. Each time I see it, it changes. Now, let's move on down a little farther and we'll set up camp."

McKay had already moved the pack animals to a sheltered area and was beginning to start to build the campfire. Raising his head to watch the guests returning from staking out the horses, he suggested quietly, "Make yourselves comfortable, we'll be here for a while."

With the fire burning well and the guests seemingly taking care of themselves; Tyler stretched out on his own blanket-roll, carelessly he drawled, "The fishing is great up here. If you would like to, the poles are right over there. If you want to hike, have at it. There is a marked hiking trail just over there. Just stay together. There are also hotdogs if any of you feel like roasting some, and cans of pop in a bag floating in the lake. The rest of the afternoon is up to you. Jessie knows where there are some baby foxes and a spot where we sighted a couple of twin fawns."

At first they just looked at each other, then Tim and Larry grinned and started off to pick up the fishing poles. The girls eyed one another for a few moments more, then Cindy declared, "I don't know about you, Linda, but if Jess doesn't mind I'd like to see those babies."

Cooper chuckled low in her throat, nodded the sunset-colored head in agreement. Linda and Cindy followed the redhead through the thick timber.

Tyler glanced at the one remaining, Joe Drake. With a grin tugging slightly at the firm mouth, he merely leaned back, making himself more comfortable by pulling his hat low over his eyes. To all concerned, he appeared asleep.

Soon Drake moved on down to where the other two were fishing, and Ty was finally able to relax. He found that he was very glad that Joe had not stayed in camp. He didn't care for the Drake man and knew that those feelings would show if he were around him long enough without someone there to ease the tension.

Sometime after attempting to relax, Tyler must have dozed off. At the sound of loud, frantic shouting, he was jerked rudely awake. Springing to his feet, he met Linda running into camp, fear apparent on her features. Reaching out he grabbed ahold of her shoulders, pulling her up short. "Linda, calm down. Now tell me what's wrong?"

The woman's face was pale beneath the tan, dark eyes were swimming in tears as she choked out, "It's...uh... Jessica! She's in a...uh...trap! You've got to hurry!"

"What? Hell! Where at, Linda?" demanded McKay in a clipped, tight voice.

"It's where the horses are." Mumbled the dark-haired woman on a frightened sob.

Not waiting any longer, Tyler took off at a dead run. Pushing his way through the underbrush, he stumbled forward into the clearing where the horses stood tethered. Glancing to his left, he caught sight of the redhead. She was slumped on the ground, her slender body hunched over her right foot. The ankle appeared lodged tightly between the jaws of a steel trap.

The delicate lips were drawn tight over clinched teeth, attempting to keep from crying out in pain; but large tears nevertheless rolled down the pale cheeks. Quickly Tyler was at her side, speaking calmly as he gripped the trap with lean, tanned hands. Anger simmered in the soft masculine voice as he whispered near her ear. "Hang on, Jess, have it off in a jiffy."

In a few brief minutes, the steel jaws inched open and the girl pulled the injured foot out. As the jaws snapped sharply together; Tyler found himself holding onto Jessie as she silently cried against his chest. In a short time, she pushed herself back away from him and lowered the autumn-colored head. "Sorry, Ty, didn't mean to cry all over you, like some baby. But, damn, it hurts."

"Forget it." Whispered McKay softly as he bent forward, tilting the small face up so that he could look into the pain-darkened gray eyes. "Now, let's have a peek at that ankle. Good thing you had your boots on."

Just as he was about to remove the mangled boot, the others arrived and unnoticed, one extra. At first no one saw the intruder as everyone tried to talk at once. Linda Winters rushed to Jessie's side, kneeling down on her knees and taking the redhead's small hand. "Is she alright?"

The husky male voice was grim as he answered, "We will know in a few minutes. What I'd like to know is how in the hell a trap got here in the first place."

"That's easy enough to answer, McKay." The strange deep voice grumbled from behind the gathered group.

Slowly Tyler looked up as the others moved nervously to see this new threat. McKay's rugged features hardened into angry lines, the usually friendly hazel eyes turned decidedly dangerous. The intruder was mounted on a large bay that shifted nervously. Roughly handsome, if one would go that far. At the moment his face carried an ugly sneer.

Leaning back slowly, his voice hard and dripping with ice, McKay stated, "Dave Hunter. Alright, if you have the answers, let's hear them."

"That's an easy one. The trap belongs to me."

McKay started to rise, but Hunter's voice halted him mid-way. "Stay put. I'd hate to have these nice people see their head guide get himself shot for being just plain foolish."

Tyler's lips curled back, jaw muscles bunched with suppressed anger. Anger so hot that the cowboy almost ignored the leveled gun pointed directly at his chest. He more than likely would have tried his luck at charging Hunter, if Jess's small hand hadn't stopped the move. Sighing shakily, he glanced down into her small oval face.

Such a worried little face, and pale. Suddenly a deadly calmness swept over him. Throwing a quick glance at the clustered guests, he saw them standing almost motionless; except for Larry, who was eyeing Hunter with wary, cautious eyes.

McKay grinned disarmingly, yet the gold-green eyes still held the hard glint of anger. Slowly, very slowly, he stood up and managed to keep the grin planted on his stiff lips; as a bullet kicked up the dirt near his booted feet.

Involuntarily taking a step forward, Larry Connors stopped when he heard McKay speak in a quiet, deadly calm voice.

Tyler was perfectly aware of his danger, but exaggerating his western drawl, stated pointedly, "This is Dave Hunter. Wes Wilcox's foreman and henchman."

Not quite able to understand McKay's grin and coolness, Hunter tried to sneer his way on. "I said to stay put, Tyler Boy. Any closer and I'll have to do you some bodily harm."

"I don't doubt it." His voice was rough. "But, I'll warn you right now. If I catch you over or anywhere near here again...I will personally beat the living hell out of you."

Hunter laughed nervously. "Look who's talking. I could k---." Glancing quickly at the ranch guests, he substituted, "You are in no position to be making threats, Ty. I've got the gun and the upper hand."

Tyler smiled again, no humor showing, only sustained rage. "Guess you're right about that. But remember, Dave, I don't make idle threats."

As a flicker of unease slid across the dark-featured face; McKay leaped forward like a swift moving cougar, reaching for the man's mount. The sudden attack, not only caught Dave Hunter by surprise; but also startled the man's bay horse into a decisive side step that caused Hunter to go off-balance. It gave Tyler the advantage he had needed and savagely he grabbed the bigger man and jerked him from the skittish horse.

Hunter somehow managed to hang on to his handgun, an old fashion revolver. As he fell against Tyler, he used the weapon as a club. Slashing down on McKay's left shoulder, causing the younger man to stagger under the brutal impact to his knees. The shirt ripped and after a couple more hard blows, blood started seeping down his arm.

Still on his knees, Ty decided to take the last and only alternative he had left. So ramming his good shoulder into Hunter's mid-section, they crashed over backwards. Hunter landed hard under Tyler; and McKay took full note of the fact, grabbing the gun from Dave Hunter's fingers, then tossing it out of reach.

With a quiet savageness, McKay slugged Hunter in the face. Not once, but continuously; not letting the bigger man gain any kind of advantage. In a matter of moments, his face bloody, Hunter threw up his hands yelling defeat.

Breathing heavily, Tyler leaning back, slowly pushing himself up off the larger man. Glancing up, he singled out Larry and Tim. "Help him on his horse."

Weaving unsteadily over to where he had tossed the gun, Tyler returned and handed it to Larry to empty any shells. Throwing a freezing angry glare at Hunter. "When Larry, here, gives you your gun, get the hell out of here. And, Dave, next time things might be different; I might be wearing one of those, too. Just remember."

His face a mass of bruises and drying blood, Hunter mumbled under his breath. "I won't forget, McKay."

The trail foreman's features were as if made from stone, the eyes cold as he warned through stiff lips, "Good. Just so you know."

Uncertainty caused the husky-built man to let his glance linger on McKay's handsome, but chilly, closed features. Then with a savage jerk on the reins, he turned the bay and bounded away through the timber.

Without further discussion on the incident, Tyler turned round and was again working on Jessie's injured foot. "Now for that ankle." Looking up once at the silent, gathered group, he remarked quietly, "Better tend to the camp. And what about the fish?"

Larry Connors took the hint and made sure that the rest started back toward camp. Linda was the only one to remain behind to help McKay with Jessie's injury.

Before he could get the boot pulled off, Jess questioned, "Ty, your shoulder? It's still bleeding. Don't you think you should do something with it first?"

McKay flicked a cool glance over her lovely face. "After we bandage your ankle."

No bones appeared broken, but the ankle was cut and swollen. Not as bad as they had at first thought. With the combined help of Linda and Tyler, Jessie was able to limp painfully back to camp. Cooper was feeling much better by the time her ankle was neatly bandaged. A quick glance at McKay and she stiffened in concern.

His usually dark-tanned features had drained of color, leaving him quite pale. The shirt sleeve was stained with dried blood and apparently he was in some pain as he had the injured arm held close to his body keeping it very still. From the looks of him, Jess was afraid that he was going into shock.

The blonde-haired Larry appeared at Tyler's side at about the same instant that Jessie's quiet voice sounded, "Ty, it's your turn to be taken care of. No arguments, just sit down."

McKay managed a weak grin and then sank to the ground with a tired sigh.

Chapter Three

By late afternoon Jessie had decided that Tyler was well enough to start the long journey back to the ranch. The condition of his shoulder looked to be very serious; but being decidedly stubborn, McKay insisted that it was fine. A long ragged tear extended from the top of his shoulder and across the blade to below the underside of the band of muscled ribs.

Cooper was afraid that he would need stitches; and the sooner they returned to the ranch the sooner he could be treated. But try and tell that to Tyler McKay was like talking to a brick wall. A thick brick wall at that.

In what was only minutes, that seemed more like hours, they were all saddled and ready to be underway leaving the lake area behind. Jess led off with Larry beside her and Tyler riding on out ahead with the two pack horses. Connors glanced over at the silent redhead; she was intently watching McKay with worried gray eyes. Leaning forward slightly, he remarked softly, "He's quite a guy, isn't he?"

"Yeah...I guess you could say that. Stubborn as all-get-out." Murmured Jess quietly, a slight smile in her voice.

"He was very...uh...angry while he was fighting with that Dave Hunter. I don't believe that I have ever seen a man that close to beating another senseless with his bare hands. You do know that Hunter would have killed or at the very least, have shot McKay if he hadn't had an audience."

The young woman sighed, leaned back in the saddle just a trifle to ease stiff muscles. "I know. It goes back a long time. I'm sorry, I shouldn't be bothering you with all of this."

Connors shook the blonde head. "Seems to me that I started this conversation. I'd like to know. I already like Tyler. And I'd like to know the reason for the violence we seen earlier."

Turning a pensive, thoughtful face toward her old friend before saying quietly, "Alright. Like I said it all began quite a long time back. I heard it from one of the older cowhands that told me a lot about the past. Tyler's past. Ty doesn't talk much about himself. Like he isn't just the trail foreman and also the horse trainer. He is in charge of buying all the saddle stock for the ranch as well as the pack animals and draft horses. He is also a stock holder in the guest ranch. He owns a large section of land up in the mountains where he is building a cabin by himself."

Grinning slightly, she continued in a soft patient voice, "He's really very talented. Did you know that he has a very good singing voice? Yep, I'm not kidding. But back to the distasteful Hunter. Tyler's father, Taylor McKay, had been one of the first cowhands to work for the guest ranch when it first began. In fact, he was working for the ranch before it became a guest ranch. Tyler, of course, grew up around the cowhands and horses. His mother had died when he was just a little boy, so he had grown up with mostly adult males. He was a top contender at bareback and saddle bronc riding at some of the best rodeos. Then he started to train and gentle the young horses for the ranch; and stopped competing on the rodeo circuit.

"At first he did all the little odd jobs around the stable along with the horse work. Shortly after he had started working with the horses, he was promoted to head wrangler. He was just out of high school, can you believe that? Over six years later his father, who was then foreman of the working part of the ranch, had went out to the far edges of the ranch to check out some problem and while out there had an accident. When they found him a few hours later, he was unconscious. He never came out of the coma before he died.

"Hunter was one of the trail guides and one of the men next in line for the trail foreman position. The older trail foreman retired and Phil, the ranch manager, chose Tyler over Hunter. After Tyler's Father's death Phil took over both phases of the ranch. And Taylor had been Phil's best friend. But that wasn't why he picked Tyler; the owners of the guest ranch had the final say."

"And Hunter, not liking to be out-done by a twenty-sum-year-old-kid, went to work for Wilcox." Interrupted Larry sharply.

Cooper slowly nodded her head. "Well, uh yes, something like that. Except that Hunter stayed on. He figured Ty would fail or make a serious mistake; or just not be able to handle the job. But of course, McKay didn't fail.

"He not only trained and then rode Confederate to victory, but also broke and then trained Rebel. That horse had everyone figuring that he would never make a saddle horse. Rebel has won quite a few championship trail courses and also a number of endurance races. The main owner of the ranch presented Tyler with Rebel the same afternoon of the first race that Con won for the ranch. He also gave him shares in the ranch and made him the horse buyer for the whole ranch. That was when Hunter went to work for Wilcox as foreman. Ever since there has been trouble of some kind, either between McKay and Hunter or the ranches. That is about the time that Ty's father died.

"So far, though, McKay hasn't completely lost his temper. And believe me he does have a temper. Or so I've been told. Tyler isn't in the habit of wearing a side arm; especially while guests were around. But I have heard that he is real fast with one; you know, like fast guns of the old west? He's also a sharp-shooter. He's won a number of competitions here in Wyoming. I'm just afraid that Ty will start carrying a gun. He hasn't even competed in any marksmen contests for a number of years."

Larry's tanned features paled slightly. "I can see why you would be worried. But, don't you think that Hunter might be more cautious of pushing McKay if he were armed? Tyler was unarmed today and it didn't seem to stop Hunter. We did. Too many witnesses. If it were me, I'd think twice before provoking a man that was armed and had a rep with a gun. I'm fairly certain that Hunter isn't completely stupid enough to take that kind of risk."

Cooper frowned in concentration. "I hope you're right, Larry."

Glancing at the powerfully built back of McKay, Larry Connors sighed to himself. He hoped so too.

It was nearing dusk as once again Phil found himself going to the office window. He just kept looking out across the valley to the foot of the mountain trail.

A sigh escaped him as finally Tyler's group was on their way in. Phil Holden by nature was not the worrying kind, but for some odd reason he had this strange, uneasy feeling all afternoon? Besides, Tyler's group wasn't even late. He just couldn't seem to relax. A restlessness that was very unusual for the older man. Ty was almost like his son, and for that matter, so was Jessie like a daughter. They were his family. And for some unknown reason he was worried about them?

Before returning to his cluttered desk, he threw one more glance toward the nearing group of riders. It was then that he noticed the bootless foot of Jessie and then the torn, sleeveless shirt on McKay.

Stepping out of the door, he sent one of the cowhands for the doctor. Proceeding on into the yard, he met Jess first. Without preamble he asked bluntly, "What happen?"

Cooper's cool storm-gray eyes flew to Tyler. A worried frown forming between the gold-flecked brows. "I'll explain later. Get Ty to Doc's."

McKay slowly and very stiffly dismounted. Then he told the others to head on over to the barn and that someone would help them unsaddle. Larry Connors moved his horse up close to McKay and took the pack animals from the trail guide's tired grip.

Leaning wearily against Rebel, Tyler sighed deeply. Then Phil's deep voice reached him and he forced his sore body straighter.

"Ty, come with me."

Hazel eyes, sharp with pain, settled on the ranch foreman's worried features. Tyler managed a weak grin. "Okay, Phil, I'm just too tired to argue. But, you had better take Jess, too. She caught her foot in a steel trap."

Holden stood for a brief moment; first looking at McKay, then back to Jessie. His face taking on a puzzled expression, mumbled something to himself, then turned to the doctor as he appeared, "Take them both, Bob."

Sitting around the large oval-shaped cement pool, Tyler McKay flexed his left shoulder. A dull stiffness still lingered, even after a week of careful healing. The warm sun felt wonderful on his sore, torn muscles and flesh. His whole body welcomed the comfortable warming rays.

In the days preceding the encounter with Dave Hunter and in the last few days, more guests had arrived; and soon the ranch would be filled to capacity. With the unusually warm, sunny days the younger people seemed more inclined to cling close to the pool area. But right then he could have cared less, nothing seemed to matter; he would just close his eyes and soak up some more sun.

Hearing a squeal of surprise and followed by laughter; Tyler snapped open gold-green eyes in time to see a pretty girl in a very brief blue bikini, get thrown in the deep end of the pool among laughing friends. A careless smile touched the firm, male lips as he watched the playful scene before him.

Appearing from the patio, Jessie let her cool glance travel over the guests, coming to rest on the relaxing Tyler. Unconsciously she let the misty-blue gaze linger on the lean, bronzed features.

She liked the way the male lips curved into a gentle smile, the way the greenish eyes turned soft with tawny-gold flecks. He was wearing a brief slim-fitting gold-brown swimming trunks that accentuated the dark-bronzed, well-built body. Very male body.

Moving with a graceful ease, Jessie made her way toward the reclining cowboy; who at the moment did not look at all like a cowhand. Still unnoticed, she leaned down beside him, whispering huskily in his ear. "Hello, Lazy."

McKay grinned, looking up at the slender young woman from under lowered lids. She was wearing a rust-colored one-piece suit that was about the same color as the reddish hair swirling around the slim shoulders.

"Lazy? Me?" He chuckled softly.

"Yes. Why aren't you in that pool having fun?" She challenged with a laugh.

A blush crept over his lean features, but his smile widened. "Why aren't you in there having fun?" he countered.

Before she could form a reply, he rose leisurely to his full lean, muscled height. Bending slightly, powerful arms scooped her lighter frame up close to the deep chest and he headed for the pool. Realizing his intent, she let out a lusty yell of objection. "Oh!! Tyler! No, you wouldn't!!"

The arms were gentle, yet strong; no matter how much she struggled, he only had to tighten them to hold her. Coming to the edge of the pool, he lifted her out away from his body and as she gave a last slim effort to hold on; they both went into the water.

Laughing and choking, they both surfaced at about the same instance. Tyler managed to find his voice first. "Well, we are both in now. Are we having fun, yet?" He added with a chuckle.

Mischief flashed in the stormy-gray eyes as she splashed the clear, cool water in the laughing face, chuckling softly. "Yes, Sir! Can't you tell?"

He was after her in a flash; his sleek bronzed frame skimming effortlessly through the clear, blue-green water. Just as he was about to reach her, she dove under the surface heading for the bottom of the pool. Taking a deep breath, he went after her. The clear water enabling him to see her slim shape as it gracefully tried to elude his searching hands. With a strong kick, he closed the distance and caught hold of the tiny waist, then he headed for the surface. With a heave, Tyler lifted her to the side of the pool; then just as easily, lifted himself out of the refreshing water to sit beside her. With their legs dangling over the side, their feet swirling the water. Turning the teak-tan face toward her, he asked in a light, joking tone. "That was fun. Shall we try it again?"

Gray eyes with blue sparks dancing in their smoky depths, looked over his features. Cooper shook her head, the dark-red hair sending a shower of water around her and the fine spray touching McKay. "Are you kidding?" Then with a grin, "Never mind, I don't want to know."

Unconsciously she stretched the slender, softly curved body back; emphasizing the small, firm breasts and flat, smooth belly. Hazel-green eyes narrowed as they took in the sensual body and slightly teasing expression that lightened the lovely small oval face. A sudden unexpected warmth uncurled itself through his lower body up into the muscled stomach. Desire, pure and simple. A stillness settled over the hard features, hopefully hiding the realization of the desire he had just discovered. Forcing a brittle smile to his now stiff lips, he tried a soft chuckle that sounded more like a choking sensation deep in his throat.

Jessie must have caught something of his tension for she frowned and studied the ragged scar. "Ty, how's the shoulder? Still stiff? Looks painful."

He smiled gently. "Not so much anymore. So lose the frightened look on your face."

Color stole over the delicate features. "Well...Ty..."

"Never mind, little one. I understand. Say, there's Joe and Larry. You know I really like Connors. He seems an alright guy."

Seeing the small face turn pale, then feeling the bite of slender fingers on his lower arm; he turned to where she had been looking.

Cooper had turned at Tyler's brief words, prepared to see Joe and Larry. But her glance had picked out another figure. Tall and broad shouldered with light-brown hair. He could have been very handsome, if it had not been for the cold, cruel pale-brown eyes and hard, thin lips.

Tyler looked past the two guests and then, he too, sighted the man. Both of them rose to their feet slowly as the man started toward them. McKay let his fingers gently enclose Jessie's smaller hand and he more or less felt her looking at him. Flashing a reassuring smile at her tense little face, he noted that her features were no longer pale; but that her expression was that of a cold mask, as aloof as his own.

McKay spoke quietly as the man neared. "What can I do for you, Wilcox?"

Wes Wilcox eyed the two people standing before him, his expression unreadable except for the faint sign of impatience. "It seems Holden is away and so that leaves you, McKay."

"So it does." Tyler grinned slightly, not humorously, but knowingly. The greenish-gold eyes were steady as they stared at the rancher's hard, smooth face. "I know you are not here for a visit, so just what is your reason?"

The rancher glanced quickly at Jessie, then returned the cold reptile gaze back to the trail foreman. "It concerns my foreman and some lost or stolen property."

McKay's look was inscrutable. But before he could reply, Cooper stepped in, her husky voice soft and quiet. "Your property was neither lost nor stolen. You see, the property, a steel trap, just happen to entangle itself onto a foot. It's just terrible about Hunter. What awful thing happen to that poor man?"

Jessie's cool mockery brought a rush of color to the rancher's face. And it was several seconds before the man could bring himself to answer.

"That 'poor man' as you call him, was beat up. And I don't have to tell you by whom. If the trap caught an unsuspecting horse, I'm terribly sorry; but it shouldn't have been on Lazier land. But I want," and turning to face Tyler, he added, "you to make a formal apology and pay Dave's doctor bills."

Jessie gasped. The gall of the man! She clenched her small hands into tight fists, eyes blazing. "Of all the nerve! On your land! For one thing, Wilcox, it was on Jute Valley land and it was 'my foot' that your beastly trap sank its teeth into. And it could have just as easily been one of the guests." She was moving steadily toward the rancher, her voice slashing with a biting edge. "And as for Hunter; if he was that hurt, he must have fell off his horse a couple of dozen times before he reached Lazier. He held and fired a gun at an unarmed man. And threatened that unarmed man that was surrounded by innocent guests, who could have been injured. Now, I suggest that you go talk with Sheriff Cradling and get your damn trap back and pay some expenses of your own!"

She turned so sharply that Wilcox backed away from her and stepped into the pool. Hearing the startled yell and then the splash, Jess spun back around. Her delicate mouth fell open with surprise as she watched the tall rancher pull himself up out of the pool.

Tyler stood beside her, a grin playing across his lean features. Completely embarrassed and enraged beyond speech, Wilcox glared at the girl, then hurriedly departed.

Larry Connors joined them remarking, "Wow! When you get mad, you don't fool around." Then turning to Tyler, "Did I hear right? Was that Wes Wilcox?"

McKay nodded. "That's right. Jessie, my girl, I'm proud of you." At her startled glance, he continued, "You gave that man an honest-to-goodness tongue lashing. And one he'll not likely forget in a long while."

She smiled hesitantly. "I...It was funny when he fell in the pool. But I hadn't intended for that to happen. Or for that matter, to get that all fired up. I was going to be so... cool." She whispered on a soft sigh.

Both men just looked at each other and smiled a knowing smile.

Chapter Four

By evening the entire incident with Wes Wilcox was all over the guest ranch. Guests and employees alike were discussing it.

After eating, Jessie silently left the large crowded dining room and drifted out into the growing darkness. The stars were brightly twinkling and the moon was just topping a set of mountains in the near distance.

Walking out into the shaded confines of the nearby stand of tall trees, Cooper leaned back against the rough bark of the solid fir tree. Her gray eyes were dark shadows and the even darker hair fell in a riotous fall of curls about the small oval face. Standing there she looked like a lost shadow. Very small and very alone.

Her thoughts were churning around in her head until they were giving her one hell of a headache. First, the surprise of Joe and the others turning up here of all places. Then the thing with Hunter; and now, having more or less, pushed Wilcox in the pool. Fate was sure dumping a load of crap on them big time. It wasn't fair, but when was life ever fair?

Jess had put the memories of her family and home far back in her mind. But the unexpected arrival of her old friends had brought them surging to the surface. As vivid as ever. Two years, no; more than that. Closer to three. She had been twenty-two when she had thought that she was in love with Joseph Drake. He had ignored her at first, but later something had changed and he had started taking her out. By the time she was nearing her twenty-third birthday, they were to have been engaged to be married.

Now she was twenty-six. A lot older twenty-six. But still, what did age mean? At twenty-one or so a person was considered an adult. But she had been a very young twenty-two and an even younger fool. Naïve and a fool.

What did the years in between mean? While she had been here at the ranch? Had she learned anything? Then she knew. She had developed her own rules for living. Her own self-worth. And it didn't mean to cower to or to be used by others. She had grown up, no it was more than that. Matured. She had matured over the years. Not just in looks, but in outlooks. She had also found out the difference between friends and real friends. And there was a very big difference.

Nevertheless, the old memories hurt. No matter how hard her outer shell had become. They still managed to penetrate and tear at the soft, tender heart. She remembered when she had tried to explain her shattered feelings to her mother; but she just couldn't seem to understand. So Jess had left, supposedly on a vacation.

And that is what it had intended to be. Just some time for herself. To get over the hurt and humiliation.

But she hadn't counted on the lure of the towering mountains that put their majestic spell over her. She had fallen in love with the towering giants, the ranch life and everyone. So she stayed.

Tears ran slowly down the smooth, lightly-tanned cheek. Silently she cried. Jessie, who never cried. But of course she had, only in private. Not around others. Tears that had to force their way through tightly shut lids. Tearing themselves from her very soul.

Careless of the misty evening dampness that had settled on the pine-needled covered ground, she sank sadly onto their fragrant softness. The tears still made a damp trail down her cheek and silently dripped off the edge of the small, stubborn chin. In the moonlight, they glistened and the large dark eyes caught and held the moon's soft glow in their shadowy gray depths.

From the entrance of the now empty dining room, Tyler leaned a shoulder against the outside wall, the hazel eyes scanning the empty darkness. For more than an hour he had been searching for Cooper.

Suddenly a thought struck him. Maybe she had walked into the small forest near the two cabins that they used? With purposeful strides, he headed into the quiet vastness. About to turn back after not seeing her, he caught a glimpse of something white at the base of one of the tall firs.

With careful, quiet steps he neared the tree. To his relief, he saw that it was indeed the redhead. A glance and he realized that she was sound asleep. Kneeling down beside her, he gently lifted the slender form into his arms.

The red-gold head nestled snug against his chest and looking down at her, he again felt the uncurling warmth of desire.

For a moment he stood silent, just watching the lovely face and wet-tipped lashes that rested like a fan on the smooth, lightly-freckled cheeks. What had caused her to cry?

Taking a deep breath, he turned and headed for her cabin. Walking along in the darkness, he felt the soft warmth of the small body against his skin. A sudden impulse to kiss the upturned lips, caused him to halt once again. After a few calming deep breaths, he shook his dark, curly head and continued swiftly on his way.

He made his way cautiously, but in no time at all he was pushing open the screen door of her cabin. Gently laying the sleeping form on the soft, over-stuffed couch; Tyler straightened, then turned to the small fireplace.

The only light came from the glowing embers of the dying fire. Turning, he watched as the fire's light made delicate patterns on her light-gold features. The reddish hair caught and held the amber glow, firing the color to a burnished copper. She was beautiful, he suddenly realized. Lovely and desirable. And his friend. And she meant more to him than just a friend. A lot more. When had his feelings for her changed? Should he say something of his feelings? No. The discovery had been a shock for him, it would be even more so for her, wouldn't it? The last thing he wanted to do was frighten her and lose her trust.

Walking back over to the couch where Jessie was sleeping, he just stood and watched her for a brief few moments. He hated to wake her, but she shouldn't really sleep in her clothes. So kneeling down close to her, his hand touched her shoulder.

"Jess honey." No response, so shaking her gently, he tried again. "Jessie, wake up."

Thickly fringed eyelids flickered open. A slim, small hand caught ahold of his sleeve; unconsciously he noted the strength of the fine-boned fingers. The sleepy gray-blue eyes settled on his face and she smiled softly. "Sorry, Ty. How'd you find me?"

With his free hand, he pushed back the silky fall of hair from the smooth forehead. "It took me a while. Sort of stumbled onto you. Not to worry. It was a pleasure, little one. Now, you had better get changed and into bed. You have those kids tomorrow, don't you?"

A smile touched the fine lips. "Yes, I sure do. But, I really enjoy doing it."

Gaining his feet, his left hand lingered on her shoulder. Turning his face slightly away so as to hide the desire he was feeling for her, he sighed, "Well, I better head for bed myself. I've horses to hoof trim in the morning. Thrilling."

Stifling a yawn, she remarked, "You love it." Then a slight frown dulled the half formed smile. "What about your shoulder? Do you really think you should tackle the trimming yet?"

"Of course, silly. It's still a little sore, but I've got to use it so that it doesn't stiffen up. Besides, half-pint, I carried you here. Didn't hurt a bit." And he grinned sheepishly.

Jessie looked up from under long, gold-tipped lashes. "That's not the same thing as a twelve hundred pound horse."

"No, guess not. But, I still have to do them. Now, good-night, Jess, I'll see you in the morning."

Cooper watched as he left, still feeling worried about him. His shoulder had not healed enough to be safe. She would have to think of something. But what? Finally deciding that it was a lost cause, she got ready for bed and once between the cool sheets, it wasn't long before she was sound asleep.

Waking earlier than usual, Joe Drake found himself walking alone beside the large buildings that held the saddles and other equipment. He had seen Jessie Cooper a few minutes before, leading seven or eight little kids in the direction of the horse corrals.

With her new changed attitude, he did not know exactly how to approach her. Hearing a voice he thought he recognized, he looked across the corral fence and spotted the lean, hard muscled back of Tyler McKay. The cowhand was doing something with one of the horses.

Slipping between the railings, he headed to where McKay stood working on a large, bay horse. Watching the man, Joe decided that when it came down to getting Jessica back; Tyler would be one of the major obstacles, possibly the main one. He vaguely wondered if the two had been lovers or for that matter were? He couldn't tell by their attitudes toward each other, though at times it seemed to be one of protection.

Joe had never in his thirty-odd years cared about anyone but himself, so couldn't really understand it in others. Because he was of a slender build and until he was almost seventeen had remained on the short side, he had always used the old excuse that he could not match up with the bigger guys. And McKay represented the very example that he himself could have been if he had tried. Joe had never tried to better himself if he had to work at it. Never had to, for others had always done everything for him one way or another. He was good-looking in a dark way, and he knew it and used it. He never had to take the responsibility for his own actions or choices, let alone the mistakes.

Before reaching McKay, the black-haired cowboy turned to face him; apparently he had heard or sensed his approach. Seeing who it was, a dark brow lifted in question. "Hello, Joe. Up early, aren't you?"

"Guess so." Joe answered dryly. "What are you doing?"

Greenish-gold eyes ran carefully over the other as he spoke. "Trimming the horse's hooves. Actually, I'm finishing up."

When he moved to the horse, he unconsciously rubbed his shoulder and upper arm, a faint grimace on the handsome features. Joe, seeing this, remarked with the barest hint of selfish pleasure in his voice. "It...your shoulder...does it bother you very much?"

McKay glanced at the dark-haired Drake, the hazel eyes looking for something beneath the sudden show of concern; but the husky voice retained the unconcerned coolness. "The trimming was a little more than I had bargained for. Four horses with four feet each made quite a job."

Walking along beside Tyler as the cowboy led the bay back to its stall, Drake glanced cautiously at the lean-built man. When the horse was safely in the enclosure, Joe questioned slowly. "Did you know Jessica when she first arrived?"

"Jessie? Yes, I met her the very first day that she arrived. In fact, I went to the airport to pick up the guests that day. I grew up on this ranch, just about. About Jessie. I guess we are pretty good friends." He drawled casually. Then facing the guest, he eyed him coldly. "Remember that."

Joseph swiftly glanced at McKay. But there was only an unreadable expression on the hard features.

Pulling on his shirt, Tyler questioned in the cool western drawl. "We are having wrestling matches this morning, while it's still cool. Are you going to join in on the fun?"

"I don't know. I've never done much of that kind of thing." He answered hesitantly.

Tyler chuckled softly. "Oh, I think you'll enjoy this. The girls participate in these events."

Joe halted and stared at McKay. "Are you kidding?"

"Nope. You'd be surprised at how tough those females can be. It's fun. Even the little kids get to compete."

"Who started this? You?" asked Joe dryly.

"Sorry to say that I didn't, Jessie did. We were having fun one day just horsing around. Us fellas, that is. And the girls were watching, when Jess ups and challenges one of the winners. She really gave Jeff the go-around. She thought it was fun and the other gals did too. So the next round, they tried it out." Drawled Tyler, hazel-green eyes carefully studying Drake's dark face. Then he added, "The girls wrestle each other, then the winners wrestle the male winners. We try to keep it in the weight category. As close as we can anyway. Sometimes it's a little difficult, but everyone seems to have a good time. And that of course is the main reason we do it. We also have an Indian Wrestling competition."

Joe remained silent for a few moments, then he muttered slowly, "I think I might just try my hand at this,"

"Thought you might." Declared McKay in a quiet voice. An odd smile touched his lips. Then nearing the grass-covered park between cabins and lodge, he halted saying, "I have got to go change. I'll see you in about twenty minutes. Back here. We'll help put down the large mats."

Joe nodded and started for his room. Tyler watched him walk away, then chuckled softly to himself. "You'll be damned surprised when Jessie tangles with you, Mister Joseph Drake. Real surprised. And that, my friend, is a promise."

Chapter Five

Tyler sat Indian-fashion on the ground in front of the mats with everyone else; when glancing up he caught sight of the slender redhead as she moved toward the gathered group. The sun caught the fiery sheen of her hair as the long braid swung back and forth. Snug-fitting powder-blue corduroy jeans and a soft T-shirt of the same color emphasized the soft, gentle curves of the slender woman.

Smiling, she sat down next to Tyler and then carelessly pulled off the soft-leather boots. "Thought I'd never make it. Did I miss much?"

"Nope. Just that almost everyone has finished wrestling each other. The winners have just about all been decided. Say, your friends are pretty good. Larry is one of the winners. Lucky for me, he isn't in my weight class."

Concern-darkened gray eyes swept his lean, handsome face. "You aren't wrestling?"

He tried to grin disarmingly, "Sure, I am. In fact, I wrestle Drake in about five minutes. By the way, you don't have to wrestle any of the girls. They elected that you would do the wrestling for them. You, my dear, are the smallest."

Jessie was still frowning at the trail foreman. "You will ruin that shoulder, yet." She stated in a flat voice.

"Ah, cool it, Jessie. I'm fine. Well, here I go." He said as Joe appeared on the large mat.

Smoothly, with apparent ease, McKay approached the dark-haired man. It was Drake who made the first move, hitting Tyler low about the hips. Together they hit the mat. Ty rolled clear, then before Joe could get set, he managed to knock him off-balance. Using the advantage, McKay got Joe onto his back intending to pen the man's shoulders.

Cooper watched with a knowing grin. The match was going to end fast and clean. But even as she watched, she saw Joe's doubled-up fist sharply strike Ty's injured shoulder. Not once, but twice!

McKay's face paled. The injured arm gave way and in a moment; Drake was on top, easily penning Tyler's shoulders to the mat. Anger surged hotly through Jessie's slender frame, as she watched McKay slowly make his way back beside her.

Apparently no one else had noticed the nasty by-play or wasn't about to mention it. As Tyler sank down on the ground, his features tight with pain and a sickly gray color. He still hadn't said a word.

"It hurt, didn't it?" She muttered harshly. As the pain sharpened hazel eyes met stormy gray, she added, "I want to see you after this is over."

Before he could form an answer, she gracefully climbed to her feet. Studying the pretty face, Ty glimpsed another side of Jessie Cooper. And he wondered? As he made an attempt to catch her hand, he heard the cool, pleasant voice.

"Chuck, how about taking the lighter weight ones first? I haven't been able to get any action yet."

Chuck grinned. "Sounds good to me."

She fastened cold, icy-gray eyes onto Joe's dark-tanned features as she asked with a thin smile. "And who do I get?"

Watching her intently, Tyler noted the chilled look enter the usually soft blue-gray eyes. He knew behind that gentle-appearing façade the anger was building. And he felt an icy sliver run down his spine.

Chuck's southern drawl sounded. "Joe, guess you tangle with Jessie."

"Yes, guess I do." Smiled Drake.

Jess eyed Joe carefully. He was a lot stronger than most people realized, but that was one thing that she remembered from the past. By the self-assured grin, she knew that Joe thought he had her beat. Silently, she chuckled to herself; that misjudgment would help her in the long run.

Cooper knew that Joe out-weighed her and of course, was taller; but she was determined to make him pay for the dirty trick he had used on Ty. Caution fell into play as the two circled each other, each looking for an opening. Cold, calculating precision moved Jess as Drake made the first move once again.

Because of that, he couldn't seem to get a very good grip on her and with very little struggle, she twisted free. Now they both were on their knees, and once again she twisted out of his insecure hold, making her move on him.

Totally. And with force. Instead of closing in and trying to force him to the mat, she swung her compact body up and against his chest, flipping him solidly onto his back.

Instantly he whirled, his hand catching her upper arm and with his added weight, managed to pull her over onto her back. He would have penned her if she hadn't pulled her legs up to her chest and lifted him bodily over her head. Joe landed hard and dazedly he twisted into an upright position. He saw Cooper launch herself at him and before he could move he felt the impact of her small solid body, as it struck him. Turning unconsciously, he by chance managed to get her small, slender frame under him.

Looking down at her, he grinned with the light of triumph flickering in the dark eyes. She twisted under him like an eel and it was all he could do to keep her in that position. The triumph slipped a fraction as no matter how he tried, he couldn't manage to pen her slim shoulders to the mat. She struggled with every muscle in the slight, yet strong body. She was breathing heavily and he could feel the taut muscles shiver under him. Then suddenly, she just relaxed and he thought that she was finished.

Tyler edged as close to the mat as he could. Tim and Linda were close beside him and when they saw her small body seemingly go lax, Tim whispered, "Looks like she is giving up."

McKay didn't think so. He was watching her right leg. He had an idea of what she was going to do. Hell, he had taught her how to Indian wrestle and had seen her use it a couple of times.

Just as Joe Drake thought he had her beat, relaxed somewhat himself; her right leg shot up and hooked him around the neck. Twisting her upper body to the left, then bringing the right leg down yanking Joe over backward.

In a flash, she was on top of his chest forcing his shoulders to the mat with strength she hadn't even known she possessed.

Before she would let him up, she leaned forward and whispered next to his ear. "We don't play dirty, Joe. I saw what you did to Ty. I wouldn't like to see it happen again. Remember that."

Drake's face stiffened and paled as the slight woman rose to her feet. He remained silent as he, too, rose and followed after her. Then moved a little farther down the side of the mats.

Cooper gave the others a disarming grin, then sat down between Tim and Tyler. While the next two competitors took their turn, she fixed smoky-blue eyes on the trail foreman. "Alright, Ty, come on. I want a look at that shoulder."

Tyler was about to argue the need to leave, when Larry Connors came up behind him, his voice low with concern as he asked, "Does it hurt very much?"

McKay threw a hard glare in Drake's direction, then reluctantly moved to follow Cooper. "Yeah. Must have landed on it too damn hard. Good luck, Larry. Do your best."

Connors flashed him a smile. "Thanks." Then turning to the redhead, he added, "Say, Jess, that was some wrestling."

"Nothing to it. Piece of cake. Tyler taught me that Indian wrestling part. Take care." She answered calmly, then walked off towards the cabins.

Linda glanced up at Tim. "I wouldn't have believed that she was the same person we used to know. Did you see her flip Joe?" She remarked in an awed voice.

As Tim Winters nodded in agreement, Larry spoke up. "You don't know just how right you are, Linda. She has changed and I'd say for the better." His voice was unusually hard. He stood for a moment longer, then turned and walked over to Cindy.

Tim raised somewhat confused blue eyes at his friend's outburst. Linda frowned to herself. "What did he mean by that remark?"

McKay had to lengthen his stride to catch up with the still angry Jessie. Her small oval face was set in stubborn lines, with lips stiff and pulled tight over small, even white teeth. With an effort at lightness, Ty called, "Slow down, Jess. Take it easy."

Her step slowed, but she remained stubbornly silent. As she stepped into her cabin, McKay followed. With her back still to him, Jessie ordered roughly, "Sit down."

Shrugging his broad shoulders; then as a faint knifing pain shot through the torn muscle, he wished he hadn't. He slumped slowly onto a nearby chair. "Jessie, it wasn't that bad. For heaven's sake, the shoulder is fine."

A burning darkness glowed in the gray eyes as she turned on the seated cowboy. "It was nothing? You can say that, Ty, after what happen?"

Dark color crept over the teak-brown features, but he held her gaze. "Jess, I know that you are angry and worried. Cool off. You're really beautiful when you're angry, but you are much nicer when you aren't."

"Men!" She spat in exasperation. "You can get yourself shot at; and for no reason. Get sucker punched by a bully, but,"

Cooper stopped and sighed heavily. "Never mind. Now, strong man, peel off the shirt."

Ty started to object, but Jessie stepped closer. "Now."

Slowly McKay removed the shirt, his face showing mixed traces of embarrassment, anger, and pain. His shoulder was once again swollen and darkly discolored. Exactly where Drake's fist had landed.

With gentle fingers, Jess applied the soothing and cooling antiseptic cream and then wrapped it with a light-weight bandage. Glancing at her face, Tyler knew she was still angry. Her eyes, which were usually a soft dove gray, were instead dark with blue fires in their depths. The fine lips were into a tight grim line. Even so, he had a hell of a time not to lean forward the few short inches and touch his mouth to hers.

She straightened and eyed him carefully, some of the anger melting from the tense features. "There. All fixed, but no work for you until that shoulder is better. And no back talk. Phil will agree with me. And you know it."

He leaned back in the chair and the greenish-gold gaze slid carelessly over her slight figure, then slowly returned to the small oval face. "You know, little one, you really are beautiful."

Soft color stole across the delicate features. Smiling softly, she remarked lightly, "I've never had a brother; but, if I had, I'd bet he would be just like you. You are really great for a girl's ego. Always knowing just what to say to make her feel special. Of course, you could be suffering from a fever. Think so?"

The handsome face hardened, seeming to close up. "You see me as a brother? Well, it comes with practice. Not to worry, no fever. I guess I had better be going. See you later, huh?" Tyler muttered abstractly as he pushed himself up out of the chair and headed for the door.

Just as his hand reached out to push open the screen door, Jessie called softly to him. Hesitating briefly he turned back toward her slight figure. "What is it?"

She smiled impishly. "How 'bout having lunch with me? I'm not such a terrible cook. Nothing fancy, but it should be edible."

He stood undecided. Finally he replied almost cautiously, "Okay, sounds fine. I'm not real hungry. I'll be right back in a few minutes. I want to talk with Phil and I should change."

Jessie nodded and moved into the small, compact built kitchenette. "Alright, it should be ready by the time you get back."

McKay grinned slowly as he stepped outside. Striding towards the manager's office, he kept thinking of what the redhead had said. A brother? That's what she considered him? Shit, that was worse than being a friend. He also remembered how her face had looked as she had fought with Joe. It had to be. It had to have been Drake that had hurt her years ago. Hurt her bad enough to cause her to pack-up and leave home and friends.

Reaching the office, he stepped quietly into the small, cluttered room. Phil glanced up and seeing his top trail guide, smiled. "Ty, how's the shoulder? Heard that you got roughed up a bit again."

Tyler nodded slowly. "Yep. Sort of. Is it alright if I take today and tomorrow off? There isn't anything that Chang can't handle over tomorrow. There shouldn't be anything of importance until Wednesday."

Holden laughed with a deep chuckle in his throat. "I was going to make sure you did. Glad you asked. Sure thing, go ahead." Then as McKay was about to leave, he questioned, "What's troubling you, Tyler?"

Tyler grinned wearily. "Does it show that much?" At Phil's nod, he sighed and slumped back into a wire chair next to the door. "What do you do if the woman you care about only thinks of you as a brother or best friend? A brother, Phil."

Holden leaned forward on his cluttered desk top, his eyes studying the troubled features. "It's Jessie, isn't it?"

McKay nodded.

"Well, you can remain her friend. Things and feelings change. She thinks the world of you, but for some reason known only to her, she is afraid to get involved with anyone. Give her time."

"That's not easy to do, Phil. It's hard not showing how I feel. But, I guess there really isn't too much else that I can do. Guess I knew you would say that. Thanks, Phil. See you in a couple of days."

Holden watched as the younger man left. Tyler usually could hide his emotions pretty well. His deepest feelings. But today, Phil had seen them clearly on the handsome face and in the greenish-gold eyes. That man was hurting, it was obvious. Not to everyone, not to very many at all; but to those that were close to him, yes.

Chapter Six

After fixing a fresh green salad and then getting them ready to put in the skillet, Jess decided to change clothes before Tyler returned. Slipping on a cool, silky short-sleeved white blouse that exposed the creamy-tan throat. Pulling on a pair of navy-blue shorts, she surveyed herself in the full-length mirror. The fiery hair was loose and tumbled in a riot of curls about her shoulders. She liked the innocent affect that it created and tossing the curls back, a secret smile touched her lips, and then she went back to the kitchen area.

Reaching up into the cupboard, she brought down a container of potato chips and another of a cheesy variety. Placing them on the table and the salad in deep, round bowls, she went to place the steaks on a low flame. Taking two cans of soda out of the refrigerator, the screen door opened and Tyler strolled in. He was dressed in dark-brown corduroy jeans that hugged the narrow hips and strong thighs. A soft green shirt with dark-brown lines running through it, encased the broad shoulders and deep chest. The green of the shirt made the hazel eyes appear more green than usual and emphasized the dark, thick lashes. Jessie sighed to herself, women would pay dearly to get lashes like his. The shirt sleeves were rolled up to his elbows and the front left open at the throat. She could see the dark, curling chest hair that peeked out of the opening of the shirt front. Without turning, she called, "Grab yourself a seat and the steaks will be ready in a couple of minutes." Then after setting the cans of soda on the table, eyed him slowly, "There's salad dressing in the fridge, if you want some. And steak sauce."

McKay rose easily from the hard-backed chair and opened the refrigerator door. Finding what he was looking for he stuck his dark-curly head above the door and asked, "Anything in particular that you want while I'm in here?"

Glancing at the bottles in his hands, she shook her head, "No, you've picked the ones I like." From under long, thick lashes, she watched him slide back into the chair. "How do you want your steak?"

"Medium well is fine." He answered, the strange gold-green eyes watching as she placed the sizzling steaks onto a small platter and turned to the table.

As she set the platter on the table and looked up, her gray eyes ran full tilt into the gold-green of his. A tightness formed in her chest, and the palms of her hands became moist. What was the matter with her? "Would you like a glass for your drink?"

A dark eyebrow rose at the huskiness of her voice, but he answered quietly, "Sure."

Turning to the cupboard and reaching up on tip-toe to reach the tumblers there on the high shelf, she suddenly felt the warm masculine body of McKay as he leaned in behind her to reach up and get the glasses for her. She could feel the hard, solid body the length of her softer one. Warm color ran up her neck and onto the smooth cheeks. "Oh... thanks. I don't know why I leave them up there. I always have a time reaching them..." Geez, she was babbling!

Ty looked down on the top of the red-gold head and as he slowly let his arm come back down with the glasses, he noted the heightened color in her face. For a brief moment longer he let his larger body stay close to hers, until he was afraid that she would feel the desire that was coming to life being so close to her and so he backed off and turned to the table.

As he moved away, Jess turned slowly and without looking at him managed to slide into her chair. "Help yourself. Hope it's done to your liking?"

A light chuckle. "Most likely. It would be real hard for me not to like steak. Almost anyway it's fixed."

Lifting the tumbler to her lips, Jessie let her gaze run lightly over the tall man. The muscled forearms were tanned to an almost copper-brown and as the hand and fingers moved, she could follow the movement of muscles in his arms and under the soft material of his shirt across the shoulders as he shifted in his seat. They rippled with grace as well as strength. Vaguely she wondered what it would feel like to have those very same arms wrapped around her own slender form; or to have the lean fingers touching her heated skin.

A flush swept up over the delicate jaw and cheek. She was heated all right. What had happen to her for her to look at Tyler with those kind of thoughts?

McKay took his last bite and picked up the paper napkin, "That was good. Really hit the spot. What would you say to a walk?"

Cooper agreed quietly. "Fine. Sounds fine to me."

Stacking the dishes in the stainless-steel sink, the two of them left the small cabin and walked into the bordering woods. Perhaps fifteen minutes later they came across a narrow, rapidly rushing mountain stream.

Jesse ran forward, a squeal of pure delight issuing from the smiling mouth. "Come on, Ty! Let's wade across. It can't be very deep."

McKay bent, pulled off boots and socks; then rolled up his pant legs. Cooper just stepped out of her thin sandals and grinned impishly at him. McKay grinned in return and together they entered the icy-cold water. Half-way across, mischief flashing in the smoky eyes, Jess showered him with the frosty water. It splashed squarely in his face, sprinkling the dark curly hair with flashing crystals.

"Why...you little vixen!!" he inhaled sharply. Then shaking his head he bent to the water and retaliated in full.

Laughing she tried to hurriedly scramble out of the narrow stream over the slippery flat rocks that lay scattered about the shifting bottom. Just gaining the grassy bank, she looked back to see Ty right behind her. With a last ditch effort, he made a grab for her arm, his fingers closing around the slender wrist; she slid to the ground, pulling him down beside her. "Oh....that...was...fun. But I'm all out of breath."

"So am I." Whispered Tyler, his voice husky and slightly labored.

McKay watched as she leaned back against the cushiony thick grass and closed her eyes. His warm glance swept over her slight, soft curving body; finally coming to rest on her delicate face with the light dusting of pale freckles across the small nose. Sighing softly, he sank back against the ground, his arms folded behind his dark head, staring absently at the cloudless, deep-blue sky.

Just how long they lay there like that, McKay didn't know. He wasn't sure if Jess might have fallen asleep. Then she was raising herself up on one elbow to look at him, her expression thoughtful.

"Isn't it about time to bring Fed down to the lower pastures?"

Tyler nodded assent. "Yeah. Probably the end of this week." Shifting the lean frame slightly, he added, "I suppose we should get back. You do have a swimming class at three, don't you?"

Cooper nodded agreement. "Yes." Then looking up at Tyler, she found herself asking, "Won't you come and watch? You could help with the younger ones."

McKay shook his dark head. "Sorry, not right now. Maybe...I...can drop in a little later though."

"Good enough." Smiled Jessie.

By evening though, Jessie had yet to see any sign of Ty. At first it hadn't bothered her; figuring he had something else to do. But now she began to wonder. She had met some of the wranglers and other friends, but none had seen anything of McKay since before she had went to teach her swimming class. So finally she went in search of Phil.

Jessie found him in his office, writing out reports and signing supply lists. As the screen door swung closed, he glanced up. At seeing her standing just inside the door, he pushed the mounting paper work to one side and smiled, "Jessie, how's the wrestling champ of the JVG Ranch?"

"Okay, I guess." Cooper said. Then swinging astride a chair close to the desk, she asked bluntly, "Phil, do you know where Tyler disappeared to?"

"Not exactly. He did ask for the rest of today and tomorrow off."

Gray eyes opened wide. "He did? Why didn't he say something at lunch?" then hesitating, "Phil, did he act sort uh...uh...troubled when he talked to you?"

Phil eyed the tense, lovely features. "Yes, I did notice that he acted; well, not quite himself."

The redhead nodded slowly, a small frown on her lips. "Yes. Wonder what is causing it? It's just not like Ty."

Light flashed in the gray eyes. "Phil, let's have a large all night camp-out? The guests would love it."

Phil smothered a grin. "That'd be fine. Except we can't possibly without Ty. And there is no way he will be back in time by tomorrow."

"Oh, yes he could. Especially if a certain someone went after him." Grinned Jessie.

Holden still stalled, not quite sure that this was the thing to do. "But even so, how would you find him? You don't even know where he has gone?"

The slender, small woman rose from the chair. "I haven't been friends with Tyler McKay for over three years and don't know some of his most favorite places to go. You just get everyone and everything ready for the camp-out tomorrow. I'll take care of the rest." With a wave of a slender hand, she called from the doorway, "Bye, Phil, see you tomorrow before noon. Promise."

As she disappeared through the screen door, Phil leaned farther back in his desk chair. A thoughtful look had crept into his eyes. Jessie was in love with McKay, or damn close, but he didn't think the redhead realized it.

Not for what it was. Something would have to happen to cause her to acknowledge how she really felt about the trail foreman. But what?

Hurrying to the corrals, Jess found Rebel still there with Shiloh. Leaning briefly on the top rail, she frowned. Then as she slid off the fence, a smile touched the fine lips. Without Rebel, Tyler had then hiked. And there were only two likely places in which McKay could get to on foot. Twisting around at the sound of her name; she saw Tim Winters and standing close beside him was Joe Drake.

"Yes? What is it?"

Winters stepped forward smiling. "We wanted to know if you would like to join us for supper?"

Cooper glanced first from one face to the other, before answering, "I'd like to, Tim. But there's an errand I have to do. It'll have to be another time. I'm sorry. Now if you'll excuse me; I'm in kind of a hurry."

"Sure, no problem." Remarked Tim as she moved off at almost a run. Turning to the man beside him, he added, "She's some gal. Course you know that, don't you, Joe?"

Drake nodded jerkily. "Yes. But I think I like the old Jessica better."

Winters glanced briefly at the brown-eyed Drake. Frowning, he remembered what Larry Connors had said earlier. "That's sort of funny. Connors thought that she was better because of the changes."

Joe looked up quickly, but couldn't read his brother-in-law's expression. Shrugging carelessly, he mumbled, "Everyone to their own tastes."

Jessie wasted very little time in getting what she needed from the cabin. A canteen of water, a sack of sandwiches and she was on her way. She had debated on taking a horse, but then had discarded the idea with the feeling that some of the terrain would be too rough and it would be much simpler on foot.

The pale light of dusk was descending about the ranch buildings as she walked out at a brisk pace, pushing her way through the thicker underbrush; she vaguely wondered why she was doing this. Except for the odd fact that when Tyler was away like now, she found herself uneasy, nervous...Missing him. Slowly she shook the copper-colored head in frustration.

Switching her wandering thoughts, she grinned. It would be fun surprising him. And she just bet he would be surprised, really surprised. And very possibly a little angry. She had yet to feel Tyler McKay's anger directed at herself. Jess smiled knowingly, she had seen him in a flaming rage of anger; but he had never been angry with her.

Watching the softly glowing embers of the campfire gradually lose their intensity; Tyler pulled off his shirt and threw a disgruntled glance in the direction of his bedroll. He was tired, bone tired and it sure appeared inviting. Swiftly he tugged off walking boots and jeans, then eased the lithe frame into the warm comfort of the blankets.

There was still a chill in the air, but as he pulled the thick, micro-knit cover over legs and narrow hips, decided he was warm enough. The glow of the dying embers still gave off enough warmth to be comfortable.

Folding his arms beneath the curly, blue-black head; he gazed up at the star filled night sky. To his surprise he found that sleep was the farthest thing from his mind. He was deathly tired, but not sleepy.

For the first time in a long while he actually wished that he was no more than a wrangler again, no responsibilities of importance. A sudden empty, loneliness swamped him. A feeling he had not experienced since the death of his father.

Phil Holden's words came drifting back to him. Give her time. Stay her friend. Tyler frowned. Sounded simple enough. But, for how long could he hide his true feelings from her? If he didn't show her just how he felt, how would she ever come to find out? If he did, it could possibly ruin the friendship and companionship they now shared.

Once again he lifted his dark gaze to the night sky. One large, very bright star seemed to out-shine all the others. Watching it, an old rhyme he knew as a child came to mind. Sighing hopelessly, he mouthed the old verse in a raspy whisper. "Star light, star bright. First star I see tonight; I wish, I..."

"What would you wish for, Ty?" interrupted a soft, slightly husky voice he knew so well. And it came from almost directly beside him.

Startled, he rose to a sitting position; but stopped instantly when he felt the cool, gentle fingers touch his bare chest. And then the faint, soft light of the fire fell across the lovely, pale features before him.

"Jessie!" McKay stammered. "What the hell! How? What are you doing here?"

A gentle, musical laugh sounded and he caught the flash of white teeth as she smiled.

"Hunting for you, silly. I hadn't expected you to have come quite this far. I had hoped to catch up with you long before this."

"Why were you looking for me? And how did you get so close without me hearing your horse?"

"Well...uh...I didn't ride a horse. And there is to be an all-night ride and cook-out tomorrow." She confessed.

McKay frowned. "That doesn't make sense. Phil said there wasn't anything planned."

"Something must have come up. Anyway, the guests decided that they wanted a bar-b-cue. So here I am." Declared the redhead. Then with a teasing tilt of her head she bantered, "You wouldn't dream of me doing all this just to be with you and ruin your time off? Do you?"

Under her finger tips, she could feel the chest muscles stiffen and laughed lightly, "Ty, I missed you; and then when I couldn't find you I went directly to Phil. That was when the bomb was laid almost in my lap."

He had not relaxed and a faintly uneasy feeling crept slowly over her. She hadn't meant to hurt him with her careless teasing. Why, if he only knew that it had been all her idea...? And just to get him back, he would more than likely laugh his handsome head off.

"Well, better get your sleeping bag. Where'd you stash it?" He asked and Jessie felt a warning chill run up her spine.

"To tell the truth...I...well, I...uh...didn't bring one." She faltered.

"What!" He roared. And would have come to his feet if Cooper hadn't forced him back down.

On her knees, Jessie forced all her lithe weight onto Ty's chest until she had him laying down once again. He shook the dark head in exasperation.

The husky voice came out on a groan. "Of all the stupid. It was foolish enough to be up here alone; but to not bring a sleeping bag. What were you thinking? Or were you thinking at all?"

Anger stirred a low flame in her belly, she tried to curb it as she returned in a tight, small voice. "Ty, cool down. I didn't think that it would take me as long as it did to find you. So the thought of a bedroll never entered my mind. There's no reason to act this way."

His eyes narrowed on her face. "Just how do you expect to sleep? It's too rough of terrain to go traipsing off on foot in the dark."

"I know that. I'm not totally stupid. You have plenty of room. So move over and share a little."

"In this bedroll! With me! Together! Girl, are you crazy?" demanded McKay in a shocked, choked voice.

This time the slim control she had on the short temper failed. Clenching the small hands into tight fists, she stammered furiously, "Oh, for heaven's sake! I'm over twenty-one. And if 'we' can't trust one another...well..." Taking a deep breath, she continued, "So now if you can't bring yourself to share your blankets; I'll just go sit over there under that tree and...and..." Struggling to rise, she flared, "Oh! Go to hell!"

A strong, bronzed arm shot out and steely fingers clamped around the slenderness of her wrist. "All right, little one, you win. I'm moving over." Sighed Tyler resignedly.

His voice was still hard and tight, but he was having a tough fight with his flaring temper. Jessie felt near to crying as she stared down into the glittery green of his eyes. But still she managed a weak, watery smile.

Swiftly removing her boots and the heavy jacket, she settled down next to Tyler's long hard frame. Snuggling deeper under the warm cover, she could feel the heat coming from his lean, almost naked body. Whispering smugly, "See, it's not so bad. You didn't have to use that big brother stuff."

She gulped as narrowed eyes swung to her face. "I might seem like a brother to you...but, others know I'm not." And my body knows the fact also, he added to himself.

Silence engulfed them then. Both were quiet with their own thoughts. Just the feel of her small, softly curved body up against his hard angles, brought a hot searing through his body, pooling low in his belly. He could hear the slow, steady breathing as she fell into a deep sleep and tried to calm his ragged, shallow one. Then just as he felt he was gaining some sort of control, the slight frame moved closer, the small, slender fingers curled into the dark, thick mat of curly chest hair. Slowly he closed his eyes as a shudder of desire rippled through his strong body.

Chapter Seven

After a restless and frustrating night that produced very little sleep, Tyler awoke feeling decidedly worse for wear. Glancing at the watch on his wrist, the lighted digits showing up palely in the still early morning darkness. Not quite four o'clock. Hell of a time to be getting up. But if they left now they would reach the ranch before anyone else was up, and hopefully before anyone would see them arrive. Carefully turning his head so that he could see the sleeping girl's. Girl? No, woman's peaceful appearing face.

Gently, he touched the pale, delicate cheek; then with a heart-felt sigh, he shook her awake. "Come on, Jess. Wake up."

Red-gold curls tumbled over her shoulder, spilling onto his arm as she mumbled and opened sleep-dazed eyes. "Hell, it's still dark. You must be crazy."

"Very possibly. I know it's dark, but light enough to see our way back to the ranch. So come on and quit belly-aching." Muttered McKay.

Cooper tilted back her head to look more closely at him, a frown formed between pale-gold brows. "Why?"

Tyler stiffened. "What do you mean, why?" he demanded.

"Why do we have to leave so early?"

A stillness swept over the hard, muscled body and it seemed like minutes before he answered in a tight, almost whispery voice. "So no one sees us come in. So that no one thinks we slept together."

Shock flashed briefly in the smoky-blue eyes and then she smiled softly and Ty felt an uneasiness crawl over his skin. The small hand moved slowly over the muscled planes of the hard chest and the fingers played with the curly black hair they found there. "Why would you care if anyone thought that? I'm a big girl; not a child. And I don't give a tinker's damn if anyone thinks that or if they even notice that we were gone."

His breath stopped somewhere in his chest. And before he could find an answer, she raised up on an elbow and moved over him. Even before he realized just what she intended, her warm, soft lips touched first his chest, then his chin, moving to his tightly held mouth. But as their warm moistness brushed against him, he felt as if he were unravelling, coming apart at the seams. Those soft lips settled over his and unconsciously he opened to her, drawing the kiss deeper.

Jessie felt her heart beat increase in tempo and at the same time she could feel his beating furiously under her hand. His warmth engulfed her, turning her body soft and tingly, sending the blood rushing through her at a dizzy rate. She had to stop before it got out of hand. Out of hand? This was good old Ty, her best friend. But something more and frightening was happening and she didn't think that she was ready for that. Stiffening her arms, she pushed up away from his warmth and at the same time she could feel the tenseness rippling through his lean, muscled body.

Looking down into his handsome face she found his eyes closed. But before she could think of anything to say, he was speaking. In a low, tight, almost painful voice, "Don't say anything. Not a word, Jess. Or you might say something you'll regret."

Briefly she closed her eyes and then opened them to stare into the gold-green ones below her. Hot, searing eyes.

Forcing a tight smile to her face, she carelessly shrugged slim shoulders. "So, I liked kissing you. No big deal. And seeing as I'm awake now, we can leave. Just like you wanted."

His eyes closed and he took a deep breath. "Right."

Pinks and yellows were just peeking above the mountain tops as they reached the dawn-drenched ranch buildings; but everything seemed to be still asleep. McKay dropped Jessie off at her small cabin then headed for his own. Maybe if he hurried, he could manage a few quiet minutes of extra sleep. Shit, who was he kidding? Not after that kiss; hell, he'd be lucky if he ever slept again.

Entering the front room, Jessie stopped, leaning back against the closed door. Staring unseeingly at the small kitchen that was set just off to one side, she found herself unable to believe that first, she had to get McKay back; second, that she actually kissed him for heaven's sake! But, oh he had felt so good. Fleetingly, she remembered the curious yearning sensation that had assaulted her whole being while lying next to Tyler's lean length. A soft warmth rose over the high cheek bones. With a confused shake of her head, she slowly made her way to the small bedroom at the back of the cabin. At the memory of that feeling and the necessity to have McKay back, her face clouded momentarily; but she was just too tired to try and figure it all out. Especially not at this moment.

After stripping off his clothes and climbing in between the cool sheets of his bed, Tyler found himself staring unseeingly at the ceiling. He had known he wouldn't be able to sleep. Damn. What was he going to do about his feelings for Jessie? What about that kiss? What had she been doing? She had never ever done anything like that before. He had thought that he would lose it. Totally. And he almost had. So what did he do now? Should he ignore that kiss? That hot kiss. No matter what he decided to do it was going to be difficult. He feared that his body wouldn't be able to withstand the strain.

The pale pinks had turned more yellow and gold as the ranch personnel came to life and activity came into motion. Linda looked at the clear deep-blue sky and felt a moment's sadness. As she walked past Shiloh and Rebel's corral, she once again went over the words she was going to say to Jessica Cooper. Coming to a halt at the cabin's screened door, she inhaled a deep breath and knocked softly on the door, then waited.

"Come on in." came a husky, sleep-filled voice from within.

"Jessica...uh...Jessie, it's me, Linda."

Jess turned around, putting the slender back against the counter and smiled softly. "Linn. What brings you here this early in the morning? Sit down and have some hot chocolate with me."

Nervously the model-thin woman did so, the dark-brown eyes serious with what she needed to say to her one-time best friend. "Jessie, I...uh...I came to tell you that Tim and I have to leave tomorrow evening. Something to do with his business. But, I wanted to tell you how wonderful it has been to see you again." Then pausing, "Do you think that you could come to the airport to see us off? Tyler, too?"

"Well, sure. And I'll see about Tyler. It's too bad you both have to leave so soon." Sighed Cooper sadly.

"It sure is. I was hoping to see Confederate. But…." And the dark-haired woman shrugged slim shoulders.

Jess looked at the solemn face of her friend, then suggested softly, "We'll see. Maybe I can do something about that. Now you better get back to the lodge. I've got a lot of work to do before we go on that large cook-out tonight."

Linda smiled. "Right. See you later, Jess." Then with a wave she went out the door.

Jessie watched until she was out of sight, then she pushed away from the counter and walked into the front room. A frown marred the usually creamy smoothness of her brow. Why couldn't it have been Drake that had to leave? But, no; it just had to be Tim and Linda. She hoped that it wasn't anything serious with his business.

Leaning a slender shoulder against the door frame, she stared out at the cloudless sky and remembered last night with Tyler. Suddenly an impish grin touched her lips. Poor Tyler. He had been so angry. And then this morning. The poor man hadn't known what hit him. Actually she didn't know either. Where to go from here? With a shake of the sunset-red head, she returned to the kitchen to take care of the few dishes that were left to do.

About the same time Tyler was starting for the corral. His step not quite as light as usual; his handsome face set in weary lines. The usual smile lurking at the corners of his firm male mouth and in the depths of the greenish-gold eyes were not apparent. Instead there was sadness.

Even though the features looked tired and sort of haggard, there was a quiet anger in the greenish eyes. His voice was faintly husky as he talked to Rebel. The horse eyed him carefully because of the strange sound of his voice and tone. Also his body language. It appeared aggressive, agitated.

From behind him came a quiet, softly feminine voice. "Morning, Ty. Poor Reb, he thinks you are mad at him. Better tell him that it's me you're angry with. Excuse me." And she moved past him to the misty-gray Shiloh, who she easily bridled.

McKay glanced at the small oval face and caught the glint of laughter in the smoky-blue eyes. To her, apparently, last night hadn't meant anything at all, or that kiss; except he had acted like a fool. Tyler was facing the red roan as he forced his voice through stiff, unbending lips. "What time do we leave on this cook-out trail ride?"

"Around noon, I guess. But they may decide to leave earlier." Jess answered softly.

"Thanks for the information. I truly appreciate it." He answered sarcastically.

Anger seeped into her laughter as she watched him lead Rebel toward the gate. "Tyler McKay, I hope Reb gives you a good toss. And the harder the better. You deserve it."

McKay stopped and turned to face her defiant small figure. "If you weren't so damn little, I'd tan your backside."

Eyes turned smoky and flashed blue anger. "I might be little; but I'm way too much for you to handle, cowboy!"

"Is that so?" he flared.

"Damn right. I'd like to see you try it!" she dared hotly.

"Oh you would, would you?" countered Ty as he dropped the reins and started back toward the redhead.

Jessie eyed him stonily and involuntarily backed a step, also dropping Shiloh's rein. Cautiously she edged out away from the gray gelding; trying to keep Ty's oncoming figure in front of her. But still she was not prepared when McKay did make his move. He lunged, catching ahold of her forearm tightly, pulling her body toward him.

Twisting and turning; not forgetting to slug, she fought like a cornered bobcat. Tyler was finding out just how much of a handful she was, but at the same time Cooper realized that she was no match for McKay.

Wrapping his arms around her waist and sinking to his knees, Ty flipped the light-weight woman across them. He then proceeded to whole-heartily spank the small bottom. Jess kicked and yelled until she was released to sit ungracefully in the soft, powdery corral dust.

Tyler rose, dusting off the knees of his faded denim jeans, his greenish eyes sweeping over her mutinous features. "Don't underestimate me, Jess." Then turning on his heel, he gathered up the gelding's loose reins and headed for the barns.

Cooper watched him leave, feeling very near to tears. Tears of anger, not at Tyler, but herself. She had asked for that. She knew without a doubt that she had pushed him too far.

Carefully picking herself up out of the dust, she wondered if she really did know Ty as well as she assumed? He definitely wasn't acting his usual self. It just wasn't like him to be obstinate. She had always used him as her confidant, knowing that he would listen to all she had to confide and not judge her. But had she ever really listened to him? Or had she been too wrapped up in her own little world of self pity? Had she used Tyler like she confessed that others had used her? Not intentionally, but...?

One thing for sure there was no way that she could ask him to go to the airport to see Linda and Tim off. At least not in the foul mood he was in.

Slowly she led the sleek blue-gray gelding toward the first large barn. Nearing the gaping doorway, she happen to glance in the direction of the large indoor arena. At the same moment, McKay swung into the saddle. To Jess's dismay, she watched as Rebel cut loose with some real bone breaking bucks. Tyler, who had not been firmly in the stock saddle, lost his balance and landed with a noticeable thud on the hard-packed ground.

The other wranglers burst out laughing. Surprised at seeing the usually docile red-roan gelding do such a trick and to one of the best bronc riders on the ranch.

Cooper had to forcibly suppress the laughter that was rising at the back of her throat, as blazing green eyes glared directly at her, if not through her; just challenging her to even snicker. She turned abruptly away and led Shiloh into the adjoining barn, muttering under her breath, "Why did Rebel have to choose today to be overly frisky and ornery?"

By the time Jess had saddled Shiloh, Ty was returning from seeing Phil. Looking up as McKay pulled Rebel to a halt before her, she found his features strangely hard and unreadable. She also discovered that it was difficult to meet his cold, direct gaze. "What is it?" she questioned cautiously.

"We'll be leaving in about an hour. I want you to see about food and all the girls' bedrolls and such." Hesitating briefly, he added, "Don't want a shortage now do we?"

Color swept over the delicate features to her hairline as she snapped, "Yes, Sir. I'll make damn sure not to forget 'mine'!" Then she spun on her heel, swiftly leading the gray gelding away.

Now why had she said that? Nothing like putting your foot in your mouth clear to the knee. Would she ever learn to curb that temper of hers? Or her mouth? It was too bad that she had never been able to give a tongue-lashing to Drake. He had needed it. But she had been too shy and insecure at the time to say how she felt. And now there just wasn't any point. But why cut loose on Tyler?

The next half an hour was filled with so much preparation that she had little time to dwell on her feelings. Everyone was busy trying to get ready for the ride and cook-out. Jess would catch a glimpse of Tyler as he moved from one chore to another. But neither spoke to the other.

Children giggling with excitement, horses snorting with impatience; they wanted to be on their way. Jessie had made sure that the Winters group were altogether; and as McKay joined her, she reported carefully, "Everyone is here except for the Fisher group, who decided not to go at the last minute. Parker is in charge of the children along with Saylor. And Stan is driving the lead supply wagon, Peter is handling the second."

The dark-curly head nodded, he kept his comment to a monosyllable. "Fine."

Pulling his horse around, he started back to the rear of the convoy. Cooper glanced up, then turned Shiloh after the trail foreman. "Tyler, Ty..."

He halted, turning his lithe form in the saddle to wait for her, his face wearing an expression of impatience. "Yeah? What is it?"

At first she hesitated, not knowing if she should ask him or not. Then with a stubborn set to the small chin, she stated calmly, "Do you think that there might be some way that we could show Confederate to the groups? You see... uh...well, Linda and Tim have to return home tomorrow and well, I...uh...thought that it would be nice if they could see him."

Tyler's stern features remained noncommittal. "We'll have to see."

Without another word, he moved Rebel off at a slow lope toward the two supply wagons. Jessie brushed the red-gold hair back off of her face with shaky fingers. Sighing to herself, she went to catch up with her group.

Larry Connors frowned to himself as he watched Cooper and McKay interact with each other. There was something decidedly wrong between them. What could have happen so suddenly? Almost overnight. Turning the almost white-blonde head, his eyes fell onto Joe Drake. He had found that the more he was around the dark-haired Joe, the less he found to like about him. He had never been around him much over the years and now didn't have the inclination to change that fact. Besides Cindy didn't like the man at all. She said that he was in love with himself.

It was more than just Connors that noticed the strained attitude between Jess and Ty. The wranglers, their friends, and other guides had never seen the two at odds with each other before and just didn't know how to react.

Roy Parker shook his head, muttering quietly to Saylor. "Jeff, what is going on with Jess and Tyler? Any idea?"

The tall, slender Jeff Saylor leaned back in the stock saddle. "I don't have a clue. I've never seen them like this. Guess even the best of friends can have a falling out now and again. They'll get over it."

Roy grinned tightly. "Well, I sure hope that it's soon. Can't take it, myself."

Jeff laughed softly. "Come on. You'll live."

"I hope you're right."

"Mister Roy, could you fix my saddle?" interrupted a small girl with a shaky smile.

Just then Tyler rode by and as Roy glanced up at the handsome, unsmiling face; he couldn't help wishing that he could fix the dent with Ty and Jess's relationship. But some things just can't be helped by others no matter how much they want to.

Chapter Eight

Jessie slumped dejectedly in the saddle. The gray-blue eyes once again seeking out the lean figure of the trail foreman. Sighing, she wished that they were back on friendly terms. What had caused Ty to suddenly become so distant and uptight; and herself so short tempered and insecure?

The only thing that she knew for sure was the sick, chilled feeling that rested in the pit of her stomach. Almost like fear. It was fear. Fear of losing Tyler's friendship? After having him being there for her from almost the very first day that she had arrived. She would be lost. Suddenly, steely fingers caught hold of her upper arm, bringing her slight body into a stiff, up-right position.

"Wake up, Jess! This is no time for day dreaming." Snapped McKay sharply, his bronzed features almost stony.

An apology leaped to her lips, but she said instead, "Yes, Sir. So sorry, won't let it happen again."

The tawny-green eyes were dark, unreadable. "See that you don't. We'll be making camp in the clearing."

Once again her voice came out bitingly as she answered, "Right. The usual place, isn't it? What's the matter, do you think that I'm so scatter-brained that I'd ride right on by?"

A dry grin twisted the straight lips. "Gave it a thought." Then turning the red roan gelding around, headed for the first supply wagon.

Cooper's hot glance followed him. She had done it again. What was the matter with her?

A number of hours later the campfires were glowing, sending out pale amber light to displace the settled darkness. Most everyone were relaxing on or near their bedrolls. The night was quiet with the soft sound of a few harmonicas being played by a couple of the wranglers. Jessie was lying back on her blankets and staring tearfully up at the velvet-black sky.

She had spread her bedroll farther away from the wagons and campfires. Only moonlight and the faintest glow of the fires reached her slight shape. A guitar rested across her flat stomach and absently she strummed a few cords. She felt isolated; completely alone and lonely. She wanted to cry, but knew that she wouldn't. Without thinking she began to whisper the words to the song that she was softly strumming.

From his position leaning against the main supply wagon, Tyler heard the soft strains of the guitar. Turning the dark head, he could just barely make out the still form of the redhead. About to set down his coffee mug, he stopped at hearing the first, sort of sad words of the song. Jessie sang with the gentle, husky voice that showed a depth of feeling for what she was singing. And like everyone else, he stood very still and listened.

Jeff Saylor, who was sitting near the fire, was the first to speak when the redhead had finished. "Hey! Jessie! Come on out here and play some more."

Others soon joined in trying to convince her to continue to sing. Slowly the slight figure stepped hesitantly into the ring of pale firelight. The red-gold hair tumbled in wild array about her shoulders, the smoky-gray eyes glowed darkly with an inner light.

Tyler swallowed hard. A warmth uncurled in his lower gut and spread throughout his body turning it hard with wanting.

"Alright, what do you characters want to hear?" demanded Cooper as lightly as she could manage.

Roy Parker and the other wranglers exchanged looks, then when all seemed in agreement, Parker drawled, "I... that is, we think the guests should hear you and Ty sing. Isn't that right?"

"Alright!! Yes, we want to hear them!" came the shouted answer.

McKay froze in his spot as Jess managed a grim smile. "You'll have to ask our fearless leader about that."

All eyes turned in Tyler's direction, and he silently thanked the darkness for hiding the red blush that was washing over his face. "Well...uh...I don't know..." he stammered.

"Come on, Boss." Laughed Chang with a wide grin.

But still Tyler could not seem to move. Cooper threw him a swift glance, then suggested quietly, "If we do; you guys have to join in. All of you. What do you want to hear?"

The others promised, then Chang Cole drawled slowly, "Do that one by Reba McEntire and Vince Gill. We've heard you guys singing along with song on the CD jukebox in the bar."

Jessie nodded the red-gold head. "It's okay with me. Tyler," her gray gaze slid to his shadowed features, "I'll start, you come in where Vince does. Okay?"

McKay managed a brief nod and stepped closer to the slender redhead. The wranglers and other ranch workers sighed contently knowing what was coming and sat closer to the couple. The guests seeing the ranch personnel move in closer, followed and waited anxiously for the man and woman to start.

Jess started out the country duo hit 'The Heart Don't Lie' in her husky-soft alto, with Ty's rich, baritone voice blending in beautifully. His voice was the sort that caused women to melt inside and had men envious. Her voice at times could range into the lower soprano area. She had a fairly large range and was a clear, clean intense voice. The guests were completely captivated by both of them.

From a little way off, Linda turned to her husband whispering softly, "My word, they are good. I didn't even know that Jessica could play the guitar, let alone sing."

Tim shook his dark-blonde head, a frown marring his clear-cut features. "I didn't know she could either. She's really good at it. They both are. Didn't you say she was in choir when you guys were in school?"

"Yes, she was. She just never wanted to be singled out. Just one of a group."

After the last strains of the song died away, Tyler turned to the wranglers and guides that were sitting nearby. Jeff, Roy, Chang, and you, too, Toby. Now, it's your show."

The four cowboys moved together and Jeff smiled pleadingly at Jessie, "Care to join us with your guitar?" Then looking over at another young man not far away, he asked, "And how about your harmonica, Juan?"

They started out with an old song that told of the legend of a large white mysterious buffalo. A very pretty old song. Afterwards everyone joined in on a few of the more popular melodies. Others sang folk songs, even a few of the guests sang solos.

All through the entertaining, McKay let his guarded glance linger on Cooper's soft features. He had seen her play many times before; but--tonight something was lacking. At least on the happier songs. On the sad ballads she seemed to enhance the very essence of their meaning. Always before she had seemed to radiate with laughter and life. Tonight, she was so still and pale. Almost withdrawn, even though she was surrounded by people.

Finnley, one of the older cowhands, spoke up suddenly, "Jess, will you sing 'The Night They Drove Old Dixie Down'?"

The redheaded woman smiled gently. "Don't see why not." Glancing at Juan and the other four wranglers, asked hintingly, "I'll need backup."

Chang nodded affirmatively. "You've got it."

Everyone listened to the rousing song and before long were singing along. As she sang the Civil War melody, the gray eyes shuttled from Joe's dark features to Ty's bronze, lean ones. Unconsciously she compared the two men; but found that there was no comparison because one man had it all and the other had never had it. Poor Joe.

After the song finished, McKay called a halt to the music and suggested that everyone should head for bed. To most it was more than welcome. It had been a long afternoon and they found themselves comfortably tired.

From where he stood, Tyler watched as Jessie rose from her previous position to return to her secluded bedroll. Before she had moved very far, however, Drake stepped up beside her. McKay frowned.

Jess was in no mood to talk with Joe. Least of all, him. But good manners caused her to force a grim smile on her stiff lips as she looked up at his face. "Joe, what is it?"

Drake flashed a brilliant smile that never reached his eyes. "You were great. When did you learn to play the guitar?"

Cooper was tired, and couldn't seem to keep the hard edge out of her usually soft voice. "About a year or so. But for that matter, you wouldn't have known if I had been playing it when I knew you. Now, if you don't mind, it's late. Excuse me."

The flashy smile had faded, but his voice was still level. "Sure thing. Good-night, Shrimp."

Sudden fire leaped to life in the gray eyes, as she spun on Drake. "Don't call me that."

A hardness settled over the handsome face. "Right. But tell me, Jessie, who taught you to play the guitar? That cowboy of yours? What else did he teach you? Tell me is he as good at riding you as he is at riding a horse?"

A red haze flashed before her eyes, without thought, her hand slapped his face hard. Then she turned and stalked toward her bedroll.

Joe stared after her retreating figure. His cheek and jaw ached where she had hit him and an anger built in his chest. The little bitch. Then from behind him a quiet voice sounded.

"She's way too much for you. And way too good for you. I suggest a good night's rest. Far from her bedroll."

Drake faced McKay a brief moment, but could not meet the steely tawny-green eyes of the trail foreman.

Tyler remained where he was until Joe reached his own bedroll. He had been in position to see the altercation between the two. He had seen Jess start to lose her calm façade, and had been tempted to step in; but she had reacted so quickly that the slap had taken him by surprise as well as Joe. From the look on her face, it had taken her by surprise also. He wondered what Drake had said to make her react so violently? So totally not Cooper's style.

Moving over to his own blankets, the handsome features hardened into a frown. Whether Drake knew it or not, Ty considered him a threat. McKay hunched his shoulders and rested his arms on the top of his drawn up knees, his thoughts returning to what had glinted in the smoky-blue eyes as she had looked at Joe. Was it good or did it mean something else? Something that could hurt himself? Or even possibly Jessie?

With a last glance in Jessie's direction, he slid under the blankets and closed his eyes.

Jess was up early; but found that the younger children had awoke before her. Breakfast was a fun affair and the cooks knew how to do it up right. Even children that would hardly ever eat at home were now heartily stuffing themselves.

A good two hours later they were all again mounted and on the wood-bordered trail. Like she had been doing all morning, Cooper again looked around for any sign of Tyler. She had only seen him once that morning and knew he had not eaten any breakfast, which was not like the trail foreman. Was he still angry with her?

Juan Mendez pulled his horse in beside her, remarking as he did so, "We'll be nearing Lost Wind Canyon. Do we go through or around and above?"

The woman frowned. "I'm not sure. Where's Ty? Have you seen him?"

The Hispanic man shook his head. "Nope. Haven't seen him since before breakfast." Giving her a steady look, he asked, "What is it between you two? He was as grumpy as a wounded mountain lion yesterday and he was acting strange this morning."

"Oh...I don't know really. We're both so stubborn and neither one of us wants to be the first one to give in. Juan, let's go through the canyon. If Tyler says anything about it, send him my way." Suggested Cooper slowly.

Juan nodded agreement and turned his mount toward the wagons that were farther ahead. Jess silently let her gaze follow the young man, a slight frown forming on her light-tan, pale-freckled face.

What had caused McKay to change so? Ever since the arrival of her old friends, there had been some kind of discontent. If not with each other, then with outsiders.

"Hi, Jess. Hey, why the long face?" Called Larry Connors as he moved the large Warsaw up next to the rain-gray gelding.

She managed a cheerful smile, but her voice revealed the hurt puzzlement. "Nothing, I guess. Oh, Larry, it's just not like Tyler to be this way. I don't understand at all." She finished with a sigh of despair.

Larry remained quiet for a while before asking cautiously, "Maybe he is worried about certain people?"

Troubled gray-blue eyes flashed to Connors' face. "Maybe Dave Hunter and Wes Wilcox?"

Larry looked at the delicate, worried features and then acknowledged hesitantly, "Yes, I would imagine. That and his shoulder and very possibly you." And to himself he thought it would also include Joe Drake.

Confused eyes looked up. "Me?"

"Of course, you. He has some very strong feelings for you and he's worried about you. Same as you are for him."

Connors was no fool. He felt pretty damn sure that McKay was fighting a battle with himself over his feelings for the redhead. Larry had seen the faint image of desire flicker across the trail foreman's bronzed features. Only momentarily, but he had noticed it. And of Jessie? What were her feelings for the tall, lean man? Just how far should he, Larry, go? Should he ask Jess what her feelings were for McKay? Or should he tell her what he thought Tyler felt for her? No, he couldn't do that. That had to be Ty's choice.

Just how would a person go about helping the two friends without possibly hurting them? He'd have to play it by ear. Be a friend. A buffer.

Whether Larry wanted to realize it or not, Joe Drake bothered him. A lot. Joe was a different sort of threat; mainly because neither Connors, nor McKay knew just how much Jessie cared for the man?

Chapter Nine

A stream ran directly through Lost Wind Canyon. Trees and thick underbrush bordered the steep grassy slopes and near the cold, winding stream. At a shaded, grassy clearing, Jessie had the group make camp; since Tyler hadn't shown up yet.

Pulling the gray gelding to a halt near the main camp wagon, Cooper slid to the ground. She had decided to make the rest of the rounds on foot. Walking past the different cowhands and wranglers, she knew from their questioning glances that they too were wondering what had become of McKay.

Her temper was crowding the boiling point, the gray-blue eyes were dark with suppressed anger. And guilt? Whether Tyler was boss or not; she was determined to tell him a few home truths.

By the time lunch was ready, McKay still had not shown up and Jess moved over beside Jeff Saylor. Her voice was stiff with annoyance. "Jeff, since our boss hasn't bothered to show up, and hasn't left any orders, we'll just let everyone relax and do as they please. Tell them they can fish if they want to." Then with a sigh, she added, "If you need anything, I'll be over there near the small grove of trees."

Saylor watched the worried woman walk off toward the shaded, secluded spot. For the first time since he began working with McKay, he found that he was angry with the trail foreman. Worried, also. It just wasn't like the boss to disappear with no reason or word.

A good long while later, Jessie heard a twig snap behind her and without turning, said, "What is it this time, Jeff? I'd really like to get my hands on Tyler...I...I'd..."

"You'd what?" questioned a familiar quiet drawl.

Stiffening and cautiously rising to her slender height, she slowly turned to face, not Jeff as she had assumed, but McKay. His handsome, tanned features were unreadable as the cool, hazel-green eyes slid over her slight frame and came to rest on the small oval face.

"I'd ring your neck." She retorted just above a whisper.

"You would, huh?"

"I would." Jessie nodded shortly.

"I could go so far as to call that a form of mutiny or better still, insubordination. To get rid of your boss by force." McKay's tawny-green gaze remained steadily on her face, his voice soft, calm.

Jess could feel the hot color flood her cheeks and neck; yet, she forced her own gray gaze to meet his as sharp words broke from the stiff lips. "Some boss. Goes off and doesn't leave word or any orders with anyone. I want you to know that I got awfully tired of having to give or better still, getting asked questions that I had no clue about, since I'm not the trail foreman."

Not giving him a chance to answer her demands, she snapped with renewed fire. "And while I'm at it; if I hadn't done it, right or otherwise, we'd still be back at morning camp! And if you don't like the way I did things, well, next time stay around and be the boss!"

The bronzed features paled, but the voice belied any anger as he replied dryly, "Thank you for the lecture. But, if you're not going to ring my neck and you haven't anything else to submit to my character analysis... I wish you could go get the younger kids and your friends and then bring them over to that tree-bordered draw. Thanks." He very deliberately turned his back on her and walked away.

Jessie stood and watched him, the gray eyes with blue sparks boring into his broad back. Shrugging her shoulders, she went to find the people he wanted. The reason why he wanted them never entered her mind.

Walking ahead of the redhead, Tim Winters glanced at the taller Larry Connors. Tim's handsome features were carrying a depressed frown. "Larry, wonder what this is all about?"

Connors shook his white-blonde head. "No idea. Jess didn't give any details." Hesitating briefly, he added, "Sorry you two have to go home tonight."

"Yeah. Worse luck." Muttered Tim. "Would have liked to have seen Confederate and the race."

Larry laughed softly. "From what I've heard, there's only one possible winner."

"Sure hope it isn't that Wilcox horse."

"I doubt it, Tim." Spoke up McKay. His lean form was standing almost next to them.

The hazel eyes traveled slowly over the small group before he continued quietly, "I had Jessie bring you over here to see something. Since Tim and Linda are leaving; someone suggested that it would be nice if they could see Confederate."

Larry glanced at Jess just in time to catch the delicate features change from cool indifference to shocked dismay. The trail foreman's cool, honeyed voice once again penetrated to pull his gaze back to the tall, lean man.

"So this morning I happen to find him and brought him in so that all of you could met the pride of Jute Valley Ranch."

Every head there turned in the direction that Ty indicated with a short nod of his head. The stallion stood proudly with the narrow nose, wide-set eyes of the Arabian; the rippling muscles quivering with excitement. He was tall with a powder-white coat and unusual blue-black mane and tail. Very long and flowing.

A young girl with curly brown hair and big navy-blue eyes moved forward and spoke in a quiet subdued tone of awe. "He's outrageous! I've never seen a white horse with a black mane and tail."

At the words, Confederate turned his fine head and slowly eyed the girl with dark eyes as if he understood that he was being admired and totally agreed. Linda stepped closer to the young girl and remarked quietly, "He really is unusual."

A small girl of perhaps four or five reached up and tugged on Tyler's pant leg. Her dark-green eyes were glued on the large stallion, only looking away long enough to ask, "Ty, can I touch?"

A gentle smile touched the stern male lips. "I don't see why not. Come on, half-pint. But move slowly. No fast moves or loud yells or we'll scare him."

Nearing the stallion, Tyler carefully lifted the child onto the broad, satiny back. The little girl's face was alight with pleasure. The tiny hand buried itself into the thick, silky black mane and she cooed lovingly to the horse. Within minutes, twelve more small children advanced in an orderly fashion to be given the same amount of time on the stallion.

Carefully lifting down the last child, a small freckled-faced boy, McKay smiled, "Better head back to camp now. I've got to turn Fed over to the wrangler."

Everyone turned away and headed for the camp; the women making sure that all the smaller ones came along also. As the small group disappeared, Jessie moved up next to the trail boss.

"Why didn't you tell me?"

Tyler turned slowly to face her. "You didn't exactly give me a chance to say anything. Remember?"

The gray eyes flashed blue sparks. "Remember! I feel like a first class heel. Thanks..." Then she spun on her heel and ran back in the direction of the wagons.

McKay watched her until the trees appeared to swallow her up. His face turned grim and set, the green-gold eyes darkened with longing and frustration.

Walking down along the swift moving mountain stream, Larry stuffed his hands in the pockets of his jeans; a worried frown on his dark-tanned, lean face. Connors was very conscious of the tense under-currents between McKay and Cooper. Little did the woman realize that she was tearing apart the Trail Boss.

So deep were his troubled thoughts that he failed to see Cindy standing near the edge of the bubbling stream. That was, until he ran full-tilt into her, knocking the sandy-haired woman off-balance and plunging her into the cold water. With a startled yelp, she landed in a sitting position with the clear rushing water reaching her narrow waist. Larry stepped hurriedly in and took her hand, stammering as he did so. "I...I...geez, Cindy, I didn't see you there. I'm sorry. Are you alright?"

Reaching the grass-covered bank, Cindy sank limply to the ground. But as she looked up at his distressed features, she grinned softly, "It's alright. I'll dry out. It was really sort of fun, or maybe I should say, 'funny'? Wasn't it?" and then she laughed.

And then Larry was joining in with his deeper chuckle.

Cindy leaned back against the thick grass and motioned him down beside her. "I was feeling rather hot and sticky. But, it never dawned on me to sit in the creek. Thanks, I needed that. Now, tell me what's wrong?"

Blue-green eyes flashed to her face. "You always seem to know. How is that?" he leaned over and placed his lips on her soft, inviting mouth.

Everyone was gathered around the cook wagons and glowing fires. Fresh mountain trout was deliciously sizzling in old, black-bottomed skillets; or if the younger set preferred, hotdogs and hamburgers, were also available. Potatoes, wrapped snuggly in tinfoil and baked under the hot coals, were placed on waiting plates along with corn-on-the-cob.

Cindy and Larry sat with the others enjoying their dinner. But off to one side, away from the happy people and the aroma of good cooking; Jessie sat hunched up against a large, old shade tree.

Quietly she sat there calling herself all kinds of a fool. She had been stupid to think Tyler would shirk his job. But worse, she had bawled him out, and for nothing.

Stretching out her legs, a frown between her delicate brows, she could not figure out what had happen between them. She was finding fault with McKay where there wasn't any; and he in turn, would react with unaccustomed short temper and on occasions so very impersonal. Sudden hot tears burned behind her lids and she let them fall down her cheeks. There had not been much she could have done to stop them. Worse, she didn't understand them.

When she managed to return to camp, she was pale and tense. Others who knew her wondered; but knew better than to question her. The camp was being picked up and all were getting ready to be underway.

Saddling Shiloh, Jessie made it a point to avoid the trail foreman. Finishing with the cinch, she hurried to where the guests were saddling their mounts. If the guests were doing alright on their own the ranch personnel did not interfere. As in Jess's case only two of the younger children needed help. After checking the rest of the cinches, she once again mounted Shiloh and waited for the guests to mount. Within a few brief minutes everyone was underway.

Cooper, trying to keep her mind off the problems that seemed to engulf her at times, made herself stay busy talking and answering questions from the guests and children. As she rode up and down the long line of riders and wagons, she caught the worried glances from the wranglers and cowboys. So made certain not to get in a position that would lead to a conversation with them.

When she would catch sight of Tyler making his check of the larger groups, she would manage to disappear until he had passed by. Jess felt uneasy and knew it had a lot to do with the fact that she usually was not the sort of person to run away from her problems or people. Especially a friend like Tyler.

A sudden thought struck her forcibly, she realized that once before she had indeed ran away; and from friends. Yes, she had turned-tail and ran from Linda and Tim. Also Larry. And why? Because of Joe. Now, was she going to let him cause her to run away from another friend? And right then she finally admitted that it had been because of Joe Drake that she had left all her friends and family. And very possibly was the reason, or part of the reason, that Ty and she were having difficulties.

Was she going to run away again? No. She had changed. She was not a doormat for anyone any more, especially so-called friends. She and Tyler would have to work their problems out between them. It was a bad time all the way around. Temporarily she had pushed what Joe had said to her last night just before she had slapped him. He had deserved to have been slugged. Had he always been so crude? More than likely, she had just not looked beyond the image. But with the words he had uttered so nastily came a different image. The image of a hard, bronzed body that moved like a large predatory cat. Warmth seeped into her lower body and once again remembered the kiss that Ty and she had shared. She was noticing him in a different light. Was he doing the same? And somehow or other, she knew that Joe had been the catalysis.

Straightening up, she caught a quick glimpse of Larry Connors riding with his fiancée, Cindy Tanner. Jessie smiled, glad that Larry had found such a nice girl like

Cindy. Cooper liked and respected the honey-brown haired woman. She was a woman who enjoyed life to the fullest, but without hurting anyone else in doing so. She also didn't take any crap from Joe. In fact, Jess didn't think that the woman much cared for him at all.

They were now topping the high ridge that overlooked the guest ranch. Jessie had always enjoyed this spot. It reminded her of a western movie she had once seen. A John Wayne movie, she thought.

Without realizing it, she sighed deeply with relief. Glad to be back and that the outing was coming to an end. Yet, at the same time a little sad that Linda and Tim had to leave that evening. She could not help but wish that it had been Joe instead. Things would have been made so much easier.

Having pulled the gray to a halt to look down on the sprawling ranch buildings, she now moved him on down the ridge. Nearing the bottom, she glanced up and caught sight of Phil coming out of his office. The ranch manager waved a hand as he saw the group arriving.

Chapter Ten

Watching Tyler McKay slowly dismount from the red roan gelding, Phil Holden walked up to meet him. "Well, how did it go?"

As the lean features turned toward him, Phil was taken aback at the depressed expression mirrored in the tawny-green eyes, and even more so at the dry, humorless words that followed.

"You shouldn't ask. Jess and I have done nothing but argue and fight like two stubborn mules the whole trip." Then without any change of expression, Tyler gathered up Rebel's reins, "Excuse, me." And led the gelding toward the small corral.

Phil frowned. This was becoming major. He had hoped that something would have happen to get them back on better terms. Seeing the redhead, he was about to call to her when a couple of the guests confronted him. He would just have to wait to talk to the young woman.

Not far from Jessie, Linda and Tim stood talking. Tim glanced at the departing McKay and then at Jessie's stiff, small face before saying to his wife, "I doubt if Jess has talked to Tyler about joining our farewell outing tonight."

Linda sighed and slowly nodded her head in sad agreement. "I'm afraid you're right. All I've seen them do lately is barely tolerate each other or yell."

"Well, I'll ask McKay before it gets much later." Remarked Tim as he started to unsaddle his mount.

Just as he was wiping down the paint, Larry Connors appeared. Leaning against the side of the barn, he volunteered, "Tim, I talked to Holden and we can rent the cars to go to the airport. It's really too bad that you two have to leave."

"I'll have to agree with you. But it was something that just couldn't be helped." Answered Winters with a frown.

"Well, at least you did get to see Confederate." Stated Larry as he straightened his lean frame, turning to walk with Tim as he turned the big horse into the corral.

"Yes. Thanks to Tyler." Nodded Tim.

Then glancing toward Jess and Tyler's two cabins, he halted and replied quietly, "I promised Linda that I'd ask Tyler about this evening. S'pose I better go do it now, while he's off duty."

Connors touched the other man's shoulder with a detaining hand. "Wait. Why don't I do it? You go ahead and pack."

"Alright. I'll catch you later. I'll still have to check on the plane reservations." Winters replied with apparent relief.

Larry watched as he headed for the lodge. It was too bad that they had to leave so suddenly. Sighing to himself, he turned in the direction of McKay's cabin.

The small, compact building was almost identical to that of Jessie's. The kitchenette was located on the other side of the front room. The bedroom, too, was located on the other side. The ex-GI knocked softly on the screened door, but received no answer. The inside door was open and peering into the dusky-lit room, Larry could make out the trail foreman's lean form reclining on the low, overstuffed couch.

Stepping quietly inside, Larry walked over to the sleeping man. He almost hated to disturb him, but... "Ty... wake up. Tyler."

McKay woke swiftly, yet, when he spoke his voice was calm and normal. "What is it, Larry?"

"Well, as you know Tim and Linda are leaving tonight. We are all getting together to see them off at the airport. We wanted you to come along, if you'd like?" Smiled Larry.

Tyler sat up. "I'd like to, but I don't think I'll be able to make it. I'll try, but don't look for me until you see me."

The blonde man nodded. "Sure, I understand. But come even if it's late. Their flight doesn't leave until ten-forty-five tonight."

Tyler smiled slowly. "Alright. I'll be there if at all possible."

Grinning, Connors replied, "Good. Well, I better get a move on. See you later."

"Right." Answered McKay as he watched the tall, lean man quietly close the outside door behind him. Stretching, Ty decided to take a quick shower and go check on the new horses that had arrived earlier that morning. And also check on Fed. He needed to give the stallion his vaccinations and worming. Then if he worked it right he would only have a few more chores to finish up after dinner and still be able to make it to the airport before the two had to leave.

Walking quickly to the small shower, he pulled off his shirt and frowned slightly. Jess would be there. But, hell, he couldn't keep avoiding her. Play it cool and just stay out of her way.

It was getting late as McKay left the horse barns. It was nearing time for dinner and throwing a glance over his shoulder in the direction of the lodge, he was in time to catch a view of Tim, Linda and the rest of the group as they climbed into the two cars and headed for the airport. Silently he watched them.

He hadn't seen Cooper until the car, in which she was riding, drove past. And then it was only a fleeting glimpse of her copper-bright hair through the rear window of the second car.

For a few brief moments he just stood gazing after the tail lights of the last car as it disappeared into the evening dusk. With a slow shake of the dark head, he resumed his walk to the large, old world lodge.

Standing just inside the lodge doorway, Phil Holden let his eyes follow the lean-muscled form of his trail foreman as he walked closer to the building. He didn't like what was happening between Jessie and Ty. McKay and Jess were like his family. It just wasn't right for them to behave like they were doing. Hurting each other and their friends.

But Phil was smart enough to know that he could not say anything, but he would be there if either or both of them needed him.

Looking up as McKay stepped through the wide wooden doors, Phil greeted the trail foreman with a careful grin. "Well, Ty, how about some chow?"

"Sounds good to me." smiled the younger man slowly. Even though Tyler had professed to be hungry, Phil noted that the man barely touched his food; except for pushing it around on his plate with a fork. Knowing that he should not say anything about the fact he was not eating, Phil tried to ignore it by asking a question that had nothing to do with the meal.

"Are you going to see those two friends of Jessie's off tonight?" asked Holden absently, his own eyes remaining steadily on his near empty plate.

Leaning back in the chair, Tyler sighed softly before replying to Phil's question. "Yes, as soon as I finish up some last minute chores."

Again Phil noted the disappointment shadowing the younger man's hazel eyes, so with an attempt at a careless tone that would not show his own anxiety, he suggested quietly, "I'm sorry that couple had to leave. Ty, why don't you take tomorrow morning off? There's nothing of importance happening then. Besides you never had your other half-day off." He added quickly as McKay was about to decline.

Holden could see the hesitation as the younger man thought the offer over. Finally he answered, "I might just do that, Phil."

Holden smiled knowingly to himself. "Fine. Well, I've got some paperwork to finish up." Rising, he added as an afterthought, "We should bring Fed down out of the high meadows fairly soon. I still don't know why Hunter had traps set on our land and I sure as hell don't want Fed getting tangled up in one. Just would like to get the horse down here where he's safe."

Tyler frowned and then agreeing, "Not to worry, Phil. We brought Fed back with us this afternoon. He's looking real good. I gave him his shots and wormed him this evening. I'll trim his feet tomorrow. Okay?"

"Sounds fine to me." Grinned Holden.

The airport dining and cocktail lounge was muted in soft light and quiet music played. Jessie Cooper sighed and leaned back in the plush chair. Through thick, copper-tipped lashes, she eyed the people around the table.

Everyone appeared almost lulled by the pleasant atmosphere, yet there was a measure of sadness because of Tim and Linda's approaching departure. Whether she liked it or not, she had been paired with Joe. He seemed to be on his best behavior. Still, she found that she constantly eyed the doorway, looking for a tall, curly haired man to arrive.

Slowly lifting the cool drink to her lips, she was listening to Cindy, when McKay entered. He saw her first. The soft lighting resting on the riot of long loose curls of copper-bright hair and smooth lightly-tanned skin. The dress she wore was a pale lilac with flowing shades of muted blues running through it. A low, v-cut neckline with no sleeves showed off a small, firm bust-line and the creamy smoothness of her upper arms. Moving closer, he saw that the color seemed to intensify the blueness in the otherwise gray eyes. He also noticed Drake's presence at her side. Planting a passable smile on his stiffening lips, he greeted them all.

"Well, it appears that I made it in time."

Everyone looked up and all smiled a friendly greeting, except Joe who managed to remain politely quiet. It was

Tim Winters who spoke up. "Well, it's about time you showed up. Pull up a chair and sit down."

"Thanks, I will." Grinned Tyler.

Jess eyed McKay carefully, being cautious not to appear as if she were. She had to admit that he made a striking figure. No jeans tonight. He wore dark-brown pants and two-tone green shirt with a dark-brown tie and a sports jacket of the same color; dramatized the bronzed darkness of his tan and called attention to the lean, athletic build under its fine material.

A waitress with long, shiny-black hair neared their table and asked if anyone cared for another drink. Larry Connors glanced over at Tyler and questioned, "What will you have?"

"Bourbon and water." Answered McKay with a soft grin.

The attractive girl seeing Tyler, smiled widely and exclaimed in a voice that was colored with apparent pleasure. "Tyler McKay. Nice to see you again. It's been quite a while, Handsome. You'll have to come in more often. We've missed you around here."

Tyler winked up at the woman and smiled. "Guess, I've missed coming here, too. Have to see what I can do about that. Don't forget how to make my drink, Lana."

The woman chuckled softly down in her throat. "Would never do that to you, Cowboy." Then she turned to the other guests.

Joe spoke with some annoyance as the waitress glanced in his direction. "I'll have another bloody Mary and a whiskey coke for the lady."

Tyler caught the swift, surprised glance that Jess threw at Drake. She had not ordered the drink and the fine lips formed a grim line of disapproval.

A few of the others made their orders, then the waitress headed for the bar. McKay turned his attention to Connors who was mentioning something about the dance floor.

"When do they use it? Does anyone know?"

Tyler nodded. "Yes." Then glancing at the watch on his wrist, he added with a smile. "In about ten minutes. Earlier on weekends. When business is extremely good."

Larry smiled broadly as he looked around the table. "Good, we can dance, then. How about it? Sounds like fun, huh?"

The others agreed as the woman returned with the drinks. McKay lifted his glass to the firm lips and rested his indifferent greenish gaze on Drake. The dark-haired man appeared as if he had consumed more liquor than the rest. But Tyler had to admit that he seemed to hold it quite well.

His drink tasted rather good and as the music started McKay was content to just sit and watch. Larry had asked Cindy to dance and so had Tim asked Linda. Now Joe turned to Jessie. Tyler appeared not to be paying any attention, but his eyes were on the redhead's face nevertheless.

Jess Cooper hesitantly nodded consent to Joe's offer to dance and rose from her comfortable chair to join the gathering of dancers at the spacious dance floor.

Dancing with Joe had never been fun as he was not an inventive dancer. It was hard to match her smaller steps with his as he kept changing them or he would hardly move at all. Peering up at him through the fringe of lashes, she wondered if Drake did everything that way? Never staying with anything or anyone for very long; but changing for fear of failing?

She had never really enjoyed dancing with Drake. She had always found herself tense and uneasy. For fear that she would displease him in some way. He had been able to make her feel like a total ninny by a few well-placed nasty remarks. But not anymore. As they threaded their way back to the table, she realized that she was glad that the song had ended.

Reaching her seat, she glanced cautiously at the relaxed figure of Tyler as he rested in the chair opposite her own. His features were completely expressionless and she wondered furtively what exactly he was thinking.

Cooper was not the only person wondering what McKay was thinking, Joe Drake was eyeing the lean masculine body that was lounging with careless ease. Almost too indifferent; or maybe the cowboy had lost interest in the redhead? It would definitely be to Joe's benefit if that were the case. For whether Drake liked it or not the bronzed cowboy posed a threat to his reclaiming of Cooper.

Linda, who had been in an in depth conversation with Tim, now turned toward McKay and asked, "Do you enjoy slow dancing, Ty?"

A grin spread across the lean features. "Yes. What did you think that us 'poor cowhands' were still uncivilized? I even enjoy some of the fast numbers. What I really like to do is line dances and some of the country two-step."

Embarrassed color washed over the olive-toned features. "No, of course not, Tyler."

Then as the strains of a slow, romantic dance number began, he turned to Jessie, "How about this dance?"

Jess, astonishment blocking her throat, just nodded her bright head. The last thing she had expected was to have him ask her to dance. Moving away from the table, she stepped into his arms and felt them enclose her in warm strength. She was surprised to find that they danced very well together. Almost as one, their movements were well coordinated. But she thought to herself, she really shouldn't have thought that they wouldn't dance well together; they did everything well together, at least until lately.

Where she had found herself almost bored when dancing with Drake, she was finding Ty a delight as well as exciting. With a sigh, she pressed her smooth cheek against his deep chest and it seemed perfectly natural to be doing so. At the slight movement against him, his arm tightened about her slender form, pulling her soft curves even closer. And she wondered what it would feel like if he had wanted to kiss her and really meant it. The tentative kiss she had given him had more potential than she had expected.

Looking up into his face through the thick fringe of reddish lashes, she became confused at the amusement she found lurking in the shadowed hazel eyes. She couldn't help wondering what had caused it as the number came to a close. Tyler stepped calmly back and released his hold on her. Laughing softly, he took her elbow with warm fingers and steered her back to the table.

"Sorry, didn't mean to give you such a shock." He announced softly.

Joseph jumped up from where he had been sulking, watching them while they had been dancing. Without waiting for her to even reach her chair, he claimed her hand and pulled the slender body up against his own hard, male one. "Now, it's my turn." He stated tightly as he whirled her away onto the tiled dance floor.

Trying to catch her breath, she leaned back against Drake's restricting arms. The gray eyes had turned frosty and a mutinous expression settled about the fine lips. "That was unnecessary, Joe. I don't care for that type of man-handling. Not in the least."

He refused to take her seriously and chuckled deep in his throat. "Of course, sweetie, just relax and enjoy the music."

Her lips tightened even more. "Joe, I'm not your 'sweetie'."

Ignoring his displeased frown, she glanced distractedly over his shoulder, sighting McKay dancing with Linda. For some reason, odd though it might be, a pain tugged at her mid-section and she felt cheated. Hastily she shook the absurd feeling away. Or tried to.

Watching McKay and Linda move around the floor in time to the soft playing music, Cindy and Tim exchanged comments. Tim leaned back in the comfort of the plush chair. "McKay appears to be quite apt in almost everything."

"Well, he can dance. Looking at him now, no one would know he was a cowboy." Smiled Cindy, her smoky-hazel eyes dancing.

Winters agreed. "That's true enough. I like him. He's not conceited or pushy. I like the way he takes people at face value. As equals." Hesitating briefly, he added, "You know, Jessica has really surprised us, also. She has changed quite a bit. I can't decide if I like it or not, she seems harder somehow."

Cindy frowned slightly, her slender fingers absently turning the glass around and around. "Maybe she is harder because she is trying to protect herself? I didn't know her before. But I like her now, I like the way she stands up for herself and her friends. Don't take this the wrong way, Tim, but if you like Ty's upfront attitude, how do you put up with Joe's inflated ego?"

He looked taken aback at first, but smiled grimly. "Who says that I do? He's my wife's brother. I put up with it. Did you know that Jess and Joe were engaged once? Yep, and Joe cancelled it, by using his sister. He had Linda tell Jess. Can you believe that? No one knows, but Linda told me after Jessie had left. We had our first big disagreement."

Cindy lowered her long-lashed eyes, so he wouldn't see the sadness or anger in them. What a coward Drake was turning out to be. She would have to tell Larry about this, she knew he had not known because he had been away at that time. Gently she placed a slender hand on Tim's arm and smiled softly. "I'm sorry for you. No one deserves a brother-in-law like Joe. We're going to miss you two."

Awhile later the atmosphere was decidedly morose as they all stood watching as Tim and Linda boarded the large plane. A sad silence remained the whole period of time that the flight was on the ground. As the jet took-off, the remaining people turned from the large windows that over-looked the runway and slowly started to the front of the airport terminal.

Walking down the vast, long corridor, Larry suggested quietly, "Why don't we stop at the lobby for a cup of coffee before we head back?"

Everyone agreed. With a cup of hot coffee in each hand, except for Joe. They talked for a few minutes before figuring they had better head back to the ranch. They had brought two cars and Larry was not too happy with the return arrangements; because that meant that Jessie would have to ride back with Drake. But he didn't see any way around it. Glancing at the trail foreman, he saw that he had also noted the situation and was not pleased.

Watching Joe and Jess pull out of the parking lot, Ty frowned and couldn't help but notice that Cooper seemed very tense and on edge. He was not happy with the idea that she was alone with the man; but also because Jess was the sober one and she wasn't the one driving.

Tyler had noted that Jess was only drinking soda, except when Joe had ordered the one drink. But, she hadn't drank it. Fact was, Jess hardly ever drank.

Chapter Eleven

The night sky was dark and clear with bright, twinkling stars dotting the vast velvet blackness. A cool breeze whipped against Tyler's face as he leisurely drove the short-bed GMC pickup along the almost deserted black-topped highway.

The brisk breeze was refreshing and seemed to clear away the worried thoughts from his tired mind. The day off tomorrow would be more than welcome and needed. He had not realized just how very worn-out he had become.

Letting up on the gas pedal as he neared the Jute Valley turn-off, he swung the truck onto the narrow gravel road. Whispering along the sandy track, he came to the decision that tomorrow he would saddle up Fed and ride up into the foothills. Unconsciously he found that he was glad to be working with the stallion again, instead of having to face Jess and her old friends on a steady basis. It gave anyone who rode the lordly Arabian the feeling of freedom and power.

Once again turning onto another, slightly narrower road; McKay could make out the ranch buildings looming up out of the inky darkness just ahead. It was late and there were hardly any lights showing as he pulled the silent-running vehicle into the garage that housed the employee's automobiles.

Stepping out into the night air, he started toward his cabin. Before he had hardly covered any distance at all, he noticed one of the rental cars. Then the soft, quiet night was broken by the faint sounds of voices.

Sitting in the front seat, Jessie still had the tense edginess that was travelling up and down her nerve endings. She had offered to drive and was told to mind her own business. Though Joe seemed to be handling the car okay, except for going so very slow. And of course, if she mentioned it he would say not to worry.

Glancing from under long, reddish lashes, she eyed Joe Drake. A sudden chill caused her to wrap her arms about her body to still the shiver. A strange smile was lurking on the shadowed features. And that sent little warning bells throughout her small frame. To stop the words from coming out of her mouth and setting him off on one of his tangents, she closed her eyes and tried to shut out the tenseness.

Joe's dark eyes were watching the road ahead, but more times than not he let them sweep over the petite woman at his side. He had purposely driven much slower than the car far ahead. For by the time they were pulling into the parking area of the ranch, the other couple had already headed for their rooms.

Switching off the ignition, Joe unclipped his seatbelt, then turned in his seat to face Jessica. The redhead sat with her coppery head resting against the headrest of the seat. Her eyes were closed and moon light played softly over the delicate features. Slowly easing himself closer until his arm was lying directly above the girl's head along the back of the seat. Then as she turned her head slightly, soft gray eyes opened drowsily and he bent his dark head and kissed the tempting lips.

When she did not struggle against the pressure of his first tentative kiss, he slipped his arms about her slender frame and again found her lips in a more forceful demand. Suddenly the soft, warm body stiffened and small hands pushed hard against his chest.

"Stop." Muttered Jess. But when he failed to do as she requested, she pushed harder, saying once again, "Joe, I said quit."

Slowly he leaned back, dark eyes narrowed and still retaining his hold on her. "Why?"

"Because I don't want to kiss you."

"You're lying. You liked it at first." He stated in a calm voice, with a hint of iron in it.

Jess looked at the face she had once thought that she loved. But it was now not the same. Not at all. After that first hesitant kiss there had been nothing, no sensation, nothing. Then when he had kissed her again with more passion, she had felt – empty. Then, threatened.

An overwhelming feeling of relief swept over her. She now knew that she was not in love with Joe any more. Never had been 'in love' with him, more of a case of infatuation. Being in love with love.

"I fell asleep because you were driving so slowly. And it was unexpected. Now, I've got to go." She managed firmly as she tried to undo the seatbelt.

Joe's hands tightened. "Go? Just like that? Not yet, you don't. You used to like being kissed by me, what's changed? You can't still be on your mettle, after almost three years?"

Her mouth hardened as the gray eyes bore into cold dark ones. "You had Linda tell me that you didn't want to become any more involved, so you had your sister break off our engagement! How much more involved did you want to get? But that wasn't the worse part, Joe. The humiliating thing was that you felt I wasn't good enough for you to be seen with or good enough for your friends. You had used me, Joe, while you were between affairs. Used me from the very beginning. And then just tossed me away." She said quietly.

The dark eyes narrowed even more. "But you did love me, Jessica. You would again. Give it a chance!" He demanded as he crushed her slight frame against his hard one, forcing his mouth down cruelly on hers.

With the seatbelt still attached and her arms penned between the two bodies, she couldn't get any leverage to push him away. Swiftly he shoved his leg over her thrashing ones and his weight held them still. As his right hand moved to her breast, the left slid up her right thigh. A tight band of panic closed around her chest, fear bubbled up and lodged somewhere in her throat. She felt her body jerk stiffly at the intimate touch of the hard fingers trailing up her inner thigh. Twisting, trying to get her face turned away from his crushing and bruising mouth; she pulled her head back just far enough to pull in much needed air. Joe's lips trailed over her jaw to the small ear, his breathing harsh and rapid.

Whispering roughly, he asked, "You never did say how good your cowboy was in the sack? But I can say that no cowhand can be as good as I am."

"Stop it!" Then he covered her mouth in a brutal crush.

Suddenly the driver's door was jerked open and an icy, flint-hard voice stated, "I believe the lady has had enough."

Both struggling people froze, then Drake turned and faced the intruder. "McKay."

"That's right. Jess, get out of the car and go." Said Tyler in a deceptively quiet voice. "Joe, I think you had better go to the lodge. Now."

Jessie watched as Drake did as McKay had suggested. She tried shakily to undo the seatbelt clasp, but her fingers were shaking so badly that she couldn't get it to work. Quietly her door opened and Ty leaned in and deftly undid the clip, then helped her out of the seat and closed the door.

He put his arms around her and moved her away from the vehicle. Looking down at her small body, he noted that she had protectively wrapped her arms around her chest. The pale dress was torn at the top of her left breast and the skirt had a large rent near the lower right edge.

Tawny-green eyes settled on the pale, delicate face. At seeing the bruised and slightly bleeding mouth he felt a pain tighten through his chest. Anger simmered and burned just beneath the surface. Too close. Damn, he should have beat the bastard's face in. He also noted the trembling and the way she held herself. "Your mouth? It's bleeding."

A small shaky hand came up to touch the sore lip. "Oh. I hadn't realized...I…."

The trembling seemed to increase and if possible the already pale face turned whiter. Stepping forward he took the slender frame into his arms and held her close and warm. "I'll walk you to your cabin."

He could feel the short, brief nod, but no sound came from the bruised lips. For a long moment, Tyler held his breath afraid that he would say something he would regret later. Anger still simmered through him. He barely managed a shaky breath and slowly moved her steadily toward the cabin. Coming up to her screen door, he halted and looked down at her. "Are you going to be alright?"

Her breath came out on a mere whisper of sound. "Sure."

Then as she turned to step out of his embrace, she stumbled slightly and her voice broke, "Yes...no. Ty, please... Can you... would...Hold me, please." And the tears started to roll silently down the pale cheeks.

Swiftly Tyler stepped close and wrapped his arms about her protectively and easily moved her into the dark cabin. He left the lights off and headed for the large over-stuffed chair and sank into it and pulled her small body onto his lap, then just held her close. "It's alright, Jess, I'm right here. No one can hurt you." Then taking a deep breath, he asked quietly, "He didn't hurt you other than your lip, did he?"

"No. But it wasn't because he didn't try." She whispered huskily. "You got there in the nick-of-time. I think he just got carried away; and I don't think he realized just how fri...frightened I was." She tried a shaky laugh, but it failed terribly.

"It's a good thing that I let him go before I saw you, or I would have beat him within an inch of his life." Tyler stated in a deceptively calm, steady voice.

"I'm sorry." Mumbled Jess through shaky lips.

"You have no reason to be sorry, Jessie. You hear me? No matter what. When a woman says NO, it means NO. A man knows that or he should." Grumbled McKay flatly.

A soft sigh escaped her as she settled more closely in his arms. In them she felt safe and secure. Yet, her body tingled at the closeness of the male hardness and warmth. She was physically attracted to the man, her friend! An excitement bubbled just under her skin and she began to fidget restlessly against him.

The strong body under hers stilled, she didn't even think that he was breathing. But beneath her hand she could feel the erratic beat of his heart. Softly she murmured, "Ty? Could you kiss me, please?"

His usual drawl came out in a harsh whisper, "What? But...are you sure? I don't think that would be a goo..."

"Please..." She whispered softly as she turned the pale oval face up toward him.

A shudder swept through the hard body, but he lowered his head and took her mouth in a gentle, yet possessive kiss. Even being careful of the injured lip, he could feel the heat build in his lower gut, hardening his body in sexual awareness. Dragging a deep breath into starving lungs, he muttered softly against the tempting lips, "I've got to stop, Jess. Before...I...I hurt you. Before I lose control. You are so tempting. But, enough. You need to get to bed. Tomorrow comes too damn early as it is. I'm sorry, but I have to go."

Carefully he stood and set her on her feet. Her legs felt like liquid, but she forced them to hold her weight. Hesitantly, yet almost hurriedly, Ty headed for the door. "You'll be alright?"

Slowly she nodded. Then a soft smile touched the hurt, bruised lips. "Yes. Thank you, Ty. Good-night."

"Okay. I'll see you tomorrow. Night." He stammered as he turned and slipped quietly out the door into the night.

Turning toward the bedroom and undressing as she did so; she thought about what had happen with Joe, before he had got carried away with trying to make her want him. He had almost raped her. But the main reason was to get her to want him. The real reason he had pressed it too far. He couldn't understand anyone not wanting him.

But after that first kiss there had been nothing. No feelings, no guilt. And no anger for what he had put her through three years ago. In fact, she could hardly stand his touch. Maybe it had been the shock of discovering she no longer had any feelings for him. She was over him. Except now she had an anger at what he had almost done.

Amazing how one's emotions and feelings could change. Apparently she hadn't really loved him. Not the real thing, anyway. Or maybe he had hurt her too deeply. Not only had her heart been injured, but also her pride. A stubborn pride, too. Snuggling deeper into the cool, soft bed, she sighed softly and closed her eyes. Sleep came gently, but swiftly. The image on her mind's eye was not that of Joe Drake, but of the curly-haired trail foreman. Her cowboy.

There was a drift of breeze and the great trees swayed in their feathery foliage. Jessie gazed upwards, a satisfied, content smile touching the mobile mouth. Early morning sunshine rolled down from the surrounding mountains, flooding the valley with soft, liquid gold.

Upon hearing someone talking quietly, she stopped and listened; trying to catch where the voice was coming from. The barn that had the enclosed stalls was directly beside her and the training corral was on the far side. The voice was coming from the general direction of the corral. It would have to be Tyler. No one else would be there this early. Unless of course it was one of the horses. Then at the silly thought, she chuckled to herself.

Stepping around the corner, she saw McKay busy cinching-up the bag that carried his farrier tools. His back was toward her as she called out in a soft, breezy voice. "Hello, Handsome. What you up to, so early in the morning?"

Tyler swung around, surprise registered on the lean features. At seeing her smiling face, he too smiled. "Well, hello yourself, Beautiful."

Cooper leaned against the saddled horse, her soft, gray eyes glancing over the equipment he carried. Then she once again looked up at McKay. "Where you going?"

"Believe it or not, little one, I've got the morning off." He said. "I thought I'd take Fed out for a little exercise and loosen him up some before getting down to the hard training. Just finished trimming his feet."

"Lucky man." Grinned Jess. She would love to be able to go along, but refused to ask.

"To tell the truth, Jess, I'd thought about having you go along, but well, I just plan on taking it easy today. Besides, Phil will want you around in case something comes up." He went on to explain.

Jessie touched his arm and smiled softly. "I understand, Boss. You have a good time. But, I get to help when you start working with the big guy."

Tyler grinned. "It's a deal." Then reaching over, his fingers touched her small chin, lifting it so he could look at the bruising that was still visible. "Does it hurt?"

"Oh, a little. But it will be fine." She grinned carefully.

"Well, I'll see you back here around supper time."

Cooper nodded her red-gold head. "Right. Take it easy."

Watching him ride out of the corral area and towards the far mountains, Jess sighed and started to the lodge for breakfast. It felt really great to be back on friendly terms with Tyler. Yes, it felt really good.

After lunch Jess walked alone up to a shaded, grassy hillside and stretched out on the cool ground. Sitting there, the soft breeze gently ruffled the red-gold hair. Her thoughts unthinkingly drifted back to the past. To the night that she had confronted Joe after he had sent his sister to break the engagement for him. Linda had tried to explain his feelings. What a joke. His feelings had been no more than ego. What had really hurt her, more than the spiteful words that he had yelled at her; was the fact that friends that she had counted on had let her down. They were friends as long as they needed something from you, but as soon as the times got a little rough, they bailed. What was even worse was when they met you they acted like they didn't even know you.

It wasn't just Joe that had ignored her after the engagement was broken. His sister, her best friend? And a few other friends that they had run around with. True, Larry and Tim hadn't really known what had gone on and hadn't ignored her. Larry had been away in the service at the time.

At first she had felt that it was better to never count on friends or let them get too close, that way they couldn't let you down or hurt you. Now she knew better. You had to take that chance or life would just pass you by.

She was very grateful that she hadn't married Joe. It would have been a terrible mistake. Joe had always used his so-called limited stature as a shield, an excuse. A way to out maneuver his enemies. For who would suspect a coward to be tough or clever. But he used it to his benefit.

How could she have ever thought that she loved him? She had turned a blind eye to his nastiness, because she had thought that she loved him. How foolish. And even worse, she had thought that he loved her. He couldn't love anyone else for he was in love with himself.

With that thought still whirling around in her head, she laid back against the spongy grass and closed her eyes. Within moments the soft, regular breathing signaled she had fallen into a deep sleep. A healing sleep.

Sometime before noon, Tyler found the trail that led to his unfinished cabin. It was easy going, so he let the white pick his own way. The steady breeze fanned his face, bringing with it the fragrance of the wild flowers that grew along the mountain trails. Coming across a clear, swift-running stream, McKay dismounted and tied the stallion to the hitching post in front of the almost complete cabin. Having reached his home, he made a quick lunch.

Sitting down on the log porch, carefully sipping the hot coffee; he let his tawny-green gaze sweep over the stallion. The large horse was as beautiful as ever. The white coat shiny and healthy, the long blue-black mane and tail fluttering in the slight breeze. In all honesty the horse had never looked better. He was in his prime, age wise.

Wilcox had better train that black Gunfire to perfection. Better give him a lot of vitamins and supplements along with his grain. He was going to have to run his long black legs off to beat the white.

For that matter, Rebel would be the horse to beat in a clear-cut flat race. But Shiloh was another matter. The blue-gray gelding could run over any and all terrain, including a straight flat race. He had the agility and endurance of the Arab, but also the toughness of the Morgan. He not only had speed, but heart. A very hard combination to beat. Very hard.

Tyler had often wondered if the gray could actually out-run his sire, Confederate. He had never mentioned the possibility to anyone, not even Jess. True the gray wasn't as big as Confederate, but that had never been a winning factor in other races. He could run barrels with some of the best times ever.

The true Arabian of ages past was in actual fact a small horse. Confederate was an unusually tall horse for his breed. A lot of the Egyptian Arabs were taller, more like Saddlebreds. But Fed was unusual in other ways also, like his coloring. Everyone had believed that Fed had been a gray when born and later turned white, but he had always been powder white. It would be some race if the two horses ever ran against each other.

Taking another swallow of his coffee, he thought of Wilcox and Hunter. They hadn't seemed to be up to any mischief lately and that was extremely unusual for them. A frown marred his tanned brow. He still couldn't figure out why Hunter had put a trap in that area. Also, he could never understand why Wilcox was so eager to race a horse. They weren't a horse ranch or even a cattle outfit, they were more of a hunting lodge in the summer and fall months with a very limited hunting area; and then a ski resort in winter with ice fishing and such. Some big company really owned the outfit and Wilcox was the manager and partner. Nothing had ever been very clear on the real function of the ranch or Wilcox. A funny niggling memory whispered in his mind, but he couldn't quite bring it in focus.

Something that his father had said? A few other comments that his dad had muttered about a few days before he had his accident. He'd have to talk with Phil and see what he remembered.

Taking a last swallow of coffee and finishing the last of his sandwich, he prepared to pack up and head back to the ranch.

Turning the corner of the lodge, Cindy Tanner came face to face with Larry Connors. A smile touched her lips as she looked up into the blue-green eyes.

"Just who I was looking for. Where have you been?" she questioned.

Larry laughed lightly. "Until about twenty minutes ago, I was helping out at the barns. After that I was looking for you. Ready for supper?"

"Sounds good to me." Cindy smiled, then asked, "Has Ty gotten back, yet?"

"Don't think so. Should be coming in any time now." He answered easily.

"I can't wait to see Confederate race. The horse show and rodeo sound great, but the race is the big event. The main crowd pleaser. Did you know that the guests can participate in the events? I think I'm going to try the women's western pleasure, and maybe some of the games. How about you? Think you'll try something?"

Connors looked thoughtful. "Yes, I think I would like to. I'll have to talk to Tyler about it. Should be fun."

"You know last night while we were at the airport I was talking with Tim and he told me something that I think you should know." Then when Larry stopped walking, a confused look on his face, she continued, "He said that Joe and Jess were engaged and then Joe broke it off. But he had

Linda tell Jess. And the reason, Jess hadn't fit in with his friends. Can you believe that?"

Connors frowned. "You know, I do. Especially if it concerns Joe. But to know his sister helped him at Jess's expense is not what I thought of Linda. Jess was her best friend."

"That's not all. Tim said that because of it, Linn and he had a big fight. Their first. She wasn't supposed to tell anyone what she did, but she felt she should tell Tim." Remarked the girl quietly.

"I remember the fight. Tim wrote me about it, but never said what it was about. But by the time I came home on leave, Jess had already left. And no one would say much." Larry added softly.

Cindy sighed and took hold of his arm and said, "I thought you should know. I'm sorry."

Connors grinned, "I'm glad you did. It explains a lot. Now let's go eat something. I'm starved."

"Shoot, you're always starved." Laughed Cindy.

Chapter Twelve

The room was dark with only the shadows of pale-blue light from the television flittering against the walls and floor of the cabin. Jess sat curled-up in a large over-stuffed chair close to the window. The same chair that Ty had held her in after Joe's attack.

The television was turned down low and the window was open wide. Listening for Tyler, she really wasn't paying much attention to what was on the TV. The open window was facing Tyler's cabin, so Jess felt sure that she would be able to hear him arriving. It was getting terribly late and she kept dosing off. The chair was very soft and comfortable. Unconsciously she sank deeper into the softness and within moments had fallen asleep.

A good fifteen to twenty minutes later, McKay made his way silently across the thick grass. Glancing up toward the lodge, a flickering bluish light caught his attention. It was coming from Jessie's cabin. Curiosity had him hurrying across the grassy clearing to the cabin. Reaching the front door, he found that only the screened door was baring his entrance to the inside. Quietly he pulled it open and stepped inside.

A gentle grin touched the firm male lips as he sighted Jess asleep in the chair. The TV set had signed-off the air and was causing the ghostly light, so with a quick push of the remote he turned it off. As he did so the room was enveloped in total darkness. Taking a few moments for his eyes to adjust to the sudden lack of light, he stood motionless near the sleeping woman.

With the moonlight washing in through the open window, he found that he could see quite well. The soft moonlight blanketed the small shape of Jess as she slept in the big over-stuffed chair.

Looking at the delicate, fine featured face, he once again experienced the hungry longing low in his belly. She was so much a part of him that he thought about her almost constantly; yet, she didn't belong to him. Not in her eyes, anyway. Maybe only as a brother. But the memory of the few kisses that they had shared gave him a moment of hesitation. She had seemed to enjoy them. He knew he had. He was finding it harder and harder to hide his feelings for her. He would catch himself just wanting to touch her.

His warm glance took in the pajama-clad figure with the light-weight bathrobe covering the curled up legs like a blanket. Eyeing the direction to the bedroom, he bent down and carefully lifted the slight form into his arms. As he straightened he could feel the warmth from her soft body against his chest. And whether he wanted to admit that it affected him or not; he was very conscious of the havoc it was causing in his body.

Taking a deep, steadying breath, he hurried into the small bedroom. Then coming up next to the bed, he gently deposited his light-weight burden onto its softness. Pulling the covers out from under the slight form he then placed them over the sleeping shape. Watching her mouth curve softly into a smile in her sleep, he bent and carefully placed his against her lips.

With a shaky sigh, he rose and turned back toward the front door. One day, he thought to himself, as he stepped through the doorway; one day, Jessie girl, you'll really be kissed. Thoroughly. And you will remember.

And then he smiled.

The early morning breeze gently stirred the dark-red hair away from Jess's lightly tanned face as she stepped through the doorway of her cabin. The gray eyes went directly to Tyler's cabin. Yes, he was still sleeping. Good, she wanted to see him before anyone else.

It was just starting to get light and no one was up and about as of yet. Taking a deep breath, she started for the other cabin. As she drew closer, she began to wonder about last night. Hopefully it had been Tyler that had found her asleep in the chair. She sure hoped that it had been. She sure didn't want anyone else to have…well? A faint blush swept over her face at the thought of someone she didn't know as well as she knew or trusted Tyler putting her to bed.

But regardless, it was still embarrassing to have to be put to bed like a little kid. And by McKay. He more than likely would think her an irresponsible fool.

Just the screened door was closed and after stealing a quick glance inside, she opened it and stepped in. The small room was bathed in early morning pinks and yellows. Soft and inviting.

Without looking to either side, she walked to the back of the cabin where the small bedroom was located. Even as she neared the doorway, she could hear the soft, easy breathing of the sleeping man. Quietly she entered the dusky-dawn shaded room and found herself staring down on the lean, tanned features. He was still sound asleep, so she started to retrace her steps, but stopped and let her gaze linger on the deep chest that was exposed above the white sheets. Dark tanned and well-muscled with dark curling hair dusting across its width and disappearing under the edge of the sheet. His tanned arms lay relaxed, one along his side, the other draped across the hard, flat belly. Silently she watched the chest rise and fall with his steady breathing.

A warmth spread through her stomach and chest. Tingling started in her fingers and raced up her arms and down her legs, warm and exciting. All from just looking at Ty's very male, very sexy body? Swiftly she spun away and returned to the front of the cabin.

The small, compact kitchen was almost identical to her own; slightly larger, but otherwise, no difference. In no time at all, she had fresh coffee brewing on the stove. Then she started frying sausage, hashbrowns, eggs and fixing toast. Not sunny-side up, she remembered. Tyler was like her in that respect. Come to think of it, they liked and disliked the same foods.

Everything was just about ready as she turned to the table and her eyes slammed into sleepy tawny-green ones.

"Good morning." She smiled.

He frowned slightly, not quite taking it all in. "What in the--?"

"Your breakfast, Boss." Teased Jess softly.

"My what? Well, it sure smells good. But, I don't understand." Stammered McKay, his handsome face still clouded with sleep.

Pulling up a chair across from his stance at the table, Jessie nursed a steaming cup of coffee in her suddenly nervous hands, then placing it in front of him. "Here, drink this. Sit down, Ty, you are making me nervous. Besides, I've got your breakfast ready."

"Okay, I'm sitting." He shook his head in confusion. Then as she set the loaded plate before him he smiled and suggested, "Grab some and join me."

Then as she did so, he grinned at her in a sort of sweet, boyish way. "It tastes great. Thanks. Have you been up long?" The tawny-colored eyes flickered slowly over her face. "You're up sort of early, aren't you, Jess?"

"Yes, I guess so." Answered Cooper softly. Then from under long lashes she glanced at the man sitting across from her. "I fell asleep last night in the chair. But woke up in bed this morning. You wouldn't know anything about that would you?"

Secretly she was watching his face for some kind of reaction. When a teasing grin played across his features, she caught it. Then he leaned back in his chair and looked steadily back at her, a different light in the greenish eyes. "I could. You also left the television on. What's the matter, Jess, you are turning pink?" he commented in the familiar drawling voice.

"Nothing." She stammered, a little flustered at the strange light that still lingered in the gold-green eyes.

But if she had thought that by giving a short answer that was no answer, she was going to get him to drop it, she was mistaken. The sexy eyes narrowed as they continued to look at her steadily.

Evading that heated look, her eyes encountered the wide bare chest. More color moved over the already pink-tinted features. Struggling to get her wayward thoughts in order, she questioned in a choked voice, "Are you going to work Fed today?"

Tyler's brilliant gaze tangled with Jessie's confused gray one. A deep chuckle rumbled up from that same wide chest. "Changing the subject, Little One? Never mind, the answer to your question is, yes I am. Right now, in fact." Then with a slightly ironical set to the masculine mouth, he leaned forward, placing a finger beneath her stubborn chin, tipping her face up to meet his eyes. "Like to come?"

"Are you kidding? You couldn't keep me away." She smiled, turning the already lovely face radiant.

Swiftly they cleared-off the table and stacked the dirty dishes in the sink, he then grabbed a shirt and they left the cabin, heading for the main corral.

The large white stallion was in a sheltered corral not far from the training track and arena. At the first sound of their approach, the horse leaned the massive chest against the fence railing and gave a loud trumpet of greeting.

"He looks in great shape, Ty." Breathed Cooper through smiling lips.

McKay threw a quick glance at her upturned face, but remarked calmly. "Yeah, he's in pretty good shape. He just needs some old fashion work that helps firm and tone those muscles.

They worked the horse for almost two hours when Tyler glanced at his watch and seeing the time, remarked quietly, "Well, it's going on eight, so we better quit for now."

Jess leaned back against the corral fence, looking up at McKay from under gold tipped lashes. "Do I get to ride him?"

Green-hazel eyes swung carelessly over her from head to foot, to once again settle on her face. His voice cool and infuriatingly calm. "We'll have to see. Later on in the week, maybe."

Once again Jessie felt that disconcerting glance linger on her and the blush again swept over her cheeks. For some reason she couldn't seem to find a suitable reply, so nervously shifted her feet and remained silent.

Ty noted her confusion and had to hold back the pleased grin that tugged at the corners of his mouth. "Well, let's go see what Phil has in store for us today."

Nodding, Jess said, "I think he has some special activity he wants to do. He was mumbling something about it yesterday."

"You know Phil, he believes in something new and exciting happening all the time." Drawled Tyler as he followed the slender redhead through the gate.

The door was open as the two approached the office. Even before they could reach out a hand to push open the screened door, Phil's controlled voice drifted out to them.

"'Bout time you two showed up."

McKay leaned lazily against the screen as Jessie slipped past him into the cluttered room.

"Well, we're here now, Phil. What can we do for you?" grinned the young woman.

"As soon as your cowboy friend, there, will manage to drag his body inside, I'll tell you. Don't like to have to repeat myself." Smiled Holden.

"I'm in, I'm in." Laughed Tyler as he lowered himself into a nearby chair. "Proceed."

"Good. Now, how would a dance; or really, a sort of party and dinner sound to you two?"

Jess and Tyler exchanged glances, then McKay spoke up. "Sounds good."

"That's what I thought you'd say. I want it to be this weekend." Beamed Phil.

"What does this have to do with us? Or should I ask?" Questioned Ty slowly. He had an uneasy feeling that something was coming that he wouldn't like. Besides he didn't care for that self-important grin on the ranch manager's face.

"I want Jessie to sing a couple of numbers with our cowboys and don't look so smug, Tyler McKay. I want you to do a few also. Thought that would get you to look sharp." Chuckled Phil softly.

"But, I couldn't." stammered Tyler.

"But nothing. Jess, you haven't said anything yet. What do you think?" interrupted Holden, his eyes narrow and shrewd.

"I'm in shock. But, I'll be glad to do it. Might even be exciting." Murmured Jess quietly, her gray-blue eyes carefully eyeing Tyler's stricken face.

"I'm glad you see it my way. Roy wants to see both of you this morning yet." Glancing at his trail guide, Phil questioned, "Well, Ty, what's it to be?"

McKay rose to his full height, his handsome face almost void of expression. "Guess, we better go see Roy."

"Yes, I think you better. By the way, the guests asked for you two. Apparently they liked what they heard at the cook-out. Parker's in the lodge. I'll see you later, Ty. Want a good gander at Confederate." Remarked Holden with a pleasant smile.

Tyler just nodded, not trusting himself to speak, and followed Jessie outside. His thoughts were anything but pleasant. Hearing the door slam shut, he muttered to himself. "Damn Phil and his crazy ideas."

Cooper flashed him a quick glance, before replying, "It's not all that bad. For heaven's sake, you'd think you were getting a tooth pulled instead of just singing a few songs or so."

The tawny-green eyes glared at her, but he refrained from answering her remarks.

Soon they were entering the large dance room. Roy Parker was standing next to the piano and turning, he caught sight of them.

At seeing Tyler's dark, stony features, he voiced his questions to the woman first. "Did Phil explain anything to you?"

Jess shook the dark-red head. "Not much. How about you tell us all about it? But first what kind of dance is it supposed to be?"

Roy chuckled. "Sounds like Phil. But, I think he has a good idea. It's for everyone. All pretty much up beat stuff. Country, rock and popular music. A sort of Oldies theme. Some from movies."

Cooper nodded. "Sounds nice. Doesn't it, Ty?"

"Yeah, sure." Muttered McKay. Turning to Parker, he asked, "Where do we fit in?"

"Follow me and we can sit down and talk. How about some coffee?" Offered Roy.

"Sounds good to me." Smiled Jess.

After they were all settled and had their coffee cups in their hands, Parker started to explain.

"Jess, I want you to do at least two solo numbers. We'll be your back up." At her startled look, he continued, "Have you heard that song 'Because You Loved Me' by Celine Dion from the movie 'Up Close and Personal'?"

Cooper nodded once again. "Yes. I've seen the movie, more than once. And I have the CD. I'll have to get the music in town. You said two. What's the other?"

"It's a newer one by Bonnie Raitt called 'Thing Called Love'? Have you heard it?" Asked Parker.

"I've heard it a number of times and, yes, I will need the music for it also." Answered Cooper.

Parker glanced at both of them, then said, "We want you guys to sing two songs together. 'Almost Paradise' and then '(I've Had) Time of My Life'. What do you think?"

"Okay with me." Smiled Jessie.

Roy nodded and returned her smile. "Great." Then facing the trail foreman. "Well, Tyler?"

"So far, so good. Now, what have you got for me?"

Roy smiled, then asked, "You remember a movie with Kevin Bacon?"

Tyler sighed softly. "You mean 'Footloose'?"

"Yes, that's the movie. The song is 'Hurts So Good'. There is two more songs I sort of wanted you to do. They're from the animated movie 'Spirit'. Don't laugh, the songs are great. One is 'Get Off of My Back' and the other is 'Can't Take Me, I'm Free'. You could combine the two. They sort of go together. Well, do you think you can do it?" Parker looked almost anxious.

Tyler looked at Jess and then back to the wrangler. "I think I can manage it."

"That's it, old boy." Grinned Roy slowly. "Ah, Ty, do you think that you could do uh…Well, they aren't the standing still kind of songs?"

Heat climbed up his neck. "I didn't think that they were. I'll do my best."

"Thought so. Don't look so glum, Boss, it'll be fun." Chuckled Parker.

Looking at the other man, McKay found himself returning his smile. "Alright, you win. I just hope that you are right. Do you have to pick up the sheet music, also?"

Roy nodded. "Yeah, among a few others. Oh, we're having a regular dance band. We're just the extra entertainment. We will do our little bit in between."

Tyler agreed with the plan. Once they had the music, the practice sessions would begin. The three then sat down and started to discuss the intermingling times and different ideas. Finally Cooper rose and stretched.

"Sorry, fellas, but I for one have to get going. I've a riding class in fifteen minutes. Say, who's going in to get all the music and arrangements?"

For once, Parker looked as if he didn't have an answer. Frowning he said, "I won't have time today. We should have that stuff as soon as possible, so we can get started. At least by tomorrow, I had thought. We don't have all that much time."

McKay leaned forward. "Not to worry. I'm free for a while this afternoon and I have some ranch business in town, so I'll stop in and get what we need." Then turning to the redhead, he said, "You don't have much going this afternoon, do you, Jess? Didn't think so. You can ride along and go order all the material Roy will need while I attend to the business."

Jessie smiled, but only meekly nodded. She had other things to do, but if the 'boss' decided she didn't, then who was she to argue? Besides, she could do with some shopping. Turning to leave, she remarked over her shoulder, "After lunch then, Boss?"

"Fine. In front of the carport." Called Tyler with a laugh.

Chapter Thirteen

Standing in front of the full-length mirror in her bedroom, Jess carefully examined her reflected image. True, she wasn't tall, but the slender frame had all the right curves and located in the right places. Not too bad, she thought sheepishly to herself.

It had been an awfully long time since she had stopped, really stopped and looked closely at herself. And now that she had, she found herself pleasantly surprised.

She was wearing a pale-yellow, soft cotton sleeveless top with small buttons running down the low cut neckline. The material was silky-soft and clung to the gentle curves. It was loosely tucked into soft cotton jogging type shorts of a matching color. The outfit showed off the long, slender legs to their best advantage. Slipping on white and yellow cotton tennis shoes, then tossing the curling hair back from her face, she smiled softly to herself. "Almost a sexy outfit. Should knock old Ty on his ear."

As soon as she heard the words come out of her mouth, she wondered why she would want to do that? But, scooting out the front door, she quickly forgot about it. She didn't have time to worry about how McKay would react to her outfit or why she would want to shake him up.

Leaning against the side of the pickup, Tyler once again checked his watch. "What the hell is taking that woman so long?" he muttered to himself.

Almost on his last word, he heard the crunch of gravel. Looking up, he caught sight of the redhead. But what a sight! She looked absolutely delectable in those shorts and top. And he was supposed to act like a brother? Great. Just great.

After the first of the shock had worn off, he straightened the lean, hardening body and looked up again, the green-gold eyes were cool and distant. The bronze, handsome features were devoid of expression, except for the thin white line about the lips.

"Well, well, a new outfit, Jessie?" he asked carefully.

An impish grin touched the delicate lips as she turned the bright head up and looked at him. "Yes, sort of. I've had these for a while, but haven't had a chance to wear them till now." Then tipping the red head to the side, she asked almost absently, "Do you like it?"

Tyler bent to open the truck door for her and waited until she was seated before answering her question. "Yeah. Real...cute."

After the cowboy had slid under the wheel, Jess peered at his face from under lowered lashes. His expression puzzled her the teeniest bit, but she wasn't going to let him know that.

"I'm glad you noticed. Sometimes I wonder if you only have eyes for horses." She remarked in a cool, little voice.

McKay threw her a quick glance, but her small face revealed not a thing. With a weary grin, Tyler said in an equally calm voice, "You might be surprised on just how much I notice. Jess, buckle up."

Now it was Cooper's turn to be startled. Jessie buckled her seatbelt and leaned back in her seat. She didn't quite like the new atmosphere and wished they were back to their easy banter.

Perhaps Tyler, too, felt the same. For just then the tension seemed to ease a little as he asked about the riding lessons she had taught that morning. The rest of the trip into town was more or less uneventful, more relaxed. So gradually Jess started to enjoy the swiftly passing countryside.

Every now and then Tyler would glance at the young woman sitting beside him. The trim, evenly tanned legs were stretched out before her and her head rested on the headrest of the seat. The tawny-green eyes slid appraisingly over the soft curving lips and slightly stubborn chin to the creamy-tanned throat.

The yellow top clung in all the right places and the tiny buttons drew his attention to the low curved neckline and emphasized the slight swell of the small, firm breasts. Damn. The desire he felt uncurling in his belly was definitely not that of a brother. And pretending that he was would kill him. Maybe that would have to change? Yes, maybe he should go ahead and let his appreciation of her show. If nothing else it would prove interesting. No more big brother stuff for him. Let Jessie Cooper take her chances. Yes, maybe a little competition and jealousy would work where nothing else seemed to?

Slowly he pulled onto the main street of town and steered toward the nearest car park. After a few more minutes, he shut-off the engine and turned to Jess, who was gathering up her handbag and list.

"I'll be about an hour. Then I'll meet you over at the music store. That alright with you?"

Her clear gray-blue eyes smiled back at him. "Of course. I'll be at the front door."

As she turned to open the door, Tyler's soft drawling voice halted her.

"You know, I really do like those shorts. A person sure wouldn't mistake you for a boy in that. Yep, I like it."

Slowly she eased back in her seat, turning to face him. All the while trying desperately to hide the surprise from her face. What was behind that cool remark?

"I've been of the female gender for quite a while, Ty." She replied as calmly as she could, not sure whether to treat the conversation as a joke or not.

"No kidding? I remember one night in particular that I definitely realized that fact." Smiled Tyler with a certain gleam in the tawny eyes.

Jess blushed a rose-pink. Embarrassed at first, then angry. With a sharp retort, she countered with, "If I remember right, it was you that objected to sharing."

A slightly mocking smile touched the firm lips as his warm glance swept over her. But, before he could form a suitable reply, she had flounced out of the truck and swiftly walked off.

McKay chuckled softly. Yes, it certainly did produce effects.

Reaching the music store an hour later, Jessie had cooled off considerably. Tyler, she had discovered lately, was becoming subject to moods. At times she rather liked it.

If the yellow and white short outfit produced such a rise out of him, then wait until he saw the new clothes she had bought. Especially the very brief aqua bikini. Then there were the silky dresses and more shorts and a real classy outfit that would be just right for the dance, and of course, new jeans and such.

She had really bought quite a lot. But it had been a long time since she had bought any new clothes. She had got some really sexy silky underwear and nightwear that felt just heavenly against her skin. She really liked the simple no frills look; yet they still had a very feminine appeal. A satisfied smile played across her lips. "Just you wait, Tyler McKay."

At that moment, McKay walked up. "Well, I see you are right on time."

"Well, of course. What's the matter, Ty, didn't you think I'd be here?" She asked with a rather coy-type of smile.

"Not at all. You are always on time. Most always." He grinned. Pushing open the door, he said, "After you, Brat."

Showing a flash of white, even teeth in a smile, Jessie preceded him into the large, air-conditioned music center.

The store carried everything connected with music from sheet music to instruments. Seeing them enter, a tall, sandy-haired young man approached them with a smile.

"Hello, Jess; Tyler. Roy called and ordered some music, I suppose you are here for those?" At their nods, he added, "What about you two? What do you need?"

Tyler briefly gave him a run-down of the upcoming dance and their part in it. The young man grinned and then took the list that Jessie handed to him. "'Bout time you two got in the lime light. It'll be about an hour for these arrangements and the stuff that Roy ordered is just about ready."

McKay smiled. "That'll be fine, Kip, we'll go get something to eat. We'll be back in about an hour. Come on, Jess."

As they stepped onto the sidewalk, Cooper remarked sulkily, "You could have asked, Ty."

"Guess I could have. Well, do you want to go get something at the 'Chateau'?" Asked McKay mildly.

Cooper couldn't find anything wrong with his planning, so accepted.

"Good. We just as well make a day of it." Tyler smiled softly.

"Closer to night than day, if you ask me." Muttered Jess.

"Okay, then we'll make a night of it."

"We have to pick up some of my packages from the Village Place before seven." Remarked Jess with a sudden secret smile.

"I'll see to it." Stated Tyler as he steered her into the darkened cool interior of the dinner club.

The club was a large, well-built castle-like building. It was very expensive appearing and plush. Even though it was large it still gave the impression of coziness. Finding a secluded booth, Jess found herself on the inside with Tyler more or less blocking the only way out. Funny, but she couldn't help the slightly uneasy feeling. Something was different about Tyler's attitude. And she wasn't exactly sure that she liked it.

The cocktail waitress set down some spicy snacks and then asked what they would like to drink. Taking their order and turning away, Tyler glanced over at her. "Are you going to taste those little sausage things?"

"Was thinking about it. Are they good? Have you been here before?"

"Yes, to both questions. But, go ahead and taste 'em." Smiled the cowboy.

Right then he didn't look all that much like a cowboy. But neither did he seem like her old, dependable Tyler. Obediently she stabbed a toothpick into one of the small sausages and took a bite. It was spicy, but very good. "I like them. They are very good. What did you order to drink?"

"Wait to taste it before I tell you what it's called. The waitress is coming with them now." Remarked the curly haired man.

The waitress set the tall, frosty drinks on their table and smiled at Ty before moving away. Jess smiled hesitantly, but sipped the drink. To her surprise she liked its tangy, yet sweet taste. "Okay, I like it. It's different. Now will you tell me what it's called?"

"It's called Moon-Lite. I thought it up as a fruity mixed drink and Tony, the head bartender, fixes it for me whenever I ask. Glad that you like it." He drawled slowly.

His mood was changing again, Jessie noticed. He was becoming quiet and a strange gleam had entered his otherwise calm hazel-green eyes that did queer things to her nervous system. Seeing that her glass was about empty, he motioned the waitress to get another for them both.

When their drinks came, she noted that it took her longer to drink it, but was very refreshing.

Glancing at his watch, Tyler looked at her. "Jess, why don't you stay here and I'll go pick up the music and everything. Yes, including your packages. I'll bring the truck on down here closer and park it."

Leaning back in the seat she eyed the handsome, familiar features, then smiled, "Alright. Sounds like a good deal for me. Before you go, order me another one of these Moon-things."

Cooper watched as the tall, lean man walked out of the room and sighed to herself. Glancing around at the dimmed lighting and seeing the flickering candles that were placed on some of the tables she realized just how romantic the restaurant and bar was. Settling deeper in the plush seat, she slowly sipped her drink and calmly waited for Tyler to return. Sitting there, she found that she was really enjoying herself. Too bad Ty didn't get into this kind of mood more often.

Within a very short time, McKay appeared in the open doorway. As he entered, Jessie noted that quite a number of the female heads turned in his direction. Funny, that she had never noticed that before? Maybe she hadn't actually looked close at Tyler before. Just like she hadn't noted the difference in herself until that morning. Well from now on she decided that she would keep her eyes wide open. Unwittingly Tyler broke into her thoughts as he slid in beside her.

"I hope they bring our meals soon I'm getting damn hungry. How about you?" He asked absently.

A smile of her own uncurled inside. Wonder what he would think if she replied that she was hungry for him?? Sighing softly, she remarked, "I'm ready anytime."

Looking across at her, he asked, "What did you do; buy out the whole store? All those bags and boxes."

She chuckled, the blue-gray eyes dancing. "You'd think so, wouldn't you? It's not easy to find nice clothes in small sizes that don't look like they are for some little kid. Today

I hit the jackpot. It's not every day I go on a shopping spree."

Before he could answer, their orders arrived. The meal was superb and as they sat finishing with the dessert, Jess questioned, "Can we go in and see the floor show? I heard some of the customers talking and made it sound pretty good. Well?"

It was getting quite late; but Tyler seeing the pleading look on the delicate, enchanting face, gave in and agreed.

As the night wore on Jess's mood became happier and more relaxed, she was truly enjoying herself. Tyler, on the other hand was fast becoming depressed. Liquor sometimes had that effect on him, and this was definitely one of those times.

Finally as it neared one o'clock, McKay called a halt and without any argument from Jess, they headed for the pickup. The night air had turned cool, yet was very refreshing. Jessie's light laughter tinkled out into the night as she walked along beside Tyler to the shortbed pickup.

Carefully Tyler helped her into the seat and then slid in under the wheel. Making sure that her seat was secure and then his own, he headed for the ranch. The road was almost deserted of other cars and after a little while, McKay felt Jessie's small warm body slide over against his shoulder. Looking down he saw that she was very nearly asleep. Shifting his shoulders slightly, he made it a little more comfortable for her.

McKay was tired himself, but not really sleepy. His thoughts wandered and he wished he could picture a happy future concerning Cooper and himself. But he just couldn't quite bring it into focus.

As he turned onto the gravel road that lead to the ranch buildings, he had to slow down. When he did, she stirred, turned toward him a little more, her small face at his neck. The soft mouth touching his collar bone.

Tyler slammed down his foot hard, braking the truck to a sliding stop on the gravel. He sat unmoving, looking straight ahead; the soft, warm bundle of woman in the curve of his arm.

"Jess, why did you do that?" His voice had a break in it.

Sleepily she murmured against his heated skin. "Cause I wanted to. You are so nice and warm." And she giggled softly.

Tyler knew that the drinks were still effecting her and that she was silly from sleep. But as she snuggled even closer, he drew in a ragged breath, looking down into her moon-drenched features. The gray eyes were half closed and the soft, curving lips slightly parted. It was just too much for him.

Gently he released the seat belts and with nervous fingers took the small stubborn chin and tipped it up to his waiting mouth. Her lips were warm and as they responded to his gentle pressure, the soft kiss wasn't any longer. Hot, unthinking passion swept through him as he felt his body become hard and wanting. Her slim frame shuttered and moved against his. He crushed her to him and then just as suddenly, he released her.

He'd had no right to do that, to take advantage of her. No matter how much he wanted to. They were both too tired and too much under the influence of the liquor they had consumed. His body ached and shook with longing and anger. Anger at himself. He should have more control, he wasn't some young kid with raging hormones.

Jessie snuggled even closer, and was now sleeping soundly, almost peacefully. Slowly Tyler let the truck move forward and continued on their way. Tomorrow was almost upon them and they weren't even home yet.

Chapter Fourteen

Sunlight filtered in through the stable window as Jessie leaned back against the bales of hay. A small smile touched her lips as she remembered the events of the night before. She had enjoyed herself, quite a bit really. Though, she would not drink so many of those fruity Moon-things. Thank goodness they didn't give her a hangover or a headache.

A slight frown slipped in and replaced the smile, just momentarily. She had the most realistic dream. The dream had been of Tyler kissing her. A real kiss. In fact, she was having a hard time believing that it wasn't real. Or maybe she wanted it to be real? But of course it hadn't happen.

But she found that the more she thought about it, the more she wondered what it would be like. Then she mentally shook herself. Mustn't act like a fool, just because

McKay had noticed that she was a woman and not just a trail guide. It was about time. But she had realized that Tyler was a good looking man, also, not just a trail foreman.

Straightening up she decided to get to work. She also had a rehearsal after dinner and she meant to look her best. She had decided not to let Tyler forget the fact that she was female, not just one of his hired hands.

Later that afternoon, Roy looked up from the piano and then unconsciously let out a soft whistle. The rest of the band looked up, including McKay.

Tyler's handsome face seemed to close-up, hiding the conflicting emotions. The tawny-green eyes swept swiftly over the slender figure walking toward them.

Jessie was wearing a silky-knit slim skirt in multi-colors of blues and pinks that was short and clung lovely to her small very feminine body. The top was a pale pink soft silky top. The soft skirt showed-off the long, tan length of leg, creating quite a delectable sight.

Secretly he was wondering if she remembered about the shared kiss. When he had awakened her, she had been lucky to have been able to just make it to her cabin. From what he could see of her expression, he didn't think that she had. Hopefully?

Roy nudged McKay and remarked softly, "Pretty sexy outfit, huh?"

"You can say that again." Murmured Jeff Saylor, who was sitting at an electric keyboard.

Jessie reached them at that time. "Hello, fellas. Hope I'm not late. What's everyone staring at me for? Do I have dirt on my face or what?"

Roy chuckled quietly. "Not that you'd notice. But we sure like what you're wearing."

"What you're almost wearing." Muttered Tyler as he lifted his canned soda to his lips.

Jess chose to ignore the remark, but smiled becomingly at the rest of the cowboys. "I'm glad some people have taste. I decided it was high time I had a new wardrobe. Just wait, you haven't seen anything yet."

Pushing himself away from the piano, McKay stated in a tight voice, "Couldn't see much more." Then without waiting for a reply, turned to Roy, "Did we come here to rehearse or stare at a lot of skin?"

Jess blushed warmly and the others exchanged wondering glances. Cooper felt she could gladly strike him, but with an effort relaxed the tense muscles and even managed to smile. Her voice was quite soft and calm as she remarked, "Roy, if you would, I'll start with 'Because You Loved Me' and then go to the 'Thing Called Love'." Then added, "Some people I know shouldn't drink if they wake up with a sharp tongue as well as a sore head."

She was in time to catch the dark, angry glance McKay swung her way, but answered it with a beguiling, innocent smile.

The rehearsal went reasonably well considering. Even so there were undercurrents of tension. Evenly suppressed, but there nonetheless. Everyone felt it, but no one wanted to be the one to break the calm before the storm, sort of speaking.

Finishing up everyone stretched and Jess yawned delicately, almost like a silky kitten. "Well, it's almost time for supper. Think I'll go get washed up. See you later." And she smiled softly.

As the slender redhead walked away, the cowboys watched her for a few more minutes, then started to pack up their equipment. After the others had finished and were drifting away, Roy leaned against the up-right piano and faced McKay.

"Boss, that wasn't very nice what you said to Jess."

Tyler slowly shook his dark head. "No, I guess not."

Parker frowned. "If you want a little friendly advice from a mere wrangler, I'd tell you this much. That won't work. She almost used physical violence on you, and she would have been justified. Why not let her know that you think of her as a woman and not your younger sister."

McKay's features were stony, but he listened quietly. "How did you guess? How'd you know that was what I was feeling?"

Roy smiled gently. "I've known you a long time, Ty. And to me, it was all over your face. And something else, Ty, you are not usually subject to moods, but lately you've been a regular roller coaster. Ever since that Drake fella arrived." Then seeing the already hard features turn to stone, the young cowhand added, "Look, Tyler, you and Jess have been close, such good friends, that now it's hard for her to see you as a lover. You are going to have to show her. Just don't overwhelm her or you will scare her off. Sorry about the lecture, but just think about it. You know, I'm so smart because I have two older sisters. You learn these things."

McKay watched Parker walk out of the long, wide room and then pushed himself up, off of the piano. So Roy knew and more than likely some of the others. Oh, well, nothing he could do about that. But he would have to think about what Parker had said.

Tyler moved slowly out into the cool evening air. Yesterday he had treated Jess with a different approach and she had acted quite flustered for a while. Alright. He'd do it that way. But, he knew he couldn't just change. He was going to have to take it easy. One step, one day at a time.

After leaving the others, Jess went to her cabin. Outwardly she appeared cool and calm, while inwardly she was shaking with anger. Tyler McKay and his hurting remarks were going to get paid back for the humiliating embarrassment.

Then a smile touched her lips. If he thought that the skirt was too short, wait until he saw the very brief aqua bikini. Tomorrow would be the day. The perfect time to model it. If the man was jealous, that had to be a good sign, didn't it? But did she want Tyler jealous?

Glancing at the time, she ran a comb threw her long, red hair, then headed for the lodge dining room.

The evening supper was a quiet affair, everyone taking it easy after the warm humidity of the day. Unconsciously Jess seemed to ignore Tyler. She avoided meeting his glance and remained a distance away from him.

After the meal was finished, some of the younger people went into the dimly lit bar and dance room. A multi-colored jukebox stood against one wall and it wasn't long before it was sending lively music vibrating around the room.

Soon couples were moving in time to the latest popular rhythms. Leaning lazily against the wood-grained bar, Jessie called, "Rob, how about a cherry-coke."

"Right away, Jess." Then bringing the drink, the blonde-haired bartender added with a grin, "Sure is a sexy outfit."

"Why thanks, Rob." Smiled the redhead.

Moving away from the bar, Jessie glanced slowly around the shadowed room. It had gotten quite crowded, not uncomfortably so. As her glance swept the bar, she caught sight of a slightly brooding Tyler sitting at the far end by himself. His handsome, bronzed features were set in a hard, almost brittle way. Cooper decided she would be better off staying out of his way. It was then that a young man, one of the ranch guests, came up to her and asked her to dance.

Finishing the last of her drink, she laughed and accepted, "Don't see why not."

The slender redhead could dance. It wasn't long before almost every one of the young men there had at least danced with her once. After one of the lively dances had ended, Cindy and Larry appeared close to Jess. The sandy-haired woman smiled and said, "I sure like that skirt. And I never realized that you could dance like that."

"Neither did I." remarked a voice from behind Jess.

She knew that voice. A shiver slid up her spine. Joe Drake. With a tight smile, she turned and faced the man.

"Well, I'm just full of surprises."

At her words, his dark eyes moved over her slowly, and thoroughly. "Yes, I guess you are at that."

As a slow dance started, he said, "I think we'll try this one." Not even giving her time to reply, he swept her out onto the dance floor.

A coolness entered the gray-blue eyes as she looked up into his face. "You know you never gave me time to accept. Or were you afraid that I would refuse, Joe?"

The boyish good-looking face tightened. "Maybe." Then eyeing her closely, he added, "Would you have?"

She sighed softly. "More than likely would have told you to go to hell. But now..."

"What about now?" he asked with stiff lips.

"It's not important now, we're already dancing. But one thing, Joe, I'm no longer in love with you, if I ever was. It makes life much easier."

"I'm not sure I know what you mean. Where do I stand?" He demanded quietly.

"Look around you. You're equal with every one of the guests. And in some ways you aren't in as favorable a light. Don't ever pressure me sexually again, Joe." She said in a calm voice.

At the bar McKay watched as the couple moved slowly among the other dancers. He didn't know what they were discussing, but he was not liking it. He had never seen Jess in a mood like she was in. It was so un-Jess-like.

"Hello, Tyler."

Turning around on the bar stool, McKay made an effort to smile at Larry Connors and his girlfriend, Cindy Tanner. "Hello, yourselves. How is it going?"

"Not too bad. We can't wait until the dance." Then he added, "Jess sure is enjoying herself tonight. She looks real sharp."

Tyler's glance took in the slender redhead as he answered slowly, "Yeah. Real sharp."

Cindy eyed the handsome cowboy and then frowned slightly. Glancing at Larry and meeting his eye, she smiled softly and turned back to McKay. "Ty, could you show me how to line dance? Both of us? We want to know how to do it for the big shindig. I know a few of the other guests would like to know how. We could play the right kind of song on the jukebox."

Swallowing the last of his drink, he nodded the curly head and smiled a gentle smile. "Sure, why not."

Like a lean, graceful predator he moved over to the jukebox and punched in the song he wanted and as the music rolled about the room, Ty became the center of attention.

And soon most of the room was following the intricate western dance steps and having a good time. As the time swiftly got late, he told everyone that they were doing great, but it was time for him to head out. And as he turned to leave, Connors and Cindy moved over to his side. They both went out with him and as they stepped through the large doorway, they pulled him over beside the timbered path. Larry started talking softly to his friend and with Cindy adding parts where needed he was informed of the engagement and how it was ended. Unconsciously the trail foreman's hands formed into tight fists.

Looking up into the two sets of concerned eyes, he stated dryly, "How could a man be that cowardly and heartless? How could Linda have done that to her best friend?"

"I don't know. Except Joe is in love with himself, the only time he wants something or someone is when someone else wants it or if he thinks it will put the spotlight on himself." Answered Larry with a frown.

"We just wanted you to know. Tim told me when they were waiting for the flight. He said that Linda wasn't supposed to have told anyone her part of it. But, she felt she had to tell Tim." Said the sandy-haired woman.

"Thank you. It explains a lot. He was trying to step in like nothing had happen and it sort of blew up in his face. She was not the same timid little mouse that he had once controlled. Hopefully, she will see for herself what kind of person he really is." Sighed Ty. Then, he added, "I'll see you both tomorrow. Have a good night."

Slowly Tyler walked toward his cabin. The couple were nice people and he hoped that Jess knew how good of friends they were to her. He hoped Jess was as smart as he always thought her to be.

Chapter Fifteen

The morning air was cool with just a hint of a chill. A brilliant pink glow lit up the eastern sky as the sun made its slow way up into the still dark sky. Confederate tossed the proud white head, sending the coal-black forelock over excited dark eyes.

"Easy, boy, you'll get your run." Spoke Tyler softly.

He had the stallion saddled and bridled ready for his morning workout. The track was soft enough to give good sound footing. He had dragged it himself late the afternoon before, making as sure as possible that there were no holes or rocks. Then he had set up some brush jumps to get him ready for the higher ones later on in the training.

Just as he was about to swing up into the light-weight racing saddle, a soft voice spoke up from almost directly behind him, halting him.

"Would you like me to time him for you on the way back around the track?"

McKay turned slowly, letting the tawny-green gaze rest on the lightly tanned face with the cool smoky-blue eyes. Jess was mounted on the blue-gray gelding, faded denim blue jeans encased the slender hips and long legs. A pale-blue open-necked shirt was tucked inside the jeans. She looked like the Jess he knew, except maybe unless you would look into the now guarded eyes.

As she waited for his reply, she nervously pulled the tan felt hat lower over her face.

"Guess you can. Have you got a stopwatch with you?" questioned McKay slowly, his expression unreadable.

"Yeah." Was the short answer.

"Good. I'll take him all the way around the track first, then when I get to the far side I'll stop before I let him out. Wave your hand when you are ready with the timer." Deftly he swung up into the saddle, reining the large stallion around and sent him off at a quick trot, which soon changed to a slow lope.

Liquid grace with every movement of the large horse. Beauty in motion. The truly free spirit. To be on the back of such beauty, spirit and power was like nothing anyone could begin to imagine. It was power and control with just enough of a hint of wildness that took your breath away. The more you had the more you wanted. It was like having an addiction.

McKay had ground worked the big horse for over a half an hour before saddling him, but he still gradually worked the horse around the long circular track. As he neared the point where he would turn him and wait for Jessie's signal, he eased the horse down even more. This would be the first clocking. He could feel the power of muscles rippling under his legs and in the tensing neck, a nervousness started in the pit of his stomach and he had to take a couple of quick deep breaths to steady his nerves. Glancing back to where Jess sat on the gelding, he saw her raise her arm and then swiftly brought it down. He let the stallion go.

Unleashed power bolted forward. Flashing white legs beat a faster and faster rhythm as the sleek horse and rider swept around the track. As they exploded past the finish, Jess stopped the clock.

Glancing down at the small round instrument in her hand, she decided to let Tyler see the time first.

Walking the Arab stallion up next to the mounted, waiting woman, he questioned, "Well?"

Without a word, she handed the stopwatch over to him, her large eyes on his face. McKay took the watch in his palm and peered at the time. A smile touched the stern lips before he remarked on a sigh, "Best damn time he's ever run. Better than Gunfire has ever run in his life. Not a bad start." Then he laughed softly. Motioning them to keep moving to let the big horse cool down, he again chuckled softly.

Sighing happily, Jess leaned back in the stock saddle. "What comes next in Fed's training?"

Pushing the flat-crowned hat to the back of his head, Tyler replied, "Next we do a couple of things. First we have to take him over those jumps I have set out in the middle of the track. And then we need to do some pacing. Rebel will do for one. Say, how about Shiloh? Think he could keep pace? You know, not run full out?"

A rather bewitching smile lit up the redhead's face. "Sure, you bet. What is pacing exactly?"

"It's something like a small, controlled race; only you keep the two or three horses at an even pace. Never running full-out. That way it gives Confederate a challenge. Keeps him from getting bored. We do it over the jumps too. Builds up and tones muscles. Gives him more endurance and staying power."

"I see. Are you through with him now?" she asked.

"Almost. I want to take him over a few of those jumps. Want to take them with us? Good. Then I've got to rub him down. Don't you have a trail ride this morning?"

"Right. I'll have plenty of time to go over a few jumps. Then I'll head on over. Okay, Boss?" She responded in a cool little voice.

As the day progressed the temperature rose. By ten-thirty Cooper had managed a quick swim in the ranch swimming pool and then for the next hour had laid in the warm sun, with lots of sunscreen on or she'd burn to a crisp.

With a multi-colored beach robe wrapped around her slender shape, Jess headed quickly for her cabin and a light lunch. In an hour she had to go for rehearsal. Slipping through the front screened door, she wondered fleetingly if Tyler would be in better spirits than at yesterday's practice. She had really been more hurt than angry, but now she decided to forget the whole thing had ever happened. Well, she was going to try.

But upon reaching the lodge an hour later, she found she wouldn't have to worry about McKay's mood as he wasn't there. Roy had explained that McKay was busy with Phil over some ranch business.

In all honesty, Jess wasn't sure if she was relieved or disappointed that the trail boss hadn't been there. The rehearsal went well and the afternoon passed swiftly. As they broke up to leave, Parker moved over beside the redhead. "How do the songs feel to you now?"

Jessie smiled, "Just fine. You know to tell the truth, I think it's going to be a lot of fun. If I don't get scared to death and freeze-up."

Parker chuckled. "Don't worry, you won't. Are you going to have supper at the lodge tonight?"

"No. I thought I'd take a picnic lunch and go swimming somewhere by myself for a change. But, I'll see you later, probably." She called with a slightly teasing grin.

Parker watched as she left. She was a nice girl. A good friend. He hoped everything worked out between her and McKay.

Turning the sorrel roan into the corral, Tyler reached up and rubbed the blue-gray neck of Shiloh. The young horse laid his slender head on Tyler's shoulder and blew soft, warm air against the lean tanned cheek.

"What's all this attention for? Where's that owner of yours? Has she been neglecting you, Shiloh? Don't worry, fella, she'll come and spoil you after dinner." Grinned McKay.

As he walked tiredly toward his cabin for a quick shower before going to dinner; he thought Jess probably hadn't had time for the gelding with the rehearsals and all. More than likely had just finished in time for supper.

But on completing his own dinner some twenty minutes later and still not seeing any sign of the redhead, he began to wonder where she was. He knew she hadn't ate at her cabin, for he had walked past and no one had been there.

Seeing Jeff Saylor, Tyler went over to him and asked, "Hello, Jeff. How'd practice go?"

Saylor smiled. "Pretty well. So well, in fact, that we broke-off rather early."

"I see. Say, Jeff, have you seen Jess since then?"

Saylor shook his head. "No, come to think of it, I haven't. Why don't you ask Roy, he talked to her last."

Tyler nodded. "Thanks, I'll do that."

Turning around he almost ran into the very ranch hand he wanted. "Sorry, Roy."

"That's alright. Too bad you had to miss practice. Going to make it tomorrow?" Asked Parker with a grin.

"Should be no problem." Drawled McKay. "Roy, have you seen Jessie?"

"No." Then he added, "But she said something about taking a picnic lunch and going swimming."

"By herself?"

"Yeah. That's what she said." Catching the look on Tyler's face, he continued, "Don't worry, she can swim like a fish."

"Sure." Muttered McKay.

Chapter Sixteen

Shivering slightly from the soft breeze coming across the deep running stream, Jessie bent down and picked up her thin toweling jacket. Slipping it on over the very brief bikini, she could still feel the coolness.

It was later than she had planned on staying, but it had felt so grand to just relax by herself, that she had temporarily lost track of time. The faintly glowing sun was making its slow descent behind the towering mountains and she knew just how fast it could become dark in the mountains. Stooping down to repack the picnic basket; a dark, forbidding figure emerged from the gathering shadows.

"Oh!" she gasped, taking a step backward.

Then as the lean figure stepped closer and she saw that it was Tyler, she slumped with relief. "You scared me."

"So I noticed. Don't you think it was foolish to be out here alone? Especially swimming?" He said crisply.

She smothered a sharp retort, and instead turned her back on him, intending to gather up the rest of the picnic things. Before she could take a step, he took hold of her arm and swung her back to face him.

His face in the fading light appeared hard and uncompromising, as did the low voice. "You should know better than to swim alone. You could have drowned."

"But, I didn't." It sounded weak, even to her. She gave a laugh, and he shook her.

His hands tightened, feeling her lack of clothing through the light fabric of her jacket. "That doesn't alter the fact that it was stupid."

"Maybe so. But you are not my keeper. I'm old enough to take care of myself. I'm not a child." She whispered tightly.

"Sometimes I honestly wonder." He breathed harshly.

She stiffened and would have jerked out of his reach, if he had not suddenly gripped her chin with his fingers. Looking into her eyes, the tawny-green glance was inscrutable; but his voice was low and the drawl more pronounced than usual. "On second thought, you certainly don't look like a child."

With the fingers that had held her chin, he now let them trace the delicate curve of her jaw, down along her throat. The hazel-gold eyes, that seemed to now bore into her face, shifted to follow his fingers. His touch was warm and caused a tremor that shook her whole body, she felt them scorch their way down across the top of the aqua bikini to the deep center of her breasts. Her skin tingled and felt burned where ever he touched.

"That's a very revealing...uh...garment you're wearing." His voice was soft, silky, almost a whisper.

Panic seized her and as she tried to back away, his other hand tightened. Was this Tyler? Her Tyler?

As the other hand lowered to her small, slender waist and she felt his male warmth, she trembled violently.

"What's the matter?" chuckled the deep, silky voice. "Isn't this what you want?"

Sudden rage filled her and before she could even think, her hand flashed up and struck him squarely on the cheek. "How dare you!"

Hot burning anger simmered in the now tawny eyes as he wrenched both her arms behind her back. "You silly little fool. Too bad you never hit friend Joe like that. What do you expect when you are dressed like that? In next to nothing. I'm not your brother, I'm a man, Jess. A man." Then with a shaky sigh, he ordered, "Now get yourself back to your cabin before I turn you over my knee and give you the spanking you deserve!"

"I believe you tried that once...never mind. What about the basket..." she stammered.

"I'll take care of it. Now move." He barked.

Jessie turned and swiftly made her way back to the ranch, almost choking on the tears she was trying to suppress.

Watching her go, Tyler sank to the ground with a groan. Now she'd hate him for sure. His insides twisted and his belly churned.

The morning was gray and overcast as Jessie neared the training track mounted on the excited gray gelding. She knew the sky would more than likely clear before noon, especially with the strong wind that was blowing. But her troubled thoughts would remain, no wind was going to be able to blow them from her mind.

Shiloh was not the only nervous one. Her hands felt clammy and the pit of her stomach kept turning somersaults. She was embarrassingly afraid to face Tyler.

Catching a glimpse of the dark-haired, lean cowboy; she could once again feel the burning sensation where his fingers had touched her skin the night before. He had shocked her. Had more than likely intended to. But after a while it had worn off, and she found that it had not been so unpleasant. Besides she sort of liked the new, different Tyler. At least part of the time. She was too stubborn not to try and get him worked-up. And boy, did he get riled. He was gorgeous when he was in a temper. Vaguely she wondered what he would look like as passion rushed though that lean, hard body?

Nevertheless, as she approached him, she found that she was afraid. Her face felt stiff, and the lips tightened ever so slightly.

McKay was pulling the cinch up when he heard the gelding's eager snort. Glancing up, his gaze was drawn to the slender redhead. She was dressed in faded, slim-fitting jeans with a soft cotton pale-yellow shirt. Her hat was pulled low over her eyes, making it difficult to see her expression.

Slowly he straightened the lean, hard form and then rested against the stallion. "Morning."

"You said that you'd like to use Shiloh as a pace horse. So..." Her voice was low and tightly controlled.

Tyler nodded. "Sure. If you want. Let's go."

Deftly he swung up into the saddle and quickly reined the stallion in. Confederate, his dark liquid eyes keeping a close watch of the slender blue-gray gelding.

Jess as well as Tyler could see the challenge in the stallion's eyes and body language as Shiloh matched his springy walk to Confederate's. Yes, McKay had been right when he had said that a pace horse would give the stud a more determined will to win.

At Tyler's nod, Cooper nudged the restless gelding into a faster pace. After they had reached the far side of the track, both horses were pulled to a halt.

"When we start out get off at a gallop. But don't run full-out. Understand?"

At Jessie's nod, Tyler continued, "I'll hold Fed back and you do the same with Shi. But let him get up even, then slightly ahead. Okay?"

"Right." She nodded again.

Then glancing at each other they let the two horses out at the same time. Sustained power trembled through Shiloh's reins into Jess's fingers. The game little horse wanted to run, he wanted to win. The faster the stallion ran, the more the gelding lengthened his stride, stretching out over the smooth track. As Shiloh nudged ahead, McKay would let the stallion move. And move he did. But to the astonished redhead, so did Shiloh. The little gray gelding pulled up even with the white, then gradually inched ahead.

Tyler had a strong, but gentle grip on the stallion and could see that the girl was having a struggle to keep Shiloh under restraint.

Smiling slightly, he yelled. "Keep him even, Jess. I don't want either horse to finish first."

Jessie nodded the curly red head. She understood perfectly. It would make the stallion want to run even more in the next race.

Then it was over. Both horses were snorting and hopping up and down with more than likely disgust. Jess slid to the ground, and as Tyler stepped in front of the stallion their eyes met. Then both were laughing.

"I don't think that they liked that race." Chuckled McKay.

"No? It was all I could do to hold Shi back. He sure wanted to run." Grinned Jessie.

"It was the challenge. It makes all the difference." Remarked McKay quietly, his hazel-gold eyes dark with hidden meaning.

A challenge. Jess smiled grimly to herself. Life, itself, was a challenge. But without them it would be pretty dull. Pulling herself back to the present, she remarked, "Well, I've got to get a move on. I've a trail ride going out in about ten minutes. See you around, Boss."

Tyler pushed back his hat and watched the redhead lead the gray toward the corrals. He hadn't mistaken that set face that morning. But he wasn't quite sure just how to take her actions. He'd have to try for patience.

Taking a look at his wristwatch, he remembered that they have their last rehearsal later that day. And after talking to Roy and Jeff, decided to have it before lunch. Tomorrow night was the big show. Secretly he was hoping he didn't get stage fright or some such thing. The ranch hands would never let him live it down. Oh well, he thought, it should be rather fun.

As he unsaddled the stallion and gave him a good rubdown, Tyler's thoughts returned to Jess. It was getting him down. Others noticed it, also. He found himself irritable and short-tempered. Also, he was drinking more than he usually did. Well, he had to stop. It wasn't helping matters at all, more than likely making them worse.

He didn't know how to look at Drake. He had thought that Jess would stay away from him after the tussle the night that the Winters had left. But he was still hanging around. And worse, she wasn't stopping him. He didn't like it, but he could do very little about it.

Finally shrugging his broad shoulders, he left the closed-in corral and headed for his cabin to get cleaned-up before going into the practice.

Dismounting from the weary gelding, Jess Cooper remarked to the riders as they pulled up behind her. "Be sure to rubdown your mounts before turning them loose in the corral."

As she loosened the cinch, Cindy's voice reached her. "Have a nice ride?"

Turning with the rein in her hands, she answered, "Yeah. Was a nice morning. Want to walk with me to Shiloh's corral?"

The sandy-haired woman nodded. Walking slowly toward the cabins, Jess idly kicked a small stone out of the way with the dusty toe of her boot. Glancing up at the lovely woman beside her, she asked, "Think you'll like the dance party tomorrow evening?"

The woman's dark-hazel eyes glowed with excitement. "Oh, yes. Can't wait. What are you going to wear?"

"Oh, haven't really decided, yet."

"Sure wish we could listen in on your practice session." Wished the slender woman with a quick glance at her new friend.

Cooper laughed. "Sorry, my girl. But no go. Besides, I'm not practicing today. Did extra yesterday. Tyler missed yesterday, so he can do it all by himself today. Me – I'm going swimming. I've got a class, anyway. Say, why don't you join me at the pool in about fifteen minutes?"

Cindy smiled. "Fine with me. See you in fifteen."

After watching the girl disappear heading toward the lodge, Jess finished unsaddling Shiloh, rubbed him down and then turned him loose in the corral with Rebel. Walking back toward her cabin, she couldn't help remembering when she had always been the third one on one of Linda's dates. Until that is, when she had met Joe. Then it had been different, but not really.

Joe had just been let down by another girl and Jessica had been there ready and waiting to lend a sympathetic ear. She was someone he could moan and complain to about all his troubles. At first, she had just settled for him being around her. She had been so wrapped up with him that she hadn't seen him for what he was. Then they had gotten engaged. She had thought herself loved. Then everything had fallen apart.

Joe had decided to call the engagement off. But he had sent Linda to do the job for him. Only Jess hadn't let it end there. She had confronted Joe, asking him why? What it all came down to was he had wanted to make this other girl jealous and so he had used her. But he had asked her to be engaged for the simple reason that he thought she would go to bed with him, because she hadn't when they were sort of dating. So no sex, no engagement. The other reasons were the fact that she wasn't his type and she hadn't been good enough for him or his friends.

The awful scene, and it had been awful, had shattered her younger, insecure self. Finally she had escaped. She had left for a vacation, but had felt safe and happy at the ranch, so had stayed. She had felt like she belonged. And she still did. She was no longer a third wheel or insecure and she had real friends. They were more like family.

Shaking herself out of the past, she hurriedly slipped into the brief, aqua bikini and made her way to the now sun-drenched pool.

Chapter Seventeen

Shoving away from the side of the pool, Jess closed her eyes and floated gently on her back. After playing hard and fast games of water volleyball all afternoon, she found it great just to be able to relax in the now late afternoon sun.

The pool was almost deserted now, except for a few young couples still playing at the end of the pool. Cindy and Larry were lying beside the pool's edge soaking up the sun and dozing. Joe had headed for his room to change for dinner.

Smiling faintly to herself, Jess was glad that Cindy and Larry had stayed. She liked them both so well. Cindy had made Cooper promise to help her with the training for the fair. The woman was good, too. One of Jessie's better pupils.

Larry Connors had said that he was going to compete, also. With the help of McKay, that was.

Thinking of the trail foreman, she realized she hadn't seen him since that morning at the track. Wonder how the practice session had turned out? She knew that Tyler didn't care for the idea of singing in front of all those people, but would nevertheless do his best. At one time, she had been totally scared to death to get up in front of an audience, but not so much now. Still nervous though.

Faintly as if from far away, Jess heard the soft gurgle that the water makes when someone had made a neat, clean dive. Suddenly hands touched her and in a panic she forgot about floating and went under. Gasping for breath as she came out of the water, she saw Tyler's wet-plastered black hair and gold-green eyes.

"Well, if it isn't little Miss Mermaid." He jeered through tight lips, his glance taking in the brief bikini. "Still taking chances, I see."

At the insulting tone of his voice, anger swept over her. With eyes flashing dangerously, she choked out, "Of all the..."

"Don't say it." He cut in sharply.

"Don't worry, I won't. Now get out of my way." She snapped in a peculiarly quiet voice.

As it became apparent that he wasn't about to move, she twisted and would have made a dash between him and the side of the pool; but his hand flashed out and caught her arm in a tight grip.

"What's the hurry?" his voice was calm, but she didn't fail to miss the dangerous undercurrents.

Not paying any heed, she said bitingly, "There wasn't any hurry until you showed up."

With a sharp movement that caught him unprepared, she made her escape out of the pool. Without looking behind, she hurriedly made for her cabin.

Just as she reached the door, McKay reached her. Pulling open the door, he whisked her inside. She could feel the warm male body against the front of her. The fine dark, curling hair that dusted the wide chest was still damp as her fingers tangled in the springy silkiness. Small tingles started at the tips and spread up the fingers to hands and arms. A gasp was wrenched from her lips as she came in contact with the wall.

She tried to pull away from him, but his grip tightened, the fingers digging painfully into her soft flesh. "Let me go." She panted. "You're hurting me."

Immediately his grip relaxed, "Yes, I guess I am. Why have you changed so?" his voice low and husky.

"Me? Me, change?" she laughed dryly. "That's a joke. What's happen to you, Ty? You've changed. I don't know you anymore."

Seeing his tightened jaw, she continued in a more normal tone. "Look, Ty, I'm honestly sorry that you don't like what I wear. But no one else seems to disapprove. And regardless that you are my boss, when I'm on my own time, I'll wear what I damn please."

"I'm sure you will." He repeated. There was a little white line about the firm lips.

"Jess, I...oh hell." Tyler stood a long minute, then turned and left.

With the sound of the door closing, the woman sank onto a nearby chair, her thoughts in a turmoil of confusion. Had she changed? Of course, she had. Now no one could tell her she was second best. But, if she changed, so then had Ty. But had he changed because of her changes?

Oh – everything was so terribly confusing. At times like now, she wished for the quiet, simple life as it had been before Joe and Linda had once again entered her life. But at the same time, she found that she now seemed to enjoy the more intense feelings of late. There was more awareness of other people. Tyler, in particular. Even if at times it was frightening. Not only Tyler's behavior, but her own as well.

Yes, her own. She had been unconsciously trying to get a reaction out of Tyler; and without any doubt was succeeding. She flirted with the cowboys and even Joe, of course. But not Tyler. She, Jessie Cooper, had never flirted before in her life. But she was finding it all rather exciting. The attention was great. Besides in a very small way, she felt that she was paying Joe Drake back for using her and in a way that he would understand. It sure wouldn't hurt him any. Joe was one of those people that as long as someone else wanted someone, then so did he. It was all a game.

Why had she excluded Tyler from the flirting? Why had she left him out? Maybe it was because of that first day that they drove into town and she had worn the shorts? She hadn't been able to answer him back when he had teased her. She had been embarrassed, while at the same time pleased that he had noticed. He was able to tear down the careless, happy attitude she had acquired and then nothing but sparks would fly between them. But was she guilty of using him to fan her own worth? She hoped not.

Sighing deeply, she glanced around her. To her surprise, the room was in total darkness and she was still wearing the wet swimsuit. Moving reluctantly and loath to turn on a light, she carefully made her way into the bedroom. Turning on the soft, dim bedside lamp, she gathered up clean clothes and went into the bathroom.

Taking time for a quick shower, she let her mind wander over tomorrow night's entertainment. After slipping into one of the silky pant outfits, she glanced at her reflection in the full-length mirror. The pants fit snuggly along the slim line of her legs and over the hips. The matching silk top was in a tailored style with a soft collar and low neckline that buttoned with silk-covered tiny buttons. The color was a very dark mid-night blue with lavender winking through the darkness. Not too bad. Actually, pretty classy.

A smile touched the soft lips, and slipping on the matching slippers, she made for the door. Jess grinned, she wanted to talk to Roy right away. One more song might just add to the already planned entertainment. Yes, it just might.

The bar was dark and fairly crowded as she entered; but glancing toward the muted-colored jukebox, she caught sight of Roy Parker. As she threaded her way through the different dancing couples, a pair of hot, smoldering green-gold eyes met hers and with a frown, Jess turned away.

Tyler was drinking again. That was something that she didn't care to see happening. He had hardly ever drank until Drake had arrived. She felt the burning gaze as he had watched and apparently assessed her clothing. But strangely she hadn't found that so distasteful. In fact, she sort of enjoyed the strange feeling that his eyes had caused when he had inspected her.

Coming up next to Parker, she smiled and linked her arm through his. "Say, Roy, can I speak with you a moment?"

Looking down at her, he smiled appreciatively, "Sure, Beautiful. What's on your mind?"

"Well, it's about tomorrow's shindig..." she began quietly, a secret smile moving across the mobile mouth.

From his position at the bar, McKay watched as the redhead talked with Parker. Tyler's glance kept sweeping over the silky dark material of her outfit. She looked real classy and delectable.

Shifting his weight to a more comfortable position, he noted that others in the bar had taken notice of her also. Well, why not, he asked himself angrily? She is very lovely and with that soft, clinging material skimming over long, slender legs and the trim shape above. His lower body tightened almost painfully.

Turning abruptly back to the bar, he called the bartender and ordered another bourbon and water. Tossing it down swiftly, rose from the softly padded bar chair and without another glance at the young woman, he left.

Just as he was stepping out into the darkness, he met Joe Drake almost head-on. At first neither spoke, then slowly moving aside, McKay remarked dryly, "The field is all yours." And then he moved away into the darkness.

For a brief few moments, Joe stood and stared in the now empty direction in which the trail foreman had disappeared. Now what was that remark supposed to mean, he wondered?

Turning back toward the bar and slipping in through the doors, Joe's swift glance caught sight of the slender redhead. With a pleased smile he made his way toward her and the cowboy she was talking with.

"Good evening, Jess, and Parker, isn't it?" greeted Drake quietly.

Both woman and man looked up and Roy Parker was the first to answer.

"That's right, Drake." Then turning back to the young woman, he added, "Jess, I think we can work it all out the way you want. Even without the practice. I'll see you a little later."

Once again he nodded to Joe, then moved away.

"What was that all about?" questioned Drake curiously.

Jessie shook back the dark-red hair and managed a grin ever so faintly. "Nothing very much. Just a few changes about tomorrow night's show. Have you heard from your sister and Tim?"

Joe nodded his head. "Yeah, they made it back with very little trouble. Everything seems to be working out pretty well."

"Well, that's good. Have you seen Larry and Cindy? I thought that they were coming over." Asked Cooper.

"Changed their minds and decided to turn in early. Say, your foreman fella must be heading the same way."

"Oh, and why do you say that?" she asked slowly.

The slim-built man carelessly lifted his shoulders in a neat shrug. "I met him just as I was coming in. He was heading in the direction of his cabin. Acted sort of strange, if you ask me. He was muttering something about an open field. Well, enough of him. Let's dance."

Jess nodded absently as Joe swung her onto the dance floor. All the while she moved in time to the music, her mind was on Tyler. So he had left the bar.

Then suddenly Joe's voice pulled her back to the present and she realized that he had been asking her a question. Giving a slightly apologizing smile, she asked softly, "I'm sorry, Joe, what did you say?"

"I was wondering what time you want me to pick you up for the dance tomorrow night? I thought it would look better if I asked instead of just showing up." He remarked with a self-satisfying grin.

"Oh? And what exactly is that supposed to mean?"

"Well, everyone knows how it is between us. Of course, I'd be the one taking you."

Jess stiffened. Her lips were so stiff, she could hardly speak. But when she did, she was surprised at the calmness of her own voice. "Well, really, Joe. Just exactly how is it between us? I'm not going with you. I had no intention of using you as my escort. Besides..."

"But." Interrupted Drake in an astonished whisper. "You aren't going with anyone else. I know, I asked around. So quit trying to make me think otherwise. You aren't that high and mighty. So climb down off your high horse."

Her face paled with anger. "I don't have to try anything. I'm going with Tyler. I would have thought everyone would know that."

"McKay! You're going with him?" demanded Joe more loudly than necessary. His face was flushed with anger, and nervously Jessie looked around for Parker or one of the others.

Her small face froze, for standing directly behind Drake within easy hearing distance, stood Tyler. And by the fleeting look he gave her, she knew without a doubt that he had heard. Why had he come back after leaving? Why now of all times?

"I believe I heard my name mentioned?" drawled the quiet, deceptively calm voice.

From his expression, Jess had no idea what he was thinking. And even worse, what he would say.

Drake had spun around at the sound of McKay's soft voice.

"Tyler, we were just... I...I was just telling Joe that you...that you were escorting me to the dance tomorrow night." Breathed Jess in a shaky voice.

"You did, huh? Well." Murmured McKay as the green eyes fastened onto her still pale face. Then he turned his attention to the still stammering Joe.

"I take it that you had planned on taking her yourself?" commented Tyler ever-so-quietly.

Drake seemed a trifle nonplussed for a moment before he managed to find his voice. "Well, yes. I had just thought..."

"Yes, I suppose you did. I'm just escorting her there and safely back. Only claim I have." Remarked McKay in a matter-of-fact voice. Then his glance swung to meet the redhead's confused one. "I'd like to speak with you a moment."

Jessie nodded and somehow managed a smile for Drake. "Excuse me, Joe."

Slowly, almost reluctantly, the girl followed Tyler out of the bar and into the cool darkness beyond the large building. When the man stopped, so did Cooper, silently bracing herself for his cutting words. But instead, his voice was calm; almost mocking in its softness. "What's the matter, afraid of your old friend Joe? What did you do, get yourself in a corner and couldn't get out? You know, usually the man asks, not the other way around. You just assumed I would want to take you?"

Anger once again swept over her.

"If that's how you feel; why didn't you just ignore the whole thing, instead of agreeing with what I said? Especially since I'm so distasteful to be in your honored company."

A dry, low, rather unpleasant laugh met her words, before McKay answered with, "Oh, I couldn't possibly let the poor girl stand there looking as if she was backed against the wall. Besides, I don't have to stay in your attendance after I once get you to the dance."

"In that case, why even bother?" snapped Jess. "I'll go over alone."

Once again that low, sexy chuckle. "No, I don't think so." Stated McKay softly. Then he turned and walked back into the bar.

Chapter Eighteen

Smiling fleetingly, Jessie waved a careless hand to the joking, laughing group of young people; then slid in through the door of her cabin. Moving through the cabin she went into the bedroom. She was becoming nervous about that night's show. Glancing at the clock on her night stand, she hurried into the bathroom.

That morning and then the afternoon had been extremely hectic and now at last she had time to look to her own preparations. She studied herself thoughtfully in the mirror, deciding that the tan suited her. The brief, backless muted-colored dress, when she put it on, looked even better than she had hoped. It was soft pale-gray with light-blue and aqua whipped gently through it's soft, clinging material; and with the additional attraction of a golden skin, she looked really quite pretty. Especially for a tomboy like her. The copper-red hair was done differently than how she usually wore it. It hung down in loose long curls, but the sides were pulled back away from her face with aqua combs leaving a few loose tendrils by her small face. She added just enough makeup to emphasize the velvety-thickness of lashes, brought out the gray-blue of her eyes. Then she smiled. She still had the same scattering of pale freckles across her nose.

Glancing out the window, she saw Tyler's cabin go dark as he switched-off the lights. Hurriedly pulling on a pale-blue wrap that succeeded in enveloping her, she reached the door just as the curly-haired McKay raised his hand to knock.

"Well, what do you know, the lady is on time." Drawled the silky smooth voice.

Mischief gleamed in the smoky-blue eyes as she stepped out beside his tall, lean build. "Of course. Couldn't let you stand out here and wait."

"Oh, I wouldn't have." Was the quiet, mocking reply.

Angry color rushed over her face and she was thankful for the covering of darkness. He was really the limit. Despite her anger, her voice managed to be rather off-hand and cool. "Didn't think that you would. Maybe I should just have waited and maybe then you would have disappeared?"

McKay's features stiffened. "Never can tell. If the rest of you under that wrap is anything like the hair; well, need I say more?" he teased dryly.

"You know, Tyler McKay," she observed, "you keep up and you might just make the rating of a sidewinder."

Before he could make a reply, the redhead had entered the lodge. The professional band was already playing and the dining and dance floor area were filled with many couples. The lights were low and muted, and the effect was really quite nice. Romantic, thought Tyler with a grim smile. From then on he was only able to catch glimpses of the copper-haired girl as she danced with different guests and some of the wranglers, guides and ranch hands. She was obviously avoiding him; and he couldn't help but feel resentment, yet he knew she had every right to be angry with him. In a way though, he was also pleased. Pleased because she was going to so much trouble just to stay out of his way. At least he was on her mind.

Then as she was danced past him, McKay followed her with his eyes. As the music ended, he purposely made his way toward her and her then partner.

Jess breathlessly thanked the young man for the dance and as she was about to turn toward the coolness of the outside patio; a warm, strong hand closed over her arm. Looking around she met the chilly hazel eyes of the trail boss.

"My dance, I believe." He drawled softly, but the girl knew it meant that he would brook no arguments.

Reluctantly she went into his arms. But once there, she found that she was liking it. In fact she lost track of the time as they moved to the music, pleasant and soothing music.

As the tune died away, she became aware of his strong hand at the small of her bare back. Just the touch of his fingers sent warm ripples up and down her spine. He was steadily guiding her outside into the moon-washed darkness. Unconsciously she stiffened.

His deep, soft chuckle sounded. "Afraid to be alone with me? I don't bite, you know."

She turned angry, sparkling eyes to him, annoyed at his conceit in assuming that she was very wary of being alone with him. "I hadn't supposed that you did." Came the tart reply.

"Oh dear." He mourned with mock regret, "Did we make the little lady angry?"

"Of course not. Merely irritated." She answered with a deceptively calm voice. She was still very conscious of his hand on her bare back where the dress came to a low V.

"Quite a dress. I rather like the feel of it. Or better yet, the lack of it." He grinned mockingly, his fingers moving along her slender backbone.

"I can tell." She answered as cool as she could manage. "Besides, I rather like the color myself."

'You're right, it is a very becoming color. At least on you." He remarked quietly.

"Sort of different from my tomboy outfits." She found that she could even manage a light laugh. "Wasn't sure if I had the nerve to wear it."

"Unlike most women, you have more nerve than you need." He drawled. "I wonder what it would take to really unnerve you?" Then as if driven to find out, he jerked her against his chest, his left hand tangling in her hair drawing her head back so that her face and neck were exposed to him. She was too shocked to move, feeling his grip on her hair and aware that if she tried to pull away it would hurt. The pallor of her face gleamed against his darkness, and his eyes burned with an oddly reckless blaze as they held hers. Then as panic took possession of her she fought with him, and gave a soft cry as her hair was tugged by his fingers.

The cry she gave was snatched away, her entire being felt the flame and the fury of his down-driving kiss. His mouth bruised her and his arms felt as if they'd break her... then he thrust her away from him.

She cast him a look from under her lashes and caught the gleam of mockery in his eyes.

She stiffened and anger weld up within her. With sheer physical effort, she forced herself not to make a cutting retort. Finally she managed a weak murmur.

"I think we had better return to the dance."

His face was now hard and she couldn't read his expression as he agreed. "Yes. We wouldn't want to be late for our numbers."

As they entered; Jessie, without a glance in Tyler's direction, turned toward the powder room. While she tried to straighten the red-gold hair, she met her eyes in the mirrored image. They were wide, excited and at the same time appeared hurt. Anger made them bright and as she finished a slight smile touched the fine lips.

She was even more determined now to sing those extra songs.

The band was a very good one, but most of the guests were waiting to hear the Wranglers, Jessie and Tyler perform. Of course there were a few couples more anxious than others. Like Larry and the sandy-haired Cindy, who were now moving closer to the platform figuring that a break was about due.

Others moved in closer, also, and of course, Joe Drake. Though it couldn't be said that he was giving anything away. His dark, wine-colored eyes were not on the band, but were searching the crowd of people for the slender redhead. At first his glance lingered on the dark-haired McKay. For an instant hatred burned in the dark eyes, then Jess stepped into his line of vision.

As the woman moved slowly toward the band; the leader, Jay, stood at the microphone and made the break announcement, adding with a smile. "It seems we're to be entertained, also. So I'll just turn it over to Roy Parker."

Stepping up to the stage platform. Parker smiled and thanked the handsome lead singer. Then facing the audience as the rest of Jay's group left their instruments, "After the entertainment you have just had we're going to find it hard to measure up. But we'll sure give it a try."

The Wranglers then took their places behind the instruments and after a few minutes, Roy remarked, "As some of you know, we have some talent lurking about. So without further delay, we'll give you a good sample."

And then they went into one of the current popular songs. The guests showed their appreciation by dancing and when the song ended they cheered. Once again Roy moved up to the mike and said, "We also have some solo talent. One, a pretty redhead. Jess, come on up here and show us how it's done."

Cooper mounted the platform, the lights lowered and the band started to play. Her clear, soft vibrant voice sang the older melody, 'Because You Loved Me', while the cowboys sang the backup. She was good and everyone realized it. Her performance was flawless, and the applause was almost deafening.

Parker joined the redhead and gave her a warm smile. Then as Jess stepped down, he said, "Not bad, huh? Don't worry, you'll hear more from her in a little while. Next we've got a song from the movie 'FOOTLOOSE', 'Hurts So Good'; and to sing it, Tyler McKay. That is if we can get him up here." Then with a quick glance at Ty, "Come on, Boss."

If Jess's performance was flawless, then Tyler's was just as brilliant. If not sexy. He wore gray snug-fitting dress jeans with a soft silky ice-green shirt that showed-off a well-built body and his voice was melting every female heart in the crowded room. With the lively beat that the band was beating out he started to move in time to the song and that in turn brought the crowd to life as well. As the earthy, upbeat moves came across so did the dancers in the audience. They were dancing along with the sexy man on stage.

Once again the applause rang around the large room. The Wranglers were very good and had blended to make the most of the singers' voices. With a very masculine grin touching the firm lips Tyler declared in the smooth drawl, "And now I think it's time we heard a little more from this group of cowboys, don't you?"

And the already excited crowd shouted their agreement. The boys played another number, then Roy again announced Jess. This time she sang 'Love Sneakin' Up On You' and the band and their back-up was a key ingredient. So good had everyone been doing, that it wasn't uncommon to see Jay turn to his band members and nod his head in admiration.

McKay was standing next to the dancing crowd as Jessie finished up her second song. His tawny-green eyes had remained on her small oval face through-out the whole song. He was waiting for her to step down, when Parker once again spoke up.

"What's coming up next is strictly off the cuff. No rehearsal. Jessie, here, is going to sing another song."

Jess smiled at the cowboy and then turned it on the crowd. "It was strictly my idea, but I'm sure you will like it. At least the female half, anyway."

As they made themselves ready, Tyler's surprised expression slowly changed to one of wariness. What was the woman up to? For very definitely she was up to something. Her gray-blue eyes were fastened on his own.

Then as Parker asked her if she was ready and received her nod, he announced, "Like Jess said most of the ladies will appreciate this song. It's by Bonnie Tyler. 'Holding Out For A Hero'."

As the words of the song poured out they were intense and demanding. Her voice which had been soft and vibrant with the other songs was totally different with the present song. You could picture the white knight and his charging white stallion coming to the rescue. And the singer's determination to wait for the real hero and not a false one.

McKay could feel his blood heat. God, she was beautiful standing up there demanding that a hero must come. And she was looking at him with those gray velvet eyes that were daring him to be that hero. His own yearning eyes were fastened on the lovely, teasing features. He wasn't about to break that eye contact. Towards the end of the song, Tyler let a strange smile reach his lips. Jess caught it, and for a brief moment her satisfied expression slipped.

When she had finished, Tyler stepped forward and helped her off the stage. Bending forward so that his mouth was near her ear, he whispered softly, "Very smart, Little One. I got the hint. But now you have to wait."

High color mounted her cheekbones as she hurriedly reached the tiled floor. But then she smiled. Oh, she would. Looking back over her shoulder, she saw that Tyler was about to go back on stage to do his next number.

Picking up the cordless mike and turning to Roy, they started the upbeat rhythm of Tyler's next song. Roy's mellow voice came over the microphone as he announced, "This song is really two songs from the movie, 'Spirit'. They sort of go together. 'Can't take Me, I'm Free' and 'Get Off of My Back'. We are dedicating these songs to all our competition in the upcoming race and rodeo. Hit it, Trail Boss."

With the band's increase of sound the rhythm seemed to vibrate to the very bones and everyone was moving in time, even those that weren't dancing. Tyler's voice was rich and ringing. Getting everyone caught up in the mood and beat.

Watching him move to the sexy beat, Jess found herself loving the muscle play and the fluid movement of the soft material of his shirt as it moved over chest and shoulders. Feeling her face warm, she glanced away and found to her surprise that others, female others, were eyeing McKay with the same hungry look in their eyes. Suffocating jealousy surged through her, taking her completely by surprise. She didn't want other women to ogle her man. Her man? Sighing deeply, she thought that no one else had better lay their hands on him or they would have her to answer to. Oh, God, she was in love with Tyler McKay!!

Hearing the roar of applause and cheers, shook her out of her personal thoughts. The song was over and some of the women were giving him wolf whistles. Looking up to where he was still standing, she saw that a faint blush was high-lighting the cheekbones of his lean, handsome face. Why the man was embarrassed! That was cute, and sexy as all get-out.

Waiting for him to hand over the mike to either Roy or one of the others, she was surprised yet again as she watched them talk together for a few seconds, then Parker turned to the crowd.

"Okay, folks, this is the night for off-the-cuff music. Now you can really hear just how good we really are. Our boss, here, is going to sing another song. It's called 'Hungry Eyes'."

Jess knew this song. And as he sang the words, he was staring directly at her. One part of the song implies that the man fantasies about a woman he is in love with and he can't hide the hunger in his eyes from her any longer. Did Tyler mean him and her? Maybe, just maybe they were after the same thing.

Almost through a haze, she watched him sing the tantalizing words of the song. The guests were dancing or moving with the rhythm of the song and she felt a wave of warmth sweep over her whole body as his hot tawny-green eyes seemed to touch her with a look.

It was getting close to the time for the band to return to the stage and they still had a song to sing together; two actually. And she still had one last song to sing that Ty knew nothing about. But her big problem was trying to prepare herself to face McKay when he was finished with the sizzler of a song he was singing.

Chapter Nineteen

Tyler was pouring out the last of the song and Jessie moved a small distance away as a couple danced close to her. As she did so, she overheard two young women as one said to the other, "I'd give anything to be with him just one night. He is one sexy man, that trail foreman. I definitely need what He has." The other woman, a little blonde, nodded her head in agreement.

Maybe Jessie was going to have her work cut out for her? Then she smiled softly. But it would be a fun fight. She was still smiling as Cindy, Larry and Joe stepped next to her.

"Well, Jess, I would never have thought you could sing like that." Stated Joe with a dry smile on his rather, dark handsome face.

Jess's lips tightened just before she answered him with, "You didn't think I could do much of anything."

Cindy, seeing the danger signals, flashed a disapproving look at Drake, and asked with a slight, if not forced laugh, in her voice. "Why that Hero song, Jess?"

Once again a smile lit the pretty oval of the redhead's face. "Mostly to tell someone something; but mostly because I like it. It's one of my very favorites. Tyler wasn't bad, either."

"I should say not. You should have seen all the women when he sang. I think those that didn't fall in love with him, fell in heat for his body. If I didn't have my own hunk, I could fall hard for that sexy cowboy too." Laughed Cindy with mischief flickering in the hazel eyes.

"Glad you remembered me." Grinned Larry with very apparent love for the slender woman encircled in his arms.

Watching them, Jessie felt a moment of hurt. Pain from the past. Turning slightly, she caught Joe watching her with the same old displeasing look on his face.

"What's wrong with you?" she asked before thinking.

His dark-toned features reddened and his lips stretched tight over clinched teeth. Then as the band started the lead-in to the song that she and Ty were supposed to sing, she moved away from Drake and to the stage.

Tyler gave her a hand up and the audience applauded as they took center stage. Roy's voice drifted across the room as he announced, "We thought that you all would like to hear them do a number together. Well, how about 'Almost Paradise'?"

Tyler started the song with his rich very masculine baritone and Jess's softer, higher one blended in with perfect timing. The crowd remained quiet, listening with appreciation and totally involved with the song. It was a long song, but most of the crowd felt it ended much too soon. As the couple drew the song to a close, the applause was deafening to hear, but made the group of performers feel great.

Then as Tyler started to move off-stage, he glanced back and stopped where he was as he realized that the redhead was moving to the center of the stage again. Another song? Unconsciously he moved in closer to the band just as Parker's amused voice sounded.

"This is one of our last songs. A last minute add on, but one we feel that you will enjoy. It's one of Bonnie Raitt's songs. It's called 'Something to Talk About'." And then the wrangler looked at McKay. As he walked back past him, he whispered, "Stay where you are."

An uneasiness slid up Tyler's spine as he listened to the band start the sexy song. Looking back to Jess the feeling increased as he caught her looking at him with a mischievous glint in her gray eyes. And then the smoky, teasing words were floating out over him and that sexy smile was causing his temperature to climb.

The song was about rumors that were trying to say that two people were involved and trying to keep it secret, but then the woman feels that maybe these friends were seeing more than the two friends had realized about themselves.

And then in between the instrumental part, she looked right at him and crooked her finger at him and called him over to her. When he didn't move, one of the guitar players pushed him in her direction. So he moved slowly toward her just as she started singing the words again.

He could feel the color rise up from his neck to his cheeks. Her small body was moving in time to the seductive song and now everyone would know that it was him she was singing the words to.

She moved in close to him and whispered to him, “Sing it with me.” So he did.

The heat in his body rose even higher, but he could not take his eyes from her face. Her eyes locked with his as they finished the song together and then the applause roared over the group.

Man, he needed a drink before he talked to the small redheaded firecracker. And he slipped off the stage and through the crowd to the bar at the back of the large room.

As the professional band took over and the Wranglers and Jessie stepped down off the platform they were surrounded by friends and guests. As she moved through the crowd, she bumped against someone who closed hard hands on her shoulders.

Turning her red-gold head she looked into dark, hard brown eyes. Joe grinned without humor and as the band started to play, he swung her out onto the dance floor.

Blue-gray eyes flashed with indignation. The pretty face paled slightly with suppressed anger. “You are like a small child having a tantrum, Joe. Besides, what I said earlier was the truth, if you remember.” Stated Jess coldly.

She felt him stiffen and then he pulled her closer, his fingers biting into the soft flesh of her upper arms. “You’ve changed.” He growled.

“Oh, you think so? Took you long enough. But I haven’t really changed all that much. You just never took the time to notice. You were too busy using me as your pride-saver. I was just handy when you needed someone. And me, well I was a gullible fool and very insecure. But, I’ve learned from the experience, believe me.” Her voice was husky with feeling, but remained lowered. Pulling back from his embrace, she said through tight lips. “Let me go. I didn’t ask to dance with you.”

"You're right, you didn't. But, I didn't ask you and you can just finish this dance." He sneered softly.

She tried pulling away, but he held her tighter. There was nothing that she could do about it without causing a very public scene. And Drake knew it, and was using that fact.

Tyler, taking a sip from his drink let the hazel-green eyes rest on the dancing couple. At first glance anyone would believe they were in a world of their own, until noticing just how stiff Jess was moving. And Tyler noticed. Setting down his drink, he also caught a look at the woman's angered, set face.

Just when Jessie thought she would scream with frustration, she heard the familiar deep, drawling voice from behind her. "I believe you would say that I was cutting in, Drake."

Then she found herself being swung away in McKay's arms, an angered face fading in among the dancing couples.

"He'll hate you for that, you know." She said on a sigh.

A dry chuckle, then, "He's hated me long before now. About that last number you sang, we sang? And the Hero one? But, especially that last one."

With her face hidden from his line of vision, she permitted a smile to touch her lips before questioning with a total look of assumed innocence. "What about it? Didn't you like it?"

His arm tightened around her, and she felt him silently chuckle. "Of course I liked it. Both numbers. I got the gist of the rumors, I think everyone did. That was some sexy song. Besides, I'm pretty good at coming to the rescue. By the way, I still like your dress." Whispered Tyler softly in her ear.

Cooper could feel the warm breath against her neck and the caressing motion of his thumb as he gently rubbed it across her bare backbone. Turning her face slightly towards him; she began to sing some of the words from her last song very softly, but just loud enough for him to hear.

The last word was met with a tightening of strong arms, and with a soft gasp as she felt the firm pressure of McKay's warm lips on the soft skin of her neck, near her ear. Her whole body seemed to become inflamed from the gentle touch.

"I'm just giving them something to talk about." He sighed.

Then the music stopped and Jessie sighted Jay Reynolds heading their way with the wireless microphone in his hand. "Ty, what about another song from you two?" called the lead singer's voice.

McKay turned slowly around and with a careless shrug replied, "Why not?"

Still hanging on to Jess's small hand, he took the mike from Jay and the band started to play '(I've Had) the Time of My Life'. With a meaningful look, McKay whispered, "The second duo song we were going to do. Ready?" With a smile, she nodded.

'(I've Had) the Time of My Life' being an upbeat slow song, they danced in time to the beat as they sang the words of love found. And made quite a hit. Without too much trouble they had claimed everyone's attention.

As that song ended, a song by Rod Stewart started. A song that Ty liked, 'The Rhythm of My Heart'. As Jessie was about to move off, Tyler tightened his hold and sang the words in a husky, very sexy voice that sent shivers of temptation through the slender frame. As he moved his warm body against hers in a sexy dance step, the crowd joined in and the lights dimmed.

As the last note faded, the applause sounded and McKay winked at Cooper and flashed a steamy smile. Jay Reynolds reappeared and retrieved his microphone. A pleased expression on his classically handsome face. "Not bad, old son. Never could guess why you chose horses."

McKay laughed lightly, "I enjoy singing, but until tonight you would never have gotten me in front of an audience. Besides, most of the people here, I know. I get along better with horses. They are easier to please."

Jay shook his head. "Well, if you ever want a second job; look me up. You, too, Red. You two are one hot item together. Anyone ever tell you that?"

Tyler and Jessie exchanged glances and then laughed softly. "Not in so many words, Jay. But thanks for the compliment." Answered McKay.

Then the singer shook hands with Tyler and returned to the stage. By mutual agreement, Ty and Jess danced a few more dances and then went up to the bar to get a cool drink.

As they neared the mahogany bar, Phil and most of the cowboys were waiting for them. "Not bad, guys. Now aren't you glad that I thought this all up?" grinned Holden.

"Sure thing, Phil. But next time, you have to do a number. Isn't that right, everybody?" chuckled Tyler, and then the others joined in at Phil's expense. But he seemed to enjoy it as much as the rest.

After ordering their drinks, Phil pulled McKay over to one side. "Did you see who was here?"

Hesitantly the trail foreman shook his curly, dark head. "No. I've been a little busy. Why? Who's here that I should know about?"

"Don't look now, but you are about to say hello to him." Mumbled Phil.

McKay pushed away from the bar and stepped slightly off to one side as he faced the tall man with the strange pale-brown eyes. A hardness crept over the handsome features. "What are you doing here, Wilcox? Wouldn't think that this would be the sort of thing you would go for? Besides the fact that it was here. Last I heard you didn't much care for Jute Valley."

"Now, Tyler boy, don't be that way. Actually I had no idea that you could 'perform' like that, McKay. The women were just about melting where they were standing." Came the low voice of the rancher.

At the rancher's arrival at the bar, everyone had straightened and now it seemed to Jessie that the sudden silence was deafening. Unconsciously, the wranglers and hands moved closer in beside the trail foreman, without a word they were stating that they were behind their friend and boss. Phil Holden frowned and moved closer to his head trail guide. He didn't care for this set-up at all. It was out of character for the rancher.

Jess had the same feeling and wondering at the same instant where Hunter was. The rancher hardly ever went very far without his foreman. Or more like a bodyguard. Her eyes scanned the faces of the guests and other ranch employees, but could see no sign of the tall, husky-built foreman. That alone worried her, more than if she knew where he was.

Grinning tightly, trying to cover his distaste of Wilcox's words, Ty demanded in a low, controlled voice. "You still haven't answered my question. What exactly are you here for?"

The pale eyes narrowed and bore into the tawny-green ones of the trail foreman. A stiff smile touched the man's lips but never reached the cold eyes. "Heard that you were supposed to sing and just had to see for myself. Besides, I had also heard that Cooper, here, was going to sing also. Couldn't let that go by without seeing it for myself. Real enlightening."

"Hope you were here for the dedicated songs?" spoke up Jess with a dryness to her usually soft voice.

Wilcox turned his cold gaze on the small woman and then a slight grin appeared. "I was. I take it that it was a warning?"

Tyler's hand touched the small woman's shoulder, then answered quietly, "Yes. Loud and clear."

Still seeing the skeptical look on the lean features, the rancher shrugged carelessly, then added, "I had also heard that you had brought Confederate down. Wondered how he was doing?"

A dry laugh rumbled up from deep in his throat as Ty remarked in a low, husky voice, "I bet you do. But you know I wouldn't tell you anything about Fed's progress, whether good, bad or otherwise. So I guess we're at a stand-off, wouldn't you say?"

"Maybe so. Thought I'd give it a shot. Didn't work, but had a damn good time." Then turning to the ranch manager, he said, "Phil, maybe you should add this entertainment to your regular schedule. You might even open up the bar and dancing to the locals. Be quite good for business. Actually, if you look around, you'll see a number of the locals here now. I'll be seeing all of you soon." Then with a slight nod of his aristocratic head, he went to move away and then stepped up next to McKay and in a low, rough voice said, "I hear you've been up by the northern boundary. Fences down or something up there between Lazier and Jute?"

A stillness settled over the handsome features. "No big reason, was riding and thought maybe I'd check out some new trails. Why you so interested?"

"Just curious, Ty boy, just curious." Smiled the older man, a slight nervous twitch at his jaw. Once again he tipped his head and again moved away through the crowd to the back by the large doors.

Jessie's fingers clasped tightly around Tyler's and she looked up into his unreadable face. "He makes me nervous turning up here like that. What did he say to you? He looked a little uneasy. I didn't see Hunter around, but have you ever known Wilcox to go anywhere, especially here, without his bodyguard foreman?"

McKay looked down at her, a grim smile on his lips. "I agree with you. And the only time he was at Jute Valley alone, he had an unscheduled dip in the pool. He asked about me being up by our north boundary. Go figure? I imagine that Hunter is around somewhere. Relax, Jess, there's too many people around." Then as he went to turn back to the bar to get a soft drink to soothe his dry throat; a slim, tall tawny-haired woman moved up between Ty's broad chest and the bar. "Hello, Ty, would you care to dance?"

"Alright, just one." Murmured McKay reluctantly. He was tired and he could see the angry glitter in the redhead's gray eyes. Oh, well the price of popularity. Bother.

Cooper watched silently as the leggy blonde pulled a reluctant Tyler onto the dance floor. She was angry alright, but not at McKay. But the woman, yes, she could be damn mad at her. And glancing up she saw that the blonde was getting moved out and a model-thin dark-haired beauty was wrapping herself about Ty's lean body. Okay, maybe it was time to do some moving in on her own. Picking up the soft drink that McKay had ordered, but not had a chance to taste, she went onto the dance floor and walked directly up to the dancing couple. The look of relief on the handsome features caused a small smile to flutter across her lips. Moving right up to the embarrassingly clinging woman, Jess took her free hand and tapped the woman's shoulder none too gently. "Excuse me, but I'm cutting in."

The displeased frown on the woman's face was a definite lift for her sagging spirits. Then Tyler was guiding her to the far side of the dance floor.

"You look very pleased with yourself." Grinned McKay.

"Yes, well, it's not every day that I get to steal a celebrity away from a devoted fan." Chuckled Jess mischievously.

"Fine, not you too? Is that my soda?" and he nodded at the drink in her hand.

"Yep. Do you want it? Well, in that case, why did you sing that song 'Hungry Eyes'?" she asked holding the drink just out of his reach.

"I had to answer your 'Hero' song, now didn't I? Now, about my drink." Then he smiled that heart-melting smile and she handed him the drink.

Watching him take a sip of the cooling liquid, she frowned and asked absently, "You are drinking a soft drink?"

Taking another small refreshing sip, he answered softly, "Yeah. I decided that I had been drinking a little too much lately. I know what I was doing wasn't good for me. It just takes me awhile, I guess. How about this last slow dance?"

Cooper smiled a soft secret little smile and nodded the curly, red-gold head. "You bet."

Chapter Twenty

Walking out of the lodge doorway, Jess and Tyler were softly talking about the training of Confederate in the early morning. The pale moonlight was spilling down through the trees, across the small stream that ran just behind and between the lodge and their cabins. It also fell across the hat and broad shoulders of the tall, huskily-built man that was following slowly behind them in the shadows. Stopping at the edge of the small forest, McKay leaned tiredly against the rough bark of the tall fir.

"I think I'll start on Fed's workout around nine in the morning, instead of at dawn like usual. After breakfast and some of the chores are done is soon enough. I'm so tired that I can hardly stand upright. Don't know about you, but it's been a hell of an exhausting week one way or the other. And I haven't slept much at all and I think it has finally caught up with me. Jess, do you think you could bring Rebel over to pace with Fed? You can handle Reb, alright?"

Hiding a yawn with her hand, Jessie smiled softly afterward, then answered, "Sure, no problem. You want me there at nine or a little earlier to help with the warm-up?"

"No, nine is early enough. Come on, I'm way past sleep and have passed out. My body just doesn't know it yet."

Watching as the two walked on to the lone cabins, Dave Hunter turned and made his way back through the trees to where he had parked the Lazier Ranch jeep. The boss had been right about them working the stallion in the early mornings. Apparently they had been doing it before the rest of the ranch was awake. No wonder he had never been able to catch them running the horse. But tomorrow, he would be there. They needed to know just how good the stallion was this year. With a low, sly chuckle, the Lazier foreman turned the ignition key and started the vehicle. If he had his way, they wouldn't bother with the damn horse. Get rid of the trouble; namely, McKay. First, his old man got nosey; now the son was sticking his nose where it didn't belong.

Coming up to Cooper's cabin, McKay hesitated before pulling open the door. As tired as he was he would love to have another taste of the redhead's mouth. More, if he had his way. But he didn't want to push her too hard, for fear of scaring her away.

While he was debating, Jess stepped up into the cabin and turned back to face McKay. With her position in the doorway and him still standing on the lower step, she was almost face to face with the lean features. Bending forward she put her small hands on his shoulders and placed her mouth over his. It was meant to be a light, quick kiss; but as the firm lips responded to her gentle pressure, the banked flame suddenly flared into a blaze. The muscles beneath her fingers tightened and bunched, strong hands caught her waist and pulled her closer to the hard, male length of him. She started to tremble and the flame seemed to grow hotter and was spreading throughout her body turning it to liquid heat. She could feel her heart beating wildly in her chest, or was it Ty's? Probably both of them.

Ty's breathing was becoming erratic and he felt like he was going to burn up. He could feel his body harden and ache with a longing he had never encountered to such a degree before. God, it was just a simple good-night kiss! Only it was getting completely out of control.

His hips collided with hers. He felt her shudder as his body embarrassingly betrayed his feelings. Tearing his lips from the warm, soft ones, he took a deep, steading breath. Her eyes were dazed, and he thought that his must appear the same. "I think I better go...I'll see you in the morning, Jess. I...I..."

Jess blinked twice and tried to steady her rapid, shallow breathing. "What, Ty?"

"Well, uh...nothing. I'll see you in the morning. Night."

Then he turned and headed for the other cabin. Jessie leaned against the door frame and watched until the lean cowboy stepped into the still dark cabin. A slow smile spread across her lips, the man was definitely upset. But, in a good way. Could it be that he was affected by her kiss? Just like she had been by his? God, he was potent.

With a shake of her head she turned inside and made for the bedroom at the back of the cabin. She found that she agreed with McKay. It had been a very exhausting week. And it looked to be another one.

Charcoal-gray clouds skidded across the darkening sky, wind was whipping the branches of the trees into a frenzy of activity. Rain sprayed into the sheltered hallway of the barn where Jess was leaning against the wood-planked doorway. Looking through the raindrops that were falling in increasing numbers, she watched the white horse pace restlessly in his enclosure. As thunder rolled up through the valley, the stallion let loose with a shrill cry, then spun around and raced down the fence line. She had been on edge since right after the workout with the big horse that morning. Maybe it had been the impending storm, but something wasn't just right. Call it intuition, or just nerves, but there was a feeling that wouldn't leave her. A shiver shimmered over her body.

The workout had went real well, the stallion had ran easy with no problems and Rebel had handled well for her. Even early that morning the gray clouds had been moving around, but not until that evening had it started to rain. Tyler was on the other side of the yards, getting some young horses inside out of the weather. He was supposed to meet her at the barn to go to supper at the lodge.

A sudden gust of violent wind blew dirt and straw in her face. Turning to get out of the way, she thought she heard the stallion give another more pronounced cry. Squinting through the flying dust and debris, she looked out through the evening darkness toward the corral. A dark, large shape skimmed past the fence line and disappeared into the timber and at the same instant a ghost-white object moved through what had been a closed gate, but was now open. Confederate was loose and he hated storms, the horse would run until he dropped!

Twisting around the first horse she saw was the little range mustang, Gringo. Throwing a saddle and a bridle on the little bay gelding, she vaulted onto the saddle and headed for the doorway. Just as she reached the opening, the stable boy, Gideon, appeared. Pulling the horse to a halt, she leaned down to the boy and said urgently, "Gideon, tell Ty I went after Fed. He's heading toward the northern mountains and running crazy. Oh, and tell him that he was let out."

Gideon Farrell stood in the doorway and watched as the trail guide rode out into the pouring rain, in moments both the horse and rider had disappeared into the blurring darkness. Rain struck the lean, boyish face and unconsciously he raised a slim hand to wipe away the moisture. As he did so, the trail foreman came running into the walkway. "Hello, Giddy. Boy, is it raining. Have you seen Jessie? She's supposed to be here waiting for me."

The sixteen-year-old boy looked up, his dark-brown eyes large and anxious. The curly, dark-red hair was wet and again the slim hand raised to run it nervously through the damp curls. "She went after Confederate. Ty, you have to go after her." He then went on to tell him what she had said.

The boy had started to shake from reaction. McKay felt like a large sledge hammer had just hit him square in the chest. Jessie Cooper was out in this storm and Fed was gone. "Giddy, listen, it's alright. How long ago did she leave?" Ty's voice had lowered to help calm the frightened youth. His hands had unconsciously fell onto the boy's slender shoulders.

A firmness came over the young features. "She just left. Just moments before you came. She said that he is running crazy, Ty. He hates storms. She's on Gringo. He was handy. You're going after them, aren't you?"

"Damn, right. But I need you to go to Phil and explain what happen. Tell him not to worry, I'm taking Shiloh and I'll bring them back. If we're not here by ten in the morning, come looking. Have you got that, Gideon?" At the boy's solemn nod, Tyler asked, "You said that Jess had said that someone let him out? Did she say who?"

"No, Sir."

Glancing once again at the stable boy, Ty sighed and remarked quietly, "One more favor, Giddy. While I go get Shiloh saddled, would you go get my rifle and some shells?"

The boy once again nodded his curly head and turned to do as he had been asked. McKay would get them back, Gideon was sure of it.

It was getting darker and even harder to see. The wind howled up through the canyon and the thunder rolled down off the nearby mountains. Then as she pulled the tiring bay gelding to a halt and stared through the wall of rain, Jess thought that she had seen a faint flash of white in the grayness. The little Gringo had sensed something also for the small head turned toward the canyon floor and she could feel the trembles running through the tense muscles. "Is he down there, Gringo? Well, let's go take a look." And she urged him down the slippery trail to the narrow bottom floor.

It was even darker in the canyon. Suddenly a shrill ringing rent through the sound of the rain. The gelding slid to a halt, his body tense and tight. Then looking to the north of the canyon base, Jess saw him as he stopped and rose into the air, his long sodden mane flying about the slender neck and head. The dark eyes were wide with fright and before she could call out his name, the large stallion had spun and leaped into a full gallop down the canyon.

Jabbing her heels into the gelding's flanks they took off at a dead run, chasing the ghost-white horse. Gringo was sure-footed and fast, but he had run full-out from the ranch yard and through the mountains trying to make up lost time. And he was definitely getting tired. His head was dropping with fatigue, yet still he ran on.

She was getting close, but at the same time she could feel the falter in the gelding's stride. Then she heard what sounded like soft thunder rumbling up from behind her. Turning her head, and squinting to see through the pouring rain, she thought she could make out the blurred image of a horse and rider. And the horse was moving up fast.

It had to be Tyler, but... As the horse came up closer to the weakening gelding, she saw that it was a wet gray. Shiloh! He had rode Shiloh. Yelling into the wind and rain, she tried to make him understand her words. "Ty, he's just up ahead. Go on! He's running scared!"

Seeing his nod, and watching him urge the gray on to an even faster pace, she eased up on the bay. Knowing that he could never stand the increased gait. The gallant little horse had run his heart out.

The gray gelding was gaining on the white stallion with every stride. As the canyon floor opened up ahead of them the gray gelding lengthened his stride until it felt like he was just pouring over the ground. The slender head was still up and the ears were flattened back against the rain-soaked mane, listening for Ty's voice. The dark eyes were pinned on the running white shape just ahead of him and he was determined to reach it.

Tyler could feel the power in the sleek muscles as the gray gelding stretched out even more and made that desperate surge to gain on the larger stallion. They were moving up to the streaming black tail and on to the wet-white rump and then almost to the muscled shoulder, when McKay saw the stallion jerk away and then the loud pop of a gunshot! Swerving into a slightly timbered area that dipped down into small gullies, another shot rang out, almost mingling with the roar of the rain. Shiloh stuck to the other horse as if attached, until the large horse suddenly and violently rose into the air and started to twist and buck as if in pain. Then he just dropped from sight!

Pulling the gray to a sliding halt, he found them standing at the edge of a rather deep gully that was covered with brush. As he flung his lean body out of the saddle, he felt a sharp burning impact to his left side that spun him around and he felt himself slide downward in the direction of the tumbling horse. Faintly he thought he heard the sound of Jess's voice, and not wanting her to be shot at also, yelled up at the place he had slipped through. "Jess, get down! Someone's shooting! Take cover!"

As his body slid down to the almost level base, he came up against the stallion's quivering body. The horse was down, but still alive. Even in the rain and the mud that covered most of the white coat, Tyler could make out blood all along the flank and shoulder, running down the slim white leg. The pain in his own side was now burning and sending a knifing pain up and down his left side. And where was Jess?

Sliding legs and following close was the slight body of the redhead. "Ty. Oh, God, is he dead?"

Tyler started to shake his head then realized that she more than likely couldn't see the move in the increasing darkness, so said in a low, tight voice. "No, he's still alive, but he's been shot and I have no idea at the moment just how bad it is."

Hearing the hard, choked ring to the low voice, Jessie turned and looked at McKay. Even in the darkness, she could see that the lean features were pale and the firm mouth was in a tight, unyielding line. He was also holding his lean body stiffly. "Ty, are you alright?"

Gritting his teeth together against the sharp, burning pain that suddenly sliced through his side, he nodded carefully, "Yeah. Just landed sort of hard coming down the hill." Then glancing at the top of the gully that they had just slid down minutes before, he added, "Where's Shiloh and Gringo? Did you turn them loose or hide them?"

Trying to get a better look at the handsome face, Cooper answered slowly, "They are ground-hitched in the cover of the bordering timber."

Then seeing McKay wince as he shifted his tall frame into a more upright position, she asked, "Are you sure that you are all right?"

"Yes." Avoiding her eyes, he looked again at the downed stallion. "We need to get him on his feet and find some kind of shelter from this storm. I haven't heard any more gunfire; so hopefully, they have left."

Jess sat back on her haunches and studied the tense, still pale features, but decided not to mention anything at that time. She looked over at the white, mud-caked horse and suggested softly, "We are not far from the Wind Canyon line cabin. If we can get him up, it shouldn't be far to it if we just follow this gully. Even if whoever is still out there, they won't be able to get a shot off at us down here."

Turning her face toward the top of the gully, she placed two fingers between her lips and let a slow, piercing whistle float through the wind and rain. Shortly, two heads appeared over the top of the ledge. One, gray and the other a dark bay. Slowly they made their way down the slope to the waiting couple.

Rubbing both noses, Jessie eyed the trail foreman. "Any ideas on how to get Fed to his feet?"

Chapter Twenty-One

Squinting through the rain and darkness toward the shadowed gully below, Dave Hunter cursed under his breath. "Damn that man. I can't see a damn thing."

George Clark pulled back from the husky-built man and glanced at the silent other man standing next to him. Both men exchanged uneasy looks, then George mumbled, "Hunter, let's get out of here. The horse went down and I saw McKay get hit. You weren't supposed to shoot anyone. What's wrong with you, man?"

Hunter turned angry dark eyes on the other two men. "I did what I was supposed to do. Stop that horse from running, anyway I had to. And taking out McKay was an added bonus, just wanted to be sure that I had hit him." Hate flickered swiftly across the rugged features, as he once more looked toward the gully. Moving the large shoulders in a careless shrug of acceptance, he remarked gruffly, "Let's get out of here."

The other two Lazier hands were already moving in the direction of their tied horses. Hunter soon followed. A self-satisfied smile of sorts spread across the harsh slash of lips. Quickly they were mounted and on their way back to the Lazier Ranch. Their job was finished.

Pushing wet, curling dark-red hair back off her face, Jessie stared into the fire she had just started in the fireplace of the line cabin. The rain hadn't slackened off at all, even had come down harder just before they had reached the secluded cabin. Tyler was putting the last of the medication on the gashes that the bullets had inflicted on the stallion's white hide. The bullet hadn't entered, luckily, but had taken a couple of large hunks of flesh off of the flank and shoulder, then had nicked the bone of the horse's foreleg. Fed had walked, but with a decided limp. He wouldn't be running any race in the near future. But he was still alive and not in serious condition.

Jess wasn't so sure about McKay. His face was almost gray in color and the stiffness of movement belied what he had said about not being hurt. When he came in from the lean-to, she would have to pen him down to a more accurate answer. Besides, they were going to have to do something about their clothes. She had pulled sodden, soaked boots off and her clothes were in the same sad shape. There wasn't a dry piece of material anywhere on her body and she knew it had to be the same for Tyler.

Glancing around she saw that the cupboards were well stocked and so decided to make some coffee. At least that would help take the bone-deep chill away.

Just as the coffee was starting to boil, the side door to the lean-to opened and McKay stumbled in. If it were possible, he looked worse than he had earlier to Jess's concerned eyes.

Making an effort to keep her voice calm, she suggested, "Ty, sit down over there in front of the fire and get those wet boots and jacket off. I've hot coffee coming in just a second."

He made no comment, just moved tiredly toward the wooden chair that was close to the blazing fire. Slumping onto its hardness, he made a half-hearted attempt to pull the boots off, but found that he was just too weak, seemed to have no strength left to use. So easing his stiff, sore body down in the hardness of the chair he slowly closed his eyes. His side felt like it was on fire, and at the same time his arms and legs were so chilled that the muscles were knotting and starting to tremble and ache.

Cooper moved silently up next to where he was sitting, carefully carrying the mug of hot coffee. Softly she touched his shoulder, noting that he hadn't yet managed to remove neither the boots, nor the sodden jacket.

"Tyler, here, drink this," and she extended the mug toward him.

He didn't even attempt to open an eye, just mumbled that he didn't want any. His body trembled and the fingers gripped the arms of the chair so tightly that his knuckles turned white.

With a loud thump, the mug was slammed down next to him on the old, hardwood table. He jerked up and the fever-glazed tawny eyes snapped open. Looking up into the stormy-gray eyes, he knew that he was in BIG trouble. But before he could open his mouth, she was bending toward him, her small chin set at a stubborn angle.

As the cool, small hand touched his hot forehead, he jerked back as if burned. Anger lightened the gray eyes as she stared down into his face. With a deep, calming breath, she demanded, "Alright, Ty, I want the truth. Now, let's have it."

"There's nothing wrong, Jess, I'm just exhausted." Mumbled the trail foreman nervously.

"Well, I think that you are lying through your teeth, McKay. You are burning up with fever and I can see that you are shaking. Want to try again? And it better be the right answers." She declared through tight lips. She'd like to shake him. When he made no move to answer her, she went to her knees and shoved her face in close to his, "Okay, hardball it is."

Leaning back she grabbed his right boot and tugged it off, then reached for the other. That done she stood and went to take hold of the jacket sleeve. As her fingers closed around the end of the right sleeve, he defensively jerked his arm back close to his chest. Taking a deep breath, fire flashing in the gray eyes, she moved in between his legs and placed her hands on his bunched shoulders. "I don't want to wrestle with you, Ty, but if I have to." She then grabbed on to the left sleeve, jerking it hard, pulling it off of the arm.

A groan escaped his lips, the already pale features washing of all color. Looking at the pain-filled eyes, Jess let go of the sleeve, her own gaze roamed down over the deep chest and muscled body, coming to his left side where a dark-red stain had spread over the lower portion of his shirt and into the waist band of his faded jeans.

"Oh, God, Tyler, you idiot. You've been shot. Why didn't you say something instead of trying to make like nothing was wrong? Damn you, McKay."

His eyes closed and he whispered softly, "I didn't want to worry you. It's not so bad, really. I'll be fi..."

The body that had been held so stiffly, now slumped slowly in the chair. Jessie straightened her slight frame and looked down at the unconscious Tyler. He was fine alright, he had passed out for heaven's sake. Well, while he was out, she just as well get some of his clothes off of him and see what the damage was. And then do what she could.

Taking ahold of the jacket once again she pulled it gently out from behind him and then draped it over another chair to let it dry before the fire. Bending down she started to unbutton the wet shirt, her fingers encountering the curly dark chest hair. Sighing nervously, she continued to unbutton the shirt front until she came to the top of his jeans and the metal belt buckle. With a firm glint in the rain-gray eyes she pulled the shirt ends out of the jeans and then unbuckled the belt and released the top button of the jeans. Being careful and trying not to hurt him, she finished tugging the shirt free from his damp jeans and removed it from his body.

Placing it on top of the jacket, she took her first good look at the area where the bullet had struck. Small even teeth chewed on the soft skin of her bottom lip as she gently touched the blood-caked, swollen skin of his lower side. The skin was dry and hot to the touch. The long, still bleeding gash appeared that the bullet had taken a good sized hunk of flesh with it as it had skimmed across the fleshy part of his left side. Lot of blood, but it didn't appear to have struck anything. It was just below the ribs and above the hip. Thank God for small favors. But because he had not taken care of the wound right away, he had possibly developed a fever and the injury itself was inflamed.

Pushing to her feet, she went to the old potbellied stove that she had heated the coffee on earlier and put some water on to heat. Digging around in the cupboard, she located some white clean dish towels and decided to use them to cleanse the wound. Now if she could find some hydrogen peroxide in the first aid box. Maybe if she could get the wound cleaned and then stop the slow flow of blood, he would come around enough to enable her to get him to the cot and get his wet jeans off of him. There was no way that she could see herself doing it without his help.

Soon the water was warm and she poured some into a shallow bowl. Picking up one of the towels that she had found and the bowl, she went over by the still unconscious man, then pulled up one of the table chairs to sit in while she washed the wound. As the dried blood was washed away, she could see just how deep the gash really was. The cleaner the area became, the more it would bleed. Finally she took the bottle of peroxide and with the clean cloth placed on the far side of the wound, she poured the liquid onto the wound and watched as it foamed up. Then she patted it dry and put antiseptic on it and covered it with a bandage.

Leaning back into the hard backed chair, she let her worried glance run over the still pale features. Stretching out to let her fingers touch the firm male lips, she felt a warmth uncurl suddenly in her chest and lower stomach. The finger tips that skimmed softly over the fullness of his bottom lip, tingled. A shaky sigh broke from her lips and she closed her eyes before standing and then moving closer to his injured side of the chair. Placing her hand firmly on his shoulder, she called his name, "Tyler, wake up. Come on, Ty."

Glazed gold-green eyes opened slowly, and a faint smile pulled at the corner of his mouth as he focused on her worried oval face. "Hi. Sorry, about that. I think."

"Not as sorry as you will be once I get you well again." Grumbled Cooper in a husky voice. Then she looked him square in the eyes. "I need your help to get you over to the cot. Are you up to it?"

The smile widened slightly. "Sure. Let's do it."

Jess moved to his good side and placed her shoulder under his arm as if she were a crutch and helped as he pushed himself into an upright position. Before he had managed to take no more than a couple of steps, he had broken out in a cold sweat and she could feel the tension in the bunched muscles. Finally he slipped from her grip onto the very edge of the cot. Before he could lay down, she stopped him with a small hand on his shoulder. Looking up, he met her steady gaze with his fevered one.

"You need to get your jeans off, Tyler. They are still wet. Raise up, so I can pull them off."

A mischievous light crept into the overly bright eyes, and a sexy grin touched his lips. "You want to take my pants off? Now this sounds interesting. Tell me more."

A blush flooded over the delicate features. "Will you stop? I'm trying to keep you from catching pneumonia. And, my man, you are making it very difficult. So straighten up and help."

"Yes, Sir." He grinned gently. Then managed to raise up so that she could pull the damp material over his hips. As the denim reached his thighs, he more or less, collapsed to the softness of the cot, his breathing ragged and labored. "Jess, sweetheart, if there's anything else you need help with, make it soon or I'm not going to be awake to help you out."

Bending over him, she whispered near his ear, "Get some rest." Then she placed her lips on his, kissing him gently.

Carefully stepping back from the cot, she stared down at the lean handsome face. As he stretched out that very male, very sexy body she could feel her own blood pound in her ears. Shaking her head, she went closer to the bed and pulled the covers up over the sleeping man.

Then she went and hung the jeans up so that they could dry. Next she had to get out of her own still wet clothes. Pulling an extra blanket out of a shelf next to the wall, she tugged off damp, clinging jeans and the cold, clammy shirt. Gratefully she wrapped the warm, dry blanket about her shivering body and sat down in the chair that Tyler had just vacated. The fire was burning warmly and heated the bare skin of her feet as she stretched them out toward its warmth.

Near sleep, she was brought awake by the sound of Ty's groan. Moving over to the cot, she found that his fever had become worse, and that he was shaking violently. She went and threw more wood on the still burning fire, then went back to the cot and spread her blanket over the other covers. Taking a deep breath, she slowly crawled in beside the trembling man. Wrapping her warm body against his and pulled the covers up over them.

Chapter Twenty-Two

Jessie snuggled down closer to the still shivering male body, her arm going over the broad chest, her finger tips cushioned by the dark curling hair. The skin was dry and extremely hot, the lean face was flushed with fever and the strong jaw was clinched tight from the bone-shaking shudders that rippled over the large frame. Wrapping her body tighter to his lean maleness, her leg went over his thigh and her soft curves seemed to fit to his hard angles like they had been made for that purpose.

She could feel the shudders as the muscles bunched and jerked. Her chin fit into the hollow of his shoulder and the dark-red hair fell down over part of his chest and against his neck. His fevered body shifted, turning so that he was more on his side and almost facing her. His arms came around her and hugged her close in his embrace. The warm male lips touched her face, and nibbled down to the corner of her mouth. He was still asleep, but his body was reacting to her closeness. And her own body was reacting to his. Strongly and vibrantly. Oh, but he felt good.

Her breathing had become shallow and her heart beat had started to race. The fair, light tanned skin was flushed also; but not from a chill, but from the man that was holding her and placing soft, loving kisses across her face. Her breath halted somewhere in her chest as the male mouth covered her startled lips and as they moved softly against them a warm curling started in her lower belly and spread outward. Her own arms moved around his broad shoulders and the fingers of her right hand sank into the thickness of his dark, curly hair at the base of his head. Her breathing quickened and she found herself straining closer to his warm, male body and drowning in his kiss. An earthshattering kiss. His warm, soft tongue slipped into her mouth and danced with her own, sending tremors down her spine. If he could set her on fire when he was sick and asleep, what would happen if he were well and fully awake? She'd melt. A puddle at his feet. Trying to slow the rapid beat of her heart, she pulled back and took a couple of deep, ragged breaths; then opened her eyes. Directly across from her, glazed green eyes with gold flecks stared back at her.

A weak, nervous smile tugged at her trembling lips, "Oh, hello."

A slightly confused look crept into the green eyes as he leaned back slowly. "Hello. What's going on, Jess?"

A shaky chuckle, and she couldn't seem to meet his steady gaze. "I was just trying to keep you warm. You were uh...uh shaking and burning up with fever. Still are from the looks of you. Things got a little uh...uh...Oh, hell. Things got carried away. Sort of. I guess."

Grinning self-consciously, Tyler relaxed his taut body. "I'd say so, too. Just exactly what happen?"

"What do you mean?" stammered Jessie softly.

"What happen? You know what I mean. Ah come on, Cooper, what did, we do?" sighed Tyler.

"Nothing like that, Tyler McKay. How could you when you are sick? Running a fever and racked with chills? Men don't...they don't get aroused. Do...do they?" questioned Jess nervously.

"Well, I...I didn't think so, but I won't go on record as saying that it can't happen." A sheepish grin slipped over the male features. "If you want to know the truth of the matter, I sort of am right now. Oh, Jess, don't blush. You said that nothing had happen. That's true, isn't it?" he demanded in a quiet voice.

"We just did some kissing, really good kissing. But... but." Warm color flooded her delicate face and she looked away embarrassed.

A soft chuckle erupted from deep in his chest. "Oh, Jess honey, don't be embarrassed. God, but you are sweet." Then gently pulling her tense small frame closer to his aroused, hard one, he sighed shakily. "A good kiss, huh?" and then feeling her head nod, he added, "How good is a good kiss?"

She leaned her head back against his arm and smiled softly at him. "Curious, are you? Alright. It was fabulous. Want to try it while you are awake?" She teased lightly.

The hazel-green eyes glowed with sudden devilment. "I'm game if you are. I like kissing you. It gets the adrenalin flowing."

Jess hesitated briefly, then grinned softly. Provocatively. Tyler narrowed the gold-green eyes, wondering if he had started something he couldn't handle. Slowly Cooper leaned forward and placed her warm lips on his. The small pink tongue flicked out and traced his full lower lip, sending tremors of desire rippling over his hardened, heated body. A tightness coiled in his lower body, as she slipped her tongue into his mouth and then dueled with his.

Not thinking, just feeling, he tightened his arms around her slight frame and the strong hands moved over her slender back and ribcage. His breathing became caught somewhere in his throat and he could feel his heart beat rapidly in his chest. Heat rose up and it wasn't the fever causing it. It was this fiery small woman in his arms with her lips doing outrages things to his senses. Driving him to distraction. God, he wanted her. All of her. He wanted to taste her skin and so moved his mouth from hers and started placing warm nibbles across her cheek and down her jawline to the small ear and the soft skin of her neck. A soft, fresh scent invaded his senses, her scent. As his lips continued down the warm, creamy neck to her collarbone and lower, he encountered a soft, silky strap.

Looking up into her desire glazed eyes, he questioned softly, "What's this? It feels cool and at the same time warm." Leaning back and moving the covers out of his way, he looked at the dark-blue silky thing that she had on. Looping a finger under the edge of the strap and beginnings of the bodice, his sexy mouth twisted into a grin.

Taking a deep, calming breath, Jess closed her eyes before muttering, "It's called a camisole. They are comfortable and covers you, but not bulky or binding."

"I'll say. I like it, but it sure helps to heat things up. And to tell the truth, we don't need that kind of help. I feel like I'm going to go up in flames any minute now." Absently his thumb rubbed gently over the silky material and just happen to be the top of her breast. The gold flecked eyes followed the trailing thumb and as he watched, the nipple hardened into a tight nub. His thumb slid over it and he could feel the small, firm breast swell at the touch. His touch. Sweat beaded his upper lip and forehead, and a shudder rippled through his solid, heated frame. He felt rotten and alive at the same time.

Jessie felt the shudder and looked closer at the lean handsome features. What she saw made reality flash in on her soaring awareness of what Tyler's touch could do to her body. But his apparent fever was frightening. His face was flushed and the gorgeous eyes were glazed and not from passion, his face also bore the glaze of sweat. And more upsetting was the shudders that shook the large frame that was so close to her own.

Leaning back farther in his arms, she murmured softly, "Ty, as much as I'm enjoying this, I don't think that right now is a good time. You are not well." Enjoying it was just a touch of what she was feeling, but he was not in very good shape. His flesh burned under her fingers.

A sadness crept into the glazed eyes, and the sexy smile slipped just a little as he sighed resignedly, "Yeah, you're right. But I wish. Hell, you know, don't you, Jess? God, Jess, I love you."

Shock held her silent for a brief, hesitant moment. He loved her. Wonder of wonders. She loved him to, but she wouldn't tell him so, just yet. Not with him in a raging fever. She wanted him to remember it when she confessed her love for him. Smiling softly, she said, "Yes, I know.

Now, settle down and let me get you warm." At her words, she felt him chuckle softly against her.

"I am warm, believe me, I am. Jessie, see if there is some aspirin or Tylenol in the first aid box, would you? Maybe we can get this infernal fever down."

Cooper nodded her head, then slid out of the cot and went to the table where the kit sat. Finding a packet and grabbing a glass of water, she returned to the cot. Tyler pushed himself up on one elbow and took the two capsules, then handed the glass back to her. Jess set it on the table once again, then climbed back into the warmth of the covers and male body. Slowly she snuggled up to the long frame, wrapping an arm over the deep chest and a leg over his thigh.

Gray clouds still swirled around overhead as McKay and Cooper rode toward the ranch early the next morning. Jessie once again glanced worriedly over her shoulder at the hunched figure of the trail foreman. Tyler was still running a high fever and his tanned features were flushed and sweat glistened on his face and down his neck. His clothes were damp from the sweat also. She had made him ride Shiloh as the small mustang would have had a hard time carrying his heavier weight. So she was riding the smaller mount and leading the limping stallion. Confederate was doing better than he had appeared the night before, but they wouldn't know just the extent of his injuries until the Vet got a look at him.

They were, she figured about an hour from the ranch buildings, but hopefully Phil would have the wranglers out looking for them before the dead-line that McKay had set before coming after her the night before. She really hoped so, she didn't think that McKay was going to be able to stay in the saddle much longer. Though he would be the last one to say he couldn't handle it. He'd fall off on his head before he would admit to any weakness.

Once again she tossed a worried look at the feverish man riding behind her. The little bay, Gringo, was steadily walking and his short, but even stride would be eating up the miles, if they didn't have to slow down to let the stallion rest every so often. Shiloh was following along and walking very carefully as if he knew that Tyler was in bad shape. McKay had long since stopped reining the gray and the gelding was just following the others as if he were attached with a lead line. Jess was proud of her small gelding, the horse that everyone had said was a renegade. That's what they had said about Rebel also. They had all been wrong.

Gringo's bay head suddenly rose and he let rip with a piercing yell in the direction of the timber and a shaded trail. Then she heard an answering yell from another horse. Had to be one of the ranch horses that Gringo knew, it just had to be.

Looking toward the trail opening, she suddenly saw the head and shoulders of a dark dun appear. And the rider was Jeff Saylor and right behind him came Chang and Toby. A weak smile touched Jessie's mouth at the sight of the wranglers. But they looked beautiful to her worried eyes.

Chapter Twenty-Three

Once again Phil Holden glanced towards the nearby mountains. Damn, he wished he had went along with the search party. Even more, he wished that they would get back. He knew that he had sent them out sooner than Tyler had asked, but the ranch manager had a bad feeling about the whole situation. When the stable boy, Gideon Farrell, had run into the office and told what had happen, a chill had swept over him. He just knew there was more to it than the stallion getting out and because of the storm had run scared.

The boy said that Jessie had remarked that she thought that someone had let the big horse out. That and the fact that Ty had said that Wilcox had asked about McKay being up near the north boundary. The same area that Ty's father had his accident. He didn't like the way things were stacking up. That and he still had to tell McKay about the talk he had with an old friend of his father's. A US Marshall.

Walking to the tack shed and then turning and heading once again back to the corrals, he heard the beat of a fast running horse and looked up quickly. Roy Parker pulled his mount to a sliding halt a few feet from where the ranch manager was standing.

"Phil! We found them. They were heading back with Fed and we caught up with them on top of the ridge. Confederate is lame, but not too bad of shape, but Ty's been shot."

Holden stood still for a long moment, then letting a slow sigh escape through stiff lips, he asked, "How bad?"

The wrangler shook his head. "Don't know. He didn't look good. Jess said that the bullet appeared to pass through and hopefully missed anything important. But he got soaked in the storm and Jess hadn't realized he'd been shot until a good time later. He's got a bad fever."

"Okay. Go get Doc. Tell Bob what you know. How far are they from the ranch?" asked Phil slowly.

"They were coming along right behind me. They should be here very shortly." Replied Parker hurriedly.

As the wrangler disappeared around the back of the tack shed, Gideon stepped out of the stable walk-way. His young face was tense as he asked, "Is Ty going to be alright?" The slender fingers picked up the dragging reins of Parker's horse.

Phil stuck his hands into the pockets of his jeans. "I don't know. We'll have to see what Doctor Collins has to say once he sees McKay. Giddy, after you take care of Roy's mount, would you go get Rick Jorden? He'll need to see to Fed."

The red-haired boy nodded his head and turned to the corral with the large paint. Rick Jorden was the resident veterinarian and one of McKay's friends. Gideon didn't care for the idea that he would have to tell him about his friend. It was bad enough about the stallion, but McKay, also.

Phil turned on his heel and headed for his office. Reaching his normally cluttered desk, he grabbed up the phone and punched out the sheriff's number. It was picked up on the third ring and then he asked the lady that had answered, to talk to John Cradling. A moment later the deep voice of the sheriff came on the line. "Hello, John. This is Phil and we have a problem."

Stepping out of the office, Holden caught sight of the small band of riders as they made their way to the holding corrals. Seeing that Tyler was sliding down off the gray gelding and that both Doc Collins and the veterinarian Rick Jorden were there to help him down, Phil moved to where Jessie still sat on the small mustang.

Cooper watched intently as the two doctors helped McKay off of Shiloh. She was really worried about him. His lean face was a sickly gray and slick with sweat and he was almost unconscious. She noted the frown on the doctor's set face and the concern on Jorden's. After they had him on the ground, the other two wranglers picked up the limp form of the trail foreman and headed for the infirmary. Then looking down at her hands that were tightly gripping the reins and saddle horn, her smoky-gray eyes met the concerned ones of the ranch manager. "Oh, Phil, he doesn't look very well, does he?"

"No, he doesn't, but he's strong. He'll be fine." Frowned Holden. "Jess, give Gringo to Giddy, there; and let Rick take Confederate. I need you in my office, then when we're done, you can go to McKay. Sheriff Cradling is on his way over."

Stretching the cramped legs out before the chair that she was sitting in, Jessie looked over at the still sleeping McKay. He looked better than the last time she had seen him, about three hours before. Doctor Collins had said that he had a bad case of infection from the bullet wound and then the circumstances directly following the incident. No kidding, thought Cooper with a twist to her lips. Letting her glance flow slowly over the lean features, she noted that the flushed, feverish look was gone and he was sleeping much more comfortably. Everyone had become really worried when as he had started to dismount, he had lapsed into unconsciousness.

With a dry, silent chuckle, she thought that it would have been a good idea for her to have been unconscious when she had been in Phil's office when the sheriff had arrived. For over two hours, they had went over every little detail. Repeating it over and over so many times that she felt that she could repeat it in her sleep. But apparently she had satisfied the sheriff as he had smiled at her and told her that she had done fine. They still had to talk with Ty and get his view of what had happen. Mostly to see that all the pieces fit together.

Because of the storm, all the tracks would more than likely have been washed away, and along with them any evidence of who exactly had done the shooting. But all three people that had been in that office had a very good idea on who had released the stallion and then had tried to murder the trail foreman. Fear, with its icy fingers, slid up Jessie's spine, causing her to wrap her arms tightly about herself. Murder. It was such a dirty word. So sinister and final.

But if the gunshot would have either been higher or more to the center of Tyler's body he could very well be dead. And that wasn't because of an accident, but because someone had wanted the trail foreman dead, or hurt so bad that he wouldn't be a threat to anyone. What kind of threat? A threat to what?

A soft groan from the sleeping man drew her attention once more to the muscled, tanned frame of Tyler. He was moving restlessly from side to side, slightly shifting the covers that concealed the lower half of his body. Her gaze followed the fine dark mat of curling hair that covered the tanned, broad chest and tapered down the flat stomach to disappear under the edge of the pale-blue sheet. Her mouth turned dry as desire rippled through her slender frame.

Moving closer to the sleeping man, Jess bent and started to reach a hand out to pull the slipping sheet back into place. Just as her fingers were about to touch the cool material, Tyler twisted away from her, pulling the fabric farther away and the finger tips touched warm, hard flesh. Slowly she let them smooth over the flat stomach, unconsciously sitting down on the edge of the bed. Her breath caught in her throat as she let her touch slide hesitantly upward over the soft layer of springy hair that dusted the deep chest. A tingling started in her fingers and quickly spread through her hand and up her arm.

Taking a deep breath, she lazily dragged finger tips back down the lean, hard male body; then grasped the sheet and tugged it back into place over the tantalizing chest. A warmth spread through her lower stomach curling upward into her chest. Desire, hot and pure. When had she started to have these feelings and longings for McKay? Had she always had them? But not realized it until whispers from the past had threatened her future? Well, however way it was, she had acknowledged the feelings that she now felt for him. Sighing once again, she frowned to herself. All this desire and it just wasn't the time; again. But maybe, yes, maybe very soon.

Leaning forward to stand up, she was halted by strong fingers that curled gently around her slender wrist. Turning to look at the once sleeping man, smoky-blue eyes met gold-flecked green ones that were staring steadily up at her, a question lurking in their depths. "Hello."

His voice came out low and husky, sexy. "Hi." His fingers still held the slim wrist. "How long have I been out?"

"Oh, uh about three and a half to four hours. Doc said that you have one hell of an infection, but you should be better soon. You also cracked and bruised a rib or two. Probably when you slid down the ridge after being shot." Her voice suddenly broke and she hurriedly went on to cover it. "The Sheriff wants to talk with you tomorrow about what happen."

With a sigh, McKay leaned back against the pillows, exhausted. Raising his right arm to lay over his closed eyes, he muttered, "I figured he would. Did he already talk with you?" At her low voiced yes, he added, "I suppose they went over and over everything?"

A shaky laugh broke from her lips. "You could say that. How are you feeling? You look much better."

"Oh, I sort of ache all over, but a whole hell of a lot better than earlier. What about you, how are you? Think that you feel good enough to give me a nice kiss before you head back to your cabin?" The arm came off of the brilliant eyes as he looked directly into the soft smoky ones.

"Oh, I think I can manage that. But I'm not going anywhere for a while yet."

A slight frown touched the firm lips. "What exactly does that mean?"

"Nothing to worry about. I'm just keeping an eye on you. What's the matter, trying to get rid of me already?" she laughed nervously.

"No, of course not. But you don't have to stay here and watch over me. I'm not that bad and I'm no child that needs a sitter." Mumbled Tyler, an embarrassed grin tugging his lips.

With a sigh, Jess leaned forward and then just before placing warm lips to his, whispered, "Just shut-up and kiss me. You are in no position to argue about anything."

And before he could voice anything at all, the breath was knocked right out of him with her kiss. Everything vanished except the feel of her softness against his hardness and the taste of her on his mouth. He didn't want to complain, hell, he didn't want to stop. Not even when his battered body gave a sharp twinge at a slight movement. Feeling her slight move to pull back, he tightened his arms around her and deepened the kiss. His body flared to life, beginning with a slow throb deep in his belly, but it had nothing to do with the bullet wound.

With a reluctant sigh, he released her, closing his eyes for a brief moment. "You sure do pack one hell of a wallop. You are definitely potent stuff, woman."

Cooper was thinking the very same thing about him, but managed to keep her features in a facsimile of innocence. "Good. Then maybe you will let me stay for a while, right?"

Gold-green eyes opened, looking directly into her flushed features. A dull red rose over the lean cheek bones as he answered softly, so softly she had to lean forward to hear his words.

"There's no way that I could send you away. But are you so sure that you should stay?"

Jessie leaned back and chuckled gently. "Why, I think that you are afraid of little old me. Come on, cowboy, I won't hurt you."

"Famous last words." Grinned Tyler slowly. But he was damn glad that she was staying.

Watching him, she finally felt herself start to relax. It was a relief to have him awake and talking. Made all the scary and worried thoughts disappear as if they had been no more than foolishness on her part to even have thought such dangerous things. Except she knew that it had been all too close for comfort to not be real. And almost deadly.

"Tyler, what are you going to do about the race coming up? Now that Fed won't be able to compete?" questioned Cooper slowly, sadly.

A flicker of unease moved across the lean, handsome features. "I'm not sure just yet. But I wanted to ask you something. See what you thought."

She could feel the muscles in her face tense as she waited for him to continue. When he didn't say anything, she prompted softly, "Go ahead. What did you have in mind?"

The green eyes settled on the tense, fine-boned face. "I thought we would work Rebel and pace him with Shiloh. Before you say, that he is a flat runner; I know that, but no one else does. I want it to look that way. But, in truth we will be readying Shiloh for the race. That is, if you agree?"

Silence fell softly over the room as they stared at each other. In that single moment, Jessie knew that McKay was going to put himself and Rebel in as targets for any trouble that might come up. Again the man was using himself as bait. But Shiloh as Jute's representative in the main race?

"You really think Shi could do it? That he would have a chance?" She questioned slowly, almost holding her breath.

McKay closed his tired eyes once more, then replied steadily, "Do I think he has an honest-to-goodness chance of winning? Jess, he out-ran Confederate. Out-ran him when he was running scared. And Shi wasn't even pushing it. He had plenty more left and he was carrying a rider. Girl, that horse can run. Different terrain doesn't faze him at all. He'd make a damn good endurance horse as well. Yes, damn it, I think he stands a good chance in the race. I think he could very well win it. The truth is I think that he could win the race with Confederate in it."

She leaned back in the chair. "You really do believe it, don't you?"

Slowly he nodded his curly dark head. "Yes."

"Alright then, let's do it." She smiled nervously, yet determination burned in the smoky eyes.

Chapter Twenty-Four

Leaning up against the wood-planked fence, Joe Drake watched McKay work with a young, rebellious colt. The piebald did not want to wear the saddle or let a man on his back. A grim, yet somehow pleased smile slipped across the straight lips at the thought that the head wrangler just might be tossed on his butt. Yes, very satisfactory.

The piebald was a large, rangy horse with a lot of power and had shown his bucking ability a number of times already that day. Besides Tyler had been working with the horse for four days, gradually easing the gelding into all the new situations. The cowboy had more patience than Joe would even think about. But regardless of all the patience, the horse still fought him at every turn. He was not a mean horse, even Joe could see that; but he was not in the mood to be gentled either.

Letting the sultry dark-brown gaze move slowly over the well-muscled cowboy as he stepped back, brushing a sweaty arm over his heated forehead. The other wrangler shook his blonde head and muttered, "I don't think he'll ever make a riding horse, Ty."

"I tend to agree with you, Jeff. I'll give him one last shot and if it's a no-go, I'll get hold of Jayme Wells and see if he needs a good bucking horse." Sighed McKay with a frown.

With a determined set to the handsome features, he walked slowly up to the young horse, crooning softly to him the whole time. Even before putting any weight into the stirrup, he had the feeling that it would be a short ride. And maybe a very hard landing.

Settling gently into the saddle the gelding exploded into action. Bone-jarring action. McKay had been declared in good healing condition by the doctor just two days before, but nothing had been said about riding bucking horses. The piebald, for being a green horse, knew all kinds of top bucking techniques. The kind that tested a cowboy on his ability and on his physical endurance and strength. And right then, Ty was taking a beating. At first the bucks were the hard straight up and down type; but now the bronc was going into his second series of the dreaded sun-fishing. That was where the horse did a series of spins while still bucking and coming down on one stiffened foreleg at a time, jarring the rider twice while keeping him completely off-balance.

The still slightly bruised ribs were beginning to throb after the second bone-rattling buck and sweat had appeared on his forehead and above his upper lip. Pain was sliding steadily up his side and into his shoulder and chest. He was sure that at any moment he would go flying into the hard-packed earth. Looking up he saw that Drake was still watching. A pleased smirk was on the darkly handsome face. Oh, hell, fate was not on his side.

Once again the piebald started the dangerous sunfishing. McKay could feel his teeth rattle, along with his bones. Damn, he was getting too old for this nonsense.

Coming up silently beside Drake, Jess felt herself tense as she watched as Tyler fought to stay in the saddle of the bronc. Feeling the amused glance that Joe was sending her way, she remarked off-handedly, "Didn't think I'd see you here, Drake. Not exactly you're kind of entertainment, is it?"

A nasty chuckle erupted from the dark-haired man. "You are right, not my thing. Not usually. But the chance to see McKay eat dirt is definitely a major draw."

Cooper did look at him then, the gray eyes frosty and hard, the fine lips firming into a thin line. "I'll just bet it was. You really are hopeless, Joe. I honestly think that you will never grow up. You are like a spoiled little brat. I'd love to see the day that someone comes into your life that means more to you than yourself and then just leaves you flat."

A strange look momentarily moved over the dark features. "You don't really mean that, honey. You like me too much. And you are a marshmallow when it comes to other people. Just look how you are all twisted up inside worrying about that dumb cowboy. I suppose he's not able to service you with him being wounded and all."

A red haze swept before her eyes and anger boiled up; the next thing she knew was that Joe was sitting on the ground holding the side of his jaw and her hand was tingling unpleasantly. "Well, hell, Joe, you've got a lot to learn. What I feel for Tyler is called love. Something that you know absolutely nothing about. I care what happens to him. Right now he is acting on the stupid side, but beware, because he is not a stupid man. And I think that from now on you had better stay out of my way and my business."

With a toss of the long red hair, she turned back to the scene in the corral. Hearing the muffled groan as Joe got to his feet, she smiled smugly to herself. Then as the gray gaze slid to the still bucking horse, the smile faded and was replaced with a worried frown. Tyler's features were pale and grim, pain apparent in the straight line of his mouth. His taut body was coming farther out of the saddle. He was losing the go-around, and he was paying for it with his body. He was going to get tossed, and tossed hard.

Seeing the jaw tighten, Jess started to slip through the fence. Then with a split second of ground-breaking bucks the lean muscled trail foreman was slung violently from the saddle to the hard-packed ground. Jess was already running toward him as his body hit the ground and then laid still.

"Damn, Ty, are you alright? Answer me, damn it!" She shouted at him.

He was lying on his right side and back, his eyes were closed. Jess was on her knees at his side, her hands running swiftly over his hard body.

"I'll tell you in a few minutes. After I get my breath back." Muttered Ty in a strained whisper.

Jess sat back on her heels, her small face was stiff with worry and anger. "Just lie still." Turning to the other wrangler, she ordered quietly, "Take care of the horse. I'll take Ty to his cabin."

Jeff nodded quickly, hiding a grin as he turned to the piebald. He just bet Tyler was in for one good tongue lashing from the redhead.

Placing her small, yet strong hands on his arm she pulled him into a sitting position. "How you doing?"

"Jeeze! Just fine; can't you tell?" muttered Ty, his voice husky and strained.

"Well, growl, growl. Big tough man, huh? Looks like the horse won, macho dude. Come on get your buns up off the ground, you're going to take a shower and I'm going to make sure that nothing more is damaged than your ego." Snickered the redhead with a muffled grin in her sexy voice.

Gently she helped him to his feet, then as he stumbled slightly, she wrapped an arm around his lean waist. Flicking a quick glance at the other wrangler, she said with a dry laugh, "Jeff, take care of the piebald and maybe you should give Jayme a call about that bucking critter."

Saylor chuckled softly. "Yeah right. Sure thing, Jess. Anything else?"

"Smart ass." She muttered with a grin and then turned to the tall man beside her. "So move it, bronc buster."

Tyler grimaced when he went to move forward, his shoulder hurt and his backside was smarting, and felt sure that when he got to his cabin that Jessie would lay into him big time.

Cooper had noted the way Ty moved and the signs of pain that appeared on his handsome face. But she made sure that she remained silent. He was going to get a surprise. She just hadn't decided exactly what. But she had an idea forming in her very vivid imagination. She could feel her face heat and tried to steer her thoughts elsewhere. Finally the cabin door was before them.

Tyler pulled open the door and slowly entered with Jess right behind him. It was dark and cool inside and he would have sat down in the soft overstuffed chair, except

Jess pushed him on toward the hallway. "No, go take a shower. You'll feel better." Grinned Cooper.

"Okay, okay. Quit being so bossy. Say, what happen to Drake? He wouldn't have wanted to miss me getting knocked on my ass." Muttered McKay.

"Oh, he sort of got knocked on his ass." Mumbled Jess.

Tyler slowed and turned back to look at her. "Jess, what did you do?"

"Nothing. Oh, hell. He said something not so very nice and before I knew it, I hit him." She snapped nervously.

McKay leaned his shoulder against the hallway wall and a smile touched the firm lips. "You hit him? Open hand or fist?"

Now she was pacing, mumbling to herself, then she said, "A fist, Ty. I socked the ass in the jaw and he landed on his butt!"

In a swift move Tyler was beside her, his hands on her arms. "Jess, it's alright. He must have deserved it or you would never have hit him." Then he pulled her to him and hugged her close. "What did he say, Jess?"

Pulling away from his embrace, she looked up at him, the small face taking on a stubborn look. "None of your business."

"Aah, come on, Jess."

She looked at him with flinty-blue eyes. "You go take your shower and maybe when you are done, maybe I'll tell you."

He stared at her for a few more minutes, then turned and headed for his bedroom. His sexy voice drifted back up the hall to her. "You drive a hard bargain, Cooper."

Jessie looked down the hall and watched him disappear into the room. She started pacing again, should she do what she had thought about doing, or do something else? She was so very confused. That nasty remark from Drake had upset her a lot. Every time he became defensive, Joe would bring it down to that. She wanted to, but she was scared.

Scared she would mess it up. Scared she wouldn't be good enough. Scared Tyler would find he didn't love her. She wasn't even sure 'how' to do it. What if they made love, then...Oh, for heaven's sake! Just go for it, if it is the right time, then it's the right time; if not, well..."

Her heart was hammering in her chest, the palms of her hands were clammy as she moved slowly down the hall to the bathroom. She could hear the shower, so he was in it. Jess sucked in a deep breath and entered the bedroom. Sitting on the bed, she pulled the boots off and then the shirt and jeans; leaving the pale yellow silk camisole and matching panties. Well, she couldn't get in the shower with them on, how silly would that be? So quickly, before she chickened out, she pulled them off and grabbed up a soft towel and opened the bathroom door.

The small room and the glass door of the shower were steamy and foggy, Tyler was softly singing a song. Jessie couldn't help it, she smiled. He was actually singing in the shower. As she clicked the door closed, she moved quietly to the shower. Another deep breath and she dropped the towel and slipped in with the very wet, very male man.

He was humming softly and rinsing his hair off with his back to her. She stood for a few seconds, just letting her eyes drink him in. Oh, wow! Then swallowing hard, she stepped forward and moved her hands around his ribcage and pulled her body up close to his.

At her touch, Tyler jumped and almost slipped on the wet tiles. "Jess? What are you doing?" His voice dropped to almost a whisper. "Jessie?" And he backed up until his back touched the cool tiles of the wall; and she moved in closer and the shower spray washed over her small, soft curved body.

Her hand moved softly up the wet chest burying the slender fingers in the springy dark hair. "I'm joining you for a shower. Do you need your back scrubbed?" Her voice was soft, husky and very, very sexy.

Ty felt trapped and at the same time his body was reacting to the enticing female that was touching him. A warmth uncurled low in his belly and moved upward into his chest. Muscles tensed and hardened and the hunger for the small woman exploded. "Are you sure you want to do this?"

A soft, gentle smile touched her lips and she nodded the soaking wet dark-red head. He stepped closer to her as she moved into his embrace. The water from the shower sprayed down on their heads as he lifted her slight form up against his chest and kissed her deeply and hungrily. As the urgency grew, Tyler reached up and shut the water off. Carefully he opened the shower door and lifted Jess's body up in his arms and stepped out.

Bending down, he picked up a large, fluffy towel and then stepped into the bedroom. He pulled the covers back on the bed and gently wrapped the towel around the small form in his arms. Carefully he placed her in the bed and then followed her down into the cool softness. His fingers traced her lips and down to the small stubborn chin, which he held still as he lowered his mouth to hers. Her arms came up around his shoulders, her fingers tangled into the wet black hair at the base of his head, pulling his face closer to hers.

As the kiss intensified, he moved his hand down over her soft, warm body; caressing the small, firm breast and then moving farther down over the flat stomach. Slipping his hand from her hip under her narrow back he pulled her up against his aroused frame.

Releasing her lips from the kiss, he took a shaky breath and looked down into her flushed, beautiful face. The pale freckles danced across the small nose, and the gorgeous smoke-gray eyes glowed with desire. Desire that matched his, and as her fingers drifted down his chest to his stomach and hip, caused his breathing to become shallow and erratic. Desire rippled through his hardening body and her touch sent flames roaring into life.

"Jessie, honey, I don't want to hurt you, but I have to know that you want this as much as I do. I want you so bad, I ache with it. I want you, all of you. God, I love you." His voice rough and raspy.

"I love you too. So very much. I want you...yes, please...Ty"

She whispered against his firm, male lips.

Chapter Twenty-Five

The room was full of silence, Tyler's breathing was slowing down and he turned on his side and gently pulled the slim woman into his embrace, closer to his body. As he placed a soft kiss near her small ear, he whispered softly, his voice shaky. "Are you alright, Jess? I didn't hurt you, did I?"

She snuggled closer and opened the soft-gray eyes, "I'm fine. I am great. Fantastic. I have no idea why I was so worried, except? I did it right, didn't I? You're not disappointed with me, are you?"

Ty looked at her with surprise and love. "Jess, you could never disappoint me, never."

A smile lit up the small face. "I was so worried, you can't imagine."

He chuckled softly, "I wouldn't bet on that. You have no idea." Then he shifted and pulled the covers farther up.

Once more, he glanced at her and then asked, "Okay, Jess, you said you would tell me exactly what Drake said to you to cause you to knock him on his butt. So, come on tell me?"

She turned her face into his chest, so he couldn't see her expression. "I don't want to." She muttered.

"Jessie?" He demanded softly. "Tell me."

"He called me a marshmallow. Said I would never be angry with anyone. He said I was just being spiteful because I wasn't getting...uh...well?" She mumbled, then stammered to a stop.

"Because you weren't getting...what? Jess?" Urged Tyler quietly.

Bringing the covers up almost over her face, she whispered stiffly, "He said because I wasn't getting serve... serviced by you. He has said that kind of stuff before."

McKay became very still. He then pulled the covers off her face and moved her away from his chest so that he could see her eyes. "That's not why you had sex with me now, is it?"

The small face paled and the dark-gray eyes widened. "No! No! I was going to surprise you. I wanted to make love with you ever since the night at the cabin. And in reality, before that; I just didn't know it yet. He said that and it was the way he said it that made me mad. I didn't even know that I was going to hit him until I did. We had been engaged, him and I. The only reason he got engaged with me was because I wouldn't go to bed with him and he thought I would, but I didn't. So he had his sister break it off with me. He was using me. As a stop-gap between the girls he really wanted. I was young and stupid. I thought he loved me, so of course, I thought I loved him...Wrong! I wasn't in love with him, I was in love with love. In fact,

I didn't even like him." She smiled with trembling lips, "I told him he had no clue what love was. But I did. Because I loved you."

"He better stay away from you or he'll be knocked on his ass again." Tyler remarked, a dangerous glint hiding in his tawny eyes.

"That's what I told him. I told him to stay out of our business. I don't think he'll be a bother, but I'd keep an eye on him anyway. He's always been kind of sneaky." Replied Jessie with a slight frown.

"I believe that." Smiled McKay, then as a thought came to mind, he frowned. "Uuh...Jess? Were you protected? I didn't even think. I didn't..."

Jessie lifted her fingers to his lips, "Yes, I am. I didn't give you much warning. Everything is fine."

Tyler lowered his head and kissed her still trembling mouth. "I love you, Little One."

She gave him a soft smile. "Okay, macho man. Let's take a look at this body of yours. You better not have hurt yourself trying to ride that bronc today."

McKay leaned back and threw up his arms. "You never forget, do you? Okay, look. I'm fine. Sore, but fine."

Jess grinned at him, then pulled the covers down so that she could see his side. There would be a scar that ran from the back to the front just under the ribs. It was still sort of a reddish color, but the doctor said that it would fade in time. As she ran her fingers over his ribcage, he sucked in his breath. "A little sore, huh? There is some bruising. But not too bad. Do you want some Tylenol?"

Tyler nodded his head, then looked at her. "Are you hungry?"

"Yeah, I am. Want to go to the lodge?" She grinned.

"All right then, let's get dressed and go eat."

She started to swing her legs out of the covers, then stopped; her delicate face flushing to a hint of pink. "Uh... uh Ty, could you hand me those underthings?" And she pointed a slim finger to the soft yellow pile on the floor.

Tyler looked from the 'underthings' to the small face that was blushing even more as she waited for him. "Those, right there?" He asked quietly.

She nodded, but didn't look at him. Until that is, she heard the soft chuckle come from him. Then the features turned stubborn, "Ty, are you laughing at me?"

"You're embarrassed to get out of bed with no clothes on! Now? Don't get mad, I'm getting them." And the chuckle became a soft laugh.

She pulled the covers up tight around her chest and glared at the handsome man as he leaned over and scooped the silky material up. Turning to her, he held them out; but just out of reach. "Here they are, Jess."

"Quit teasing. Ty, you'll regret this, I promise." She whispered.

"I probably will." He smiled and then grabbed her small frame and pulled her over to him. Then leaning down he covered her mouth with his. He could feel the heat flow over his body and settle in his chest. "No, I don't think so." And he moved over her small, soft body, hugging her close as she arched up to meet his.

The lodge was starting to get busy, guests and employees coming in to eat supper. Even with hustle and activity, the dining room remained calm and cool. A good place to relax and talk with friends and enjoy a delicious meal. Phil Holden was seated at a far table away from the others. Another man was sitting with him, an impressive appearing man. He was tall, older with a slight graying at the temples, his eyes were dark, but sharp and never missed much.

Both men were watching and waiting, looking for someone in particular. Then as the tall, dark-haired trail foreman and the smaller red-haired woman entered through the doorway; Phil raised his arm and motioned the couple over. The older man straightened his broad shoulders and intently eyed the younger man as he walked over to the table.

Caution flared in the tawny-green eyes as he let his glance roll over the stranger with Holden. "Evening, Phil. What do you need?"

Phil glanced over at the other man, then back to his trail boss. "Won't you and Jess join us?"

Tyler looked down at Jess and could see the confusion on her small face, but she managed a slight smile. "Sure, what's up?"

Both of them sat down and once again Tyler asked, "Okay, Phil, what's on your mind?"

Phil leaned back in his chair and tried to relax before saying, "Ty, this is Benton Chase. He's with the US Marshall Service. He's a friend of your father."

Tyler's face hardened and the eyes narrowed. "I remember you. I was pretty young when I met you, but my dad talked about you a lot. Off and on. What's this all about?"

Benton Chase looked over at the younger man and his smile was sad. "Your dad was my friend, my oldest friend. I knew your mother, also. Just before your dad's accident, he had called me. He had some concerns and wanted me to check on some things for him. He had said that he would give me a call when he got back, he'd hoped he would have some more information. I didn't hear from him and

I didn't know that he died until later. Sorry, I missed the funeral. But like I said, I didn't know."

McKay leaned back in his chair. A frown appearing on the tanned features. "What kind of info did he want you to look into?"

Chase sat up and coughed into his napkin, then looked at Phil. "He just had some questions. He had seen some things while out checking the northern boundary that bothered him. It concerned the Lazier outfit. Then when you got shot..."

Phil leaned forward, "I had talked with Ben just before Fed was let loose. He called me because he had heard some things from the DEA and FBI. So he wanted to come and talk with us. Then..."

Jess's soft voice interrupted, "You think this is all connected? Even Ty's father? His accident?"

"We don't know. But it could be. Let's eat, then we can talk afterwards at Phil's office. Alright, with you two?" Replied the soft spoken man.

Tyler sighed and glanced at Jess. She nodded and he turned back to the older man. "Okay."

Phil Holden let his glance move around the table, then he looked up and signaled to one of the waitresses. With their meals ordered, the general conversation included how McKay was doing? Then Phil asked about the horses that he was gentling.

Jess laughed and said, "Most are doing great, but the piebald done bucked macho man on his butt. And hard. I think Jayme Wells is going to get a top notch bucking horse. Right, Ty?" And she grinned at the silent man.

"I tried my best, but he just wants to buck. And no, Phil, I didn't get hurt. Are you kidding, she'd kill me if

I did." Joked the trail boss. Then as the redhead punched him in the arm, "Ouch! See what I mean."

Everyone laughed and then the conversation turned to guests and some of the events of the horse show and rodeo. Phil then said, "Some of the guests wanted to know if we could have a trail ride and camp out? What do you think, Ty?"

"Actually, I think we could all use a break. What do you think, Jessie?" Asked Tyler.

"Yeah, sounds good to me." Then turning to the other man, "Do you ride, Mr. Chase?"

"Yes, little lady, I do. Taylor McKay and I worked cattle together until I went to work for the Marshals and he married Ty's mom." Grinned the man. Then glancing up, he added, "Here comes the food."

From another table, Joe Drake sat watching the four people at the corner table. Looks like the cowboy didn't get hurt coming off the horse. Too bad. Then he raised his fingers to his jaw and touched the bruised, tender spot from the little wildcat's fist. Man, she sure surprised him. When he knew her, she would have never done anything like that.

Picking up his drink, he downed it and then looked for a waitress. He needed another one.

Drake wasn't the only one who was wondering about the four people at the table. Parker, Saylor and Juan Mendez were wondering who the large man was. Did he maybe know what was going on? Something sure was. Tyler had Jacob Sage go up in the mountains where the horse and the trail foreman had been ambushed. Jake was a wrangler, but one hell of a good tracker. He was also a Native American and had been in the military as a Ranger.

He could shoot a fly off of a coffee cup over a hundred yards away. He hadn't come back yet. But if anyone could find something, it would be him. Ty was worried that with the storm there wouldn't be any evidence left. But Sage thought he could give it a look just in case.

Juan Mendez looked at Saylor and asked the blonde-haired man, "Did you see Jessie slug Drake? Really?"

"Sure did. Don't know what that guy said to her, but I definitely know how she answered him. With a right upper cut to the jaw. Knocked him flat on his butt. Don't want to tick her off, believe me." Laughed Jeff softly.

Parker looked over at Drake and then remarked, "If he has any brains, he'll leave her alone. I think Tyler would kill his ass if he hurt Jess."

"Damn right. We all would. For that matter, if anyone hurt the Boss, there would be hell to pay." Promised Mendez quietly.

Jeff glanced at his two friends, then said, "I heard some of the guests want to go on a trail ride and campout. Think we will?"

Parker nodded his head. "Yeah, I think so. Phil said he was going to mention it to Tyler."

Chapter Twenty-Six

Walking up the path to Phil Holden's office, the four people were silent for the most part. All four were going over their own thoughts; the past and the present.

As they reached the door, Tyler went to open it and Benton Chase put a hand on his arm stopping him. Phil remarked quietly, "I've got the keys right here, hang on." Then after he inserted the key and opened the door, "Go on in."

The office was dark and Phil clicked on the lights. Then motioned everyone to sit down. "Have a seat. Ignore the clutter."

McKay eased his battered and bruised body down into one of the chairs and pulled the other closer to his for Jess to sit in. As she did so, Ty looked up at Phil and asked hesitantly, "Since when do you lock your office?"

"Since now." Holden said in a pensive voice. His eyes were worried. "I suggest that you lock your cabins as well, let the others know. It's for safety, Ty. We are also putting motion cameras on the barns, training buildings and stables. They will be running 24/7. This is not a game. This is deadly."

"He's right, you know. The DEA and the FBI are sending two agents. They should arrive in a couple of days. They will not be advertising that they are agents, nor will I. The less people that know, the better. You can tell the men that work with you. They already know something is up." Quietly stated the Marshall.

Tyler looked over at Jess; her small face was pale, but anger simmered in the gray eyes. Then he looked back at the older man, "Some of our trail guides are women, we'll need to tell them."

"No problem. You are a lucky man. Your crew would back you through hell, if you asked them." Stated the man with a slight smile.

"You sound like my dad." Remarked McKay, with a sadness in his eyes.

Benton grinned. "We grew up together. Had the same ideals and dreams. You look like him, a little taller. The same hair, black and curly. You know that when your dad was a kid, he hated the curls; until he met your mom. She loved the curls, so guess what? He figured they weren't so bad after all. But you have her eyes. She left us way too soon. By the way, she was my kid sister and you, my boy, are my nephew. Your dad called me 'Chase' and Phil has always called me Ben. So whatever you choose will be fine."

Tyler's handsome face was pale and the gorgeous eyes were dark with memories. "And mom called you, Benty. I remember, it was my sixth birthday and you came to the party. You brought me a pony, Jackson, and you gave mom a puppy. It was an Australian Shepherd. She named him Honor. Our birthdays were on the same day. I had forgotten. Eight months later she died. That pup howled for a week. He laid on her grave and we couldn't get him off."

Chase leaned over and put his hand on Tyler's shoulder. "I remember. Your dad took it very hard. She was his life, then he realized you were too. He was very proud of you, Ty."

"Thank you. Now, let's find out what happen. By the way, I sent Jacob Sage out to see if he could find any evidence of who for sure shot at Confederate and then me. I think with the storm there probably isn't anything left, but Jake thought there might be a chance. He hasn't come back yet. I'll let you know when he does."

Phil leaned back in his chair and said, "I've talked with Sheriff Cradling and he'll help anyway he can. We'll know more when the agents get here. What have you heard, Ben?"

"Well, we've been trying to catch some mercenaries that are doing all kinds of bad stuff, from drugs, money laundering, weapons and killing. But we need to get the main people. We think it's a crime family and we think that they own Lazier. It's a go between. They sent their mercenaries to the ranch for hiding, going to and from jobs. We even think that they have been moving weapons through the ranch. They have an air field for their two or more aircraft. They even have a helicopter. It's supposed to be owned by a corporation, but it's a shell company. Taylor saw some men with horses packing some sort of weapons. They were on Jute Valley land and he told them so. They said that they must have taken a wrong turn. But after he left, he looked back and they were still there. He crossed over to the next ridge and took his field glasses out and looked back over. They were on the northern boundary trail and moving north toward Lazier, but still on Jute land. He was going back up there to check if there were more traffic. He didn't come back. He also had seen planes coming in at odd times and just skimming over the tree tops. That was the first thing he had wanted me to check on. I couldn't find any flight plans for those times."

"Wow. What now?" Breathed Cooper through her clinched teeth. She couldn't believe what she was hearing, but it explained a lot. Looking at Tyler's handsome face, she smiled at him and squeezed his hand. He smiled back and she said softly, "Ty, tell him what Wilcox said to you at the dance."

Chase looked over at the young man. McKay frowned and answered, "He said that he heard I had been up on the northern boundary. He wanted to know if we had fences down or something. And when I asked why he was so interested, he said, 'just curious'. I believe he was warning me off. He said he was wondering how Confederate was doing. He knew that we brought him down. So in other words, they'd been watching us. I've got a question for you, Chase, why would a ranch that doesn't raise horses or cattle enter a horse in a race? They went and bought this horse to race in this race. Why don't you have the DEA guys see what's up with that. You did say money laundering. What about gambling?"

Phil leaned forward, his usually kindly face hard and angry. "Maybe they have a lot of money riding on their horse to win. That would be reason to get rid of the horse that could beat theirs. They would be laundering money and gambling."

"Not only that, but when Wilcox was here; ten to one, his foreman, Hunter, was here also. Sneaking around trying to find out about Fed. Or whatever else he needed to know. Dave Hunter hates Tyler. He almost shot him when I got my foot caught in one of his traps that were placed on Jute land. If it hadn't been for all the guests there, he would have. No doubt in my mind." Said Jessie, her eyes flashing blue fire.

Tyler sighed, then he added, "Besides, Hunter not caring for me; Wilcox probably doesn't much care for Jess either. She backed him into the pool. After reading him the riot act. He had expensive boots and a suit on." And then he chuckled.

It broke the ice and everyone sort of relaxed. Then Chase looked at the petite woman and asked, "You actually put him in the pool?"

Her pretty face turned pink, but she smiled, "Yes. And I never laid a hand on the man."

Tyler was laughing, and added, "If it was anything, she might have poked him with her finger in the chest. You should have seen his face."

Phil laughed also, then said, "I missed it, but everyone told me. From guests to wranglers."

McKay looked over at his uncle and asked, "Where are you staying?"

Phil interrupted, "He will be staying in the lodge. So will the two agents if they need to. Will see when they get here."

The trail guide looked over at the Marshall and asked softly, "Chase, would you like to come on the trail ride and campout?"

The older man leaned back in his chair, then smiled, "I would love to, if it's alright?"

Everyone turned to Phil, "Of course it's alright."

Leaning back, Jess watched the three men as they talked about some of the different things. Looking at Tyler and then at his uncle, she realized that the two men had the same wonderful smile. After hearing about Ty's family, she wished she could have met his Dad. Suddenly she wondered? "Chase, did either of Tyler's parents sing? Or have a good singing voice?"

The man went silent for a moment, then smiled that smile, "Well, yes. Both of them. Katie loved to sing and Taylor? You remember, Phil. He sang at the rodeos. The opening song with the National Anthem. And he sang in church, they both did. He didn't sing much after Katie died." Then looking at the young woman, he asked, "Why?"

Jessie smiled back, "Because your nephew is a heart throb that sings and causes all the women to melt at his feet. I'm surprised at you, Phil. You should have told him."

Holden grinned and shook his head, "Sorry, I forgot to tell you. That was one of the reasons Wilcox was there that night. He wanted to see Tyler and Jessie sing. Was a great show."

Tyler's neck and lean handsome face was turning a dull red. But then he said, "You should hear Cooper sing. She had the males drooling."

But then Phil said, "You should really hear them both sing together. I had guests ask me to have the dance and that was the main reason."

"Well, I'm going to have to hear them then." Laughed the man softly. It was really good to see his nephew, and to explain so much that had never been addressed before. He should have stayed in contact with them, but life gets complicated.

Just before the meeting broke up, Tyler remarked, "Tomorrow Rick Jorden is meeting me to check Confederate out. Take some x-rays of that front leg, he's still a little worried about it. I think he has a friend, an equine specialist that is visiting. And Jorden wants him to take a look. I think Rick will also have Kim Sheldon with him. She is a physical therapist in both human and animals."

"Jorden has his practice here at the ranch?" asked Benton quietly.

"And Doctor Collins has his office here, also. We found out that with guests and employees, it was smarter to have medical attention close at hand. It's one of the smartest things we've ever done." Stated Holden.

Laying a gentle hand on Tyler's broad shoulder, Chase remarked, "Like I said, you're a lucky man."

Jacob Sage was a quiet man, handsome and smart. And very good at his job. He loved being a wrangler and trail guide, but his Ranger training never was far from the surface. He had just about given up finding anything to give his friend proof of who had tried to kill him; then as the setting sun's rays picked up a shiny metal hidden in the thick brush.

Squatting down to get a closer look, he found a shell casing, and then another. Looking up, he saw the large rock overhang that would have protected anyone from the storm. Rising, he silently moved over closer and found where horses had been tethered. Three to be exact. And looking closer, he discovered a horse shoe.

Moving to the back of the rock wall he saw some faint boot prints. Pulling out his digital camera, he took photos of the prints, shell casings and the horse shoe. Then he put disposable gloves on and placed the casings and metal shoe in plastic bags. Turning around he looked to the edge where both horse and his friend had went over. It was amazing that they hadn't been hurt worse, just by falling into that gully. And if it hadn't been for the storm, they more than likely would have died. Maybe even the redhead.

About to turn back to his horse, his boot crunched down on something. Looking down he saw another shell casing. He put it in with the others. Pulling off the gloves, he stuffed them in his back pocket then put the plastic bags and the camera in the saddlebag on the buckskin. Then with a last look around he gracefully mounted the gelding and headed back to the ranch. He should get home by dark.

As he rode, he mulled over what he had seen. Even though the boot prints were faint, he knew he had seen that left heel mark before. Reaching down he rubbed the horse's neck, "Okay, Tango, let's go home."

Chapter Twenty-Seven

The buckskin gelding picked his way carefully over the rough ground, darkness enveloped the timber and ranch grounds. Jacob could hear the sound of the running stream as it flowed over the flat stones and rocks on its way between the lodge and the cabins of the ranch yard. It was later than the young man had planned, but not too bad. As he turned the gelding toward the barn, he looked at the two lone cabins. There was a light shining through the side window of Tyler's cabin. He would put Tango away and feed him, then go over and see the trail foreman.

Hanging the saddle on the rack, he stretched his back and groaned softly. He untied the saddlebag, made sure Tango had water and hay, then headed for the cabin. As he stepped out of the barn doorway, he heard a soft click and whirring noise. Standing very still he looked at the outside of the barn and there it was, a little red glow of a camera. Something new.

Hurrying across the small bridge he went up to McKay's cabin and knocked softly on the door. He could hear Tyler moving as he came to open the door; that was new, too. Usually he just called 'come in'.

The door knob turned, the door swung open. "Hi, Jacob. You just get in?" Asked Tyler with a smile. He looked tense to the wrangler's sharp eyes.

"Yep. Just now. There's some new stuff going on. Motion camera on the barn? You, locking your door. What goes?" asked the handsome young man as he stepped quietly inside.

McKay nodded his dark head. "Yes. We want you to keep your rooms and stuff locked. All the wranglers and guides. You saw the camera, huh? Well, there are more. On the barns, training building, stables, tack area and the enclosed horse shelters. It's for safety. I'll explain more after you tell me if you found anything?"

Both men sat down at the kitchen table. Jacob laid the saddlebag on the table top and pulled out the plastic bags and the camera. "Had almost given up on finding anything, then there it was. Rifle bullet casings and a horseshoe. Took some pictures of boot prints and where three horses were tied. There was a rock face that jutted out and gave them protection from the storm. I used disposable gloves to pick them up and put them in the bags. They should be able to test everything, maybe we'll get lucky and they'll find fingerprints. The casings were suck in the underbrush, so maybe?"

Ty rubbed his hand over his face and then through his hair. "Hope so. We have to keep this quiet. Just the wranglers, guides, Phil and Doctor Collins, Rick Jorden.

Sheriff Cradling knows what is going on and Benton Chase is here, he is a US Marshall. But no one is to know that, at least for now. At least two other agents are coming, DEA and FBI. They also will be undercover. They figure that Lazier is some kind of holding station for mercenaries and more. Jake, they think my dad might have been killed. He had seen some unusual things and called to ask Chase for some help. It's everything from money laundering to weapons, to who knows?"

Jacob looked at his friend, his own dark-brown eyes filled with sorrow. Taylor had been a good man. He had hired Jacob when no one else would hire an Indian. He was a friend as was his son. "What do you need me to do? We're going to get these bastards, Ty. No doubt about it."

McKay smiled thinly, "We're sure going to try. Right now just keep it normal. We know they have been watching us. So we don't want them finding out anything is going on. Right now we are trying to get evidence to get everyone involved. We'll know more when the agents get here. We are planning a trail ride and campout. I'd like you to go along. Use that Ranger training to make sure no one is messing with us. We've got to keep everyone safe."

The slender young man rose to his feet and laid his hand on his friend's shoulder. "You've got it, Boss. We'll do this."

Tyler stood up and followed his friend to the door, "Thanks, Jake. My dad was very proud of you. Always."

"Thank you, Ty. He always was there for us, wasn't he?" sighed the young man. "I still miss him."

And then the two strong men looked at each other, tears in their eyes and gave each a hug like brothers. It was like losing a loved one all over again. Then Sage turned and stepped out into the darkness. Tyler watched him until he disappeared into the night; then closed the door and leaned back against the wall. Anger burning deep in his heart and tears of loss slowly dampened his lean cheeks.

He was still there a few minutes later when a soft knock sounded. Wiping the tears from his face, he straightened and pulled open the door. The golden light from the kitchen splashed out the door onto the small, delicate face of Jessie Cooper.

"Jess!" He stammered softly.

She took one look at his handsome face and tear bright eyes and stepped up into the cabin, closing the door behind her. "Ah, Ty. I needed to be with you. Please?"

He opened his arms and she stepped into them. He just held her for a few moments, and she held him. Then he whispered hoarsely next to her cheek. "What am I going to do?"

She leaned back in his arms, tears were running down her cheeks and she said softly, "You'll do what is right. Just like your Dad. You'll do what needs to be done. And your ranch family will be right there with you."

He nodded and guided her to the large overstuffed sofa, then sat down. But he pulled her small body over onto his lap and wrapped her snugly in his arms. She was soft and warm and her scent was like spring rain, clean and fresh. Looking down into the soft, dove-gray eyes, he lowered his mouth and kissed her. It was only going to be a gentle kiss, but as the warmth of desire flowed through his lower body, he rose with her in his arms and headed for the bedroom.

Pacing back and forth in front of Confederate's large open air stall with an outdoor dry lot, Tyler once again glanced at his wrist watch. Jorden was late, and Ty was feeling tense and irritable. Which is not how the trail boss usually was. He was fine when he woke up with Jessie lying snugly in his arms. He would have her with him every night if he had his way, but...? He wasn't sure that was the right thing to do. He wanted more, but with all the dangerous things going on, he didn't want her to be hurt. Or if anything should happen to him, what then? He didn't know how to ask her what her feelings were. Jeez! He was acting like an idiot.

"Sorry, we're late. Morning, Ty. Are you alright?" Jorden questioned after seeing the strained, tense features of his friend. Rick Jorden was a tall, lean man with caramel-brown hair and dark blue eyes.

"Yes. No. I don't know. Sorry, Rick. Too much going on, I guess. Who's this?" Asked McKay at seeing the sandy-haired man standing just behind the vet.

"This is Samuel Baivers. We went to college together. He's an equine specialist in bone and leg fractures. I thought he could take a look at Fed and make sure I was correct." Then turning to the other vet, he said, "Sam, this Tyler McKay. One of the best horse trainers around. Now let's look at the big boy."

Ty smiled at the other man and then they shook hands, "Glad to meet you."

As they opened the stall door, the large stallion walked right up to them. Tyler slipped a halter on him and led him out into the walkway. Both men went over the horse. The gashes were healing, but they were deep, so were taking a little longer to close and grow hair back. Jorden pulled the mobile x-ray machine over and set it up so they could get a picture of the front leg. It only took minutes, then a few more while it developed. Both vets compared the two different x-rays.

Sam pointed to a line that you could see in the bone. "See this line? It is slowly healing, but it is a hairline fracture. He's very lucky, the bullet could have shattered his leg. He's doing well. It just takes time. Be sure he gets some of those supplements I told you about. They will help. I have some natural topic salve and a supplement that will help those bullet scars heal and help the hair go back. The stuff really works. And no drugs."

Rick grinned. "Thanks, Sam. We'll give it to him. I'm so glad that the leg is going to be alright. I was really worried after we took the first x-ray. He still favors it, just slightly. Is that normal?"

The specialist smiled. "It is. He's smart, just giving it time to heal. But, I have a question for you? I don't see any of your horses with shoes. But their feet look beautiful."

Rick chuckled and looked at Tyler. "That's because we don't use shoes, unless of course for a special reason. It's called Natural Hoof Care. Tyler went to a clinic to learn how to trim them. It's more than just the trimming, its nutrition, learning how a horse moves. The trim is not your usual one. But Tyler knows more, he does all the horses and is teaching some of the other wranglers how to do it. Right, Ty?"

"Yes. I had seen this man do this trim and he gave me a pamphlet about it. He had a web site, so I got on line and read all I could. His name is Pete Ramey. But he has trained others. I had a friend tell me about a young man that was doing the natural trim, so I called him. He lives in Illinois and has clients in South Eastern Iowa, also. I talked with him and I went to Illinois and he trained me. His name is Eric Knapp and he was trained by Ida Hammer. She has clinics in Texas and a few other states and I believe she is going to have a clinic in New Mexico. They are great people. You can't believe how much it changes the movement of the horses. They move more freely, naturally. It's called a mustang roll. You don't have a flat edge to splay out or chip, instead the sole touches the ground and you have better blood flow and solid, strong feet. You should look into it. We need more people to know about this."

Sam shook his head. "Sounds great. I'll tell my colleagues about it. I heard you got shot at the same time. How are you doing?"

"Better. My bullet wound looks a lot like Fed's. It's still reddish, but is looking better. I had some cracked and bruised ribs from the fall. You don't have any supplements for me, do you?" chuckled McKay.

"No, I'm sorry to say. Both of you were very lucky." Said Sam quietly.

"Yes, very. How long are you staying with us, Sam?" Asked Ty.

Sam and Rick looked at each other. "Well, I have no appointments for a while and I'm done with the clinic I went to. So I'm free for a few days. Rick said I could stay at his place, so I think I will. Maybe you could show me some of the trimming you do?"

"Think I could do that. Did Rick tell you about the trail ride and campout we are going to have? I think Rick and Kim Sheldon are going, aren't you, Doc?" Grinned Tyler and then laughed out loud.

"Yes, we are and I did mention it to Sam. Didn't I?" stated Jorden, trying to keep a straight face.

"Yep, he did. And, yes, I would love to. Haven't been on a horse in a while." Sighed Samuel.

"Consider yourself invited." Smiled Tyler, then added, "Sorry, guys, but I have got to run. Great meeting you. I'll see you later." He clicked the stall door closed, hung up the halter and headed out the doorway.

Sam turned to the tall Jorden, "You have nice friends."

"Yes, I do." Agreed Rick. "We can go swimming later." Promised the vet. But as he watched McKay disappear around the corner of the barn, his face softened and he was worried for his friend.

Chapter Twenty-Eight

After leaving the barn, Tyler headed for his cabin. He needed to get the evidence that Jacob had found, over to Phil and Chase. Coming up on the door to his cabin, he dug the keys out of his pocket and inserted it in the lock. Stepping in, he bumped into a kitchen chair that was laying on the floor, just inside the door. Looking up, he saw that both rooms were a mess. Someone had been in his cabin and tossed the place; looking for what? The evidence! Of course. Wanting to run in and see if it was still there, common sense stopped him and he grabbed up his cell phone punching in the office number.

"Phil, is Chase with you? My place has been tossed, you better get over here. I haven't touched a thing. Oh, and, Phil, find Jacob."

It seemed like hours that he stood there waiting, when actual fact it was only a few minutes. Hearing them walking up the path, he turned and stepped out. "I unlocked the door and stepped in. And..."

Jacob pulled on some disposable gloves and said in his quiet voice, "I'll check out the perimeter, see how he got in."

McKay looked at the other two men, Chase handed gloves out and said, "Don't move anything, but see if anything is missing."

The men slowly moved into the room. Ty moved over to his small desk at the corner of the room. It was built into the wall and even though the drawers were all open and everything spread around, he hoped they hadn't found where he had put the evidence bags. Where the desk met the wall, there was a panel that opened, but only if you knew how to do it. Slipping his fingers along the bottom, he pushed the small catch and the panel swung open. And there inside was the plastic bags with the evidence. Carefully he pulled them out and turned to the two men. "They didn't find it."

Chase stepped forward, "I'll take it and get it to the lab. Look and see if anything is missing, anything at all." Then stepping in close to McKay, he whispered softly, "Check for bugs." And then he glanced over at Holden, who nodded in agreement.

Silently they went through each room; and not one room was left untouched. Stepping out of the bedroom, Tyler met the other two men and then Jacob Sage silently entered the hallway. "How's it going, guys?" And the slender young man motioned them outside.

Chase nodded and then answered, "Nothing, we've found nothing."

All four men made their way through the cabin and then outside. As soon as they were out, Chase asked Jacob, "What did you find?"

"He got in through the bedroom window. He jimmied the lock then climbed in. He didn't leave much sign, but there is some blood on the window ledge. Some wood splinters must have gouged his hand or arm as he climbed in or out. You didn't find any 'bugs' inside did you? Well, I did. He stuck one in the top of the window from the outside. It's still there, thought I'd ask if you wanted me to remove it?"

The three men exchanged looks, then Chase said, "Yeah. We don't need him hearing anything more, let them work for it."

A smile appeared on the bronzed features, "Will do. Do you have a DNA collector? I'll get some of the blood. Maybe we'll get lucky. There might be a fingerprint on the bug, but I wouldn't bet on it. Have you taken pictures yet?"

"Almost finished, just the bedroom and bath left. Then clean up time." Grinned Phil. He was handling the digital camera.

Benton Chase sighed softly, "Well, let's finish then. I need to get this stuff to the lab."

Tyler slowly followed the two men inside. He was angry, very angry, and also worried. When he was done with the cleanup, he needed to see Jess.

Pushing her hat to the back of her head, she rubbed the gray neck of the gelding and started to undo the cinch. Lifting the saddle and placing it on the fence rail, she turned back to the slender gray, "Bet you want to roll, Shi, old boy." She slipped the bridle off and tapped him on his hip. He trotted off and then pawed the ground before laying down and rolling. Chuckling softly, she turned around toward the gate.

Pushing it open, she walked through it, then gently closed it and moved to pick up the saddle.

"I'll get it." Came the soft drawl from behind her.

Turning around she smiled, "Ty. Sure, thank you."

He reached past her and lifted the saddle and pad up into his arms and they started walking toward the tack shed they shared. She got the keys out and moved to unlock the door. Glancing at Tyler's tanned features, she noted the tenseness about his darkened eyes. "What's wrong, Ty?"

He moved through the door and carefully set the saddle on the rack, then looked back at her, "My place was broken into and tossed. They were looking for the evidence that Jacob found. They didn't find it. They even bugged the cabin. It happen this morning while I was with Jorden at the barn."

As she watched, his handsome face hardened and the gorgeous eyes darkened to gold. "Jess, we're going to stay at your place. I'm not going to chance someone breaking in and hurting you. We'll set up my place with timers for the lights, so they won't know I'm not there. Okay?"

She hung the bridle up, then asked, "Are you asking me, or telling me?"

"I'm asking, Jess. But, I won't let anything happen to you, no matter what I have to do. You understand?" He whispered in a low, harsh voice.

"Yes." She whispered back.

"Yes, you understand or yes, you will?" he pleaded cautiously.

"How about, both." She said as she went up on tip toe, to kiss the firm mouth.

He pulled her to him and kissed her back. Then he let her body slide down his. As her feet touched the ground, he sighed, "Wow."

"Okay, let's get out of here." And he turned her around and they stepped out into the sunlight. Ty shut the shed door, and taking the keys, he locked it. "This is getting old, fast." And he handed the keys back to her.

"It's lunch time, are you hungry?" Jess asked softly as she slid her arm through his. "My place or the lodge?"

Tyler frowned and slowed his steps, "Let's go to the lodge. We can relax a little and just eat. Alright?"

"Fine with me." She nodded.

They went down the path toward the lodge and McKay let his gaze sweep the area. He even made a mental note of who he saw as they walked. Glancing at the quiet woman beside him, he found her blue-gray eyes watching him. "I'm sorry, Jess, I just can't help it. I feel like they could be lying in wait to do, who knows what?"

"I know. But that's what they want. Just do what we do best. Our jobs. We'll get them, Ty, we will." She promised as she hugged him closer.

He managed a faint smile, and they went inside. It was cool and had subdued lighting. Looking around for a table, they saw some of the wranglers and they motioned them over to their table.

"Hi, you two. They have a great hot pastrami and Swiss sandwich. You'll love it." Grinned Parker.

McKay pulled out two chairs and the two sat down between Parker and Mendez. "Okay, you won us over. Good, huh?"

"Yep. Even the Mexican likes it. Right, Juan?" Laughed Roy.

"Si, Amigo. Yes, it is good." Chuckled the handsome trail guide.

A waitress came over and took their order. After she left, Jeff Saylor asked, "Hear anything more?"

Tyler told the group about what had happen that morning, the men were silent. Then Juan said, "They must be getting worried. I don't think they realize how much we know. They are too wrapped up about the race. They were after the evidence of the shooting of Confederate and you. So we just have to make sure we don't let them know what we know. Speaking of the race, how is the training with Rebel doing?"

"We've paced him with Shiloh about four times. He's doing fine. He's not Confederate, but he'll give them a run for their money." Said McKay quietly.

Chang looked up from his plate and questioned, "When are we going on the trail ride and campout? Guests have been asking me all morning."

"Phil said tomorrow morning, around eight-thirty. Should be a pretty big group and a few old friends will be helping out. You remember, Jena? She should get in tonight with her mare. And Jacob will be one of the outriders. If any of you see Toby have him get ahold of me. I'm thinking he could be the other. To tell you the truth, I'm going to enjoy getting away." Sighed Tyler.

Their orders came and everyone just talked about the normal everyday things. And enjoyed their meal.

Leaving the lodge, Tyler and Jessie headed toward their cabins. Jess reached into her pocket and pulled out her keys. Then taking a small key off the ring, she handed it to Tyler. "Here, you might need this. It's my extra one. How are you going to move your stuff over?"

"I've been thinking on it. I'll just bring enough for a few days, then as I need things, I'll just get them. I'll just put them in a sack, like I'm bringing groceries or something over. What you think?" He grinned.

"Should work, we did that all the time. So it's a normal thing." She smiled back at him. "Was it hard telling the guy's that Rebel was in training?"

"Yeah. But I really think they know exactly what we are doing. And why. They know Rebel, but I could be wrong. I'll see you in a few minutes." Replied McKay as he headed to his cabin.

Jessie stood there a few minutes, until he disappeared inside. Quite the man. Sighing softly, she turned and moved to her cabin. She unlocked the door and then she peeked in first just to make sure that everything was as it should be. Silly. Now she knew how Ty felt. Not good. But everything was as it should be and she went on in.

Then she stopped and just stood there, Tyler McKay was going to stay with her. All night. With her. Breathe, breathe. Shaking her head, she went into the kitchen to check the food supply. Thank goodness, she had just got groceries. Then she realized he would need a drawer to put some of his clothes in; so she hurried down the hall to the bedroom. Looking at the dresser, she pulled open the large bottom drawer and took all her clothes that was in it, and put them in a box in the closet. Then she shoved her hanging clothes over to one side, making room for Tyler's things.

Shoot! She was getting nervous. Come on, grow up. It is Tyler, her Tyler. And he loved her. How great was that?

Glancing in the mirror, she started to laugh. She still had her hat on and it was at an angle. Hurriedly, she took it off and went back to the front room and hung it on the rack by the door. She needed a drink, and a cold soda would work.

Chapter Twenty-Nine

Standing at the barns, Drake was watching all the activity as everyone was trying to get things ready for the ride the next morning. As he moved over closer to the doorway, he noticed a red pickup towing a large trailer of the same color, pulling into the yard.

As it came to a stop, a number of the wranglers moved over to the truck as the driver's door swung open. "Hey, Jena! About time you got here."

The dainty woman stepped down off the tall truck and a smile appeared on the delicate face. "Would you believe a flat tire? Twelve miles out. On the pickup, thank goodness. But I got it changed. All by myself."

Joe found himself moving closer. The young woman had short, straight black hair and when she turned her head, he saw that her eyes were an unusual turquoise-color.

Jena smiled at her friends and asked, "Can you gentlemen help me get Sand out? Is there a stall for her?"

Jeff slipped an arm around the small woman, "Yes, indeed we do. All setup and ready for the golden girl. How you been, Jena?"

The dark-haired woman answered, but Joe couldn't hear her answer as they disappeared into the rear of the trailer. A few moments later, Saylor came out with a beautiful, golden horse. She pranced and jigged behind the tall cowboy. From behind the palomino the woman appeared carrying some equipment. Looking back at the woman, Jeff remarked, "The end stall, Jena. We put water and grass hay in for her. Grass hay is what she eats, right?"

"Yes. Thanks. What time is the ride tomorrow?" Jena asked quietly.

"We hope to leave no later than eight-thirty in the morning." Answered Saylor as he led the mare into the barn and her stall. "Anything else I can help you with?"

Jena smiled softly, "One more thing, where do you want my trailer hooked up? I'll be staying in it."

Jeff closed the stall door and turned to look at the young woman. "Just pull it on over along the fence, between those two big trees. You'll have plenty of shade and a good breeze. The hookups are right there along the fence and across from the tree. Want me to move it for you?

"Would you? It's much larger than my other trailer. Thanks, Jeff."

"No problem. Are the keys in it?"

"Yes. I'll be over in a minute. Just want to put this stuff away." Explained the short-haired woman.

There was a cupboard with shelves right next to the stall door and she quickly put the equipment on the shelves and hung the halter on a peg. Making sure she had put everything in and not left anything out, she turned to go outside. And almost ran into the slender, dark-haired man standing near the door.

"Oh, I'm sorry. I didn't see you there." She apologized softly, and smiled.

Drake shifted, and stammered, "No problem. I didn't see you either. Are you here for the ride?"

Jena eyed the rather handsome man, then answered, "I am. I'm a trail guide. I'm also here for the Annual Horse Show, Rodeo and Race. I'm a part-timer. The name is Jena Canota."

"I'm a guest, my name is Joe Drake. Nice meeting you." Smiled Joe hesitantly.

"Well, Joe, nice to meet you, too. Maybe I'll see you later. Got to go get set up. Bye." And she smiled once again and moved past him and out the doorway.

At the other barn, Rick Jorden and Kim Sheldon stood talking to Tyler. "We'll make sure we've got extras in the second wagon. And Doc Collins gave a list of first aid things for us to bring. He gave the list to Kim. She can handle most things, and if something really comes up, Doc will have his cell phone handy."

McKay shook his head, "As long as we have reception. We all have cell phones, but most of the time they don't work. But, shoot, we'll be fine. How's Sam doing?"

Kim answered with a grin. "He is so excited. He'll be up and on his horse by dawn, if we don't stop him." She was a slim girl with dark, straight hair cut in a 'bob' and laughing amber eyes.

"Really? You wouldn't be exaggerating, just a little?" Laughed Tyler.

"All right, maybe a little." Sheldon chuckled easily.

"Are you two riding horses or in a wagon?" asked the trail foreman.

"We decided to ride the horses, mostly because Sam has his heart set on it. I enjoy riding, it's a lot more comfortable than a hard wagon seat." Smiled the pretty woman.

Tyler smiled and said he needed to find Phil and finish up some details and that he'd catch up with them later. The couple watched the tall, lean man walk off toward the ranch office. Kim looked up at Jorden and asked softly, "How's he doing? He's putting on a good face, but..."

"I know. He's okay. He's tough, and he has 'family'." Sighed the vet.

Sheldon shifted her feet, then questioned, "You didn't tell him what else was in the wagon. Is it a secret?"

His handsome face turned a dull red, "The guys asked me to put it in there and not let Ty know. A lot of the guests have been asking them to sing at the campout, so..."

Stepping into the ranch office, Tyler found both men there, sitting at the desk. They looked up as he closed the door. "Evening, Tyler. Have a seat." Greeted Holden with a slight smile.

"Have you heard anything?" He asked shortly.

Chase looked over at the young man and frowned, "Yes and no. The 'bug' never got hooked up, so that's good. The shell casings are from a high-powered rifle. They are still checking for prints, and testing the blood for DNA."

The trail foreman slumped into the chair, his face turning hard and remote. "So not much yet. Have you heard anything about the agents? Any idea when they will get here?"

Phil leaned forward, "They thought around 24 to 48 hours. The DEA has been checking out some information that they have just received. So the more info they get, the better."

Tyler rubbed his face then leaned back in the chair. "I suppose. What did Jacob do to my cabin?"

Benton Chase laughed softly, "That friend of yours is really something. Wish I had a man like that in the Marshalls. But about your cabin; he installed some motion cameras to the outside to cover the windows and door. And believe me, you can't see them no matter how hard you try."

Tyler chuckled softly, "It's the Ranger in him. The first night he came in with the evidence, he spotted the camera on the barn. He said he heard it click. He's a good man. My dad thought so. Jake was just a kid, 14 or 15 years old. No one would give a skinny Indian kid a job, but dad didn't even hesitate. He was never disappointed. We sort of grew up together, then he went into the military. He got hurt pretty badly around his sixth year in. Was so bad, he decided to get out. He called dad and asked if he could stay with us until he got better. Dad drove all the way to the base and brought him home. When he got better, he wanted to work with the horses again, so he is one of our best wranglers and guides."

Phil stood up and stretched. "Everything going alright with the ride tomorrow?"

"Yeah, looking pretty good. Jena was on her way, she could be here by now. Everything is pretty much done. Uncle Chase, are you coming along?" Tyler asked the older man.

"You better believe it. Looking forward to being back on a horse again. If you need any help, let me know."

The lodge was full with guests and employees. Talking about the upcoming trail ride and campout. The wranglers and guides were talking about the same thing, but not the same way. Rick Jorden, Jacob Sage, Parker and a few others were standing together talking with Tyler. Jessie and Kim were not far away, talking about a new saddle pad that they had seen online; when Jena Canota walked up to them. "Hi, Ladies. What do you know?"

"Jena!" They said together, "You made it. Everything okay?" asked Jess.

"Sand couldn't be better. I did have a flat tire on the truck on the way here. But, got it changed. Jeff is going to get the flat fixed for me." Sighed the cute pixie-like woman.

Jena stood and chatted with the two women and then as she saw the dark-haired man she had briefly met at the barn walk in with another couple, she touched Jess's shoulder and asked, "Do you know that man over there with the blonde man and woman. I think his name is Drake?"

Jessie had just taken a swallow of her soda, when she heard the name. Then she choked and coughed. "Yes, that's Joe Drake and he's with Larry Connors and Cindy Tanner. They are guests. Why do you ask?"

"I almost collided with him as I left the barn. He was nice." Said Jena quietly.

Cooper didn't quite know what to say. But, Kim did. "He was an old friend of Jessie. Not on the best of terms. He's kind of in love with himself."

Jena's turquoise eyes widened, "Oh. He seemed so nice to me."

Jess found her voice, "Jena, he can be charming, but just don't get too serious. Maybe he just hasn't found someone right, yet. You make up your own mind. Okay?"

The black-haired woman nodded, "Okay." Then she smiled and walked toward Drake.

Larry and Cindy had started to move over to Jessie and passed the small, dainty woman. "Hey, Jess, Kim! How are you guys doing?"

"Fine. Are you two ready for the ride?" asked Cooper.

"Yes, yes." Agreed the couple. Then Cindy asked, "Who was that dark-haired girl?"

Jessie replied, "That's Jena Canota. She is a trail guide. She used to work here, then she started showing horses. So now she helps out when we need her. Usually this time of the year for the show. She rides for Jute Valley on her palomino mare, Sand. She does reining and dressage. Top notch rider and a top notch horse."

Larry frowned, "I think Joe likes her. He met her when she first got here, and that's all he's talked about. I see she is talking with him. Hope she knows what she's doing."

Jess smiled slowly, "I...we told her about him. She's not easily fooled. She'll make up her own mind, but she won't take any crap from him. She'll be fine."

Warm hands rested on her shoulders, "Who will be fine?" asked Tyler with a smile.

Larry and Cindy smiled a greeting. And Jess explained, "Jena. She is talking with Joe."

"What? He better mind his Ps and Qs, or she'll chop him down to size." Then he chuckled softly.

"Kim, Jorden is looking for you. He's right over there." Tyler said quietly, then he looked at Jess, "Are you about ready to go?"

Cooper nodded, "Yeah, tomorrow is going to get here early. We'll see you guys tomorrow. Night."

Jessie and Tyler walked through the crowded room toward the doors. Stepping into the darkness, Ty pulled her closer to his body. "It's gotten cooler."

"We will need to get on the trail early." Remarked McKay. Then as they walked past his cabin, he said, "Chase said that the 'bug' Jacob found hadn't been turned on. That's good."

"Yes. I think Juan was right about them not knowing how much we now know, they are concerned about the race." Whispered Jessie as the neared the cabin door.

Tyler pulled the key out of his pocket and unlocked the door. Before letting her go in, he checked the room quickly. Then they stepped inside and she closed and locked the door. Looking at the tanned features and curly, dark hair, Jess smiled and asked, "Want anything from the kitchen?"

"No, I'm fine." He answered softly, then moving up close to her, he wrapped his arms around her. Bending down, he whispered next to her ear, "I'm only hungry for you."

Her heartbeat increased, and heat crept up her body onto her face. Seeing her flushed features, he bent and swept her small body up into his arms and walked down the hall. Reaching the bed, he sat down on the edge and sat her on his lap. Then his hands moved up her creamy neck to gently hold her stubborn little chin and his lips claimed hers.

Slowly his hand moved to her shirt front and the deft fingers easily unbuttoned it, slipping it off her shoulders and arms. Then he stood her on her feet and unsnapped the jeans she wore, slipping then down until they caught on the soft boots. "Damn." He breathed softly and quickly pulled them off, followed by the jeans. There she stood in the silky black camisole and panties, with the riot of red-gold hair cascading down her narrow back and over the slim shoulders.

He pulled her in between his legs and leaned forward and kissed the lips and chin, then just above the silky edge of the camisole and between the small, firm breasts. Sitting back, he let the tawny eyes flow over the delicate face as he slipped off his shirt and stood to remove his jeans; then easily lifted her and placed her on the bed and moved in close to the soft, curved body.

His leg moved over hers and his fingers layered into the copper curls as his mouth took hers in a deep kiss. His other hand slipped down over her small breast and farther to the sensitive hip and flat belly. Her breathing was shallow and shudders rippled through her.

As desire curled in his lower body and spiraled upward, he removed the thin silky top and bottoms and pulled her body closer to his. Hard shudders raged through the lean frame and his lips moved down her neck to the creamy breast, then slowly nibbled back up to her mouth. As the kiss deepened, her slender heated body arched up to meet his.

Softly he kissed her eyelids and nose, then hugging her to him, he pulled the covers up over their entwined bodies. Gently he kissed her soft lips and whispered, "I love you, Jessie."

And together they fell into a sound and peaceful sleep.

Chapter Thirty

Pulling Rebel to a halt at the top of a rise, the trail foreman looked out over the wooded trail the riders and wagons would be entering very shortly. Glancing back, he could see the first wagon and the front or lead riders. The scene caused him to think of a cavalry unit, they even had scouts and outriders. A faint smile touched the firm, male lips. Sighing softly, he straightened and made another scan of the trail and bordering terrain, everything looked peaceful enough.

Turning the sorrel roan back down the hill, he thought about that morning. He had awoke more rested than he had in weeks. Had to be the petite person next to him, she believed in him and gave him strength. He just couldn't let her down. Not any of his extended family.

Looking up he saw Parker riding up, and smiled a greeting. "How's it going?"

Roy pushed his hat back and grinned, "Doing fine. Can't believe how early we got on the trail. Everybody was up and getting ready by the time I got to the barn."

"Yeah, I noticed. It was a good start to the day."

"Which trail do you want to take?" asked Parker.

"The wooded one, thought we'd camp at Freedom Falls. It will be a totally new place for the guests, we haven't been there this season. They can even swim and the kids can play in the falls. Adults, too." Turning his head, he added, "Let the lead riders and wagons know, I'll go down the line and let the others know."

"Sure thing, Boss."

Moving through the riders and past the wagons, Ty watched for the gray gelding and his redheaded rider. He hadn't seen her in a while, and this feeling of dread kept creeping in. He was being silly, but...? And then there she was, looking wonderful to his concerned eyes. She was smiling and listening to a little sandy-haired girl. Really listening.

Slowly he moved Rebel in next to Shiloh and kept pace with the other two riders. "Good morning, Ladies. How are you doing?"

"Hi, Ty! We doing good." Smiled the freckle-faced child.

Jessie smiled softly, "I agree with her. Doesn't she look like a real cowgirl?"

McKay pushed back his hat, exposing the dark, curly hair and eyed the little girl carefully, "Yep, she does. Handles that pony like an expert. Good work, Carrie. You have a good time."

"I will, Mister Ty." Beamed the small child with a big smile.

Looking over at the trail guide, he said, "Can I talk with you?"

"Sure." And she turned the gray to follow him back down the line of riders. "What's up? Is everything okay?"

He smiled softly, "Just fine. Wanted to let you know that we are going to camp at Freedom Falls. How does that sound?"

"Great. I love it there. We haven't been there in quite a while. Good thinking." She grinned and the blue-gray eyes danced with light.

"Glad you think so. Tell the others, I've got to tell them farther back. Have you seen Jacob yet? Or Toby?" He asked, before riding back down the line.

"No, not yet. It's still pretty early. Catch you in a bit." And she moved the gray off.

Pulling the buckskin in among the timber, Jacob scanned the surrounding area. Rubbing the gelding's neck, he moved the small horse out onto a narrow trail that wound around and came out on the trail that the riders and wagons were traveling. He should meet them just before the trail headed into the canyons and ended at the falls. Hopefully, Toby will be there around the same time.

As he rode along, he thought about some of the evidence that he had found. He was pretty sure that it was Hunter who shot Tyler. The man had a bad case of envy and hatred. And he had blamed Ty for everything bad that happen to him, even his mistakes. Even though, Ty was just a kid. It was what Hunter thought, he never said it a loud. He also disliked Taylor, because the older man had seen another side of the man, a dark and sadistic side. Taylor McKay had confided in Jacob because he had actually become afraid of what the man was capable of doing. Not for himself, but for the animals and most important, his son. Jacob had never said anything, because Taylor had asked him not to. If the need to tell either Ty or the authorities became necessary, he would. But he had died, and now they found out that most likely it wasn't an accident, like everyone had thought.

Maybe he should tell Chase? He'd know how to handle it. Besides, both Tyler and Jacob had only been seventeen years old when Taylor mentioned it to him. Also the boot print he had found outside the bedroom window was the same as one of the boot prints from the shooting. The cabin invasion was definitely not done professionally. He was after any evidence that would point to whoever shot at Confederate and Tyler. His best bet, Hunter wasn't supposed to shoot anyone, possibly not even the stallion, but he had. And he was trying to clean up his mess, so his boss didn't get angry. His boss needed to get his horse in that race and Hunter sort of drew too much attention.

Yeah, he should speak with the Marshall when they got back from the campout. That made him feel better, the weight of responsibility was becoming heavy. Silently he urged the gelding on down the narrow trail.

Tyler had made the trip all the way to the end of the line and was making his way back to the head of the line of riders. Pushing the roan gelding up to the first wagon, he nodded to Gary White, the driver and cook. "Slow it down, Gary. The trail goes down into the canyons and it's rather steep. It's pretty wide though, so you shouldn't have a problem."

Moving on ahead, he saw his two outriders enter the trail, one from each side. He smiled and rode up to them. “Hi, guys. Every-thing okay?”

“Never better.” Grinned Toby Wilson and Jacob nodded agreement.

All three rode beside each other and led the wagons and riders into the canyons. It was like going into a different world. The temperature became cooler the farther down they went. At the bottom of the first canyon they went across the wide shallow stream. Then as they came out of the basin they once again climbed up into another canyon. The canyons were very unusual as they went down then rose up higher until they reached the third canyon; it was high in the mountain cliffs, yet you had to go down to reach the beautiful Freedom Falls. There was a set of three falls that were set up like steps and the final one had water cascading into a clear deep pool.

The wagons pulled in and the wranglers unhitched the two teams and then set up a rope corral. From the first wagon, the cook started to set up and his helpers started to gather what would be needed. The second wagon was pulled in at an angle to make a half circle with the large cook-pit in the middle. There were hitching areas for the horses and picnic tables and places for tents and campfires. Everyone set about getting their campsites set up.

About an hour later, some guests were swimming and playing in the pool and falls. Others were fishing just below the shallow rapids where the deep pools hid large fish. And others were hiking on the marked trails.

The cook, Gary White, had the large fire going and the outdoor oven was setting in the corner of the cooking fire. He had a large pot of coffee going and there was a large cooler with soda, milk and juice. Also bottled water.

The wranglers and guides had set up corrals and helped the guests with their horses. The families had tents and everything went up quickly with the help of the riders and care givers.

On the far side of the main campfire, over near the tree line, Jess set up her sleeping bag and camping gear. She was leaning back watching all the activity while she sipped a soda. Glancing over to her left she made sure the two geldings were doing alright. They had water and hay and were just standing with their heads hanging down and their eyes closed. They were the smart ones.

Over near the wagons, she could see Chase and Tyler talking. Then soon, Jacob and Toby walked over. Not long after that Parker, Saylor and Chang joined the others. Juan was over checking on the horses in the corrals, and near him, she caught sight of Jena and Joe walking together. Will wonders never cease? Then she saw Rick Jorden and Kim Sheldon move toward Tyler and the others.

"Looks like a meeting, don't you think?" Chuckled Cindy and Larry joined in.

"Oh, I think it's mostly men things. See, Kim's heading this way." Then looking at Larry, she asked, "Did you want to go check them out?"

Light red crawled up his neck and the handsome face, but he smiled, "If you don't mind. Cindy?"

"Go on, we'll have a girl's chat over here and we'll talk about you men." And she laughed softly.

Kim reached them just as Larry started over. "Hey, girls. Can I join you?"

"Sure thing. What's going on over there?" Asked Jessie almost absently.

All three girls sat down and watched the men talk, sometimes with hands. Kim smiled and glanced at the redhead. "Well, it seems the guests have been asking for you guys to sing some songs this evening. Some of the people weren't here when you had the dance party and the kids didn't get to see either. So the guys had Rick put some of the music equipment in the second wagon, but we didn't tell Ty, until now. What do you think?"

"Me? I'm okay with it. I like singing, especially around the campfire. We should sing a song for us girls. Would you guys sing with me? Cindy, you too. We'll have to get ahold of Jena. She was with Joe over by the horse corral. Any ideas on what song?" Jessie asked.

"How about 'I am Woman'? It's an older one, but I like it." Laughed Kim, her amber eyes shining.

"Fine with me. What about you, Cindy?" Questioned the redhead.

"I know it. What about Jena?" She asked quietly.

Kim got to her feet, "I'll go ask her. Be right back." And she ran over to the couple.

Jessie glanced over to where the men were still talking. Looked like Tyler was slowly going to give in. He always got nervous just before singing in front of people. Kim was talking with Jena, and Joe was just standing there with a funny look on his face.

Looking at the two, she found it funny that he liked a short woman with very short hair. That's exactly what he had found fault with when they were together. He said he hated her short hair and that she was so tiny. Well, Jena was about the same size, but she was fine-boned and short coupled, dainty, but a little more body. For a short person, Jess had long slender legs and a slim body; where Jena was small with shorter legs and a more square body and bustier.

They called Jess boyish and Jena is cute. Oh, well. Tyler liked her boyish, slender body. That was good enough for her. Then looking up, Kim sat down next to Cindy. "What did she say?" Jess asked.

"She's up for it." Kim was grinning from ear to ear.

"How about we go swimming before dinner? Want to come?" Jess stood up and went over to her camp bag.

The other two women nodded yes and went to get their towels and such. Jess had her aqua suit on under her clothes, so she stripped down and grabbed a large, fluffy towel. While waiting for the other two to come back, she applied suntan lotion.

As she put the cap back on, the two women appeared. Cindy threw her towel over her shoulder and said, "Well, let's go!"

And as the three women walked over toward the pool and falls, more than one set of eyes followed them.

Tyler watched Jessie as she gracefully walked to the falls, and the two other women. But his smoldering tawny eyes were only looking at the small woman with the long, copper-red braid swinging back and forth down her narrow back.

The suit she wore was an aqua one piece that was just as sexy as any bikini. The silky material clung lovingly to the soft curves and the color enhanced the red of her hair and added a glow to the lightly tanned skin. Remembering the feel of that soft skin and the scent that was only hers, his own body hardened with hungry desire. And he could feel the warmth spread through his frame and pool in his chest. Man, he needed a cold shower. He watched a few minutes more and then went over to his bedroll that was next to hers. It was going to be a very long night.

Everyone was sitting around the large campfire and finishing up their meals. You could hear the muted voices as people talked with each other. Tyler was sitting in a camp chair with Jess next to him; they both were finishing up their plates and then he took hers along with his and put them in a large tub near the rear wagon. Then he returned to the canvas chair, but pulled her onto his lap. Whether she knew it or not, the lean, dark-haired man was staking his claim.

Parker moved over to one side, near the wagon and the rest of the band members joined him. Roy played the lead guitar, Jeff played the keyboard, with Chang on the base guitar and Jacob on the drums. They started to set up the equipment, only this time they were using a special battery power source. When they were about ready, Parker moved to the center and said with a smile, "We had quite a few of the guests ask us to sing for you tonight, so here we are. We will be open to suggestions and if we know them, we'll try our best."

Chase moved his chair closer to the campfire and next to where Tyler and Jess were sitting. "I'm nervous and I'm not the one singing."

Tyler smiled, "I get that way every time I get in front of people."

Parker stepped forward and said, "Jacob is singing this song with our help and Ty's. Get up here McKay. Jake plays the drum, but he sings too. We are going to sing this old song from the 70's. It's called 'Indian Reservation'."

Jacob smiled and did an upbeat on the drums as Ty stepped up with the guys. Then Jeff started on the keyboard making it sound like a harmonica and then both Jake and Ty started the words. The beat was a good one and the kids started to do an Indian dance with the beat and the crowd started singing with them.

As it wound down, the crowd clapped their enjoyment. Then the four women walked up and Jess said in a teasing voice, "Okay, fellas this is for the females in the crowd. It too, is from the 70's and called 'I am Woman', and you gals out there can jump in any time. Ready?"

Jessie started the song, then the other three joined in. And then the women all sang the words, including four little girls and two teenagers. The crowd loved it.

One of the younger teens asked if Tyler would sing the two songs from 'Spirit' that he sang at the dance. The tall, trail boss nodded and then said, "Sure I will. But you have to join in. Okay?"

"Yes!" They all chimed in. The second song they really got into it, so much so they had to sing it twice.

One of the older couples asked if Ty and Jess could sing the one that they did together at the dance. Turning to the couple, Jess asked them, "Which one?"

The man said, "(I've Had) the Time of My Life."

Tyler looked at the gentleman who was holding his wife in loving arms. "You've got it." And then Ty sang the opening words and Jess came in when she was supposed to.

Then someone else asked to hear 'The Night They Drove Old Dixie Down'. "Okay, we can do that."

Everyone joined in and they sang it twice. Then Parker stepped forward and remarked softly, "This will be the last song of this evening. We thought we would sing one of the songs from 'Spirit.' But one we haven't sang before. Okay? It is 'I Will Always Return.' Please join in if you want."

Tyler's voice had the melody just right, you could feel the passion of the words and the love. As the song was coming to the end; everyone sang, from the old to the young.

"Thank you, everyone. Have a good night." McKay replied softly. Then as he stepped forward, a small voice called up to him and he looked down to see the littlest of the children. Her name was Andy, and she had pale freckles on the petite nose and bright red curls with green eyes. Her little hand had ahold of his jeans, so he squatted down so she could see him. "What's the matter, Andy?"

"Nuffin'. I wanna' kiss you 'night." Her soft voice trembled slightly and she wrinkled the little nose. "Is otay?"

He smiled, then picked up the dainty girl. "You betcha'." And after her lips touched his cheek, he pressed a soft kiss to her nose. "Sweet dreams, Andy." Handing the little girl over to her dad, he glanced at Jess as she stood beside him.

"Did you look like that when you were itty-bitty?"

"Probably. Except for the green eyes." She smiled.

Chapter Thirty-One

Gray swirling clouds rolled over the mountain tops and gradually were becoming darker. Another fifteen to twenty minutes and the riders and wagons would be pulling into the ranch yard, now if the coming storm would just hold off till then. Chase, Jessie and Tyler were riding lead as they climbed a steep trail up to the tallest of the surrounding foothills.

Chase eased his body forward in his saddle and remarked, "You were really great last night. Have you been doing the singing very long?"

Jessie laughed softly, "Singing, yes. We did it for fun and on some of the smaller campouts with guests."

"But recently we have been performing. That, my friend, is new." Interrupted McKay with a frown. Then once again he looked skyward, keeping check of the swiftly moving cloud bank.

He tugged his hat down and smiled at the redhead, "I'm going back down the line and make sure everyone is staying close. Keep them moving steadily, I don't really want to get caught in a thunder storm with all these people."

Both riders watched him travel back down through the riders. Chase threw a quick glance at the small woman beside him. "Jess, how is he doing?"

Jessie turned the blue-gray gaze on him and sighed softly, "He seems to be doing alright. But until just recently, he wasn't sleeping very well. He's afraid he'll let us down. He takes all the responsibility onto his shoulders. Their broad, but that's a lot of weight. He needs to share it."

The big man was silent for a moment, then laid his hand on her arm. When she looked up at him, he said softly, "You're in love with him. You know he loves you, don't you?"

A blush rushed over the delicate face. "Yes. He was my best friend, now he's my life." Then a small smile touched the fine lips, "Did you know that you have his smile; or is it, he has yours?"

Surprise widened the dark eyes, "I didn't know, course I don't see myself smile. He's got his mom's eyes and his dad's hair and looks, and you say, my smile. He's got the best of all of us. And he has you."

"Chase, don't you let anything happen to him." Demanded the small woman, with her heart in her lovely eyes.

"I'll do my best." Promised the Marshall sincerely.

"Well, tug your hat down and we have to get these people to the ranch, those rain clouds are catching up to us. "Let's do this."

They turned their horses around and each took a side. Cooper yelled to the first wagon driver to speed up the pace, but not to run. They were almost to the ranch gates. Everyone was doing as they were told and within minutes, they were all safely inside the gates and the wranglers went to help with the horses, so the guests just needed to get inside.

Tyler met Jess at the corral gate and took the lead rope from her and led the two geldings into their shelter. "Go on in, Jess, I'll get their water and hay and meet you at the cabin."

"Okay." She smiled and turned to sprint for the cabin. She just reached the door as the large rain drops started to fall. And then she had to dig in her pocket for the key. "Damn key! Come out. Yes, finally." Swiftly she unlocked and opened the door.

As she went in, she quickly went around to make sure the windows were closed. Then coming back down the hall, the front door swung open and Tyler rushed in. He pulled off his hat and the drops went flying. He hung it on the rack next to hers, then turned to her. "Well, it's raining. So far no thunder. Confederate will appreciate that. But he's not so bad when he's inside. Did you get wet?"

"Not like you, I just got sprinkled on. You look like you ran through the shower. You better go get dry clothes on. I'll fix us some sandwiches. Go." She grinned at him, then went to the kitchen.

"Alright. You are awfully bossy." Laughed Tyler as he headed down the hall.

Jacob watched the rain fall, at least the wind had died down and so far no lightning or thunder. But that could change. Looking over at the ranch office where Benton Chase had disappeared into a few minutes before, he thought he should go over there and talk to the Marshall. Maybe they have heard more about the evidence they had sent to the lab?

So pulling his hat down on the dark hair, he sprinted to the office door. Knocking briefly, he went in. "Sorry, but I need to talk with Chase."

The ranch manager and Chase were sitting at the desk, but more men were standing near the window. "Hello, Jacob. These men are the agents we have been waiting on. The tall man with the blonde hair is FBI agent, Brandon Cord and the other is DEA agent, Kevin James. Gentlemen, this is Jacob Sage, the man that found most, if not all of the evidence that was sent to the lab."

The two agents nodded and shook hands. "Nice to meet you. That was good work." Remarked the dark-haired James.

"Thanks. But I still need to talk with the Marshall." Replied the slender young man.

Phil Holden pushed his chair back, "Ben, you two can go down the hall to the sitting room. It's private. I'll get these gentlemen some coffee while we wait."

"Thanks. Come on, Jake." Chase said quietly, then Jacob followed him down the hall to the room. Stepping inside, Chase closed the door and the two men sat down. "So what did you want to talk about?"

"Dave Hunter. And Taylor McKay." Answered the quiet Indian young man. And he told Chase about what Ty's father had feared. And a promise that a teenager had been asked to keep.

"I wondered. Taylor had called me a few times and asked some questions, but he would never tell me why. Then just before he died, he called me for help."

"The DNA came back as belonging to Hunter. You were right. We still need to get the evidence to catch the big boys. But, I'm betting that they'll give up Hunter once he becomes a liability. Let's go talk with the agents and see what they have planned. Oh, Jacob, you need to tell Tyler. It'll explain a lot for him."

Together the two men walked back into the office and the agents started laying out the plan.

Finishing up their sandwiches, Tyler and Jessie rose from the table and set the plates in the sink for later. The rain had let up and Jessie looked out of the kitchen window at the receding clouds. Then as she watched, funny looking clouds sort of rolled upward. Looking closer, she realized it wasn't storm clouds, but smoke.

"Tyler, come here. Look." And she pointed at it. He came up behind her and leaned to look where she was pointing.

"That's a fire. No? It can't be." He frowned and went to open the front door. "Damn, it's my place. I've got to get up there."

"Your place in the mountain? How?" Jess stammered, then stated, "I'm coming with you. No back talk. I'm coming."

Taking one look at the mutinous face, he said, "Okay. I'll go get the horses ready. Bring the first aid kit and extra water and anything you think we might need." And he headed out the door.

Cooper stood for a moment and watched him almost run toward the small corral for their horses. She really hoped it wasn't his cabin. He had worked so hard on it and was almost finished. Quickly she went and got the kit and put some bottled water in the saddle bag. At the last minute, she scooped up her cell phone. Should she call Phil and let him know? She'd wait until they knew for sure. With a last look around, she pulled the door closed and locked it.

As she crossed the wooden bridge, Tyler rode up and handed her the reins to Shiloh. She hurriedly attached the saddle bags and swung up into the saddle and they headed for the smoke that was still rolling upward.

They rode side by side at a speedy pace. The rain had completely quit and the dark clouds were moving off in an easterly direction. But the closer they got, the more it looked like it was the cabin. The afternoon was quickly turning into evening as they had to go single file on the narrow, rain wet trail up the mountain side. The timber was thick in this area and they had to slow down because the path was slippery under foot.

They urged the horses up the steep, slippery trail. It was taking longer than normal because of the wet conditions, which made the going more difficult for the horses.

Halting the horses on a small clearing to let them rest, Ty asked for a bottle of water. Jess handed over one of the small bottles and he unscrewed the cap and took a deep drink. Before tightening the cap back on, he asked if she wanted some.

"Yes, thanks." And she took it from him and sipped the still cool water. Then putting the cap back on, she put it in the saddle bag. "Ready, anytime you are."

"Yeah, it's going to be dark by the time we get there. Or almost." Whispered Tyler sadly.

They continued on in silence. As they got closer, they could smell the smoke and every so often, soot or ash would float down. The horses smelled it also, and they would snort and shake their heads. And then they were there, it was still smoky and you could see embers still glowing in fallen timber that collapsed to the floor of the building.

Tyler dismounted and stood silently, then handed her the reins of his horse. "Why don't you take them over by the stream away from the smoky smell? I'm going to look around and see if I can find what started the fire."

Jessie wrinkled her nose, "I smell fuel. Can't you?"

"Yes, your right." Mumbled the trail foreman.

"I'll be right back, after I tie them."

She moved the nervous horses out of the smoke and ashes, and pulled out her cell phone. She better call Phil and let them know where they were and what happen. "Phil, its Jess. Ty's cabin burned down. We're up here. What did you say? Phil..." The phone lost the signal, but at least they knew where they were. She slid off of the gray and tethered them to a low hanging limb, then started back to the burned cabin.

Moving around a large fir tree, she stumbled on some small branches and almost fell. Then as she straightened up a dark shape stepped in front of her. One second she thought it was Ty, but instantly knew it wasn't; hard, rough hands grabbed her and slammed her against the trunk of the large tree. The force knocked the wind from her lungs, then he shoved her against the rough bark of the trunk and growled, "Where do you think you're going? Shit! You're a little bitty thing. What does he get out of you? Must be a damn good lay, huh?" Then he shook her. He was man-handling her with a deadly violence.

Pulling her small body up close to his frame, he stuck his face real close to hers. She could smell whisky on his breath and a gasoline smell was coming from his clothes. The dark eyes burned with rage and hatred. Fear washed over her in waves, her body trembled and she knew she needed to stay calm. She had to get away from this man.

He laughed deep in his throat and dragged her down the path toward the smoking cabin. His movements were angry and brutal. As he yanked her forward, he snarled, "Call him."

"No!" she whispered hoarsely, then he stopped for a brief second.

"Call him!" he ordered and shook her again. And she just shook her head. "I said to call the bastard!"

"Go to hell!" she spat at him, her gray eyes blazing with blue fire.

He glared at her, "You first, bitch!" and he back handed the side of her face. Panic flared through her and she kicked out and caught him first in the knee and then she slammed her knee into his privates. He groaned, but didn't release his hold on her. This time he hit her with his large fist in her ribs, pain shot through her.

Hunter finally realized she wasn't going to call out, so he yelled, "McKay! Get out here! I've got something of yours!"

Tyler heard the rough, rage-filled voice and ran to the front of the burned-out building. He slid to a stop at seeing the man holding a twisting, fighting Jess. Her small face was pale and bloodied, rage rushed through his body. Anger so strong that he could taste it, rose to the back of his throat as he stepped forward. "Let her go, Hunter. This is between you and me."

A sneer slashed across the hard, enraged face. "You stay right there, or you'll see the end of your sexy kitten." And he slammed her into the hitching post, causing her to cry out.

Again he went to move forward, and the large man shook her, then snarled, "I said, stay put."

Fear and anger shuddered through his hard frame, the tawny-green eyes narrowed, hatred shadowing their brilliance. "What do you want, Hunter?"

"I want you to suffer. Your dad didn't know when to mind his own business, and you're just like him. Got to admit, your old man was a tough bastard. He took out two of their mercenaries before they stopped him. No, I didn't do it; but I was there. They had to make it look like an accident. It was a good thing the sheriff didn't let that Indian brat go check it out, cause he would have known. He's one damn good tracker. You sure are one lucky ass; you should have died when I shot you and that damn fool horse. But, I think your luck has run out." And picking up his rifle, he motioned Tyler over in front of the burning embers.

Moving back next to the hitching post, he shoved the injured girl down on the ground up against the post; then walked toward the younger man. Pulling what looked to be a zip tie out of his jacket pocket, he ordered, "Stick your hands out. Now."

A muffled cry came from the huddled redhead, "No! Ty, don't."

With a savage kick, he nailed her in the side. "Now, I said."

Reluctantly, Tyler held his hands out and the larger man tightened the zip tie painfully around both wrists. Then he motioned McKay to sit down and when he stubbornly refused; Hunter stepped forward and using the rifle butt, hit him hard in the chest, knocking the wind out of him. "I said sit down!"

Slowly he did so, all the while keeping his eyes glued to the older man's face. The man was crazy. Panic started to roll in his chest and fear slid its icy fingers up and down his spine.

Hunter straightened up his large frame and backed toward Jessie. When he reached her, he bent down and grabbed a hold of her hair at the back of her head and roughly yanked her upright. Tyler made a move to get up and the large, angry man turned the rifle on him and said dryly, "Don't you move." Then looking at the red-gold hair he had twisted in his hand, he jeered, "Bet she's got one hell of a temper to go with this fiery hair. Is she hot in the sack, Ty, old boy? Does that little body of hers set your male innards on fire? Think maybe I should sample the goods? Only you might not want her when I got done with her. Oh, no – Ty, boy, are you getting riled? I think I'll just make you watch."

The younger man's face drained of all color and hardened into an icy rage, "You leave her alone. Or I'll kill you."

"Well, you can sure try, but when I'm done with her." Warned the evil, sick man. As he turned to grab her, she kicked him again, and he back-handed her, knocking the slight figure to her knees.

Tyler got to his knee and rushed at the bigger man, knocking him sideways. But hunter stayed on his feet, swinging the rifle around he struck Ty in the side of his head with the barrel. Sending the younger man to his knees, then Hunter placed a solid kick in his side, cracking the healing ribs again.

Jessie got to her feet and ran for the horses, Ty's saddle had a rifle on it, if she could get to it? It was hard to breath and a sharp pain knifed through her side. But she didn't look back, just ran.

She could hear the heavy breathing before she felt his hand bite into her shoulder and she spun around, bumping into Shiloh. The gelding snorted, his dark eyes wide with fear. Then Hunter yanked her toward him, slapping her face; and she cried out in pain.

Suddenly there was a squeal and a flash of gray and white. Hard, strong teeth clamped onto the man's arm and Jess heard bone crunch. Then there was a scream of agony. The man fell and quickly tried to rise, dragging his shattered arm. But the horse wasn't finished, he rammed his chest into the back of the man and sent him rolling, then stomped with his small, solid hooves until the threat didn't move. Gently he moved in close to the small redhead and blew soft, warm air on her cheek.

Jessie leaned against the warm, satiny neck and whispered softly, "Thank you." Then she stumbled back to where Tyler was. He was staggering to his feet. She rushed up to him, tears running down her pale face.

"Tyler? Are you alright?" She was sobbing and trying to get the words out.

"I'll live. What about you? He hurt you, I saw him. Where is he? What happen?" He whispered in a raspy voice.

She hung on to him even tighter. He was holding her up, and she was holding him. Then she whispered softly, "He's dead. Shiloh killed him."

Tawny eyes opened wide, "What? What did you say?"

"I said that Hunter is dead. And Shiloh killed him. He stomped him into the ground. I tried to get the rifle, but he caught me before I could; he slapped me and the next thing I knew, Shiloh broke his arm and knocked him to the ground and stomped him to death."

"Let's go to the horses and I'll get the scissors out and cut your hands free. Come on." She encouraged gently.

Slowly they walked back to where the horses were. She gently cut the plastic tie that had bound his wrists together. Then she got the first aid kit out and cleaned up his bruised and bloodied face, then he gently did hers. She looked at the injured ribs and he was afraid that she had either cracked or broken hers, also.

"We're a great couple. Battered and bruised." She grinned carefully.

"But alive." He stated quietly.

Jess pulled out her phone and tried to call Phil again, it was picked up on the first ring. "Phil? Slow down. Is anyone on their way here? Yes, you better get ahold of Sheriff Cradling and who, did you say was there? Okay. Hunter is dead, Phil. We're hurt, but okay. We'll see you soon. Yes, I know. We do to. Bye."

Tears rolled slowly down her pale cheeks. Tyler looked at her and whispered, "What's wrong? Is everything alright?"

"Yes. The two agents were there. The DNA was Hunter's, as we already knew. Chase, Jacob, Parker, Jeff and Juan are on their way here. I had called, but the signal died, but they did hear where we were and why. So they left right away. Oh, Doc is coming with them. Then, Phil said we were to stay put. And he...he, they love us." And she laid her red-gold head on his chest and sobbed. And he just held her, a tear slowly ran down the lean bruised cheek and a soft smile touched the firm male lips.

Chapter Thirty-Two

The room was fairly dark with only one small lamp on, the soft yellow glow only reached a short distance. Tyler sighed slowly, leaning his dark, curly head back against the sofa cushion. His whole body ached and his face felt stiff and sore. He was sitting in the corner of the sofa and Jessie's copper-red head rested on his thigh, her soft regular breathing, indicating that she was asleep.

Gently he threaded his fingers through the silky red tendrils, and again he eyed the white bandages on his wrists. He hadn't even realized that they were cut. But Doctor Collins had; after taking pictures, the doctor had cleansed them with peroxide, then wrapped them. He also had six or so stitches in his cheek, near the cheek bone where Hunter had used the rifle barrel on him. They were told that they probably shouldn't have cleaned up the gashes on either of them, but the damage was very evident; so it didn't really matter. He had three bruised ribs and two cracked. Jessie had mostly bruised ribs and a mass of cuts and scratches. Her beautiful face was bruised and had some bad cuts, but she hadn't needed any stitches. Thank God. Her slim back was a mass of bruises and scratches from when she had been slammed into the tree trunk and the hitching post.

Anger boiled in his gut and he felt like he needed to destroy something. He could still feel the rage and terror. He saw what Hunter was doing to Jess, but he couldn't stop him. So helpless and so very angry. His chest where the rifle butt had struck, was a dark purple bruise, Doc was afraid that it might have damaged the ribcage farther up; but the area was too swollen and bruised to get x-rays. Both of them had been packed with ice on their ribs and faces.

Chase and the Government Agents had suggested that he continue to stay at Jess's cabin, just in case Hunter's boss got nosey. They were going to have the Sheriff's Department handle Hunter's case. Hoping that the Lazier crowd wouldn't realize that the Feds were planning a full scale sting. They found an empty gas can with Hunter's prints on it and in the timber they found the Lazier ATV that the man had used to get to the cabin. They bagged the plastic zip-tie that was used to tie McKay's wrists. They took all kinds of pictures, even of Shiloh's bloody front legs and feet. Thank heaven for that gray horse. He succeeded where the human's had failed.

If not for that small gelding, neither one of them might not have been here. The asshole had every intention of raping and beating Jessie.

Shudders rippled through his hard frame, fear and rage still collided in his chest. If he had lost her? He couldn't imagine life without her.

Suddenly the small, slight body stirred and a groan whispered from the bruised lips. He could feel the tremors as they coursed through the slender frame. A pain, sharp and burning knifed through his chest at what she went through. Gently he laid his shaking hand on her shoulder and soothed her. She settled back down and snuggled up against him.

On the ride down from the burned out cabin, Jacob had told him about his father's fear and worry for him. And the promise his father had entrusted to the young Jacob.

Looking down at the delicate features, he knew he should wake her, so they could get to bed. They needed a good night's rest to tackle the coming days. But he doubted if he would get much sleep.

With his hand, he gently touched the soft cheek and whispered, "Jess, honey, let's go to bed. Come on."

The gray-blue eyes opened slowly, then she smiled very carefully. "Did you ask me something?" she mumbled sleepily.

"Yes, I said let's go to bed."

"Alright. Ooh, move very slowly. I'm so stiff." Then she chuckled softly.

It was getting late, and his drink was getting warm. Slowly he twisted the glass with his fingers, not drinking, just thinking. He felt so terrible, it was a new experience for him. And then he realized his hands were trembling. Because he, Joe Drake, had almost lost two friends; one new one and one old one. When Larry and Cindy told him what had happen to them; he had felt a sharp stabbing pain in his chest. How could that be? After the way he had treated Jess, and the dark-haired McKay; it didn't make sense, no sense at all. But, he remembered the hate-filled face of Hunter that day on the first trail ride when Jess had her foot in the trap. He would have killed the younger man, if he hadn't had witnesses.

He jerked suddenly as a small hand touched his shoulder. He looked up and into the dark-turquoise eyes of Jena. "Joe? Are you alright?" She whispered softly.

His eyes were dark and to the young woman, appeared haunted. "I don't know, Jena. I...I have never felt this before. I always figured I didn't need friends, real friends; because then I would have to help them when they needed it. I was selfish. Damn, I was an asshole. And then I met you and something changed; and when Larry told us what happen to Jess and Ty, I felt this awful pain. I so let everyone down. My sister, Tim, and the friends I had used. What do I do now? How do I make it right?"

The petite woman sat down next to him, then leaned in and placed a soft, warm kiss at the corner of the male lips. "You tell them how you feel. Then we will help any way we can. Together, we can do this, Joe."

"You and me? You still want to be with me? You don't hate me?" He whispered in a rough voice.

"No, of course not. We're human, Joe, we all make mistakes. It's what we learn from them that counts." She smiled and laid her hand on his. "Now, why don't you come to my trailer, and we'll figure out what we can do. Okay?"

He stared at her for a long moment, then pushed the drink away and rose to his feet. "If you are sure you want me to come. Yes."

The two dark-haired people moved slowly out of the dining room, and together they went toward the large red trailer. Out of tragedy, a new future begins.

Dawn was peeking through the curtains of the small bedroom, Tyler sighed softly and turned his head to look lovingly at the sleeping redhead. He hadn't been able to sleep much; every time he dosed off, the twisted, hate-filled face of Hunter would haunt him with images of what he had tried to do to the young woman beside him. She was so precious to him, she was his life. His very breath. The love he felt for her sometimes almost overwhelmed him. Not just the desire, but love.

Easing his battered, sore body out of the warm, soft bed; he went into the bathroom and splashed cold water on his face. Fear was still hanging on to him, and he had to come to grips with it. He needed to do something, outside in the fresh air where he could breathe.

So quickly and very quietly, he pulled his clothes on and headed out to the corrals. Pulling the door closed, he tugged the hat down on his head; the tawny eyes taking on a dangerous glint.

The ranch was still asleep, as he made his way to where the two geldings stood. At seeing him, they both raised their heads and whinnied to him; coming up to the fence and following him to the gate. "Hi, guys. Just a minute and I'll get you some hay."

With his arms full of the sweet-smelling grass hay, he pushed through the narrow gate and made two piles, one each for the horses. Both walked up to him; Rebel was his usual morning self, demanding a rub between his large dark eyes, but Shiloh? The gray walked up and then, he stopped and raised the fine head, looking past Tyler to the cabin beyond. He was waiting for Jess.

Tyler rubbed the satiny neck and murmured softly, "She's alright, fella. I let her sleep in. She'll be out later." Then the horse turned his head and looked into the tawny eyes, moving closer he placed the soft nose next to Ty's cheek and blew soft, warm air. "Thank you for saving her." Tyler whispered to the horse.

Shiloh seemed to know what the man was saying, as he nodded his head up and down, then walked over to the fresh pile of hay and slowly took a mouthful. McKay turned and made his way to the ranch office, nobody would be there, but he could wait.

Just before reaching the office, a slim figure stepped out of shadows of the trees, "Can I talk with you, Ty?"

Joe Drake stepped closer, his handsome features were different, more...something? Tyler nodded briefly, "Sure, Joe, what do you need?"

A faint smile touched his lips, "Forgiveness. I was a jerk, and I'm sorry about that. More than you'll ever know. But, how is Jess? And yourself? I'm so sorry about what happen and if there is anything I can do to help? Anything? Just let me know."

Tyler stood for a moment, but he saw the honesty in the dark-brown eyes. "She's doing better. Me, too. And, Joe, Thanks. I'll be sure to let you know if we need anything."

Then before either one of them could move, a smaller form came up behind Drake. "Morning guys."

"Morning, Jena. You're up early." Said McKay with a faint smile.

The small woman moved closer to Joe and slipped her slender arm in his, then looked up at the handsome trail foreman. "We were supposed to do this together, but I'm glad he talked with you. We will be here, if you need anything, Ty."

He looked from one face to the other, then he smiled, "I will. Right now, we need to help the guests with their training for the events. Main thing is to make sure everything stays normal. Thanks again guys. And, Joe, you should tell Jess what you told me. She'll appreciate it and she'll understand. Have a good day, you two."

Silently Tyler stood and watched the couple walk toward the lodge for breakfast. Maybe it would work out for the couple. He thought they looked good together." Slowly he turned and moved on toward the office.

Like he had figured, the office was locked and Phil had yet to arrive, so McKay went over and sat down on a wooden bench to wait. The morning was calm and the birds were singing softly, peaceful and serene. But the undercurrent was anything but serene. Tragedy, fear, and death. Whispers from the past, what kind of impact would they bring to the future?

In deep thought, he almost didn't hear the crunch of boots on gravel. Looking up, he saw Phil, Chase and the two agents as they neared the office door. "Morning, fellas."

Phil stopped with the key inserted into lock, "Tyler. Didn't even see you there. Come on in." Then he carefully turned the key and the door swung open.

Chase walked over to Tyler, he thought the young man looked done in. "Haven't slept much, have you?"

Slowly shaking his dark, curly head, Ty eased his tall, lean body up off of the bench and straightened stiffly. "Not much. Have you heard anything else?" Together the two men stepped into the ranch office behind the two agents.

Chase frowned, his dark-brown eyes looking over the handsome face, "Not today, yet. Sheriff Cradling and his men brought Hunter's body down, and the evidence that we left for them. He is supposed to be going over to Lazier to report what happen and they do have a warrant to search his quarters and where the ATV was kept. Of course, John will ask all the right questions concerning their knowledge of what Hunter was up too. But of course, they will most likely deny any knowledge. We just don't want them to know that we are here."

The other two agents were leaning against the desk and watching the trail foreman as he eased his lean frame into a chair next to the window. The concerned faces turned and looked at each other and then the FBI agent, Brandon Cord, said quietly, "You think you will be able to keep up the everyday routine?"

"I'll do it and so will my people. Hunter was only part of the problem. When he was gloating, he told us that my father had taken out two of the mercenaries before they killed him. They made it look like an accident. He said he didn't kill him, but that he was there. Hunter also said that it was a good thing that Jacob didn't get to inspect the scene as he would have known it hadn't been an accident." Quietly answered the young man. "I have a question for you. What have you heard from your guys about that ranch?"

Kevin James, the DEA agent, said, "Lazier is not classified as a hunting lodge, but is a gun club. They have an extensive firing range and equipment. But they do have a hunting permit, so they can have certain weapons and can hunt in season. Just covering their butts. Of course they have a landing strip. Our guys have some intel concerning this race that's coming up. Wilcox has a lot of money riding on this. The word is that they'll be using the money that needs to laundered, that way they can get fresh money back; but only if their horse wins. We also heard some scuttlebutt about some mercenaries bringing a load of weapons at the same time. They could be stinger missiles. But the main word is that some big boss is bringing the money, or possibly two. One for sure from New York and the other from Chicago. Something big is definitely going down. We think we will need to wait until after the race. Do you still have a horse to enter?"

McKay glanced intently at the two men, then replied carefully, "I believe so. But what we are doing is; well, we are going to do a switch. We are going to let them think we are entering one horse when we are going to enter another. And I think the horse we do enter will win. But they won't have a clue, until it's too late."

The honey-blonde haired Cord, frowned and asked, "Do you think that is wise?"

Tyler's handsome face hardened, the tawny eyes burning with determination, he remarked dryly, "They already tried to get rid of the horse they thought would win, I'm making sure they don't this time. If they watch our training, they'll think the times will not be a threat to their horse. I'm making sure of that."

Phil Holden coughed softly, "Tyler, the Fair Board called and asked if you, Jess and the wranglers would do numbers for the opening show? I told them I'd ask. But, it's up to you. If you will they want it to be from the 'Spirit' movie. That's the theme for the fair this year. Also, they wondered if you'd do the song, 'God Bless the USA' by Lee Greenwood, right after the National Anthem for the Rodeo? Not just you, the whole group."

"I'll have to ask the others, then I'll let you know." Sighed the weary young man. Then looking at the tall man sitting next to him, he asked quietly, "Uncle Chase, you've been very quiet. You want to say anything?"

Benton Chase leaned back in the wooden chair that he was sitting in and then said, "What about the plane sightings that Ty's father had sent me? What did they find out?" And he eyed the other two agents.

They both looked a little uneasy. "We couldn't find any flight plans from this end, but after some digging; an agent found that they were filed in New York and then another one was set up in Canada. And once we found them, we have been monitoring them. That's how we found out about this upcoming deal."

Before Tyler could say anything, Chase said, "It's too bad that we couldn't have taken what he had said with more importance, before they killed him. Think of all the lives that would have been saved." Then the US Marshall stood up and said, "Excuse me, I need some air." And he walked out of the office.

McKay scanned one face and then the other, rising up out of the chair, "If you don't need anything else, I'll go check on Jessie."

The two agents stayed silent, but then Phil remarked softly, "I'll talk to you later. Let me know what you decide on the songs. Get some rest, Ty."

Tyler nodded, but said nothing. Then pulled the door closed behind him.

Chapter Thirty-Three

As Tyler walked out of the ranch office, Chase looked over and then rose from the bench and moved over to him. "We'll make this right. The good guys are going to win. You take care of that young woman, your father would have loved her." And he laid a large, gentle hand on the younger man's shoulder.

"Yes, he would have. He would have asked me why I took so long to realize it. Thanks, Uncle Chase." Replied Tyler with a slight smile.

Both men walked together down the gravel path toward the lodge and then the cabins. When they reached the path that went to the lodge, both men stopped. "I'm going to go and check on Jessie and if she wants breakfast we'll join you shortly. Say, Chase, do you know anyone who does specialty rings?"

The older man's dark eyes widened and then he smiled, "I might. For Jess?"

"Ah huh. But I want something special." Sighed the dark-haired man nervously.

"Let me check and I'll let you know. You might want to ask Jacob, he has a friend that designs jewelry." Grinned the tall, older man.

"Okay, I'll do that. See you shortly." The tall, lean muscled cowboy took off down the path to the cabins.

Tyler smiled. Jacob has a friend that designs jewelry. Wow! He'd have to ask him later. Right now, he wanted to get to Jess.

Stretching out her arms, Jessie turned her burnished head and slowly opened her eyes. Then not seeing Ty's muscled body, she sat up and listened. Maybe he was in the kitchen? Slowly she managed to swing her legs over the side of the bed, and eased to a stand. Her legs were so stiff that she almost staggered into the bathroom. Looking into the mirror, she flinched when she saw her bruised face. Boy! You are a beauty. Maybe I should wear a brown paper bag? Then she chuckled softly.

She rinsed out her dry mouth and carefully washed the sore face. Deciding to wait on the shower, she went in the bedroom and dug out some clothes. Even that was hard to do, pulling her socks on caused a knifing pain to stab through her right side. At this rate, it would take her hours just to get dressed.

Sitting there looking at the second sock dangling from her fingers, she heard the front door close. Hopefully it was Tyler. And then she heard his voice, "Need some help, small fry?"

"Small fry? Well, maybe not." She frowned. "Yes, I need help."

Tyler moved to the foot of the bed and took the sock out of her hand, slipping it on, his hand softly moved up the smooth, slender leg to her thigh. Seeing the soft gray-blue eyes widen, he moved his body in between her legs, leaned down over her forcing her to lay back. He smiled gently and leaned even closer, placing a soft, warm kiss on the corner of her mouth where there were no injuries. "Morning."

She smiled carefully, her hands on his chest, "Morning, yourself. What time did you get up?"

"Early. Took care of Reb and Shi, then went over and waited for Phil to get to the office. Chase and the two agents were with him. We talked a little while, then I came back to see if you were up and if you want to go get breakfast?"

"As soon as someone helps me get dressed. How do you do it? I can hardly move with my sore ribs. And they're bruised; yours are cracked?" she mumbled.

"I'm used to it and I didn't get slammed into a tree or post. But the bruised ribs almost hurt worse than the cracked ones. The bruising is more extensive." Then he picked up the jeans, "These?"

She nodded the red-gold head. "Yep."

Very gently he slipped the legs of the jeans over the small feet and then carefully stood her up and pulled them to her hips. He picked up the soft aqua shirt with sleeves and slipped it on her, then he slowly buttoned the front. "Where's your boots?"

She grinned and pointed to the closet. "The taupe ones. They're easier to get on. I'll need you to do a couple more things for me."

He grabbed the boots and looked back at her, "Well, sure."

The boots went on fairly simply and then he asked, "So what next?"

She lowered the small face and stared at the toe of her boot, then mumbled quietly, "Could you brush my hair?"

He stood and looked at the small woman, then went over to the dresser and picked up the brush she used on the long wavy hair. Walking back over to the bed, he sat down behind her and as he went to apply the brush to the copper hair, hesitated. "Uh...uh, Jess, how do I...?"

"Just start at the front and pull the brush straight back, go from one side to the other; do the front half and then do the rest. When you get done with the brush, just take your fingers and run them through it. That loosens the hair so it falls into place. You're doing fine." She chuckled softly.

As he pulled the brush through the silky hair, he discovered he enjoyed brushing her hair. Then he ran his fingers through it and just as she had said it bounced into place. Getting off the bed, he set the brush back on the dresser and went back to her. "Okay, what else?"

"Can you roll the sleeves up to my elbows? That should cover the bruises, or most of them." She asked softly, almost in a whisper.

"Sure." He did the right one, then the left. "There, all done. We better go, Uncle Chase is waiting."

"Well, Jeez! Why didn't you say so?" She grinned.

Leaning back in his chair, Chase set his coffee cup down. Then he glanced at his watch, he hoped the young couple came soon. He had just put his order in, but it wouldn't take long to fix. Once more he looked at the doors and there they were. Silently, he watched them walk toward his table. His nephew's handsome face was stitched up and bruised and the little redhead's delicate face was bruised and scratched. Anger bubbled to the surface and the older man quickly put a damper on it. Now was not the time or place. He turned and smiled at the couple as Tyler pulled out a chair for Jessie, then sat next to her.

"Morning, you two. I just ordered and here comes the waitress for your orders." Stated Chase softly.

Connie, the waitress came over and took their orders, then before leaving the young girl said quietly, "We're so glad that you two are okay." Then she turned and went to the kitchen area.

Looking at the couple, the older man asked, "Ty, have you told Jess what Phil asked you?"

"No, not yet." Smiled McKay.

Jessie looked first at Tyler, then his uncle. "What's up?"

"The Fair Board wants us to do the opening show. Then at the rodeo, after the Anthem, they want us to sing 'God Bless the USA'. The theme for the Fair is 'Spirit' from the movie. I need to ask the guys, yet. What do you think?" Softly explained the trail foreman.

"It's alright with me, if the fellas agree and if my face looks better. What about you, do you want to?" she asked.

"I think it's kind of nice to be asked. I would if everyone agrees." Sighed Tyler.

Then Connie came with their orders. And all three started to eat their breakfast. While eating, the two men informed the young woman what the agents had said about Lazier. And then Tyler told her that they had asked if they were going to enter a horse in the race. She had agreed with him when he told what he had said.

Then Jessie asked, "What do you think about doing something at the rodeo?"

Tyler raised an eyebrow. "What kind of something?"

"Well, Jena was going to do a demonstration; but we were wondering if we could do a western version of a dressage drill team show. About six to eight of us. We'd have to practice, and Jena could teach us what we need to know. We'll do it to music. What do you think?" Jessie asked as she absently brushed the red hair back off of her face.

"I don't know. We'll talk to Jena and then we'll see who will want to do it. We'll see. You know that's a lot to do, and a little time to do it." Sighed Tyler.

Chase leaned forward, "And the agents wanted to know if you could keep up the everyday routine? Wait until they see what all you do."

Tyler looked over at the older man, then said softly, "It's better to be busy."

"That may be true; but you, my boy, need to get some sleep. See that you do. Now, I've got to go. I'll talk to you later. Take it easy, you two." Smiled the tall man.

Watching Chase walk out the doors, Jessie looked at the weary features of the dark-haired man. "Is that why you were up early?"

The young man leaned back and closed his eyes, "Yeah, couldn't sleep. Kept seeing Hunter's face and what he tried to..."

"But we made it. He didn't." Stated the redhead softly and laid her small hand on his.

The tawny-green eyes opened and he smiled. "I know."

After finishing their breakfast, they went outside and walked silently down the path. Finally Tyler said, "You better go see Shiloh, I promised him that you would see him this morning."

She smiled at him. "Okay. Don't want him to think that you lied to him. Where are you going?"

"I'll go talk to the guys and see if they want to do the songs for the fair. And then when you get done, we'll go talk with Jena. Okay?" He asked.

"Sounds good to me. See you shortly." And she headed for the corral.

Tyler watched her go and then he decided to find Jacob first, then the other guys. He wanted to ask him about that friend of his. Quickly he headed for the barns. Coming around the corner, there was the very man he was looking for. "Hey, Jake! I need to talk to you."

The young slim man set down the bridle he was working on and walked over to the trail foreman. "How are you two doing?"

"We're doing. But I heard that you have a friend that designs jewelry. What about rings?" Asked Tyler almost impatiently.

The Indian looked at his friend, then smiled slowly, "Yes, I have a friend that does that, and she does rings. She is very good. You need a ring? Or is it a friend?"

"It's for me. For Jessie; but you have to promise not to tell anyone, especially Jess." Pleaded the tall young man.

"You going to ask her to marry you?" Asked Jacob quietly. His face breaking into a smile.

"Yes!" Whispered the trail boss. "I want something special for her. Do you think your friend would make one for me?"

"I'm sure she would. I'll give her a call and I'll let you know. You know her, Ty. It's Skye. She does amazing work." Grinned Sage.

"The little Navajo girl that was always following us around?" asked Tyler.

"Yep. But she's all grown up. Still not very tall. Little taller than Jess." Acknowledged the slender young man.

"Okay, you get ahold of her and then let me know. Do you know where the other guys are?" asked McKay.

"Over in the training barn helping the guests with their horses for the show. What's up?"

"Well, the Fair Board wants us to sing at the opening and at the rodeo after the Anthem. Can you come with me and I'll explain more?" Questioned the trail foreman.

"Sure, let's go." Grinned the young man. "It's getting interesting."

Chapter Thirty-Four

The lodge was humming with soft chatter, from the guests, from the employees; and all were talking about the upcoming horse show and Rodeo and of course, the race. The lighting was muted and soft music was playing in the background.

The days had seemed to fly by, the second day after the cabin fire, Tyler was surprised by the insurance agents that had been up to the burned out structure. They had a check for him, not a large one, but it would cover the materials he had used to build the cabin. The ranch owners had put insurance on it and he hadn't known.

The insurance agents had asked him if he would rebuild, but he hadn't even thought about it. Thinking for a few moments he had looked up at the two men and slowly shook his head. "No, I don't think so, not there anyway. I really don't want to remember that night."

The agents nodded sadly, then had left. But before they had got into the car, they had stopped at the ranch office. Now, sitting at the bar, he thought about it once again. No, not up on the mountain again. He had another parcel of land closer to the ranch; maybe that would be better?

Sipping his soda, he glanced again at the doors. He was waiting on Jacob and Skye; and hoping that they would get there soon. Before Jessie arrived. She wasn't due for another twenty to thirty minutes; but he had been waiting for the two for over thirty minutes.

He had talked with Skye and had told her what he had wanted, well, sort of. She had made some drawings of rings and one in particular had caught his eye. Then they had to decide what kind of gem to put in the recessed setting. She had used Black hills Gold. And if the rings turned out half as good as the drawing, it would be perfect.

Jacob had been right when he had said that Skye had grown up. She had long straight, blue-black hair and the most gorgeous chocolate-brown eyes. Ty grinned, as he had watched his friend and the young woman together, he knew. They were a couple, even if they didn't know it yet. It must be in the air? And then he chuckled softly to himself.

Looking up once again, and to his relief; the couple was walking toward him. Both were smiling as they stepped up close to him. "About time, you guys. So did you get them done?"

Skye, her beautiful face aglow, whispered softly, "Yes, I finished them late last night. Here is her ring." Her small bronzed hand held a tiny cream-colored box.

Tyler took it from her and opened the lid. It was lying on an aqua satin cushion. The band was the pinkish and white gold colors of the Black Hills gold that she had made into delicate leaves; one on each side connected to two open hearts that were linked together. A frosted turquoise was set in the middle of the two hearts where they were linked. It was both, delicate and strong.

The gold-green eyes moved up to the designer's face, "It's beautiful, Skye, its perfect." And then he smiled the beautiful one that his friends hadn't seen in a long while. Then asked quietly, "You said rings. Did you get the bands done, also?"

Skye Light-Feather nodded and smiled, "Yes, I did. Here, what do you think?" And she handed him another matching box.

As he opened it, a soft sigh escaped the firm, male lips. "I had no idea, they'd be so...wow." They were wedding bands, his and hers. Hers would fit to the delicate heart one, and his band had a small matching frosted turquoise set in the band with softly etched leaves on either side of it. "Yes, Skye, I love them. They are unbelievable."

Carefully he placed them in the jeans pocket. Looking at his friend, he asked, "Jacob, can I give her a hug?"

Surprise widened the dark eyes, "Sure. If Skye doesn't mind."

"Good." And McKay wrapped his arms around the slight young woman.

"You let me know how much and I'll pay you tomorrow." Grinned the trail foreman. Then eyeing his friend, he asked, "You ready to practice those numbers? The guys are here, somewhere. And Jessie should be here in a few minutes." Then turning to the slim Indian girl, he asked, "You're going to stay and listen, aren't you?"

She smiled and nodded her head. She stepped closer to Jacob and put her hand on his arm. "I haven't heard you play. This should be good."

Tyler moved closer to his friend and whispered softly, "You better hang on to her, my friend."

Once again surprise showed in the dark-brown eyes, and he looked at Tyler, then down at the vibrant woman at his side. A soft smile washed over the lean, handsome features. Love did sort of sneak up on you, he thought. And he smiled wider.

The two men went to gather up the rest of the group, and placing Skye at a table near the stage, began to set up. A crowd started to gather near the stage also. Chase and Phil walked in together and got themselves a good table. A couple of minutes later the two Government Agents joined them.

They had to practice for the opening show at the fair, and some of the guests said they would like to hear them. They couldn't see anything wrong with it, so here they were. Jessie walked in with Larry and Cindy, Joe and Jena. As they made their way through the crowd, the redhead looked up and caught Tyler's eye. He straightened and moved over toward them. "Hi, everyone. There's a table right over there for you. That is Skye Light-Feather, she's an old friend of Jacob and me. Jena, you know her. Introduce everyone will you?"

The dainty woman smiled, "Sure thing."

Smiling down on Jess, he said, "Come on, little one. We are giving a show. Do you know the words?"

"I better by now, don't you think?" She laughed softly

"Good evening, everyone. We are going to try and do all the songs for the opening show. The theme this year is from the movie 'Spirit'. So, here we go. Have a good time." Smiled McKay, then turned to the group, "Ready?"

They all nodded. And the music started to fill the packed room. The first song was 'Here I Am'; then they did one of everyone's favorite, 'Can't Take Me, I'm Free', which went into 'Get Off of My Back'. And the audience started to sing with them. As the song drifted to an end, Tyler moved forward and spoke to the crowd. "This next song is going to be different. It's about the Lakota Indian that befriends the stallion, they save each other. And become brothers of a sort, it is called 'My Brother under the Sun'. Jacob will be the singer and the drummer on this."

The music flowed over the crowd and Jacob's voice carried the passion and longing that was in the words. The crowd roared as it ended. The group decided to take a short break, and some of the guests came over asking questions. Ty and Jess walked over to where the others were sitting at the table. "Well, how are we doing, guys?" McKay asked with a grin.

"Pretty damn good." Smiled Joe with enjoyment evident on the handsome face.

Jacob walked up to the table and went to stand by Skye's chair. But she stood up and hugged him, saying softly, "You did so well. I had no idea." Then turning to the trail foreman, "You sing! Man, do you." Then her musical voice laughed softly, and everyone joined in.

Tyler turned to Jessie, "Do you know Skye?" The redhead nodded, then said, "I've never met her, but I've heard of her. So nice to meet you, Skye." And the two shook hands.

Glancing over at the stage, Cooper sighed and said softly, "Time to go back. See you in a bit."

The three turned and walked back to the stage. It was only minutes and they were ready to sing again. This time Parker spoke up and said to the crowd, "Guess what, we're back. This next song is a sad, soul searching song and our boss is doing this one. It is 'Sound the Trumpet'."

As Tyler sang the heart wrenching melody, he thought of what they had just been through and you could hear the pain and sorrow in the baritone voice. The audience was silent as the words poured out and then as it came to an end, the crowd roared with applause. A faint red tint swept up the cowboy's neck and into the lean cheeks. He smiled softly. "Thank you. The next song is a duet between Jess and myself and it is called, 'Don't Let Go'. We hope you enjoy it."

The couple moved together, then turned to face each other. Tyler started out, with Jess joining in. His voice soft and husky and hers crisp and clear that just pulled the words up to a higher note. So magical. Couples in the audience were holding each other and swaying to the music.

Then as it finished the crowd cheered and applauded for minutes. As it died down, a voice called from the guests, "Hey, Jessie, sing 'Holding Out for a Hero'!" And then the crowd started chanting.

Large blue-gray eyes looked at Tyler, then back at the band. Parker nodded and McKay smiled, "Alright. The majority rules. Sing, my girl!"

The tall, dark-haired man stepped back out of the light and Jessie settled in the middle of the stage, she took a shaky breathe and looked back at Roy, then nodded the copper-red head. The music rolled out and she cut loose with the opening words. Then as it was about half way through, the crowd started singing the chorus with her.

And as the song was coming to the end, she turned and looked at Tyler. The crowd went wild.

The well-built trail foreman moved over to join the small woman on the stage that was smiling softly at him and he was blushing to no end, but he was smiling. "Well, it sounds like you enjoyed that, are you ready for another?" And the audience yelled, "Yes!"

McKay took hold of Cooper's small hand and he smiled down at her, saying softly, "Stay. We'll do this together."

Then the tall, lean muscled man turned to the gathered crowd and said easily, as the main light softened to a pale glow and encased the two of them. "Okay, this is the last song, 'I Will Always Return'. Hope you enjoy it. It's a charming song."

The music started out soft, building up to when Tyler started to sing. As he poured out the words, he still held her small hand and he was singing the words to her. As the music died away, he knelt down, pulling out a small cream-colored box, then looked up at the now trembling redhead. His voice was husky and low, filled with love and longing, "Jessie, my love, will you marry me?"

The silence was loud, as everyone seemed to hold their breath, waiting for the small, flame-haired woman to answer him. Her soft gray eyes filled with tears and she nodded her head, then whispered brokenly, "Yes...yes!"

Tyler rose to his feet, picking the small woman up into his arms, kissing her lovingly. Everyone rose to their feet, cheering. Slowly he lowered her to the stage, but held her close to his side. Turning to the band, then to the crowd, he smiled widely, "She said yes!"

Everyone was cheering with happiness. People were talking to each other and the ranch family were congratulating the couple. With everyone talking to each other, Tyler pulled Jess over away from the crowd. "Do you like the ring?" He asked in a whisper.

She opened the little box and gave a soft gasp at the delicate, beautiful; yet unusual ring. "Where ever did you find it?"

"Skye designed it for me. You like it?" He asked hesitantly.

"Oh, yes. Almost as much as I love you." And she stood on tip toe, kissing his mouth with trembling lips. His heart felt like it would explode as he drew her closer against him and just hugged her.

Laying his cheek on the silky, soft vibrant hair, he gently touched his lips to her forehead. Then feeling a hand on his shoulder, warm tawny eyes looked over into dark-brown ones. "Does she like the ring, Ty? Skye is worried she wouldn't."

The redhead turned and smiled at Jacob, "You tell her, I don't like it, I love it. And then tell her thank you."

"I will. Congrats, you two." Grinned the slender trail guide as he turned and headed back to the small woman at the table.

"I suppose we better go see Phil and Chase." Suggested the tall man gently.

"Yes, we better. Tell me, Ty, did everyone know; but me?" She asked with grin.

He shook his head, then said carefully, "Not everyone. Phil and Chase, the guys. I'm not sure about Larry and Cindy, but Jena knew, so I imagine Joe and the others did too. You're not angry, are you?"

"Hell...no. I just don't know how you pulled it off." She frowned, then chuckled. "Don't look now, but here comes Phil and Ben Chase."

Turning to meet the two older men, Jess gave them both a hug. And Chase told the dark, curly-haired young man, “I knew she would. Your dad would be so very proud of you right now. Just like I am.”

Tyler couldn’t speak, his throat was all choked up, so smiled softly. Phil stepped closer and hugged the small redhead again, turning to Tyler, “You’re like my son and I love you both.” And then he wrapped his arms around the tall young man. Quickly he stepped back and appeared embarrassed, so Jessie leaned over and kissed his cheek, “We love you, too.”

Then turning to Tyler’s uncle, she said, “Both of you.”

A voice from behind them spoke up, “Best wishes you two. Say, McKay, you’re good at keeping secrets, we never figured it out at all. Sure you don’t want to join the agency?” Grinned Cord.

The small redhead moved up to face the FBI agent. “No, he doesn’t. But, thank you.” She smiled, but the gray eyes had blue sparks shining in them.

The other agent grinned and said, “We get it!” Then turning to Tyler, he added, “My boy, you do have your hands full.” Then the two men went back to their table.

Rubbing his hand through the dark, curly hair, Tyler muttered softly, “I’m sorry, but it’s been a very long day. I will talk to you gentlemen tomorrow. You have a good night. But we’re going home. Night.” His arm went around the slight figure, pulling her gently against him and headed for the doors, “Come along, Little One.”

She never said a word, just waved a small hand to the two men and let the tall, lean man guide her away.

Chapter Thirty-Five

Pale yellow sunlight filtered into the bedroom and flowed over the bed sheets and cover, touching the bronzed lean face of the sleeping man. The small scar on the cheek bone where the stitches had been, only made the chiseled features look ruggedly handsome. Dark eyelashes laid softly on the male cheek and the face appeared relaxed. He was finally able to get some rest. The well-muscled frame was lying comfortably with one arm at his side, the other was across the firm, flat stomach.

The small, red-haired woman laid on her side and just watched the man sleep. She wanted to run her fingers through the silky dusting of chest hair and feel the warmth of his skin; but was afraid it would wake him. He needed to rest.

Closing the gray eyes, she sighed softly. They all have been training and practicing, trying to get ready for the show and race. The guests were doing great with the training and the guys have been helping them and also getting ready for the opening show. Then Jena helped everyone get ready for the horse show with the special western dressage dance. The song they chose was the Magnificent Seven Theme. There were seven of them; Tyler, Jena, Jacob, Chang, Toby, Juan and herself. They would come out in a V formation and do spins, side passes, and a standing-in-place trot. Jena choreographed the whole routine like a dance with horses. It was really beautiful.

The last thing they had worked on was the song for the Rodeo, 'God Bless the USA'. And Tyler was the main singer. The band members had practiced very hard to get the true meaning of the song to be heard. All the members were singing and would be on horseback. They would be using an instrumental CD of the song because there was no place to setup a band in the arena. At the time when the words of the song says 'I will stand up for her yet today', Tyler would ride forward and the others would move their horses up beside him. Who knows, maybe the audience would also stand up?

No more training until show time, the next day. One whole day of doing nothing but the basics and of course last minute bathing of horses. Would be sort of nice to just relax. But underneath it all was what was going on with Lazier and of course, the race. She knew Tyler was trying to decide whether to let her ride Shiloh in the race; or ride himself, depending on the amount of danger there might be. Shiloh was ready for the race, he was in the best shape he had ever been in. She would love to be on him in the race, but she would do whatever Ty thought was best.

Then there was the surprise that the ranch owners had done. They were building a beautiful cabin with an attached stable and corral for the horses; not too far from the main ranch buildings, but far enough to be private. They said it was a wedding present. The couple got to choose the design for the cabin, all the appliances. The owners said that it was only a small token on how much they owed for all the support and loyalty and sacrifice. Then they told the young couple that the ranch was a family. Maybe an extended family, but a family. The ranch owners were also going to pay for the wedding and it was to be held at the ranch. The generosity of the owners was overwhelming and wonderful at the same time.

Opening her eyes she turned the small, oval face to look at the handsome man that was to be her husband. Warm tawny-green eyes were staring back at her, and she blushed. "How long have you been awake?"

"Not long." A gentle smile touched the firm, male lips and humor lightened the hazel-gold eyes. "Like what you see?"

And her blush deepened, but mischief danced in the blue flecked gray eyes as she leaned closer to the long, lean male frame. A slender finger traced the firm lips and over the stubborn chin, then on down into the silky chest hair, where the fingers splayed out and tangled into the curls. "Have to check out the merchandise, you know."

"Oh, you think so?" He moved swiftly, shifting the long, lean body over her smaller, delicate one. His fingers tangled in the fiery mass of silky hair at the back of her head, as he placed his lips over hers. At first he teased, then the warm tongue slid into her soft mouth, sending a groan of desire whispering from her lips. His hands weren't the only ones tangling in silky hair, her slender small hands buried fingers in the black curls on his head. Warmth swirled through the slight frame as she arched her body closer to his muscular hips and stomach.

Desire rippled through his tightening body, as the warmth of her soft skin tantalized his senses. A hunger to have her closer, drove him to tighten his hold as he moved his fingers over the silky skin. Gently he touched and caressed the small, firm breast, his thumb rubbing over the pale rose nipple. The creamy breast swelled in is hand and he groaned with desire, shudders raged through his body and as his lips trailed over the slope of the firm breast, tremors feathered over the slight delectable frame of the woman in his arms. "Ah...Jess, I want you, all of you. I need, need to be deep inside..."

Her slender arms went around his shoulders, the small fingers digging into the muscles. Her lips were kissing him and the small teeth nibbled his collarbone, sending flames licking through his lower belly and into the wide chest. The small body rose to meet his larger one, coming together with an intense desire.

A few minutes later, he gently moved the damp red hair from her delicate face, placing a soft kiss at the corner of the love bruised mouth. "Sweetie, you are going to be the death of me yet."

Slowly she opened desire clouded eyes and smiled ever so slightly, "Never."

Tyler chuckled softly, then leaned over and placed a quick kiss on her pouting lips, "You want to go first in the shower, or me?"

Cocking the copper-colored head sideways, she appeared to think about it, then grinned mischievously, "How about, us?"

Faint color rushed up into the lean cheeks, "Why not? Just remember, it was your idea."

A few hours later, they found themselves leaning against the corral fence railing, watching the dainty black-haired Jena working the butterscotch-colored palomino. It was like floating, the feet never seemed to touch the ground. The flaxen mane and tail flowed out like a banner in the wind.

"She makes it look so easy." Sighed Jessie.

Tyler smiled softly and looked down into the gray-blue eyes, "She sure does. Looks like the mare is dancing." Then as the man glanced over at the other side of the rider, he saw the lean dark-haired Drake. "Have you noticed the difference in Joe? It's almost like two separate men. I couldn't believe it that morning when he approached me by the office. He looked so...so...sad. Even confused. And then he asked for forgiveness."

She frowned slightly, "Yeah, that's what he said to me also. He said that you told him he should tell me in person. I think you did the right thing. It was hard for him, but he did it. Do you think it will last?"

He shrugged the muscled shoulders, "Don't know, but he looked like he was being truthful. I think it has something to do with Jena. He was acting different right after he met her. He was more real?"

"I know what you mean. She was everything that he had said he didn't like and then, wham! Head over heels! Love, maybe?" She asked softly.

"Maybe." He grinned, then pulled her slight form up against his strong one. "Seems to be a lot of that going around." And he chuckled. "I think Jacob and Skye realized that they were more than friends. Like us."

Jessie's red-gold head came up and a gentle smile touched the fine lips. "I wondered. I knew they were friends, but the looks they were giving each other were not of friendship."

"That's what I saw, also." Agreed the tall, dark-haired man. He gently laid his strong hand on the slim shoulder, looking down into the soft dove gray eyes, he added, "We should go and see if the agents have any more news about tomorrow and the race."

She nodded and they walked toward the ranch office. As they walked they talked about the guests that were going to enter the different events. And then she mentioned that Shiloh was doing very well and ready for the race coming up. Tyler nodded, but still didn't say anything about who would be riding him. She fell silent, she knew he would do what was best, but she was worried that if he did ride the gray, they would maybe hurt the trail foreman, just because. But she kept the thoughts to herself.

Stepping up to the office door, Tyler knocked softly, and a low voice called them to enter. He opened the door and they went inside. All four men were there, and Chase looked up and smiled at the couple. "Pull up a chair, you two. We've heard from the agency. The word is that there will be a big shipment coming in from Florida; weapons, most likely. Possibly Stinger missiles, along with some mercenaries. Quite a large group of them. Then there are two important men coming for the race with a large amount of money; from New York. The planes should be arriving around the same time. Which should be sometime tomorrow, possibly early evening."

The DEA agent, Kevin James spoke up quietly, "Our inside informant said that the two VIPs and the money would be coming to the race with Wilcox when they bring their horse in for the race. We won't take them down, until after the race."

"But we have a special team that will go in at Lazier during the race. Then we'll have a unit here at the race to catch them when it starts to go south." Grinned the FBI agent. His chocolate-brown eyes going to the silent trail foreman. The young man's face was hard and the gold flecked green eyes were narrowed and smoldering. Cord glanced at the other agent, then over to the Marshall.

Brandon Cord brushed the honey-blonde hair back off his forehead, then said, "Tyler, we'll get them."

Jessie saw the narrowed eyes and the tightly clinched lips. Fear slid up her spine, the man she loved was very near to the breaking point. She'd only seen him that angry twice before; when Hunter had threatened him after she had her foot in the trap and when Hunter was hurting her, the night he died. Slowly she leaned forward and placed her small hand on his arm. He turned his head and glanced at her worried soft-gray eyes, "I'm alright, Jess. I'm just very, very angry." Then with a deep sigh, he glared at the agents, "You better get it done right. Or I will."

Before the two agents could say anything, Chase straightened in his chair and remarked in a deadly calm voice, "They will, or I'll go with you. Isn't that right?" The dark eyes were eyeing the two men steadily.

They nodded, then the DEA agent asked carefully, "You have any questions?"

Jesse looked over at them, her small face stiff and the beautiful gray eyes were hard. "What should we be careful of with the race? Will they try something, if it doesn't look like they will win?"

Instead of the agents, it was Phil Holden who spoke up, "Wilcox will do anything to win this race. I've dealt with this guy, he thinks he can do anything he wants. Just ask Sheriff Cradling. Remember, it wasn't Hunter that killed Taylor McKay, then made it look like an accident. And just because Hunter got out of hand and shot Ty, more than likely it was Wilcox that ordered them to turn out and run off Confederate. Now, he's trying to show off to his bosses and make a name for himself; he's not going to let anything or anyone stop him. That's what I think."

Chase looked at his old friend, then smiled. "I agree with Phil. I think you guys better get ahold of Sheriff Cradling and work out a plan with him. They will be there for the fair anyway, so their presence won't be unusual." Glancing over at his nephew, Ben asked, "Have you decided who is going to ride?"

The red-haired woman sat back and watched the handsome face as he looked up at his uncle. "I've been thinking about it a lot. I think I'll have Jessie ride. He'll run best for her, and then I can keep an eye out for trouble." Turning the bronzed features to the small woman sitting next to him, "Okay?"

She nodded. "We won't let you down."

"You're entering the small gray horse?" Questioned the FBI agent. "You think he'll win, really?"

Anger simmered in the blue-gray eyes, her small hands formed into tight fists. But before she could say a word, Tyler's husky voice answered the question, "I'd say he'll blow them away."

Chapter Thirty-Six

Among the hustle and bustle at the ranch with cowboys and guests trying to get everything loaded and ready to go to the horse show, Jessie leaned against the corral fence and rubbed an arm over her damp forehead. Looking up at the eastern mountain tops, she could see the large golden sun just rising above the craggy peaks.

Still early, just a little after dawn and with all the activity you would think it near noon. And still so much to do. A dark gray nose gently pushed against the lightly tanned face, "Morning, fella. Are you ready for today?"

The smoky gray gelding bobbed the fine head as if to say, yes indeed. Soft, musical laughter slipped from her lips. "You think so, huh? Do you remember our new trick? Okay, show me. Up!"

She raised a slender arm up and the gelding rose in the air, the white mane and tail flowed out behind him. Then he lightly came back down and pranced around, showing off for her. "You're such a good boy. Go eat your breakfast, then I'll be back in a little while and get you all ready to go."

Smiling, she turned to go back to the cabin to eat a light breakfast herself. There hadn't been time earlier that morning, now she was hungry. "When did you teach him that?"

Looking up, gray eyes met gold flecked green ones, a slight smile touching the firm male lips. "A week or so ago. Just playing around. He can walk on his back legs, too." She chuckled softly, "He likes showing off."

"You are just full of surprises. Are you hungry?" Tyler asked quietly.

"Was heading to the cabin for some breakfast, what some?" Jess looked at the tall, lean man and wondered? "Is everything alright, Ty?"

He moved in close to her, smiling dryly, "Yeah. It's just that everything is coming to a climax, and I'm worried how it will all go down. Just nerves, I guess." He muttered huskily.

"We'll be fine. We're not alone in this. We have family and the very best friends." She put her hand on his arm and they walked to the cabin.

Two hours later, McKay backed the truck up to the last trailer. Cooper was standing at the back of the trailer with both Rebel and Shiloh. Next to her was Jacob with his buckskin, Tango. Then as Tyler got out and went to hook up the brakes and lights, Chase appeared beside the truck, smiling he said, "Can I ride in with you folks? I'll help."

The dark-haired man smiled in return, "You bet."

The two men went to the back and they started loading the horses, equipment, saddles and clothes. Just as they were checking that everything was loaded, Skye Light-Feather arrived. "Hello, I'm not late, am I?"

Jacob stepped up, putting his arm around her slim shoulders, "You are right on time. Just getting ready to get in and leave."

Everyone climbed into the pickup and Ty eased the pickup out, pulling the trailer through the wide drive toward the Fair grounds. As they rode along, Chase asked, "Are you guys ready for the opening show?"

Everyone laughed, and Jessie said, "We sure hope so. I think we're more nervous about the dressage dance routine, I know I am." Both Tyler and Jacob nodded that they too felt that way. It was something that they had never done before.

It took about forty minutes to pull into the fairgrounds, then find the hookup spot for the trailer. The horses were unloaded and tied to the side of the trailer. Next to them were three more trailers, all from the ranch, including Jena's big red trailer. The opening show was at two o'clock. Some of the events were due to start at ten o'clock; so after making sure the horses had water and hay, they went to watch some of the events.

When Jess and Tyler got to the main arena where they were having the gaming events, they saw the guests that were trying their hand at barrels and poles, key-hole and flags. A number of Jute Valley guests did very well. The younger kids were thrilled with their ribbons and trophies. And then it was time for the Performance classes; Western Pleasure, Ladies and Men's classes, also trail classes and horsemanship.

Cindy Tanner placed second in her western pleasure class and Larry Connors came away with a first place trophy for the trail class. And Joe Drake surprised everyone, including himself, when he received a second place trophy in his western pleasure class. Jess hadn't even known that he had practiced for that class. Tyler explained that Jena had coached him.

Then it was time for them to get ready for the opening show that would take place at the Grandstand. They went and changed clothes. Jesse pulled on a cotton skirt of ivory and pale aqua with a matching laced-up top that showed off her trim slender waist. The aqua colored western boots with the higher heel, gave her slim, petite form a few inches. The long wavy red-gold hair was a riot of curls falling about the slender shoulders and narrow back.

Tyler stepped out with snug fitting denim jeans and a silk aqua colored shirt with a denim vest that matched his jeans. Looking at him, she had to swallow hard before she could speak. The muscular frame and handsome features were very apparent and had her heart racing into overdrive. They both just looked at each other, then that wonderful smile of his appeared.

The cowboys were setting up the instruments and making sure that everything was ready to go. The fair board had brought them the new head set microphones and they all had to put them on and try them out. Then it was time.

The crowds of people filed in, then the Fair Board announcer came up on stage and started the show. They opened with the song, 'Here I Am' and it flowed into the following songs, the crowd sang with them on the choruses. Again, like at the ranch when McKay sang 'Sound the Trumpet', the crowd went silent, then roared their pleasure. As the final song ended they got a standing ovation that lasted minutes.

Then it was time to get ready for the western dressage dance. The seven met at the gate and Jena looked up at them and smiled, "You'll do great, just go with the music and have fun!"

They entered the arena and formed a line at the far end, then the music started, all seven horses started their exaggerated in-place trot, with Tyler moving Rebel out first in the middle, they formed a V and moved to the center of the arena. The music increased in volume and beat, the horses spun, and side passed, then like partners dancing, the horses spun like in a waltz. Forming into a cavalry line, two abreast with Tyler in the lead they did figure eights and spins with slides and all in time with the music. Coming to the end, all the horses went to the center and formed a line, then bowed.

The crowd roared and cheered. The seven riders calmly turned the horses and left the arena. As they gathered outside the arena, everyone was trying to talk at once. Jena smiled at all of them, "What can I say? You did great!"

"Shoot, you were the teacher. Thank you." Praised McKay with a grin. The others agreed. The rest took the horses back to their trailers, except Jena. She had a competition in a few minutes in Free-style Dressage.

She came out with a first place and two of her students placed second and third. Her training and showing stable would be well represented along with the Jute Valley Ranch. A good day all around.

Everyone got together for lunch and talked about the events, the winnings and the programs. Most of the guests were staying for the Rodeo and the Ranch hands were taking the guests' horses back and were going to do chores. Some were coming back for the rodeo and fair rides.

After eating, Tyler went looking for the two agents with Ben Chase, to find out if the planes had arrived at Lazier. The Sheriff was talking with the two men as McKay and Chase stepped up. "Howdy, Ty, Chase. Say, that was quite the show, Tyler. Where's Red?" Asked the Sheriff with a smile.

"She's at the trailer. We've got a show to do at the rodeo. What have you guys heard? Anything?"

James and Cord nodded slowly. "Yeah. We just got word that two planes landed there about twenty minutes ago. About twelve mercenaries, four to six extras; bodyguards, most likely for the VIPs and funds. And three large crates. As soon as Wilcox leaves in the morning, with the other two and the horse, our guys will move in." said Cord.

Then James remarked, "As soon as we get an all clear from our agents at the ranch, we'll start setting everything into motion here. As soon as Wilcox pulls in, he will be under surveillance. We'll move in as the race ends."

Sheriff Cradling spoke up softly, "I'll keep you informed on what's going on as it happens."

Tyler glanced over at his uncle, "Ben, is the Marshalls in on this, too?"

The tall older man straightened up and said quietly, "Yes, they're working hand in hand with the FBI and DEA. But I have two of my best men coming tomorrow and will be here before the race. We want the man responsible for killing your father."

The FBI agent, Brandon Cord asked absently, "You going back to the ranch tonight?"

Tyler's hazel-green eyes narrowed on the agent. "No. We have the horses here for the race tomorrow. We'll stay in the trailer. The others will take the ranch horses back and the other trailers, then be back in the morning after chores. Jacob rode in with us and his horse. He's staying with friends. He plans on being positioned on the track for the race. Over where there isn't any cameras or personnel. Sort of a backup. Why?"

"Just wanted to know if we should put men at the ranch, but if you or the horses weren't going to be there. Won't have to." Added the agent, then looking at the US Marshall, "Need a ride back to the ranch, Chase?"

The dark-haired man looked over at the tall, lean trail foreman, then said easily, "Sure, that would be fine. I'll see you in the morning, Ty."

McKay nodded and said, "Give me a call if anything changes."

Chase smiled. "You got it."

Tyler watched them move off toward the parking area, then turned to Sheriff Cradling, "Did any of that sound strange to you?"

The man's dark-gray eyes narrowed. "Something not quite ringing true, you think?"

The handsome features hardened. "I'm not sure, but the look that the DEA agent gave the FBI agent, says something isn't. Or maybe I'm way over my head."

John Cradling eyed the young man. "I'll be watching the rodeo. Good luck tonight."

Tyler came around the back of the horse trailer and found Jessie saddling Shiloh, then glancing over at Rebel, saw that he was already saddled. "Wow, you've been busy. Thanks, Jess."

She looked up, a gentle smile on her face. "No problem. Jacob helped. He just left on Tango and was heading for the Rodeo Arena. He said he'd meet us there."

"What else is left to do?" McKay asked.

"Well, the horses are ready, so I guess just us. We need to get our hats and I need a drink. Let's go, huh?"

They both ran inside, and scooped up their hats, and Jess decided to take a bottle of water with them. As they came out, Tyler made sure the door was locked and also the pickup truck.

When they rode up to the arena, the others were there waiting. Looking around, the stands were filling up with people and then the announcer walked up to the group. "Evening. As soon as the Anthem is over, move on in, at this end. We'll put the CD in and it's all yours."

The trail foreman glanced at the gathered group. "Are we ready?" The riders nodded and smiled. Then the lights dimmed and a spotlight zeroed in on a young girl from the local high school. And her voice was fabulous as she sang the Anthem. A very big voice from a small person.

A man came over and opened the large gate for them, as soon as the girl finished. Quietly they moved the horses through the opening and made their way to the center, where another man stood.

He advised them where to stand, and then McKay leaned down and told him that they would be moving around during the song. The man nodded, and said that they were all set up for that. Then he smiled and wished them good luck.

The lights again dimmed, then three spotlights zoomed in on the group of riders and the announcer introduced them. The music rolled out of the large speakers and Tyler started to sing the words to the song with the others joining in. As the song's words say 'I love to be an American' and then 'I'll gladly stand up next to you and defend her, today'. The lights rose up and shined all over the arena and the seats. With the audience joining in; Tyler moved forward and the other riders moved up next to him, and the crowds of people rose to their feet and sang with them. Then on the last notes of the song, all the riders removed their hats and the horses bowed; except for Shiloh, who rose straight up in the air with his small rider on his back and then he too, bowed.

The audience roared and cheered and applauded as the lights came up and the group rode off. As they came out of the arena, a large man with a big smile met them. "Thank you so much. It was great. We'll have to do this again." And then he walked up to the main Grandstand VIP Box.

"That my friends was the Fair Board President." Beamed Tyler. "Good job, everybody. Jess, that horse is...wow."

The others all agreed. Ty looked at the men, and smiled softly, "Thanks, my friends. Have a good night and we'll see you in the morning."

The group split up and moved off. McKay watched them go, except for Jacob and Jessie. "Jake, you're staying with Skye, right?"

The dark-haired man nodded, "Yep. I'll put Tango at the trailer and make sure he's taken care of. I'll be here early tomorrow."

Tyler stepped down from the saddle and handed the reins to the Indian, asking, "Would you take Rebel and go with Jess? I've got to touch base with Sheriff Cradling and try and catch Phil before he takes off." Then looking up at the slender woman, he added softly, "I'll be back in just a few minutes, Okay?"

Cooper nodded and smiled, "Sure. Jacob and I will take care of the horses. I'll lock the door, so be sure to knock. Tell them hello for me."

He moved off toward the Grandstand. Jacob looked at the redhead, "He'll be fine. Let's go take care of these boys." And they walked the three geldings toward the trailer.

Tyler looked back and saw them ride off, then glanced toward the viewing stand, he caught sight of the Sheriff. As he moved over to him, he realized that the older man was talking with the ranch manager. "Hello, you two. How'd you like the program?"

Phil smiled widely, "Yes, you all were great. And when Jess's horse rose up in the air. Wow." Then turning to his old friend, "Wasn't that something, John?"

The sheriff grinned. "I'd say so."

McKay leaned against the railing, "Jessie said to tell you two, hello. Phil, have you heard anything else?"

The ranch foreman said, "Some. They have a team at Lazier ready to go in after Wilcox and his 'guests' leave in the morning. Chase is keeping his eye on things, he has men stationed all over. And they blend in real well."

Sheriff Cradling nodded, "I trust Chase. That man knows things. His declaration that he planned on nailing the person who is responsible for your dad's death, sort of upset a certain FBI agent."

Ty's husky low voice said, "Brandon Cord?"

"Yeah. All the way back to the ranch, the man kept trying to get more information on his plans, and Chase told him, he'd let him know, when it was right. I guess, the DEA agent wasn't pleased. He told Chase that they hadn't come together, that Cord was already here when he flew in." Informed the Sheriff dryly, "I guess that feeling you had maybe right. We'll keep our eyes on him. And Chase told me to tell you that both the DEA agent and he would be making some calls. Now, my boy, you better go take care of that special woman of yours."

"Thanks, guys. I'll see you in the morning."

Chapter Thirty-Seven

Jessie sat on the queen-sized bed in the trailer, hugging the pillow in her arms. She had taken a shower and pulled on a silky nightshirt while waiting for Tyler to return. He was taking longer than planned, she hoped nothing was wrong.

Jacob was staying with Skye tonight, but would be back in the morning. Skye's place wasn't far away; in the front was her jewelry shop and the living quarters were in the back.

Looking down at her left hand, she stared at the delicate, beautiful ring on her slim finger. It was so unique. And the wedding bands were gorgeous too. Just thinking about being married to Tyler had her heart doing a slow pound. God, she loved that man.

A soft knock at the trailer door, startled her. "Ty?"

"Yes." He called softly and she jumped down from the bed and unlocked the door. He no more than got inside the door and she wrapped her slender arms around his warm, hard body. "Hey, what's the matter?"

"Nothing...I just missed you. Is everything alright?" she stammered softly. Her large gray-blue eyes were searching his face.

Tyler smiled and said calmly, "Of course." Then he turned back to the door and deftly locked it. "What are you wearing?"

"It's a nightshirt, silly. Don't you like it?" She asked hesitantly.

"It's damn sexy. Yes, I like it." He grinned, then touching the still damp hair, "So you got your shower, I need to take mine. I'll just be a few minutes, then I'll tell you what has happen so far."

Jess nodded her head and watched him disappear into the tiny shower. Climbing back onto the bed, she hugged the pillow and laid down with it under her chest. She could hear the shower and closing her eyes, she could picture his delectable body with the water running down over the hard, taut muscled frame. Her breathing became shallow, heat swept up her slender frame and seemed to settle in her lower body.

The shower shut off, the door swung open and the tall, lean man stepped out with a towel wrapped around his hips and he was using a smaller towel to dry the black, curly hair. She looked up into the bronzed face with dark curls laying in disarray. How handsome he was! Feeling the heat crawl into her face, she sat up, still hugging the pillow.

Tyler lowered the towel he was using on his hair, looking up and seeing her watching him; his lower body tightened. A raw hungry look flickered in her warm gray eyes. Excitement drummed through him, and he bit back a groan of need. A need of her, her touch; the feel of her skin against him.

He stepped toward her, the towel slipping off his hips and to the floor. Her dark gray eyes continued to roam hungrily over his body, he moved in next to the small woman. His body responded immediately as he dragged her against him. Their hips collided; he felt her shudder as his body embarrassingly betrayed his feelings. Swiftly he tugged the silky nightshirt over her head.

As he placed his mouth on hers, lips teasing hers open to his invasion of her moist warmth. A throbbing need tugged at her and she felt on fire. Then as she felt him shudder against her, she reached out and pulled him closer. Raising the silky black, curly head, he gazed down into her small, oval face with smoldering, tawny eyes. With a husky voice, he asked her, "Do you have any idea what you do to me?"

Color washed into the delicate face, hunger burned in the gray eyes as she whispered. "Show me."

He moved his heated throbbing body over her slight frame, thrusting himself deep inside her warm, moist center. Hearing the soft groan whisper through her lips, he sank deeper, his body shuddering with a burning desire.

Long minutes later, Tyler gently eased the sleeping woman's slight body over, slipping out of the warmth of the bed; to check the locks and then shut off the lights, except for the small nightlight in the tiny bathroom. Quickly he slipped his still heated body back into the soft bed and pulled the covers up over them both.

Jerking awake, Tyler laid still and hardly breathed. Something had wakened him; then he heard the horses.

They were snorting and blowing, stomping their feet. Something or someone was out there. Glancing at the softly glowing clock on the small stove, four in the morning! Quietly, he grabbed up some pants, slipping them on he headed for the door. Slowly he eased the door open after quietly unlocking it, squeezing through the opening he looked toward the horses. They were totally riled up, and suddenly Ty made out a shadowy figure stalking close to Shiloh, who was throwing a royal fit.

Straightening up, McKay started toward them, shouting, "Get away from there!" Suddenly the sound of a gun went off, he saw the flash and then a bullet hit the ground near his bare feet. Throwing himself up against the trailer; he heard the gray gelding squeal, striking out with his rear feet. Hearing a human's groan of pain and sounds of a body falling; he approached the excited horses. "Easy fellas, good boys."

Reaching Shiloh's side, he rubbed his hand gently along the lean shoulder and back, "Easy, boy." Then looking behind the horses, he searched the ground and area, but couldn't see anyone. Must have gotten away. But more than likely, with some injuries.

"Tyler! Are you alright? Ty!" Jessie's worried, frightened voice called from the doorway.

"I'm alright, Jess. Turn the outside light on and get dressed. Then call the Sheriff." Answered Tyler in a quiet, but hard voice.

With the outside light on, he looked closer at the surrounding area, making sure not to walk on any signs that the intruder might have left. After calming the three horses down, he removed the gray's water bucket and set it by the door. He didn't want Shiloh to drink it until it could be checked. Then with a last look around, he went back inside.

Jessie was sitting on the bed, she had pulled on blue jeans and a T-shirt. "I woke up John, but he's on his way." Then she handed him the cell phone. "Do you want to call Jacob?"

"Yes, very smart thinking." Grinned the tall, lean man.

Jessie slid socks on and then her boots as she listened to Tyler talking to Jacob. It had been a gunshot that she had heard! And someone was trying to get to Shiloh. But nobody knew that they were racing the gray? Or even if he was that he had a chance to win. They wouldn't think he could run times any faster than the ones they had made sure were good times, but not as fast as Gunfire. So it had to be someone...they trusted... She looked up at Tyler as he was still talking with Jacob; her small, delicate face hardening and the fine lips tightening into a thin white line. The usually soft gray eyes turning dark and icy.

Tyler glanced over at the small woman and his voice faded, a chill slipped up his back as he looked into the small angry features. Whispering into the phone, he told Jake to hurry over, then clicked it off. "Jess? What is it?"

Her lips were so stiff, that she could hardly move them. A shaft of pain entered the angry eyes. "Only very few people knew we were going to enter Shiloh, even fewer knew he could win. Ty, it's someone we trusted."

Green fire darkened the tawny eyes, as what she said sank in. Shit, they hadn't even told the wranglers, not because they didn't trust them, just that it was safer that way. Besides, none of them knew how fast Shiloh was. He was the only one to even hint that the small gray horse had a chance to win. He had said, 'He'll blow them away'.

He raised saddened, icy-hard eyes to her pale, angry face. "I'm pretty sure I know who, but have no idea – why? We have to have evidence. And we'll get it. But don't say anything, he has no reason to think we know who it is, uh...might be. I should call Chase, let him know what happen."

Jessie nodded the red-gold head, but said nothing.

Tyler punched the Marshall's number, and listened to it ring. Two rings and a sleepy voice answered. Ty spoke carefully, yet urgently, "Chase, its Tyler. We had some trouble, they were messing with the horses and took a shot at me. No, I'm fine. John and Jacob are on their way here. Okay, I will."

"He's on his way. He told me to tell you to hold tough."

"You better put some more clothes on, don't you think?" And she gave him a soft, small smile.

The tall, broad shouldered man nodded the dark, curly head, "Yeah, I suppose so." He picked up some clean clothes and went into the bathroom. A few short minutes later, he came out and moved over and sat down next the small, sad woman. "It'll be alright, Jess." She laid her burnished head on his arm, "I know, but I am so very angry."

There was a soft knock at the door. Jessie rose from the bed and went over to the door. A voice from the other side of the door called, "It's Jacob and Sheriff Cradling is right behind me."

Cooper opened the door and the dark-haired man stepped in and hugged her, then looked over at the trail foreman, who was pulling on his boot. "You alright?"

Tyler nodded, "Yeah. He missed, but Shiloh didn't. Whoever was out there, got kicked by the gray. It was too dark to see much. But I set Shi's water bucket by the door to be checked out. I was barefoot, so if you see footprints, they're mine. When he got kicked, I heard him groan and fall to the ground, but by the time I got to Shiloh, the guy was gone or hiding. Let's go out and see if we can find anything."

The Lakota man nodded his head, smiled softly at Jess; and then followed his friend outside. The Sheriff was just pulling in as they stepped outside. "Why were they going after Shiloh? I thought it was Rebel that you were entering."

"We were going to change horses at the last minute, but the times were not a winning time, so they had no reason to stop him. Except someone that knew we were entering him and that he had a good chance of winning. Yes, Shi can outrun Confederate. He flies."

Jacob frowned, "So who did you tell?"

"How about FBI agent Cord?" Grumbled the Sheriff, as he came up next to them.

Tyler sighed, "We're pretty sure, but we don't want to let on that we know. Something still doesn't fit. But, John, I need you to have that bucket of water tested. Can you do that?"

"Sure. Got anything else?" he asked.

Jacob was squatting down, scraping in the hard dirt, when he picked up a damaged bullet with his gloved hand. "Looks like a service weapon. A hand gun. Got a bag, John? Good, there you go. Let's go look where Shiloh kicked the son-of-a-bitch." He was eyeing the ground, then made the two men wait where they were, while he checked closer. "I see your footprints, Ty, but there is some boot prints, also. Oh, yes. I'd say Shi did a number on our guy. I found where he fell and I have blood. He either split the skin, or he may have broken something. From the looks of this, I'd say he has an injured arm. When he got to his feet, he only used one hand. I'm figuring it is the left arm. John, I need a DNA collector and do you have a camera? Good, can you get a picture of the boot prints, where the bullet was and where he fell?"

"Do you want a second job? Yes, I believe I have one. Chase gave me some of this stuff the other day, after uh... uh what happen with Hunter. I'll take this stuff and be right back." Muttered the Sheriff as he walked back to his patrol car.

As he turned and looked at the trail boss, Jacob asked, "Has Jess been out here, yet?"

"No. Thought we should take care of the scene first. I wanted to get a good look at Shiloh before she sees him, just in case. Shall we go check him out?" questioned Tyler.

"Yeah, would be a good idea." Smiled the young man.

Slowly they walked up next to the gray gelding. He was acting calmly, just turning his head and eyeing them with curiosity. They checked him all over and didn't find any marks of any kind. But they did find a damaged area on the trailer, near where the bucket was hanging. The two men looked at each other, then the Sheriff's voice reached them, "Here you go. Did you find anything else?"

"We need a picture of this." And Jacob pointed to the damaged siding. "Let's see if it's from the perpetrator?" As they looked closer they found small pieces of hair and skin embedded in the material. "I'd say, yes." Remarked Jacob with a grin.

"Let's get this stuff out of here, before we get visited by an unwanted person. John, Chase is on his way. When he gets here let him see the evidence, he could possibly get it to their lab without Cord knowing. I know it could be the DEA agent, but I doubt it. Let's go inside. You have everything locked up, don't you, John?" Asked Tyler quietly.

"Sure do. How is Red handling it?" questioned the Sheriff.

Jacob looked at the Sheriff, and grinned, "Does Jess know you call her that?"

"I think so. Why?" Wondered the older man with a slight frown.

The trailer door opened, and Jessie smiled at them. "Come on in, gentlemen." As they filed into the small trailer and found seats, she asked, "Do I know what?"

"That I call you Red." Laughed the Sheriff.

"Oh. No, I don't mind that. I don't like being called 'shrimp', or even worse is 'runt'. I'll put up with shrimp, but not the other." And she laughed also. "Did you guys get everything done out there? And Shiloh, he's okay?"

"He's fine. And, yes, we got everything." Answered the dark, curly haired man. Then the green flecked gold eyes met her gray ones. "Are you going to be able to face Cord, if he shows up, without killing him or otherwise do him bodily harm?"

"Yes, unless he says or does something stupid. Unless, of course, it wasn't him and the ranch office was bugged?" She murmured.

Jacob looked from one face to the others, then said, "Don't think so, I went through the whole building. But, we'll know if we see him. Shiloh got him good, and we have proof. We'll know for sure once we get the results back." Turning his head, he added, "Here comes Chase."

A knock sounded and then in walked the tall, dark-haired older man. "Okay. What did you find?"

The other men took turns telling him the whole findings, then Sheriff Cradling said, “I've got all the evidence locked in my car. Can you get the results from your lab in quick time?”

“Yes. Let's do it right now. I'll be back. What time is the race?” He asked.

“We have to be checked in by ten.” Answered the redhead softly.

“I'll be back in about twenty minutes. Come on, John. Let's do this.” He smiled at his nephew, then went over and placed a kiss on the small woman's pretty face. “Stay sharp.”

Chapter Thirty-Eight

The minutes seemed like hours, but of course, that wasn't the case. Tyler had decided to take a quick shower to rinse off the dirt he had on his bare feet. While he was showering, Jessie loosely braided the long copper-red hair. It was better to have it under control while racing at fast speeds and with all the jumps, it would be out of her face. She dressed into her softest pair of jeans and was wearing a soft aqua long-sleeved shirt. Tyler had gotten her a safety vest to wear, which he had stated that it was not negotiable. It fit like a glove and was very comfortable. He also told her, that she had to wear her helmet. And seeing the kind of terrain they would be running over; the jumps and everything, it was a good idea.

Hearing the bathroom door open, she looked up and met his green-gold gaze. "You look ready. Does everything fit well?"

She nodded, then said, "They feel good. You were right about wearing the vest and helmet. What is your idea of strategy for the race?"

He calmly put on his clothes, then frowned slightly, "I thought that instead of going to the front right off, you should keep him just off the leaders. He's got a hell of a finishing run. It seemed that the more he ran, the faster he'd go. And if he sees a horse ahead of him, he gets it in his mind to catch him. That's what he did the night he ran down Confederate. He got him in his sights and then that was it. He just stretches out and lengthens his stride, sort of flows over the ground."

The redhead nodded and moved over to the counter and sat down. "It should be better for him with that lightweight saddle, and then my smaller size. How much does that saddle weigh?"

Ty chuckled, "Would you believe about ten pounds? If that. Jess, don't take chances. It not worth it to injure either you or Shiloh. You understand?" He asked seriously, his expression grave.

Again she nodded. She slid off the stool and stepped up to him, placing her strong, slender arms around him.

The tall man groaned and pulled her up into his arms and kissed her long and deep. "Ah, Jess, I love you. Just do your best and trust that little gray horse. He won't let anything happen to you if he can help it, he loves you too." Then stepping back, he sighed softly, "We better go get Shiloh saddled. I'm bringing some bottled water. It's warm out there. Ready?"

They stepped outside, locking the door behind them. Swiftly Tyler put the close-contact racing saddle and breast collar on the gray, then saddled up the red roan and they led the two toward the starting area. Jacob had taken Tango and went to check out locations, then he would meet them at the gate before the race.

While they walked, Tyler kept looking around. An uneasiness had settled in his stomach. They still hadn't seen the FBI agent, and Chase hadn't returned yet with the results. Turning his head to look at Jess, he realized that she was doing the same thing.

The staging area was off to the right of the gate. Seven of the twelve horses were there, getting vet checked and checking in. Gunfire hadn't been checked in yet, but their trailer was there and the big black horse was standing quietly, watching the activity all around him. Jess's small hand held Ty's larger one. Looking down he could see the tension in her stance and on the small face.

McKay tethered Rebel over in the shade, not too far off. Then moved over to the small woman and gray horse. Just before he reached her, Parker and Saylor appeared. "Hello. Boss. How you doing? Is she okay?" At his nod, they added softly, "We're all here. Juan and Chang are going to be over by Rebel, the rest of us will be on hand. Jacob is coming, he thinks he found a good spot to watch the race. Give us a shout, if you need us."

"Thanks, guys. Say, let me know if Chase gets here." Smiled the tall, lean man. Then he walked to the young woman, just as the officials and vet came over.

A tall, gray-haired man smiled at the redhead and then turned to the tall, dark-haired man standing protectively beside her. "Morning, McKay, Cooper. How's it going?"

Jessie tried to smile, but barely made a small one. Tyler grinned, then drawled smoothly, "Just fine, Carrington. How goes it with you?"

Carrington chuckled softly, "Fine, here too. So, little lady, you are riding in this race?"

Jess looked at the older man, the she smiled, "Yep."

"Okay, it's Jessie Cooper from Jute Valley Ranch, right?" At her nod, he continued, "And the horse's name?"

"Shiloh. He's a Morab. Gelding. Here's his vaccination records and all his papers. I'm the owner. Anything else, Mr. Carrington?"

He grinned at her, "No, Miss. Here's your number. Say, I heard that you are soon to be a Mrs.? Congratulations, you two. And good luck with the race."

Tyler smiled back, "Thank you, Hank." Then turning to the redhead, he asked, "What's your number?"

She held up the card, it was the number eight. "Have you seen Chase, yet?" Then looking past Ty, she said, "Here comes Jacob."

McKay turned around. "Hey, Jake. Parker told me that you found a good spot."

"Sure enough. It's at the turn, just before the riders head back. It's where it's the hardest to see from this end. I'll be able to watch them coming to the curve and heading back down the track. Then I'll move towards the finish line." Looking at the small figure standing next to the gray, he said, "You take care, Sweetie. We'll be watching." She smiled back at him.

"Heard anything from Chase? No, damn. I haven't seen Cord anywhere either. Or the Sheriff. Do you have your cell? I'll call if I see anything. Okay, I'm heading out now." Then before turning away, he laid a hand on his friend's shoulder, "She'll be fine. We won't let anything happen to her."

Tyler nodded and said softly, "I know. You be careful, too."

"Always." Grinned the Lakota as he moved over to the buckskin and swung up into the saddle.

The trail foreman jabbed his hands angrily into the back pockets of his jeans, then paced back and forth with frustration. "Damn, where are they? It's almost time for the race." Then he turned smoldering tawny eyes on the delicate face. "I'm sorry, Jess. I just hate not knowing what's going on."

Looking toward the parked horse trailers, Cooper noticed that the last four horses were being led into the staging area. "Wilcox is on his way in here with Gunfire." Muttered Jessie softly.

Tyler stood still, almost like a statue, except for the blazing gold flecked green eyes that narrowed to mere slits. Silently he watched the large, black Gunfire walk by and then the tall, well-dressed man following. As he came abreast of the couple, he stopped and looked smugly at the broad shouldered trail foreman.

McKay moved over closer to Jess, his larger body protecting her. Wilcox eyed the two, then grinned dryly, "Too bad what happen with your stallion. So you are sending in the little guy and with the fiery Miss Cooper on board." Then a serious frown appeared on the dark, handsome features, "Sorry about what Hunter tried to do. I hadn't realized that he had a vendetta against you. It's not an excuse, but I am sorry. Miss Cooper, McKay." He nodded his dark head and moved off to where his horse was standing.

Jess and Tyler looked at each other with surprise. "Wow, never expected that. I think he really meant what he said. Do you?" Questioned Cooper quietly, her smoky-blue eyes searching his face.

Tyler frowned. "Yeah, I think the same thing. Maybe he is just the manager of the gun club. And he is just following orders. God, it just gets worse. Well, sort of."

From behind the tall trail boss, a soft, hesitant voice asked, "Boss, I'm to help you and Jess."

Turning around, Ty looked at the sixteen year-old stable hand. "Hi, Gideon. Yes, would you make sure Shiloh has some fresh water?" The boy smiled and nodded the curly red head.

The redhead glanced over at the young teenager and asked, "Gideon, who sent you?"

"The ranch foreman, Jessie. They brought me from the ranch when they came. We just got here. They are parking, he just dropped me off." Picking up the water bucket, he added, "I'll be right back."

"Thank you. We'll be here." Smiled the young woman. Then she faced Tyler. "About time." He agreed and looked toward the parking area, suddenly he smiled. A group of four men were heading their way.

The redheaded boy appeared with a full bucket, and Jess touched his shoulder and asked, "Gideon, will you watch over Shiloh while we go visit with Phil?"

"Sure, no problem." He smiled ear to ear.

The couple walked over to meet with the men. Even as they neared, they could see the worry etched on their faces. Tyler and Jess slowed and waited for them to reach them. "What did you guys find out, and don't tell me 'nothing'." Demanded the tall, black-haired man, his arm going around the young woman.

Chase frowned, then said, “We found out a lot, but still don’t have who.”

“What the hell, is that supposed to mean?” He snapped, the hazel-green eyes burning.

The DEA agent stepped up and explained, “We got the results from the DNA tests, but they weren’t agent Cord. And agent Cord is not the man we have been talking with. They found the FBI agent’s body in Chicago. He was to leave from that office to come here. The fingerprints belong to an ex-military man by the name of Jackson Wyler. He is a mercenary, not like most of them, but he’s the planner, handler; he is also a freelance operator. He gets paid up front, then makes sure the job gets done. We believe he has been working here off and on for years, doing jobs for the owners of Lazier. They are based in New York and Florida. He is based in Canada and Chicago.”

Tyler’s face hardened, then after looking at Jess, he remarked, “Wes stopped and talked to us when they brought Gunfire in. He apologized for what Hunter tried to do. We both believe he was not lying. We think he is just the manager of the gun club, so follows orders. So if he isn’t trying to move up, who is doing the betting?”

“Wyler!” All four said together.

Kevin James added carefully, “They’ve raided the Club. They will let us know what they find after they go through everything.” Then looking at the young woman, he said in a soft voice, “Ride safe, Jess. We’ve got men stationed all along the track, and Chase’s men have been here since you called this morning. He’ll surface sooner or later. And we’ll be ready.”

Phil stepped up next to the couple. “We’re very proud of you two, no matter what happens. Now, you better get over there, it’s about time. Best of luck, Sweet Girl.”

Jesse leaned forward and kissed the weathered cheek. And winked at Chase. Then grabbing Tyler's hand headed for the small gray gelding. As they neared the horse, he turned the fine, chiseled head and cut loose with a loud call. Then the tension was swept away with the soft laughter from the three young people.

Tyler went over and checked the saddle, breast collar and last, the fleece-covered cinch. Looking at the redheaded young man, he asked him for the bitless bridle. Then he gently slipped it on and adjusted the strap around the nose, made sure the single rein was securely fastened, then flipped it over the gray's head. Turning to the small woman next to him, he asked, "Ready?"

Jess nodded, then stepped up next to the cloudy-gray horse. Tyler bent and she put her slender knee in his hand and he eased her into the saddle. Taking a deep breath, she looked down on the handsome face, leaned down and placed a kiss on the firm male lips. "For Luck."

Gideon's young freckled face blushed red and he smiled widely, then gave her a thumbs-up. Tyler's handsome face had softened, and the gold flecked green eyes warmed with love.

Jessie reined the gelding around and with Tyler at his head they walked to the gate. As the horse in front went through, she moved Shiloh into the opening, then stopping when the official at the gate put up a hand. They were checking to make sure no one was using outlawed bits or cruel equipment. As the man smiled at them, and then checked the saddle and moving up to the bridle, seeing no bit; he looked up at the woman sitting on the horse. "No bit?"

Tyler stepped forward, "Is there a problem?"

The man frowned. "Is it safe to race without a bit?"

The trail foreman smiled, "Yes, Sir, it is. More and more endurance riders are going to these bridles, they're more humane. So is everything okay?"

The man smiled and replied, "Sure. Have a safe trip, Miss."

"Thank you." Smiled Jessie as they went through the gate.

Tyler put his warm, firm hand on her thigh and looked up into her beautiful face, "Be very careful, Jess." Then he went to Shiloh's head and placed the strong hand on the space between the large dark eyes, and whispered softly, "Keep her safe, fella."

Stepping back, he watched the redhead move the sleek, gray horse into his spot in line. Turning he hurried out through the gate and joined the young redheaded, Gideon.

Jessie settled deeper in the saddle and sank her hands into the silky, snow-white mane. The other horses had started to dance and fidget nervously; but the gray appeared calm as he stood there looking into the distance. But, she could feel the tremors that feathered under the satiny coat. He was excited, but didn't let it show; just kept staring straight ahead. Feeling another tremor, Jess felt herself tighten her hold in the mane and her slender legs snugged up on the gelding's sides. He was going to explode when they all took off; and Ty wanted them to hang back until the last half. She needed to be ready, had to keep him under control.

All of a sudden, it got very quiet; the starter raised the flag and then, down it came! And all twelve horses surged forward, Shiloh would have been in the lead, but he obeyed her touch and held just behind the two leaders. She looked around and spotted the black Gunfire charging up on the outside, he was heading for the lead; but they hadn't come to the jumps yet.

It was a lot like a steeplechase race, only western style. The gray was settled into an easy mile-eating stride, and he knew how to handle the jumps without even breaking that stride.

Looking up she saw the first set of jumps loom ahead, she could feel the small horse gather himself to make the jump. He never slowed, just sailed over the brush and headed for the next one. Some of the other horses almost hopped over and then broke their stride, then they would speed up and run into the next set of jumps. Shiloh would gather himself and then just skim over the jumps, keeping himself in an extended stride that never slowed. The other horses from behind them were trying to make their runs. Too soon, and even though they were now ahead of the woman and the gray, they were not even to the half-way point. They would have no game left to finish the race in a winning form.

Looking up the track, she could see the curve coming up, no jumps were in the curve; the other horses would be pushed for more speed, but Jess was just going to let her horse out. No pushing needed. Jumping the last set of three jumps, before the flat curve; she glanced up and saw Jacob sitting on Gringo back in the trees.

He saw her too, and waved slightly. Then motioned for her to turn the gray loose. And with a wide smile, she did; and he leveled out and exploded! He went to the outside and started passing horses like they were standing still.

Then the larger jumps were coming up and the track was now a winding one over some gullies and rough areas. He never slowed, he extended the stride and she felt like they were flying! He sailed over the taller and wider jumps like they were only bumps in the road.

There were only four horses ahead of them, and the last set of jumps were coming up and then it was a flat race to the finish line. Of the four, one of them was the black, Gunfire; she had to give the horse credit, he was running his best. He definitely was trying, even if it wasn't the kind of race he was used too.

Now the jumps, and the gray seemed to excel at them as if he enjoyed it. He swept past two of the horses and then there were just two left, and now it was just an all-out flat race. Gunfire started opening up the distance from the big sorrel and the gray breezed past on the outside.

Jess leaned down over the gray's neck, the white mane streaming back whipping her face. She laid the small hand on the neck and whispered to him, "Go, Shi, go!"

And just like Tyler had said, the gray set his eyes on the black and went for him. It was like a switch was flipped. The wind caused her eyes to tear; but it was exhilarating! Stride by stride the gray gained on the black, eating up the distance; until the black tail was at the gray's nose, then his shoulder. Two more strides and they were running head to head. The black's nose was starting to drop, the big horse was tiring, but still he fought on.

The two straining horses, running side by side, turned their heads slightly and eyed each other; then the gray straightened out and blew past the large blue-black horse!

His refined head was up and he was running because he loved it! And then the finish line was there and he flashed past into a record breaking time that broke his sire's best time ever! The young woman on his back sat up and threw her arms in the air, a beautiful wide smile on her lips. Slowing, the gelding eased down and gently turned back and trotted to where everyone was standing.

Gunfire ran in second, and the purse would not be bad. Then the big sorrel came, followed by the rest of the field.

Everyone was rushing forward to surround the gray horse and small, slender redhead. Tyler reached her first, his handsome face was beaming with pride and love. She could see Phil and Chase just a little farther back. Tyler's hand was on her leg and his other was laying on the warm shoulder of the gray gelding.

Suddenly a loud commotion erupted a short distance away, people started to scatter, screams rose above the sound of cheers. Jessie could feel the gray tremble and the lean muscles bunch. Glancing down at Tyler, she whispered, "Ty, something is terribly wrong!"

His hands came up and he was going to lift her off the agitated gelding. Then the crowd spilled out just to their right, a woman fell and her husband dragged her out of the way of a blonde-haired man, carrying a rifle. He was yelling and with the rifle butt snugged into his right hip with the barrel resting on his left arm that was in a sling; he was firing it above the heads of the panicking people. He was striding straight for the gray horse and the man and woman. The brown eyes were burning with black anger, the twisted face in a sneer of rage. "You just wouldn't give up, neither one of you! You just had to know the truth! And that damn little gray horse has to have wings and the heart of a lion. Well, I'm going to stop you! Both of you!"

Tyler pulled Jess from the gelding and she yelled, "Shi, up!" The gray was already going for the threat, but at hearing her command, up he rose! Front feet pawing the air, ears penned back, and white teeth snapping; all the while he is walking on his hind feet. Then he squatted down and pushed up with his back legs, like war horses of old. He sprung forward and the rifle went flying, the man's face paled as he staggered back and tried to run. Again, as once before, the gray slammed into the man with his chest, sending him crashing to the hard ground. Then lowered his head and grabbed ahold of the man by his left arm, and shook him like a dog would shake a rag.

"Shiloh, no! That's enough, boy!" Jessie's trembling voice called weakly from behind him. But, he heard her soft call and stopped. The man swore, and the horse stomped his front feet just inches in front of the man, the man went silent.

People moved in closer, then the Sheriff and his deputies came in and the people moved back. Chase and Phil, along with the DEA agent and the Federal agents moved in and took charge. Jacob rode up and slid off of the buckskin by his two friends.

"I've never seen anything like that before. I'm sure glad he's my friend." Remarked the bronzed slim man.

"Me too." Breathed the slender redhead, "Me too."

Chase and the DEA agent had Jackson Wyler taken into the Sheriff's jail. Where they would interrogate him to find out what he knew.

McKay had his arm around the slender, small shape of the woman he loved; then their friends encircled them, and they made room for the smoky-gray horse that came up and lowered his head to the two people he loved, and blew his warm breath on their cheeks. Then everyone broke into soft laughter.

Epilogue

Early September, the mountains were alive with the brilliant colors of fall. People were gathered from all over the Wind River Mountain Area and beyond. The Jute Valley Guest Ranch was dressed up in its finest autumn colors for the special occasion.

All of Jessie's friends had traveled from their homes to be here. Linda and Tim Winters, Larry and the now Cindy Connors, and Joe Drake, who had not left; but decided to stay in the area and would soon be marrying the petite, turquoise-eyed Jena.

And of course, the Jute Valley family. Every single one of them. Jacob had been Tyler's best man, and the lovely Skye had been the maid of honor at the beautiful ceremony. Rick Jorden and his new bride, Kim had handled the reception and dinner.

Phil Holden had walked the bride down the aisle and Benton Chase had stood up for the groom. The ceremony had been simple, but lovely. Nothing could compare with the beauty of the small, slightly built woman with the cascading fall of burnished copper hair.

The ceremony was over a short while before, and now everyone was gathering in the lodge dance hall. The Jute Valley Wranglers were playing music, and the young couple were about to dance. The band was waiting for the couple to choose the song they wanted to hear.

Jessie looked up into the gold-flecked green eyes and smiled softly, "Would you like to sing 'our song', Ty, Darling?"

The tall handsome man grinned down into the face with the light-dusting of pale freckles across a small nose and whispered, "Sounds good to me." Then glancing up at his friends, he said, "Toss us a mike and play 'Almost Paradise'."

Parker grinned, then said, "Sure thing, Boss."

The band started to play and the wedding couple began to dance and then Tyler started singing the words, with Jessie coming in and joining him. Their guests loved it, starting to dance with them. Then as the song ended the band went into the faster paced song that Jessie had always sang, 'Holding out for a Hero'; and grinning up into her husband's smiling face, she let the words roll out over the dancing people.

And as she sang Tyler danced her around the floor in time to the music. Pulling her close he twirled her around and as the song ended he dipped her. Throwing a quick glance at his friends, he grinned up at them and remarked in a silky-smooth voice, "Well, if she can sing her song, I guess I should sing mine. How about 'Hungry Eyes'?"

Parker nodded and grinned, "Here we go."

Jacob started the drum beat and the music rolled out, and the tall, broad-shouldered man started to sing the words and they moved in time to the sexy music. As the song finished, Tyler danced her around the dance floor and ended up by the band. He had Parker come over and then he asked, "Could you play one more song for me? How about 'She's Like the Wind'? Please?"

"Boss, it's your night. Anything." Smiled the tall, cowboy.

The guitars started the song and then Tyler's soft baritone voice sang the words and slow danced his bride around the floor; among the other dancing couples.

Chase moved over by his old friend, Phil and smiled as he laid a large hand on his shoulder. "I believe Taylor is sitting up there in heaven, looking down with the biggest smile ever." The older man nodded his greying head and smiled softly, "And very, very pleased."

Then Sheriff Cradling stepped over and joined them. "Beautiful wedding. Any idea when Jacob and Skye are getting married?"

Phil grinned, "In two weeks."

John turned his head and motioned over by the bar and remarked, "Even the DEA agent, Kevin James is here. Is that his wife?"

Chase smiled and nodded, "Yes, it is. They are taking their vacation here for the next two weeks. He was talking about transferring out here, then moving his family here. Have you heard anything about Wes Wilcox?"

The Sheriff nodded. Then he said, "Yeah. He turned state's evidence and helped in any way he could. He didn't know that Taylor had been killed. And when he had told

Ty that he knew he had been up on the north boundary, he was warning him off. But to try and keep him safe. He'll be back in a couple of weeks. He is starting up a horse ranch. I guess Gunfire is his horse."

"What all did you find out from Wyler?" John asked quietly.

"He is the one that was handling most of the business for the Corporation. But he was only interested in the money. He's the one who had Taylor killed. I guess Taylor had seen him a couple of times and had put two and two together. Anyway, he felt he was getting too close, so..." Sighed the Marshall. "Then he sort of manipulated Hunter to go after Tyler. That's why Hunter set fire to the cabin, to draw Ty up there; but Jessie came with him and of course, Shiloh. We're thinking of giving that gray a badge. Ha! Only Jessie won't let us. Have you seen their new place? It's gorgeous." Grinned the tall, dark-haired man.

"What about the two VIPs and the money? The mercenaries and the weapons?" Questioned the Sheriff.

"The two VIPs were the main money men. And they folded real easily and gave us lots of information. The mercenaries are going away for a very long time. Yes, the weapons were stingers and they had NVG's, grenade launchers and some high-powered sniper rifles with scopes. We confiscated the helicopter and the two aircraft." Announced the US Marshall.

Phil Holden turned to his two friends and said quietly, "Both Tyler and Jessie told me something, just the other day. They said 'The Whispers from the Past have made a Path to the Future'."